To Kirsty

ONE GOOD REASON

EMMA SALISBURY

*from
Emma Salisbury*

Hope you enjoy it!

Copyright © 2025 Emma Salisbury

The right of Emma Salisbury to be identified as the Author of the Work has been asserted by them in accordance with the Copyright, Designs and Patents Act 1988.

Re-published in 2025 by Bloodhound Books.

Apart from any use permitted under UK copyright law, this publication may only be reproduced, stored, or transmitted, in any form, or by any means, with prior permission in writing of the publisher or, in the case of reprographic production, in accordance with the terms of licences issued by the Copyright Licensing Agency.
All characters in this publication are fictitious and any resemblance to real persons, living or dead, is purely coincidental.

www.bloodhoundbooks.com

Print ISBN: 978-1-917705-02-8

To my big brother Del, who is the inspiration behind a certain scene in this book.

Prologue

The young woman staring through the windscreen of the Mercedes SUV wore a high-necked blouse with ruffles around the collar, designer sunglasses perched on the top of her head. Her companion was dressed more casually. Bucket hat and baggy sweatshirt, a fat gold chain around his neck. The bullets that killed them had entered through the driver's window, catching the woman side on, in the temple. Her companion, who must have turned in his seat as though trying to make sense of what was happening, had been hit between the eyes.

SOCOs in protective clothing had erected a tent over the vehicle to screen the occupants from the crowd that had gathered. Uniformed officers had put a wide cordon across the junction of Westward Street and Abraham Road, squad cars blocked access at both ends. News agency drones circled overhead like vultures smelling carrion.

'Who's the SIO?' the crime scene manager asked an officer with a face that looked like it hadn't been near a pillow in days. There'd been a shooting in neighbouring Hulme, all the hallmarks of a drug deal gone wrong. The teenage victim gunned down as he ran. Before that, a fatal stabbing in Whalley Range. An argument in school that had escalated outside of it.

'DI Fucked If I Know,' the officer answered, shrugging his shoulders.

ONE

'We don't want this turning into something it isn't.'

– CHIEF SUPERINTENDENT CURTIS

Detective Sergeant Chris Ashcroft was halfway through a 10k run when his mobile rang. He slowed his pace to answer it, checking his heart rate on his Fitbit. He'd been a promising sprinter in his teens. The unbroken records at his old running club were testament to that. Running came natural to him. The grace of it. The opportunity it gave him to test himself. To push his body to its limits. Getting to the training ground had been a less than graceful affair. Stopped and searched more times than he cared to remember, in those moments he was no longer a promising athlete, just a black boy on his toes.

'Nice trainers.'

'How did you pay for that tracksuit?'

'They're all bloody sprinters.' When he'd tried to explain.

His love of running didn't extend to the showmanship that had become almost a requirement of modern track and field athletes. He was there to run, not strut around like a peacock. By the time he realised his heart wasn't in it, he was no longer winning races, did well to make it through the heats. His sprinting career was done.

He'd been awaiting the results of his 'A' levels when he

attended a careers fair put on for the schools in the area. Before he had time to think about it, he'd wandered over to the Greater Manchester Police stand, the recruitment officer's grin splitting his face in two when he caught sight of him.

'I take it I don't need to empty my pockets this time,' Ashcroft had replied when asked if he had a few minutes spare to speak to him.

That seemed a lifetime ago as he spoke briefly into his phone then listened, the designer beard that circled the edge of his mouth forming a thin line. 'Give me an hour,' he said, before turning and running back the way he had come.

He changed out of his training gear. Showered. Ran a hand over his face, decided a shave was in order. He selected a slim fitting blue suit, checked shirt and the Paul Smith tie his sister had bought him the previous Christmas which he saved for special occasions. It wasn't everyday you were summoned to the Chief Super's office, especially when you were on a rest day. Decided he'd better look sharp.

Salford Precinct station

He took the lift, bypassing his own floor which housed Salford Precinct's Serious Crime and Murder Teams, carrying on to the floor above which Chief Superintendent Curtis had turned into his hallowed ground. His promotion to Chief Superintendent the previous year had given him the ways and means to upgrade the entire floor to one befitting an officer of his status. Walls had been knocked through to make his office larger. The room beside it had been converted into a briefing room for senior officers from the cluster of stations he was now responsible for, to gather weekly to have their backsides kicked or hands shaken, depending on performance. The rest of the time it doubled as a press briefing room. It was here that

Ashcroft had been told to report, which forewarned him their meeting was not going to be *a deux*.

'Chris.'

Ashcroft turned to see Detective Chief Inspector Mallender hurrying behind him in the corridor. He slowed his pace, waiting for his boss to catch up. 'You've been summoned too then,' he stated.

Mallender looked pained. 'Listen, I need you to know that none of this was my idea.'

Ashcroft's brow creased but there was no time to ask anything further, they had drawn level with the briefing room. He threw a quizzical look at his DCI before he knocked on the door and stepped inside.

'Ah, DS Ashcroft,' said the Chief Super, as though his presence was a treat.

Ashcroft, aware that the senior officer only stood for visiting dignitaries, looked on as Curtis got to his feet and moved towards him with his arms outstretched as though about to wrap him in a hug. Ashcroft thrust his hand forward to curtail his approach, relieved when Curtis pumped it back.

'Let me introduce you to Superintendent Isaac Duncanson.'

Curtis propelled him towards a bespectacled man who was also now on his feet. Ashcroft took the senior officer's hand.

'Sir,' he said, nodding, giving Duncanson the once over. Late forties, strawberry blond hair long enough at the front to style into a quiff. He gave Ashcroft an appraising look, followed by a slow smile.

'Please, let's sit down,' said Curtis, returning to his seat.

Ashcroft selected a chair on the other side of the table; for all their friendly demeanour he knew not to overstep boundaries. He was surprised when DCI Mallender chose to sit beside him, rather than opposite with Curtis and Duncanson. Was he restating his point that he had no part in what was about to unfold? He turned his head towards him, eyebrows raised.

Mallender pursed his lips in response.

'Unblemished ten-year record at the Met,' said Isaac Duncanson, stretching his face into a smile. 'I understand you transferred there with your wife, who is also a serving officer.'

'Girlfriend, sir,' Ashcroft corrected him. 'Ex, now, since I decided to move back.'

'Their loss was our gain. Your five years here have been exemplary,' said Curtis, beaming as though this was a direct result of his management.

Ashcroft looked from one senior officer to the other. Waited.

'Superintendent Duncanson is based at Moss Side station,' Curtis informed him.

Ashcroft said nothing.

Manchester's notorious Moss Side became a by-word for gun violence during the 1980s and 90s. Ferocious clashes between rival gangs over the supply of hard drugs led to the area being dubbed "Britain's Bronx". There'd been riots, before Ashcroft was born. Racial tension, due to the excessive force used by the police when dealing with black youths, along with low unemployment, cited as the cause. Forty years on and the situation hadn't improved. Following a recent surge in violence-related crime it had once more become a political powder keg.

It was Duncanson who spoke next: 'This morning a young man and woman were gunned down in broad daylight on Abraham Road. The assailant ran off on foot, but it has all the hallmarks of an execution.'

Ashcroft, who'd been listening intently until DCI Mallender began shifting in his seat, lost the thread of the Chief Super's words as he took over from Duncanson:

'...the after-effects of COVID and long-term staff sickness have left us somewhat depleted...'

'...acutely aware of under-representation...'

He watched Curtis's mouth move. Noticed how he ended every sentence with a smile. Superintendent Duncanson leaned forward in his seat. Time for his two pennorth again, Ashcroft guessed.

'The family of the female victim has significant social standing in the Black community. We're conscious this may well be a case of wrong place, wrong time. We cannot afford to make damaging assumptions.' Unlike his smiling counterpart, Duncanson ended every sentence by jerking his head forward, like a chicken pecking for corn.

'It's important this investigation doesn't start on the back foot,' Curtis concluded, smile at the ready. 'Wouldn't you agree?'

'Go by the book, there'll be no danger of that,' said Ashcroft. He had no intention of making this easy.

'The girl's family is being difficult,' said Duncanson.

'Grief can do that,' Ashcroft stated.

'We don't want this turning into something it isn't,' said Curtis.

'And what would that be, sir?'

'Any suggestion of a lack of care. Racial profiling. Bias. You know the sort of thing. The Force has only just clawed its way out of special measures. The Chief Constable won't take kindly to unwelcome allegations.'

Ashcroft bit down on the inside of his cheek.

'I'm attaching you to Moss Side for the duration of this investigation.' The Chief Super's tone was matter of fact. His face a lot less smiley. 'I am confident your presence will be invaluable.'

'These are not the same circumstances as when you were in the Met, Chris,' said DCI Mallender, turning to face him, his gaze searching for the middle ground. 'We understand — and respect — the reason you turned down similar...*opportunities*... during your time there...'

Ashcroft doubted that. Three weeks after he'd transferred there, the Met had wanted a photoshoot for a media campaign, to show how they were committed to equal opportunities. It might have helped with their PR, but he hadn't joined the police to have his face plastered around bus stops and shopping centres. It didn't occur to anyone that the publicity could put him in danger and jeopardise any future operations he was involved in. He'd told them he didn't want any part in it, though the damage had already been done. Some of his white colleagues perceived his being singled out to take part as special treatment, creating tension where there had been none. There'd been other instances, positions offered in trouble spots no one wanted, dressed up as an opportunity to use his skills...

'However, this is a specific case that would benefit from your experience-' Mallender said, searching his face for a reaction.

'-Do this and who knows,' Duncanson butted in, 'next time the promotions board meet to review their minority quota, you could find yourself looking at inspector's pips. This is a good opportunity for all concerned, too good to miss.'

Ashcroft levelled his gaze at him. Fuck you. The words unsaid.

Duncanson heard them anyway. Read them in Ashcroft's expression, his stance. He got to his feet. Waited while Curtis walked him to the door.

'I'll let the SIO, DI Daniels, know to expect you in the hour,' he said before leaving.

One Good Reason

Moss Side station

Ashcroft knew without a shadow of a doubt there were some stations it still wasn't safe to go into without a police lanyard round his neck. It bothered him less than it used to. Some things you couldn't fight against, unless you wanted to spend all your time ducking and weaving. You had to hope, that in the grand scheme of things, the attention, the suspicion, the attitude would tire.

The station corridor was full. A woman in a hijab stood at the counter translating for an elderly couple. The room was full of angry men, sheepish women, all shades of brown.

He knew that at first glance, regardless of the suit he was wearing and the close-cropped hair, the officer behind the desk would take one look at him and think *just another one*.

He waited while the woman in the hijab led the elderly couple away. Stepped up to the counter.

'Can I help you?'

The question was aimed at the pad the officer was writing on. Ashcroft bided his time. Waited for him to look up. He smiled but got nothing in return.

'Detective Sergeant Chris Ashcroft, I'm here to see DI Daniels.'

The officer made a point of glancing down at the ID hanging from his lanyard as though checking he really was who he claimed. He looked up, flashed Ashcroft a smile. 'Welcome to the mad house,' he quipped. 'One moment, please,' he added, picking up the internal phone to call Daniels' extension. A couple of grunts and a 'Sir', and he returned the receiver to its cradle. 'Someone's coming down for you now,' he informed him.

Five minutes later a woman wearing a grey trouser suit over a scooped necked blouse opened the door marked *Authorised personnel only.* 'DS Ashcroft?' she asked when he stepped towards her. 'This way please,' she added, marching towards a set of double lifts, and jabbing the call button.

'You in DI Daniels' team?' he asked as they stepped inside.

'Yes. Sorry, Sarge! I'm forgetting my manners. I'm DC Nazia Latif.'

'Were you expecting me?'

Latif's brow creased as she shook her head. 'I'm too far down the pecking order to know what's going on around here. I just do as I'm told.' She paused, put a hand over her mouth in embarrassment. 'Sorry, I probably shouldn't have said that!'

'S'all good,' Ashcroft told her. 'Don't suppose your Super's about as well, is he?'

Latif nodded eagerly. 'I saw him step into DI Daniels' office before I came down for you.'

That was something, he supposed.

'Here we are,' she said brightly as the lift doors opened. He followed her along a corridor into a large room on the right. A dozen detectives and plain clothes officers sat at desks or milled about the room carrying files. The room was as untidy as any CID office he'd worked in. Reports to be read. Bins overflowing with paper cups and food wrappers. Desks laden with typed up statements to be filed away. Phone messages written on post-it notes stuck to computer screens.

A small office was set back in the corner of the room. Glass walls on two sides. Blinds down. Raised voices coming from the interior.

'That's DI Daniels' office,' Latif informed him, though he'd worked that much out. 'I'm sure he won't be much longer. Can I make you a coffee, while you wait?'

Ashcroft eyeballed a water cooler and made a beeline for it. 'I'm fine,' he said, helping himself to a paper cup from the dispenser. He caught the eye of a detective speaking into his phone. Pushing fifty, he had the look of someone more suited to working in a council office than a serious crime team.

Greying hair sprouted unevenly across his scalp like a lawn that had been mowed with blunt blades. His beard, which had been allowed to grow unfettered, showed more promise. His desk consisted of an overflowing in-tray. A rubber stress ball. A Tupperware box containing a sandwich and fruit. He was doodling onto a pad in front of him. Nodding as though trying to hurry the person on the other end along. He caught Ashcroft's eye, looked up at the ceiling as though saying *what can you do?*

Ashcroft scanned the murder boards which occupied the length of one wall. Dead boys mainly. Knifed. Shot. None of them looked older than 20.

Some of the same faces appeared on several boards. First as a suspect, then several boards along they'd re-appear as a victim. Drugs had a stranglehold across the whole of Manchester, more so in deprived areas like this. For some it offered escape, for others it offered a way out for entirely different reasons.

Like Salford, where Ashcroft had been stationed for five years, Moss Side had its share of criminal gangs. Turf wars were rife, which meant that reprisals for any form of attack — or cooperation with the police — were never far behind. This wasn't the entire story, though. These fiercely fought battles had sickening consequences. Innocent youngsters caught in the crossfire. The six-year-old girl fatally shot while walking home from church with her grandmother. The seven-year-old boy blasted to death while cycling through his estate to get to football practice. Gunned down by teenagers too scared or angry to aim straight.

A photograph on one of the boards caught Ashcroft's attention. A child's body dangling over the edge of a skip. The name at the top of the board said Kamali Harris.

'What happened here?' he asked Latif when she returned with coffees she'd made for herself and the DC on the phone.

'Six weeks ago, Kamali was thrown off a third-floor balcony. We haven't found the person responsible.'

'Suspects?'

A shrug. 'His dad's a small-time dealer. He'd changed allegiance to a rival gang, though we've no evidence to link the boy's murder to his dad's old boss.'

'How old was he?'

'Five.'

Ashcroft dipped his head, moved it from side to side. Some things would never make sense.

'You don't know the half of it,' said the detective he'd eyeballed earlier. His call finished, he turned to give Ashcroft his full attention. A jagged scar snaked from the edge of his mouth to just under his eye. The skin was smooth, plastics had obviously been involved at some point, though the line from mouth to eye was haphazard.

'Never mind what the politicians say, violence here is on the up again. I never thought I'd look back with nostalgia to when we just had the Yardies and Triads to contend with.'

The Jamaican and Chinese gangsters had been notorious in their time for being as dangerous as the Italian Mafia in controlling their trade.

'Now we've got over thirty crime groups, composed largely along ethnic lines, working with or against each other. Moroccans, Somalis, and Eastern Europeans, all vying for a piece of the action. Some of the Albanians fought in the Balkans in the 90s. They're as hard as fucking nails.'

'DS Ashcroft.'

He turned at the sound of his name being called out. Superintendent Duncanson stood in the doorway of the glass walled office, beckoning him over. Ashcroft glugged the rest of his water, tossing the cup into a nearby bin. As he walked across the room to join the Super, he noticed the window blinds that shielded the tiny office's occupants from prying eyes were now open.

'Let me introduce you to DI Daniels,' said Duncanson, his head jutting forward as he spoke.

Daniels was leaning against the front of his desk, one leg crossed in front of the other, arms folded. You could tell a lot from body language and Daniels wasn't hiding that he was hacked off. Ashcroft placed him at around forty, though his mullet hairstyle made him look older. There was a chance, he supposed, that he was a fan of Aussie rules football and was emulating his heroes, though he couldn't for the hell of him think why. They shook hands as Duncanson looked on, like scrapping schoolboys forced to get along. Daniels greeted Ashcroft with a grunt, leaving the Super to explain how things were going to work.

'While DI Daniels remains SIO on this case, he will benefit a great deal from your guidance and occasional steer. What I want you to do is get over to the family as quick as you can. Reassure them that we're giving this case our utmost attention.'

'Which family, sir? I recall you saying there were two victims in the car. I'll need to speak to both families.'

DI Daniels failed to contain his impatience. 'Speak to the girl's family first! Aisha Saforo. They're the ones jumping up and down since the moment I delivered the death message.'

'Hardly surprising,' said Ashcroft. 'What about the other victim's family?'

'Jamal Deng. His mother's not giving us any trouble. She's distraught, obviously, but is letting us get on with our job.'

Ashcroft shrugged. 'I'll need to speak to her anyway if I'm to compile a full victimology report.' He saw the look that passed between both officers. Decided to let it go. If this case was anything close to straightforward his presence wouldn't be required.

'What time's the PM?' he asked his new boss.

'Pathologist reckons she'll get to them tomorrow afternoon, barring acts of God.'

Ashcroft nodded. 'What do we know so far?'

'A member of the public dialled 999 at approximately 9.15am this morning to report they'd heard shots being fired. Firearms officers discovered both victims in a vehicle registered to the young woman.' Daniels swallowed down his irritation. 'It's got all the hallmarks of a gangland shooting! They were killed in an area considered to be Troy Mellor's patch.'

'Who's Troy Mellor?'

'An ambitious mid-tier dealer. Runs the supply on the Abraham Road Estate from Appleton House to Windward Tower. Other estates too if the rumours are right. He's had run-ins with rival dealers on the neighbouring Langston Estate, so there's a history of friction.'

'The kind of friction that blows two kids' heads off?'

'If these people think someone's pushing their way in, anything's possible.'

From where he was standing Ashcroft could see the row of murder boards in the incident room. The broken body of the little boy dropped from a balcony.

He watched DC Latif wipe one of the boards clean before placing Jamal and Aisha's crime scene photos at the top of it.

'Was there any evidence of dealing in the car?' He was referring to the possible presence of large quantities of drugs or cash. Of multiple mobile phones or weapons.

Daniels shook his head. 'Shooter could have cleaned them out.'

It was possible, Ashcroft conceded, but executions were normally aim and run. The sound of shots firing would have brought maximum attention. The killer, high on adrenaline, could not be relied upon to clear the contents of a car without leaving their own trace.

'Any witnesses?'

'What do you think?'

'What about the weapon?'

'I've got officers searching the locus but I'm not holding my breath. It'll have been stashed away somewhere by now by some misguided schoolboy soldier. When he gets the signal he'll move it on, pass-the-parcel style, until it's returned to its owner.'

Ashcroft nodded. Par for the course.

'SOCOs found a bullet casing in the footwell of the car, which the team are following up,' Daniels added.

'Is the vehicle still at the locus?'

'Yes.'

Ashcroft considered this. 'First thing I want to do is take a look at it while it's in situ. Familiarise myself with the area. If that's alright with you sir?' he asked, addressing the question to Daniels.

The DI lifted the case file from his in-tray and handed it to Ashcroft. 'Knock yourself out...' His tone suggesting he had no say in the matter.

'Let me introduce you to the others before I head back upstairs,' said Duncanson, stepping into the main office and clapping his hands to get everyone's attention. Ashcroft followed him back into the main room.

'Ladies, gentlemen, and everyone in between, this is DS Chris Ashcroft. He's going to be working on this morning's double murder, alongside DCs Brian Potter and Nazia Latif.' Duncanson nodded towards the detective Ashcroft had been speaking with earlier, and the woman who'd collected him from reception. Several detectives looked up from their computer screens long enough to give him the once-over. He hoped the Super didn't expect him to say anything other than 'Hi,'. He'd got no icebreakers or motivational speeches up his sleeve. When he'd woken that morning, he hadn't expected to be jettisoned to another station to investigate a double shooting.

'OK, that's the ticker tape parade out of the way. Now go get a bloody result.' With that the Super left him to it, standing at the front of the room like a debut warm up act.

'Glad to have you with us, Sarge,' DC Latif called out from her desk.

'Welcome aboard and all that bollocks,' said Brian Potter, once the Super had gone. 'We've been shorthanded for months; Christ knows how they've managed to magic you out of thin air.'

'The way your Super sold it to Chief Superintendent Curtis, was that Aisha's family were questioning the lack of representation from BAME officers.'

Potter shrugged. 'They've got a point, but then so has everyone else who's made that claim over Christ knows how long and nothing's ever been done before. Not sure what's got Duncanson's tailfeathers quivering over this one.'

'Aisha's mother is a professor in Black Cultural Studies at Manchester University,' said Latif, coming over to join them, '*and* her dad's a human rights lawyer. If they decide to make a fuss they're well positioned to be listened to.'

'Well, I'm here now, might as well get on with it,' said Ashcroft, not one to bear grudges.

'Where've they transferred you from, Sarge?' asked Potter.

'Salford Precinct.'

'I've come across a few bandits from there during my time, and I don't mean the villains,' Potter informed him, grinning.

'You should see it when there's a full moon.'

'I'm guessing you'll have dealt with your fair share of gangs, then?'

Ashcroft nodded. 'There and at the Met.'

'You'll be right at home here, then. Everywhere you look the drug syndicates are ruining the place. For every dealer you put away another steps into his shoes.'

'We're keeping an open mind on this one, though?' asked Ashcroft. 'From what I'm hearing it's too soon to call.'

'Someone with access to a firearm wiped out two teenagers in broad daylight. I'll stake my pension that it's a gang behind this,' said Potter. He saw a look flash across Ashcroft's face. 'Though that's not to say the victims are involved.'

Ashcroft tipped his head in acknowledgement. 'The Super said a bullet has been found at the locus.'

Potter nodded. 'I'm waiting on a call back from NABIS to see what they've got.'

NABIS was the National Ballistics Intelligence Service. Based in the Midlands, its database provided real time information on where weapons and ammunition recovered from crime scenes had been previously used. It helped establish any patterns and compiled an audit trail that could lead to the shooter.

Ashcroft nodded. 'Give me a shout when you hear back.'

'Will do, Sarge.'

'I'm heading over to the locus. I want to take a look at the vehicle and get a measure of what happened.' He needed to get a sense of the place. Although less than five miles from his old patch it was light years away in terms of culture. The territory he was in was completely unfamiliar. He felt as though he'd been thrown in the deep end from a great height, with the weight of expectation on his shoulders.

'Want me to come with you, Sarge?' offered DC Latif. 'We can take the scenic route, help you get your bearings,' she said as an afterthought.

'Lead the way,' said Ashcroft, tipping his head towards the door.

'So, how long have you been based here?' he asked as Latif edged the unmarked pool car into the late morning traffic, the station building receding behind them.

'Since I completed my probation, two years ago.'

'DI Daniels alright to work for?'

Latif shrugged. 'He's the only DI I've worked under. Not like I've got anyone else to compare him to, is it?'

'Suppose not.'

Ashcroft was enjoying being the one driven around for a change. Gave him an opportunity to take in his surroundings. The station was slap bang in one of Manchester's most ethnically diverse communities. The fact that it was also one of the most deprived didn't help. Poor housing. Non-existent job prospects. Those that worked were trapped in zero-hour contracts or casual work. Residents living hand to mouth. The older ones accepted it as their lot. The younger ones resented it. Wanted more. They were easy prey for the gangs that operated on every street corner. The promise of a sweet life if they did as they were told.

In the Met he'd refused point blank to move to stations in areas like this. Where officers like him were seen as sticking plasters. A quick fix to an ingrained problem. The powers that be in London had started to see him as difficult. He hadn't been as malleable as they'd hoped. Not quite so eager to please. Nobody seemed to grasp how insulting it was, after spending so much of his life working at blending into his surroundings, that it was his 'otherness' that caught their attention. In the end, returning to Manchester had been his only option. Oh, the irony.

They passed an African supermarket on the left, beside it a Kurdish Cultural centre. After the traffic lights, Alexandra Park, where a Caribbean Carnival was held every August. Ashcroft had never been inclined to go, but his sister took her son along. Made it into some sort of cultural pilgrimage.

He glanced at Latif. 'What made you join?'

Latif let out a mischievous laugh. 'You mean why did a good Pakistani girl like me join the police?'

'Your words, not mine.'

She laughed some more. 'I'd run out of things that pissed off my parents. I stopped wearing the hijab in my teens. I jilted the nice doctor they'd picked out for me to marry. Thought I might as well go the whole hog and join the boys in blue. "*With your education you could have been lawyer*",' she said in a stilted accent. 'My mother tells me the same thing every time I visit.' The grin slipped away from her face. 'We've become a bit entrenched in our positions. Not much middle ground, I'm afraid.'

'If it's any consolation my dad wasn't too happy about my career choice either. It took a while for me to realise he wasn't angry with *me*. He was angry at the situation I might find myself in. Couldn't see how an institution that treated him one way would treat his son any different.'

Latif made a sound that suggested she knew where he was coming from. When she spoke next her voice had a more serious tone to it. 'Was he right to be worried, Sarge?'

There'd been plenty of digs over the years. Subtle and not so subtle put downs and assumptions that most people of colour in any job experienced, not just in the force. Abuse in the canteen laughed off as banter. There'd been sinister overtones too. An investigation hindered by an unwillingness by colleagues from a neighbouring station to treat him as an equal. A resentment deep rooted enough to put him at risk. Only the quick thinking of his partner had saved him from serious injury. He wasn't about to heap all that on Latif's shoulders.

'Would've been nice if he'd trusted my judgement,' was all he'd say on the matter.

She'd find her own path.

He opened the case file Daniels had handed him and studied the crime scene photos. The bullet wounds would make identification harrowing, but not impossible. It was amazing the damage that could be concealed by the careful fold of a sheet. He lifted out two recent photos the families had given to Daniels, preferring to focus on them. He dropped them back into the file, before closing it.

They passed the West Indian Sports and Social Club on the right. Behind it the Indian Senior Citizens group. A Somali Support Centre. The shops and retail units gave way to red brick housing units set back from the road.

'Here we go then,' said Latif, indicating left before pulling up behind a van with *Scene of Crime Investigating Unit* on the side of it.

SOCOs were in the process of dismantling the tent from around the vehicle. Ashcroft approached the crime scene manager first, asked to see the chain of evidence list. He skim read the items that had been catalogued and placed in sealed evidence bags, now stored in the boot of the SOCO's estate car. There was nothing untoward on the face of it. Items removed from the vehicle included a backpack found in the passenger footwell, belonging to Jamal. Contents included a mobile phone and a games console along with several school textbooks.

Aisha's mobile phone had been found in the car's central compartment. Her bag had been left on the back seat. A designer brand going by the logo. Valentino, if he wasn't mistaken. Several cosmetics were listed, alongside a purse containing eighty pounds and change. No rolls of twenties bundled up, drug dealer style. Ashcroft thanked the SOCO manager and headed over to where Latif was waiting. Together they walked towards the Mercedes.

'Aisha's the registered owner?' asked Ashcroft.

'Yes, Sarge. Alright for some, eh?'

'I don't suppose she'll be needing it now.'

Latif's face clouded over. 'Sorry, Sarge, I wasn't thinking.'

'No harm done. How old was she?'

'Eighteen,' Latif replied, clocking the frown that crossed Ashcroft's face. 'Wait until you see the family home,' she added. 'Makes perfect sense after that.'

'Any idea what she was doing here?'

'No. Her parents reckon she doesn't have any friends in the area.'

'Apart from Jamal.'

Latif's features remained in neutral, as though she hadn't worked out the contradiction.

'Any idea what the cause of the breakdown was between Aisha's parents and DI Daniels?'

''Fraid so. I was there.' She pulled her mouth into a line. 'They accused DI Daniels of making out Aisha must have been known to her killers, rather than a victim of a random attack.'

'I'm sure he didn't make it sound as clumsy as that.'

'I think he did, to be fair. But then he'd taken the same approach with Jamal's mum, and she hadn't batted an eyelid.'

Ashcroft walked around the car, inspecting it. 'Showroom condition,' he said to no one in particular. ''23 plate.' He stepped gingerly towards the driver's window, careful not to tread on stray shards of glass. According to the crime scene photos DI Daniels had shown him at the station, most of the glass had shattered onto Aisha after the first bullet had been fired. There'd been glass over her face, in her hair, like she'd had diamonds scattered over her. Ashcroft stared at the smears of blood. The crevices in the car's leather upholstery caked in brain matter and fragments of skull.

He stepped back from the vehicle. Turning, he placed his hands on his hips, looked up and down the street. There were no skid marks on the road, so there'd been no forced stop by an accomplice. They were already stationary, and the shooter had walked right up to them.

'What were they waiting here for?'

Latif shook her head.

The car was parked outside a row of shops. A laundrette. A nail salon. An African clothing store that sold women's hair wraps in bright coloured patterns.

'We've got statements from all the shop workers — they don't start work till 9.30am. Most were in the back getting ready to open up. No one saw anything till they heard a commotion and came to look. One worker reckons they saw someone dressed in black, wearing a ski mask.'

Ashcroft looked beyond her to the shops currently standing empty. Staff had been evacuated for their safety, there'd been no time to lock up. The metal shutters on one unit were closed, signifying its occupants hadn't arrived yet. The sign over the door said *To Let*.

'Do we know who this place this belongs to?' he asked.

'I'd need to check,' Latif answered, taking a photo of the letting agent's details on her phone.

'Come on, let's go,' said Ashcroft, heading back the way they had come. 'Time for me to meet both sets of parents.'

'It'll be interesting to see if they say anything different to you than they were willing to tell DI Daniels,' Latif observed as she unlocked their car.

'I'm more interested in the things people don't say,' Ashcroft replied, opening the passenger door and climbing inside.

TWO

'If it was all going swimmingly, I guess you wouldn't be here.'

— DC NAZIA LATIF

Aisha Saforo's home was a stone's throw from the university. The house was detached, double fronted, within a small, gated community. A four-wheel drive Jaguar and a customised mini, both with private number plates, were parked on the driveway. Across the narrow access road, a visitors' parking bay was full of haphazardly parked cars.

'Looks like a full house,' Latif observed as they approached the property having left their vehicle on the main road.

'Who is the FLO here?'

'The family didn't want one, Sarge. Said they didn't want a stranger infiltrating their home.'

'Was this before or after DI Daniels suggested their daughter was involved in criminality?'

Latif's expression was all the answer he needed.

'Great,' said Ashcroft. 'Nothing like being on the back foot the first time you meet a grieving family.'

'If it was all going swimmingly, I guess you wouldn't be here,' Latif observed.

Ashcroft conceded her point.

He rang the doorbell and stepped back. A girl resembling

Aisha, but a couple of years younger, opened the door. She regarded Ashcroft briefly, her gaze settling on Latif.

'You're the detective who was here earlier?' she asked.

'That's right, and this is DS Ashcroft. He's been assigned to the investigation,' stated Latif. 'Sarge, this is Aisha's sister, Sika.'

'Looks like the rocket Mum put up your boss worked after all,' the girl observed, stepping back to let them enter.

The hall was large, square, with several rooms leading off it. A round table stood at its centre, with a super-sized potted palm on top of it surrounded by several framed photographs.

They followed Sika into a large open plan kitchen come living area with floor to ceiling windows looking onto a manicured garden. Glossy units had been built into one wall, a bank of appliances on another.

Several people were gathered around a kitchen island gripping mugs of strong-smelling coffee. All looked as though they'd come straight from their place of work. Boardrooms and lecture theatres going by the way they were dressed, though whatever confidence they normally exuded had deserted most of them. They stood around, staring at each other, shell-shocked and red-eyed. One man had removed his jacket and stood at a stone sink rinsing plates. No one looked in Ashcroft's direction although Latif attracted several glances.

'My aunts and uncles,' explained Sika, 'Came as soon as they heard.'

The open plan seating area was an oasis of statement plants. There was a framed print on the wall where in other homes a TV might be. A black and white print of The March on Washington.

A man and woman were seated side by side on a sofa. Ashcroft didn't need to ask if they were Aisha's parents. He could see it in the slump of their shoulders. In the hooded eyes that were open yet saw nothing. He moved over to them.

Waited for Latif to make the introductions. He crouched down in front of them so that he was in their line of vision.

Aisha and her sister had inherited their mother's looks. Professor Abena Saforo had high cheekbones and almond shaped eyes. Long hair braided and perched on the top of her head in an elaborate 'up-do.' Even though she'd cried most of it off, her make up looked professionally applied. Striking. She was someone who under normal circumstances commanded attention.

'I'm sorry for your loss,' he said.

'The inspector not with you?' Abena asked. 'DI Daniels, wasn't that his name? Couldn't get out of here fast enough earlier...' She looked Ashcroft up and down. 'I guess all his Christmases came at once when you showed up.'

'I wouldn't know about that,' he answered.

Going by Daniels' reaction when they were introduced to each other, Ashcroft was a gift he couldn't wait to return.

'I'm told you don't want a family liaison officer?' he ventured. Better to hear it himself rather than rely on the say-so of others.

'Your colleague here explained how they are supposed to help,' Abena said, nodding in Latif's direction. 'But I can't see how that would work for us. We are broken, DS Ashcroft. We need people around us who understand that.' Her voice was deep, undulating. It drew people in. He imagined her students were captivated by her.

'Have you taken over this investigation, or will DI Daniels be pulling your strings?' she asked him. Across the room, several pairs of eyes looked in their direction.

His silence spurred her on.

'I don't know what he was expecting when he turned up at our home this morning, but it wasn't this,' she stated, sweeping her arms wide to indicate their surroundings. 'He started asking us a lot of personal questions without bothering to justify them, like he was more interested in how we could afford to live here rather than finding who killed our daughter.'

Nice trainers.

Abena spoke her mind and spoke it clearly. Had probably given up caring about being described as difficult years ago. Ashcroft was nowhere near that stage. Too young and too athletic to get away with showing anger in case it was perceived as threatening, he'd spent most of his career being agreeable. Showing how damn reasonable he could be, even when the situation didn't merit it. *Especially* when the situation didn't merit it. There were worse crosses to bear.

Ashcroft's voice was firm. 'Although I report into DI Daniels, this is my investigation, and I will do everything I can to find out who killed your daughter. If it helps reassure you, information relating to family background, social groups and influences paint a vital picture of each victim and really helps move the investigation forward.'

'And why is that exactly?' Ozwald Saforo spoke for the first time. A large-framed man with a shiny bald head. Under normal circumstances his presence would fill a room, thought Ashcroft, pitying those who came up against him in court. 'A young woman is randomly gunned down and the police want details of our socio-economic background. She's the one who's been killed, but this terrible thing has happened to all of us…' he regarded the family members standing quietly, '…why must we account for ourselves?'

Pumping grieving family members for information was a brutal affront made worse by officers who didn't read the room and change gear. Unused to accounting for their actions, many perceived questions from the public as threatening. Even so, kid gloves or not, some of the dots here needed joining up.

'Your daughter was found in an area rife with criminality behind the wheel of a forty grand car.' Ashcroft's tone was matter of fact. 'Of course we need to know how her lifestyle is funded. And if it's funded by you, we need to understand how you manage that. None of it's about race.'

Abena regarded him. 'It's always about race.'

Ashcroft got to his feet. Moved around the room to give his legs a stretch. No one had mentioned the young man Aisha was with when she'd been shot. He wondered how much information DI Daniels had divulged before bailing on them.

'Is there somewhere more private we can go?'

He eyeballed Abena, having marked her as the one he needed to get on-side. He'd expected her to object but instead she nodded. She looked done in, as though the sorrow in the room was starting to suffocate her.

'Come through to my study,' she said, pushing herself to her feet. 'He means you as well,' she said to her husband, who showed no sign of moving.

They followed her into a room crammed with books on civil rights, African sculptures, and wall art quoting poetry by the Harlem Renaissance. A Dream Deferred. Mother to Son. Poems Ashcroft's mother had read to him, but he'd scorned. He'd found it embarrassing, the constant harking back to a past that should be forgotten.

A desk with a reading lamp on it sat in the middle of the room. Beneath a large bay window two overstuffed sofas had been placed either side of a wooden chest used as a coffee table. Aisha's parents sat on one sofa. Ashcroft and Nazia sat on the other. A quick glance in her direction and she pulled out her notebook and pen.

Abena angled her face towards him. 'Where are you from?'

Ashcroft shifted in his seat. He felt exposed by her scrutiny, her gaze sweeping over his broad nose and full mouth as though trying to guess his answer. He'd hated this question most of his life, for it was a reminder of how others saw him. That however much he felt at home, they assumed he didn't belong. 'I was born here,' he'd say stubbornly but that wasn't enough. *Yeah, but what about your parents?* They'd press when what they really meant was *why aren't you white?*

This same question felt different today. The context had changed. Why, when this woman asked it, did it feel like she was making a connection?

'My parents are from Jamaica, but I was born here,' he answered.

'Where are they now?'

'Back home.' He found himself copying the term his father used when referring to his motherland. A place where Ashcroft felt no such connection. He cleared his throat, readying himself to move the conversation on.

'When did you last see Aisha?'

'This morning of course, before she left for school.'

Yet that's not where she'd gone.

'She wasn't wearing uniform.'

'We leave for work before our daughters leave for school. They're old enough to be trusted. Aisha's been driving them both in since getting her car.'

'I know this will be hard, but I'd like you to tell me about your daughter, what she was like. I want you to tell me about her friends, people she spent a lot of time with. Anything you think might help me get a better understanding of her.'

Their faces relaxed as they were transported to how their life had been before the knock on the door that shattered it.

'She was so clever,' began her mother. 'You know she got an unconditional offer from Oxford to read chemistry?'

Ashcroft nodded. He'd read it in the case file notes Daniels had taken that morning. *Chemistry* had been underlined several times.

'Was she looking forward to going?'

'Of course she was! It was going to be a whole new chapter of her life. It's why we bought her that car. A reward for working hard at school.'

What happened to success being its own reward? he wondered. He had grown up in a comfortable home, though nowhere near this level.

'How was she at school?'

'She was very popular. She had lots of friends.'

'We'll need to speak to them, and her teachers. If you'd be able to provide us with a list of their names?'

'Of course.'

They already had Aisha's phone and would be able to see who she contacted frequently. It would do no harm to see how this compared to the list her parents put together.

'What about boys?'

'She had no time for boys,' her father responded, quick and firm.

'Can you be sure of that?'

'She'd never have got into Oxford if she'd been stuck to someone like glue.'

'We're not a family who keeps things from each other,' explained Abena.

Even one quick to show their disapproval? Ashcroft wasn't so sure. He decided not to pursue the matter, he was more likely to find out what Aisha was really like from her friends.

'Jamal Deng. The young man found in her car. Did you know him? Or why he was there?'

'We've already told your colleague we've never heard of him. Perhaps Aisha was giving him a lift. That might explain what she was doing on that stretch of road when she should have been in assembly. She was kind like that. Keen to help others.'

It didn't explain why she wasn't in uniform, other than suggest she had no intention of going to school after performing this act of kindness. Ashcroft filed that thought away.

'You've never seen Jamal then? In passing?'

Aisha's father bristled at this. 'Where exactly would we expect to see him? In my wife's lecture theatre? In my chambers? Where do you expect this passing place to be? It's possible our paths may have crossed at the supermarket checkout or when I've filled my car up at the garage. Maybe he delivered a takeaway to us, your guess is as good as mine. What I am certain of is that we don't KNOW him – is that clear enough for you?'

Nazia threw Ashcroft a look, but he kept his attention on both parents. 'Yes, thank you, it is,' he said, nodding slowly. Grief made people unrecognisable. Even though Ozwald was giving a good impression of a pompous arse, it didn't mean he was one.

'Had you noticed any change in Aisha recently? Was anything worrying her? A change in behaviour or attitude that seemed out of character?'

'Nothing!' her father snapped.

Ashcroft nodded. He turned his attention to Abena. Waited for her to reply.

'Of course not!' she said, her voice matching her husband's irritation.

'I know this is hard. But can you think of anyone who she'd fallen out with recently? Anyone at all who might have wanted to hurt her.'

'Why are you not listening to us?' Ozwald demanded, slapping his hand down on his thigh. 'She wasn't that kind of girl. Didn't mix in the kind of circles where a disagreement ends in murder!' He looked around wildly, as though searching for someone to blame. 'As for that boy…' he spat, his words trailing off.

'Well, it's got to be something to do with him, hasn't it?' stated Abena. 'He's got to be the reason she's dead. Have you questioned his family yet? Made the same accusations?'

'No one's accusing anyone of anything. I'm just trying to get a better idea of their relationship.'

Abena glared at him. 'Why aren't you listening? There was no relationship!'

Ashcroft took a slow breath out. He was here to make sure the investigation was conducted with an open mind. That meant treading on everyone's toes, rather than a few. In for a penny, he thought, readying himself. 'Can you tell me where you both were this morning…'

'When our daughter was shot dead, you mean?' Abena's voice had risen, there was a tremor in it that hadn't been there before. 'I was at the university, preparing for a day of lectures and my husband was on his way to Liverpool to meet with a client. Neither of us have access to guns or had any reason to kill our daughter or the people she engaged with.'

'Thank you,' said Ashcroft.

The couple were exhausted. He didn't want to badger them more than he had to, but there was still something he had to ask.

'We're going to need a formal identification. I can send a car to pick you up…' He left *the sooner it's done the better* unsaid.

'I'll do it,' Ozwald said.

Ashcroft looked pointedly at Nazia.

'I'll take you,' she stated, picking up on his unasked question. 'We can go together. Why don't you try and get some rest first?'

Ozwald nodded, his head dropping back onto the chair behind him. Abena placed her hand on his and gave it a squeeze. With her other hand she rubbed her eyes with her forefinger and thumb.

'Do you mind if we take a look in Aisha's bedroom?' Nazia asked, keeping her voice low.

'I can take them up.' Sika was hovering in the doorway,

keen to stay out of everyone's way but not wanting to be on her own.

Ashcroft wondered how much she'd heard. 'Thanks,' he said getting to his feet. He turned back to Aisha's parents. 'This won't take long, I promise, then we'll leave you in peace.'

'There's no peace here, DS Ashcroft. Not anymore,' said Ozwald quietly.

'Are you as tidy as this?' Ashcroft asked.

They were standing in Aisha's bedroom. Her bed was made. Clothes put away. No food spilled or festering. Ashcroft didn't have kids, but as a murder detective he'd stood in enough bedrooms to know what normal looked like, and it wasn't like this.

Sika shrugged in reply.

Nazia had slipped on a pair of nitrile gloves and was checking the contents of a chest of drawers and several wardrobes. A discreet shake of the head told him she'd found nothing remarkable.

Ashcroft knelt down and looked under the bed. 'There's a laptop here.' He watched as Nazia placed it in a large evidence bag.

'That's her old one,' Sika informed them.

'Any idea where the new one is?' Nazia's gaze swept over the room.

'Maybe it's at her boyfriend's.'

Ashcroft angled his head towards her.

'I heard what Mum and Dad said but they don't know about Tobi,' she told them, squirming, hoping she wasn't in trouble. 'Aisha knew they'd go mad, so she made me promise not to say anything. I guess that doesn't apply now.'

'No it doesn't,' said Nazia. 'If there's anything you can tell us that will help us find out what happened to your sister, well, that's got to be a good thing, hasn't it?'

She closed the bedroom door quietly. 'Do you know this Tobi's surname, or where he lives?'

Sika shook her head.

'Any idea how old he is?'

'I don't know, in his twenties, maybe?'

'You've met him then?'

'No, but she showed me videos of him.'

Ashcroft's brow creased. 'What do you mean?'

'He's a DJ. That's how they met. He was playing at a club called Rizla she went to with her mates.'

'How does she get to see him if your folks are dead set against her dating?' asked Ashcroft.

'I can tell you don't have daughters,' Nazia answered. 'Ways and means,' she explained enigmatically. 'Isn't that right?'

Sika nodded. 'We'd all cover for her. Me and Jess, her best friend from school. Aisha would tell the rents she was staying at Jess's, and they never questioned it. Sometimes she would sneak out after Mum and Dad had gone to bed. She'd text me when she was coming home so I could unlock the back door for her.'

'I take it you knew she wasn't going into school this morning?'

Sika's nod was slow.

'Did you know Jamal, the boy who was with her?'

'I've no idea who he is. Sometimes she'd tell me I had to make my own way in. I just assumed she was off seeing Tobi.'

'Sounds like you were close.'

'Not really, she could be a bitch sometimes,' she admitted. 'But I never wanted her to die or anything!' she added quickly.

'We know that,' Nazia soothed. 'Now this club. Can you tell us where we can find it?'

'You were good in there, with her sister,' Ashcroft commented when they were back in the pool car.

Nazia laughed. 'Thanks, Sarge. I'm the middle of three girls so I know all the moves in terms of scamming your parents.'

'So, since you've appointed yourself resident teenage girl expert, what do you make of Aisha?'

Nazia's mouth turned down at the corners as she considered this. 'I'd have said she seems pretty normal. A bit wild perhaps, though she was probably making up for lost time. I mean, come on, eighteen and not allowed a boyfriend? Sounds like they were trying to make her live my life and trust me, it was no fun — on the face of it. Makes me wonder what else she kept from them.'

Ashcroft nodded. 'That's been going through my mind as well.'

'Where next, Sarge? We going to track down this boyfriend?'

Ashcroft shook his head. 'That can wait. First, I want to speak to Jamal's family. Try and get a measure of the young man Aisha's family are adamant she didn't know.'

'No problem,' Nazia said, indicating right as they approached a mini roundabout before following the flow of traffic away from the town centre.

THREE

'If you want to do some good today, you do it in there.'

– HANNAH ASHCROFT

Appleton House was a six-storey block of council flats beside a row of maisonettes in the centre of the Abraham Road Estate. It was part of a cluster of mid-seventies built concrete dwellings that had been threatened with demolition until the developer contracted to renovate the site went bust. The council hadn't wanted to waste money on maintenance during the intervening years, resulting in run down blocks with an increasing number of empty flats as tenants who moved out weren't replaced.

The children's playground had been upgraded by lottery funding, though the only people using it were youths loitering by the swings, hoods up, scrolling through their phones while passing a rolled-up joint between them. The pungent whiff of skunk caught in Ashcroft's throat as he stepped out of the car. No point arresting them for possession, causing ructions for the sake of it when there was a murder to solve.

A poster stuck to a lamp post at the entrance to the playground had Kamali Harris' face on it. The five-year-old thrown off a balcony six weeks before. The text below his name said *Can you help Police find his killer?*

'Was this where he lived?' asked Ashcroft.

'Neighbouring block,' replied Nazia, inclining her head towards an identikit building behind the block of maisonettes. 'Though his family have been re-housed now. There are posters throughout the estate, at his primary school and one in the local shop.'

'Anyone come forward with information?'

'I'll give you three guesses.'

As they approached Appleton House a young man in his late teens stepped out of the block. He wore a padded North Face jacket over a zip up top. His gaze raked over Ashcroft as they levelled with each other, his interest turning to his phone when it rang.

'Jamal's mother lives on the fifth floor, Sarge,' Nazia informed him, pushing the lift button.

'I'll see you up there, then,' he told her, taking the stairs. He preferred to be on the move, to keep his Fitbit happy. So much of the job was sitting about, when he got the opportunity to stretch his legs, he took it.

Nazia looked surprised when he stepped onto the fifth-floor landing not long after she'd exited the lift. 'Did you run up all the way?'

'Might have done,' he answered, enjoying the impressed look she threw in his direction.

'What can you tell me about Jamal?' he asked as they walked along the landing.

'He was in the sixth form studying for his A levels. Wanted to go into engineering. Dad's not around.'

Ashcroft threw her a look. He knew that much already from the sparse file he'd been given. 'Is that it?'

'DI Daniels was delivering the death message, Sarge. He wouldn't have wanted to bombard her with hard questions.'

Yet that was exactly what Aisha's parents had accused him of.

'Which family did he break the news to first?'

'We came here first. It's closest to the scene. Then on to Aisha's family.'

'Who by comparison, didn't match the profile in Daniels' head.' Unable to pigeon-hole them quite so easily, he'd asked clumsy questions which they'd challenged, making them appear difficult. 'You see where I'm going with this?'

Nazia shifted uncomfortably under his gaze.

They'd reached Jamal's front door. Nazia was saved from answering as the door opened and a woman all too familiar to Ashcroft stepped out.

'What are you doing here?' he asked her.

She lifted her medical bag by way of explanation. 'I called in to see Safia the moment I heard. Wanted to check she was OK.' She shifted her gaze from Ashcroft to Nazia then back again, gave them a thin smile. 'Sadly, I don't need to ask why you're both here.' Her brow creased for a moment, 'Hang on, have you moved jobs again without telling me?'

'Just helping out,' Ashcroft replied, holding his hands up in mitigation. 'This is my sister, Hannah,' he said to Nazia, then, turning to his sister, 'DC Latif is helping me get the lay of the land,' he explained as the women shook hands.

'How long are you planning on being around, then?'

Ashcroft shrugged. 'As long as it takes,' he said, indicating they'd better be getting on.

'Call by the house sometime, Theo would love to see you.'

Ashcroft nodded, his gaze dropping to the medical bag she carried, then onto the car park below and the youths gathered around the swings sharing a spliff. Estates like these were intimidating for a reason.

Hannah followed Ashcroft's gaze. 'You're not going all protective big brother on me, are you?' She tutted. 'It's a tad too late for that if you are.' There was a ring of steel in her voice that hadn't been there before. 'See the tall boy in the middle of the group?' She pointed to the youth he and Nazia had passed as they'd entered the block of flats. Ashcroft nodded. 'Nezim Hassan, though his friends call him Nozza. I treated his mum when she had a stroke. He'd dialled 999 but when the paramedics arrived they wouldn't get out of the ambulance until their police escort turned up, yet no one had been dispatched. He rang the surgery in a state, and I came straight away. She's fine now. And the young boy on the bike, dressed like his mini-me? That's his brother Muktar, known as Mikey.'

Ashcroft eyeballed a boy on a BMX, no older than ten, wearing a matching padded jacket.

'Those boys will stay there until I get back to my car. They're not a threat, Chris, they're looking out for me. Now you go on in and see Safia,' she added, angling her head towards the open door, 'If you want to do some good today, you do it in there.'

The flat smelled of allspice and plug-in air freshener. Chunky white trainers had been kicked off beside the doormat, footwear Ashcroft doubted belonged to the hushed voices coming from the living room. The hall was narrow. A semi open door led off to a kitchen, small but functional. Two casseroles had been left on the countertop, supermarket flowers still in their wrapper beside them. Ashcroft followed the voices. A woman sat at a drop leaf dining table, her fingers worrying at the tablecloth as though trying to remove a loose thread. She sat hunched forward, face drained, oblivious to the people around her. Two older women, dressed as though they were going to church, sat on a fabric sofa balancing teacups and saucers on their laps. A woman with coiled hair tied back in a bun got to her feet when he and Nazia walked in. Early thirties, she was dressed in plain clothes, a GMP lanyard hung around her neck.

'WPC Anita Lam, Sarge,' said Latif as she made the

introductions. Ashcroft approached Jamal's mother to express his condolences. He remained standing while the women nursing their tea got to their feet.

'We'll call in on you later,' one of them said, patting Safia's arm before gathering their belongings. 'We'll see ourselves out.'

Anita cleared away the tea things before returning to Safia's side.

'I grew up not far from here, Sarge,' she said, nodding her head in the direction of the maisonettes below. 'I attended the same church as Safia, until I left home.' She patted the woman's arm the same way her visitors had.

There'd be a lot of arm patting, over the coming weeks, Ashcroft imagined.

'I used to babysit Jamal sometimes when you were working a late shift, didn't I?' Anita added, looking at Safia. 'When he was a lot younger, obviously. Such a sweetheart.' She forced a smile, looking to see if Safia would join in. Whether she was ready to talk about him in the past tense.

Safia said nothing. Just kept moving her hands over the tablecloth. Pick. Pick. Pick.

'Let me get you a blanket, like the doctor said. You're in shock. You need to keep warm.' Anita left the room briefly, returning with a crocheted square which she placed over the woman's shoulders. 'How about I make us all a drink? Give you a chance to talk to the detective sergeant. I'll be in the kitchen if you need me.' She was good at her job, thought Ashcroft. Sympathetic, not patronising. Intuitive.

'Mrs Deng...' he began, moving into the dining chair across from her, motioning for DC Latif to take up position on the sofa. He watched while she pulled out her notebook and pen. Wondered whether she'd find much use for them.

'Call me Safia. Calling me Mrs makes me feel old...'

'Thank you.'

In a moment of strength, she jutted out her chin at him. 'I

suppose it's pointless me tellin' you he's a good boy. I bet they all say that, don't they? The mothers…'

Ashcroft waited, carefully constructing the questions he wanted to ask, in his head. 'I'm sorry to be bombarding you with questions at a time like this. I know this is the last thing you need right now. If there was another way, I promise you that I'd take it.'

He took a breath. Waited for her to respond.

'I understand,' she said, nodding.

'When did you last see your son?'

Safia thought about this. 'Yesterday morning. He brought me a cup of tea before he left.'

'How did he seem?'

'Like his normal self.' She shrugged. 'We don't talk much in the mornings. Save our conversations for when we eat together in the evening.'

'You didn't see him later then, for dinner?'

Safia shook her head. 'No. I had an evening shift at the hospital. I'm a cleaner. He'd gone out by the time I got home. I heard him come back in, but I was too tired to ask about his day. I slept right through until your inspector knocked on the door.' She turned to Ashcroft. 'Every night I lay awake waiting to hear his key in the lock. He teases me for it. I normally call out to him and he pops his head around the door, tells me what he's been doing. Maybe if I'd spoken to him he'd have told me where he was going this morning, why he wasn't going to school. I could have made him change his mind…'

'Don't torture yourself. There's nothing you could have done that would have made a difference. If I had a pound for every time a parent in your situation blamed themselves for something they did or didn't do…'

Safia nodded, pulling the blanket tighter round her shoulders.

'Did you know the young woman who was found with your son?' asked Nazia.

It was as though she hadn't spoken. She raised her voice a little to bring Safia back to the present, even thought that was the last place she wanted to be. 'Aisha Saforo, that's the name of the girl who owned the car they were both found in, did you know her?'

Safia shook her head. 'He never spoke about any girl. Then again, they don't at that age, do they? Like they're embarrassed to admit their feelings. The inspector who came this morning, he told me they were in some fancy car. I can't see what a girl who owned a fancy car would want with a boy from this estate.'

She had a point there. Even so. 'Aisha went to Mary Seacole Academy. Did Jamal mention knowing anyone who went there?'

'He never said anything to me about any girl or school.'

Ashcroft considered this.

'Any idea why he was on that particular stretch of road at that time?'

Safia was already shaking her head. 'No, like I said, he should have been at school. He's never missed a day, so it doesn't make sense.' She paused, as though remembering something. 'The inspector said he thought they were waiting for someone.'

'Did he?' asked Ashcroft, turning to DC Latif who responded with a quick shrug of her shoulders.

'He must have said that while I was making a drink,' she said quietly.

Ashcroft turned back to Safia. 'What else did the inspector say?'

'He said he's seen this before when kids stray onto the wrong turf. That someone must have taken offence to them being there.'

Entering another gang's territory was treated as provocation, to be met by violence or the threat of violence, but only if you belonged to an opposing crew. There was no evidence to suggest Jamal or Aisha were affiliated to any gang. It was too early in the investigation to rule it out, Ashcroft accepted that, but he was reluctant to flag it as the only possibility. Granted, their murder had all the hallmarks of a gang retaliation — had this simply been a case of wrong place, wrong time? Either way, there was no place for closed minds on an investigation.

It was as though Safia could hear the thoughts tumbling round his head. 'The inspector asked me if Jamal belonged to any gang. I told him no, never! He knows it doesn't lead to anything good. We spoke about it often. You think I walk about blind? I see groups of boys hanging round the estate. I know some of their mothers. We're not a generation of stupid women, you know. We just hope for the best, every single day. Besides, he's always been a kind boy. A good student. He works hard because he wants to get a decent job so he can look after me when I get old.' She laughed then. Kept on laughing until she remembered why she had the police in her home.

Resisting the urge to pat her arm, Ashcroft got to his feet, decided to leave her be for the moment. He looked around the tidy living room, at the photos on the wall and along the top of the mantlepiece that charted Jamal's progression through school. There were more school photos than he expected. He narrowed his eyes, took a closer look. In some of them the boy was heavier than the photo on the incident board. A lot less willing to smile at the camera.

'Does Jamal have any siblings?' he asked.

Safia raised her head. 'Abdel Johannes, though everyone calls him AJ. He's twenty-five. He's in the army now.'

'Has he been informed?' He exchanged a look with Latif but she stared back at him blankly.

'I-I can't break news like that to him over the phone. It'll break him,' Safia stuttered.

Ashcroft swallowed down a sigh. It wasn't much to expect that every investigation, no matter where, was conducted in the same way, but it wasn't realistic. The press referred to the way services in the NHS differed depending upon where folk lived, referring to it as the 'postcode lottery', yet policing was no different. He'd been brought into this investigation after the 'golden hour' had passed, only to learn the initial fact finding was incomplete. In murders like this — that had all the hallmarks of an execution — the background of family members was pivotal. Especially older siblings. Even more so if they'd moved away, left those that came behind them to deal with any fall out that they'd caused. The way things were shaping up he'd need to double check every detail to make sure he got to the facts. That took time, but there was no other choice if he wanted the job done properly. It might not be what the powers that be had in mind when they decided to transfer him there, but it was what they were going to get.

He kept his tone level. 'Nazia, perhaps you could take down his brother's details while I go and help Anita.'

Nazia nodded, turning to Safia: 'I'll take care of all that. Can you tell me where he's based?'

In the kitchen Anita had placed three mugs onto a tray. She turned as Ashcroft walked in.

'I forgot to ask whether you'd prefer tea or coffee,' she asked, lifting an empty mug.

'Water'll be fine,' he replied, picking a glass up from the draining board and filling it halfway with water from the tap. He gulped it down, rinsing the glass before returning it to the drainer. Anita placed the mug she'd been holding onto the countertop.

'What about your colleague?'

'She takes coffee,' he said, remembering the drink Nazia had made herself earlier at the station.

Anita placed a tea bag into one of the mugs, spooned coffee granules into the other two. She lifted the kettle, filled each mug with boiling water, shaking her head as she did so.

'It's a crying shame. I've known Jamal since he was a small boy. He's a good kid. I don't know whether he's got himself mixed up in anything, but if he has, I'm certain it won't be of his own doing.'

Ashcroft regarded her. 'What do you think he's mixed up in?'

Anita frowned. 'I have no idea. Not dealing, I'm certain of it. But I accept it doesn't look good.' She glanced into the hallway before pushing the kitchen door to and lowering her voice. 'I mean, it's not like he was standing in line at the local takeaway and was hit completely at random. He was sitting in some rich girl's car. A rich girl his mum didn't know about, and why wasn't he at school? Day or night, you came round here and he'd have his head in a book. Does that seem like a kid involved in gangs to you?'

Ashcroft, reluctant to commit to anything at this stage, moved his head just a fraction.

'Did DI Daniels know of your involvement with the family when he assigned you?'

'Of course he did. I was straight with him from the outset.' Her face was pinched, resenting his insinuation that she couldn't be objective. 'I accompanied Safia to identify his body. I think it helped her. Not having to deal with a stranger.' Her sentiments echoed those of Aisha's parents, who had declined the offer of an FLO for that same reason. Anita moved to the fridge, lifted out a carton of milk which she splashed into each mug. 'I'd better nip out later and stock up,' she said, giving the carton a shake, 'The rate we're getting through this stuff.'

Something niggled away at Ashcroft. He'd spent the last

five years partnering a DS at Salford. A big bloke who never knew when to keep his mouth shut, though he'd covered his back on more than one occasion. Salt of the earth or a right royal pain in the proverbial, depending on your perspective and which side of the thin blue line you operated on. He had this theory about sticking to basics. Would quote the ABC of detective work in the same way the Chief Super spouted guidelines from PACE.

Assume nothing. Believe no one. Check everything.

'You knew about his older brother then?'

Anita nodded, her pinched face turning sheepish.

'Yet you failed to pass on that information.'

'I'm sorry, Sarge, Safia was in a state. She was worried how he'd take it. I didn't think-'

'You see, that's what I'm worried about. Because of your involvement you've started making decisions about what information to pass up the chain.'

'You're right. I'm not normally like this. It was a temporary lapse, that's all. Please don't assign someone else to Safia, I think it would set her back. Isn't she going through enough? Look, I was playing up my relationship with the family a bit earlier to help make her feel more at ease. I've not seen them for years, in truth. Our connection is tenuous, but it's a connection all the same. One that I think can work for the investigation, not against it.'

'What about this brother then. Do you know where he's stationed?'

'No, Sarge.'

'Can you remember anything about him?'

'He got into a few scrapes growing up, caused his mum no end of shame for a while. Stealing cars, joyriding. Was brought home by the police on more than one occasion. The army seemed to straighten him out, though I don't know any more than that.'

'Did he and Jamal get on?'

'He doted on his brother and vice versa. Safia's right. Christ knows what this'll do to him.'

Ashcroft nodded, satisfied for the time being. He'd need to speak to DI Daniels. Didn't want to assume he was as clued into the relationship history here as Anita claimed he was. With careful managing, her relationship and knowledge of the family could prove to have more benefits than negatives.

'Could you show me where his bedroom is?' he asked.

'Yes, of course, just let me take these through to the other room.'

Ashcroft opened the door for her. While she handed a mug to DC Latif, he crouched in front of Safia, asked for her permission to take a look round Jamal's room. She blinked at him slowly. Nodded. Her fingers picking at the tablecloth once more.

He followed Anita into a room at the back of the flat. Small. Two single beds, one unmade. A desk and chair beside it with diagrams and notes stuck onto a notice board on the wall. Ashcroft put on a pair of nitrile gloves, leafed through the textbooks stacked beside a laptop. He held each one up by the spine, flicking the pages to dislodge any loose sheets. Apart from scribbled details of an assignment, nothing else fell out. He returned the books to their pile. A quick look at the jotter on Jamal's desk showed his handwriting was neat and when he was bored he doodled on the corner of each page. He pulled an evidence bag from his pocket. Slipped the laptop on Jamal's desk into it. The wardrobe was crammed with clothes folded into piles. Jeans. Sweatshirts. An old pair of trainers. Ashcroft pulled out his phone and took a photograph.

A look under Jamal's bed found nothing other than dirty underwear. He lifted the mattress. Found nothing.

'It isn't easy, is it? Unpicking someone's life like this,' said Anita.

Ashcroft shrugged. He pulled off his gloves, placing one inside the other before putting them in his pocket. He ran a hand over his closely shorn hair. It didn't help that TV shows made solving murder look like piecing a jigsaw together when in truth it was nothing like that. His job was to find who killed Jamal and Aisha, nothing more. He may never find the answers the families wanted. Murder cast a shadow over the victim. Created a mystery where there wasn't one, purely because every action they took was put under the microscope. Why did someone take a day off work without telling their partner? What made them take the train instead of catching their regular bus? Were they planning a special surprise or making plans to leave them? Some questions never got answered. Once the killer was found, second guessing the victim had to stop. Look at Jamal and Aisha. If someone walked into the station tomorrow and confessed to their murder — and the evidence corroborated it — it'd be case closed. They might never know what brought them together. It was something you learned to live with, or you'd go nuts. He picked up the laptop and put it under his arm.

'What's it like living round here?' he asked.

Anita blew out a sigh. 'You wouldn't if you had a choice,' she admitted. 'Dealers started taking over the empty flats when I was still at school. They used to be places where the junkies went to get high. They've turned them into trap houses now. No one wants that going on next door to them, do they? My family just learned to make the best of where they were. Good people live here too, and when you find decent people, you hang on to them, create your own little community, the same way the dealers create their gangs. We learned to look out for one another. Parents kept an eye on each other's kids, that sort of thing. The truth is, people on this estate have been left to fend for themselves. Residents go about avoiding eye contact with one another for fear of something kicking off. It's not just pensioners that are too afraid to go out after dark.'

Safia raised her kids the best she could and yet this still happened. Was it enough to track down the person who shot her son? Didn't she deserve answers too?

DC Latif appeared in the doorway with the empty coffee mugs. 'Safia's going for a lie down,' she told them.

'Our cue to leave,' Ashcroft said to Anita, 'Tell her we'll be in touch.'

Latif turned to Ashcroft once the flat door clicked shut behind them. 'AJ's in Cyprus. I managed to get a message through to his barracks, so I'm just waiting for him to call me back,' she told him breathlessly. 'Safia was able to give me the name of Jamal's best mate, too. He works in his dad's takeaway after school. I can take you over there, if you'd like to speak to him?'

Ashcroft nodded his approval.

Latif hesitated. 'I was off my game earlier and I want you to know I'm not normally like that.'

That was the second time someone had said as much to him in the last hour. Was he being hyper critical? He didn't think so, though he supposed he *was* covering his backside. Making sure no one on his team dropped the ball in case his management was reviewed and found wanting.

He smiled to put her at her ease. 'Don't let someone's rank stop you from doing your job properly. Just because someone else starts cutting corners, doesn't mean you should too. You've got to treat each day like your driving test. Check your mirror, indicate, manoeuvre. Get that bit right and everything else will follow. Now where's this takeaway?' he asked, his rumbling stomach reminding him he'd missed lunch.

FOUR

> 'What do you do for an encore, walk on fucking water?'
>
> – DI DANIELS

The café was situated between a Vietnamese nail bar and Afro Hair salon on Walcott Precinct. A short drive from Appleton House, it accommodated a market on Thursdays through to Saturday, selling everything from fresh fruit and vegetables to knock-off designer gear.

Mikey Hassan, one of the kids Ashcroft had seen minding his sister's car earlier sat astride his bike near the parking bay. He watched Ashcroft and Nazia climb out of their vehicle before pedalling towards the clustered stalls shouting 'Feds! Feds! Feds!' his North Face jacket flapping around him. Dealers languishing against the perimeter wall disappeared into the neighbouring tower block. Another scooped up bin bags from the pavement, before disappearing down a side street. Two men on the first-floor landing, who'd been overseeing the dealers, stepped out of sight when they heard the boy's shout.

'Nice to know our presence has such a positive effect on the environment,' said Ashcroft as they headed towards the cafe.

Nazia's phone began to ring. She glanced at the screen. 'Sarge, it's an international call. Probably Jamal's brother, I'd better take it,' she said, hanging back from the shop's entrance.

Ashcroft nodded before stepping inside.

The place smelled of cooking oil and vinegar, making his stomach rumble even more. He'd wait though, buying something here wouldn't be appropriate, given the nature of their visit. Besides, he liked to take care of his body. He was in good shape. Wanted to keep it that way.

He walked up to the counter which ran the full length of one wall. Stood behind a pensioner who'd given his order and was busy counting out coins, placing them on the countertop in piles. Satisfied he'd counted out the right amount, the old timer folded his arms and waited.

An olive-skinned man with dark hair and a hooked nose stood at the fryer, turning battered fish occasionally before placing them into the warming cabinet above it. Behind him an identikit youth Jamal's age cut slices from a rotisseried lamb, placing them into pitta bread already stacked with salad and peppers.

'What can I get you?' asked the man, wiping his hands down the front of his apron.

'I'd like to speak to your son,' Ashcroft told him, holding up his badge. 'I'm afraid I've got some bad news regarding Jamal Deng.'

The boy turned quickly at the sound of his friend's name. He was tall, skinny, long dark eyelashes over the family nose. He stared at Ashcroft, waiting. His father grunted, said something in Turkish which had the boy hurrying to wrap the kebab in paper and hand it to his customer.

'What is it?' he asked once the old man had gone. 'I've been messaging him but I'm not getting any answer.'

There was a small seating area. Plastic tables and chairs bolted to the ground like a prison visitors' centre. Not entirely welcoming but served a purpose.

'Let's go and sit down,' said Ashcroft, choosing the table furthest from the entrance.

By the time Nazia joined him, Fahri — who preferred to be called Faz — had been informed of his friend's fate and was drinking a small cup of mint tea which his father brought out in a silver pot from the back room.

'Please, call me Refik,' he said when Ashcroft thanked him. He'd poured a cup for Ashcroft which he sipped at slowly, then one for Nazia when she joined them. 'I cannot close the shop; I have to keep working — the rent on these units are too high to shut even for one hour — but I will leave Fahri to answer your questions.' He placed a hand on his son's shoulder, 'I'm sorry about Jamal. He was a good friend to you.'

Fahri's eyes were red-rimmed. A trail of snot had snaked its way onto his top lip. He swiped at it with the heel of his hand.

'His mum told me you were really good mates,' said Nazia.

'He was the best,' he hiccupped. He leaned his elbows on the table, placed his head in his hands. Stayed like that until his breathing returned to normal. 'Jamal was the only friend I had, to tell you the truth. The kids at school used to make fun of me. Claimed I stank of rancid meat. The first time he heard them yelling at me he told them to shut up, then insisted on walking me home. Made a point of calling for me on the way to school the next morning and every day after that. It's not even like he was a tough guy or anything. The others just liked him. Or at least they didn't hate him. Even the cool kids gave him no trouble. I guess some of that rubbed off. Either way, no one touched me when I was with him and after a while they started picking on somebody else.'

'How come you're not in school?' asked Latif.

'Sometimes I have to help my dad. He can't afford to pay someone regular, so I step in whenever he needs me. My teachers turn a blind eye as long as I keep up with my schoolwork.'

'Did you know Aisha Saforo? The girl that was killed with

him. Ashcroft showed him a photo of Aisha that he'd saved onto his phone.

Faz shook his head. 'Not really. I'd spoken to her once or twice, when she picked him up in her wheels. She was the full package; you know what I'm saying?' he looked at Nazia and reddened.

'How did they meet?'

'Dunno. He was always a bit cagey about that. It got me wondering if she was some sort of exotic dancer but then I got to thinking — what was he doing going to somewhere like that without me?' He glanced at his father quickly to check he hadn't heard. Refik continued frying fish, oblivious. Faz reached for his cup, then realising it was empty, let his hands fall onto his lap. 'I told him she must be up to something dodgy to drive a car like that, but he told me her parents had bought it for her.' He shrugged, 'That only made *them* dodgy in my eyes. I was worried about what he might be getting into. I warned him to stay away but it was a case of little head ruling big head, I guess.'

'So they were an item, then?'

Faz gave them a look.

'How long had they been seeing each other?'

A shrug. 'Coupla' months.'

'Did they meet up much?'

'Not really. Not as much as he'd have liked, going by his mood swings. But whenever she called, he went running.'

'Any idea why they were on Abraham Road this morning?'

Faz shook his head. 'Maybe they'd planned to bunk off school together and she'd arranged to pick him up there. Whatever the reason, it'll have been her suggestion. Like I said, whenever she called, he went running. I reckon he'd fallen for her big time. Some guys have all the luck, eh?' His face grew pale as he realised what he'd said.

'You thought she was trouble, though?' Nazia clarified.

'Yeah.' Faz nodded, his face clouding over. 'Turns out I was right, innit?'

'When was the last time you saw him?'

'Yesterday. He came round here after school. Said he had a whole stack of assignments to do so he couldn't stay long. Dad gave him a pizza to take home. Jamal always reckoned I was lucky having a dad, but then I don't have a mum, so I guess that made us even.'

'You said he wasn't answering your messages. When was this?'

'Round about midnight, then this morning when he'd have been up getting ready for school.'

'Were you worried?'

'No. I mean, he'd got a thing going with a hot looking girl. If he was too busy to talk to me then he had to be with her, innit?'

'We're asking everyone we take statements from to account for their whereabouts at the time of the shooting. Can you tell us where you were this morning around 9am?'

'It was my turn to go to the cash and carry for supplies. There'll be a receipt somewhere that I can show you. Give me a minute while I go and have a look.' He got up from the table, headed into the room behind the food preparation area where his father had made the mint tea, returning with a canvas jacket over his arm. He shoved his hand in to one of the pockets, then another, before pulling out a long slip of paper which he handed to Ashcroft. The time on the receipt said 9.12am. Ashcroft looked at the address at the top of it. The store was approximately twenty minutes' drive from the shop. 'Did you set off from here or home?' he asked.

'We live upstairs so it amounts to the same thing.'

Ashcroft put the receipt in his pocket. 'Thank you,' he said, satisfied.

'Had Jamal made any other new friends recently?' asked Latif. 'Started mixing with a different crowd at all?'

Faz shook his head. 'No way. That's not how it works round here. There are too many roadmen trying to get you to sell drugs or be a runner for them. If someone new starts being nice you give them the side eye, you know what I'm saying?'

'Those bastards act like they run the streets!' Faz's father called out from his side of the counter. 'Every week there is something. A shooting, a beating, someone gets knifed. It barely makes the news, but this is our life. This is what we have to deal with day in, day out. Ordinary people are already frightened to leave their homes, what's it going to be like when this gets out? You must find whoever did this, and find them fast.'

'I think we'll leave it there for now,' said Ashcroft, getting to his feet, signalling for Latif to do the same. He handed a card to Fahri, thanked him for his time. He moved over to the counter to hand another to the boy's father. 'I've been brought in from another area to give this investigation the attention it needs. You're right though, incidents like this traumatise the whole community. I'll have a word with my inspector. See if I can get more officers patrolling the streets, at least in the short term.'

'What, from the safety of their vehicles?'

Ashcroft considered this. 'I don't want to make promises I can't keep but I hope we can do better than that. Look, I'd be happy to speak to the residents. Reassure them that we're putting all our resources into this.'

'That's a lot of people you'd need to speak to.'

A thought occurred to Ashcroft. 'Would they come to a focus group meeting? A safe place where they can air their views and we listen?'

'Bah!' Refik made a swatting motion with his hand. 'The police have done things like that in the past and it's a waste of time. They do not listen to what we say. They just hope letting us get it off our chest will keep us quiet for a while.'

'Don't write something off just because it didn't work the first time. I wasn't involved then, but I am now. Do you think people would be willing to give it another try?'

Refik shrugged. 'I don't know.'

'But they could be persuaded. If someone like you said you thought it was a good idea?'

Refik hesitated before nodding. 'I could sound them out, I suppose. I cannot promise any more than that,' he said eventually.

Ashcroft nodded. 'That's all I'm asking. Leave it with me. Let me speak to my boss, see what we can do.'

Moss Side station

'What do you do for an encore, walk on fucking water?' DI Daniels lambasted after Ashcroft had walked into his office on his return to the station and repeated what he'd said to Refik Gemici. 'Community meetings are a waste of time. The only people that turn up are activists intent on causing trouble. Stirring things up for the good of social media. Before we know it we'll have a riot on our hands.'

Some people thrived on finding fault, a trait Daniels seemed to excel at.

'So, we get them to show proof of address before we let them in,' Ashcroft countered, 'This is about reassuring the residents that we haven't forgotten about them.'

'What's with all the 'we'?' Daniels sniped. 'You've been here for what?' he looked at his watch, 'half a day. Think that's long enough to get a measure of a broken estate? To tell the chief constable where he's going fucking wrong?'

Easy now, thought Ashcroft. 'There's no criticism sir,

certainly not of this station, or the division, but half a day is long enough to see what isn't working in a community.' He kept his tone level. Didn't want to be accused of being volatile. Situations like these didn't play out well when it was one person's word against another. It didn't pay to be angry or too smart. He swallowed down a sigh. 'I only saw one pensioner the whole time I was out, barely any parents with toddlers, and far too many kids hanging around on street corners who should be in school. There's no sense of community, because the community is scared to go out.'

'You're here to solve a murder, nothing else.'

'So you want me to wear blinkers? Ignore everything that's going on around me, no matter how much it perpetuates the problem?'

'Why not? It's good enough for everyone else.'

Both men looked at each other.

'I didn't want you here, Ashcroft. I'm not going to pretend otherwise.'

The feeling was mutual, but there was no need to get into a squabble about it.

Daniels took a breath. 'The Super's twitchy because the new Chief Con keeps making bold statements to the press about *cohesion*. He's anticipating questions from Top Brass about how he's going to improve it and you, my friend, will be offered up as his answer.'

'All the more reason to hold this meeting, then. Show the effort we're making. Find out how we can help the community with the resources we have.'

'It's not happening, now drop it.'

Ashcroft gave his shoulders a shrug, like an athlete approaching the starter's block before a race. 'The FLO placed with Jamal's mother. Anita Lam. You know she's got history with the family, right?'

'Yeah, she told me. She's a good officer and I trust her not to let it get in the way of her job. Feel free to replace her if you don't agree.'

Daniels was a smart cookie. As long as he gave Ashcroft enough rope to hang himself he couldn't lose. A bit of a steer might have been nice, but it was obvious he wasn't going to give one. Ashcroft wondered whether he was expecting too much. Being pedantic was a cheap way to score points, but there was no sense in cutting his nose off to spite his face. It would be beneficial having someone known to the family in situ when Jamal's brother returned home, especially if Anita's comments about his troubled past were true. He decided to keep things as they were for the time being.

'There's no reason to move her,' he conceded.

'Thank Christ for small mercies,' Daniels muttered, checking his watch once more. 'Now, you've got fifteen minutes to bring me up to speed on the investigation. The Super's sat upstairs like a parent waiting to hear how their kid's first day at school went. Let's hope you don't disappoint him.'

Back in the CID room Ashcroft wrote up the team's actions for the following day. This included going to Jamal and Aisha's schools, to see what the teaching staff and their friends had to say about them, and if anyone could shed light on their relationship. He'd put in a request to their mobile network providers for their call logs, though he wouldn't hold his breath. Retrieving this information was notoriously slow.

Then there was the matter of Aisha's official boyfriend. Or at least the one she had her sister help keep secret from their parents. The victimology report he was compiling — the process of finding out what the victims were like — was getting more interesting by the minute. They'd taken a statement from Aisha's parents and sister, along with Jamal's mother and his best friend, but had yet to speak to his brother. He looked at his watch. Nazia had taken Ozwald to the mortuary to ID his daughter. She should be on her way back by now. He gave her a call. 'How was he?' he asked once he'd checked she was alone.

'He didn't say much. I think he was holding onto his emotions until he got home.' She fell silent.

'What about Jamal's brother? Any idea when he's arriving?'

'AJ's going to let me know what flight he can get booked onto. Reckons he'll be back the day after tomorrow at the latest.'

'How did he take it?'

Nazia paused. *'It was hellish, Sarge, to be honest.'*

'Let's hope we've got something significant to report to the family by the time he arrives.'

'I hope so.'

She sounded tired. Like Potter, her shift had ended hours ago. 'Why don't you call it a night,' he said. 'Nothing that can't wait until tomorrow.'

'I'd prefer to come in and get those statements typed up tonight, while everything's still fresh,' she insisted. *'Besides, I'm not ready to go back to an empty flat just yet,'* she admitted.

'Your call,' said Ashcroft, relenting. Sometimes the office doubled as a decompression chamber. Routine tasks provided an opportunity to unpack an overloaded mind. He made a mental note not to leave until he checked she was OK.

Brian Potter's head popped up from behind his computer. 'Sarge, I've just had a call back from the officer I've been speaking to at NABIS.'

He sounded pleased with himself, as though he'd made a breakthrough, of sorts.

'The bullet casing taken from Aisha's vehicle is linked to a haul of illegally imported Glock pistols and ammunition seized by officers from Cheetham Hill during a raid on a warehouse last year. It's possible a consignment slipped through undetected.'

'Who does the warehouse belong to?'

'It's derelict. Nothing inside to tie it into any particular gang. There were the usual rumours, and a couple of informants not willing to go on record pointed the finger at the Berati Crew, a local Albanian gang, but that's as far as it went.'

'Could they have been responsible for bringing the guns in?'

'It's possible. The members of this gang are slick. Well connected. They don't leave a trail.'

'Apart from the blood of the victims left in their wake, you mean.'

Potter nodded, conceding his point.

'Have you checked to see if the bullet casing matches any others found in the locality since the shipment arrived?'

'Yep. There's no match.'

Ashcroft smiled ruefully. 'Would have been too much to hope for, discovering that a local crew had handled the gun before.'

'The good ship Hope sailed a long time ago in these parts,' said Potter, putting on his best sea farer's accent.

'Does the boss know about it yet?' asked Ashcroft.

Potter shook his head. 'You've heard it literally hot off the press. Besides, there's a chain of command and it's my job to follow it.'

Ashcroft nodded his thanks. 'I'd best go upstairs and update him then while he's briefing the Super.' The last thing he wanted was to be accused of sitting on information. He didn't blame Daniels for being bent out of shape by his arrival. Top Brass had a habit of making unilateral decisions without giving thought to the repercussions. Daniels seemed a decent sort. Short-sighted maybe, and like everyone at his rank, under pressure to achieve more with less. No reason why they couldn't rub along together just fine once the swelling had gone down on his bruised ego.

He took the stairs two at a time to the next floor, moving briskly along the corridor until he found Superintendent Duncanson's office. He knocked sharply. Waited for the barked permission to enter.

'Speak of the devil!' said Duncanson, greeting him with a broad smile. 'I hear you've made a great first impression.'

'I've met with both families, if that's what you mean, sir. They know I'm their first point of contact if they need any information. Speaking to Aisha's family has thrown up some discrepancies that I'd like to check out before I flag up as an issue.'

Daniels had been following the discussion with an odd look on his face. Ashcroft didn't know him well enough to decipher what it meant.

'Sorry for the interruption. I stopped by to let you know NABIS has identified the bullet found in Aisha's car.' He repeated the information Potter had given him. 'It has to have been used by someone with access to stolen hardware,' he summarised.

'I said it was gang related,' Daniels reminded him.

Ashcroft met his gaze. 'Now we have evidence of that it's a line of enquiry we can take further, though it doesn't mean Jamal and Aisha were complicit. I'll know more when I've been to their schools.'

'Great start,' stated Duncanson, 'I knew you'd be a positive influence on the team.'

Ashcroft sensed it was time to make his exit. He didn't want to overstay his welcome, though as far as Daniels was concerned he'd already shot that bolt. He made his way towards the door.

'Actually, Chris, before you go, there's something I want to float by you. DI Daniels here has been telling me about his

One Good Reason

idea for a neighbourhood meet and greet. The spike of shootings in the area has understandably put the fear of God into the community. He's proposing that we put steps in place to redress that. We've tried reaching out to the community in the past with varying degrees of success but he's rightly suggesting we mustn't be put off by that. Fresh faces and all that. I take it you'd be happy to get involved. Even run the first one?'

It was one of those situations where the way he responded would scar the way the Super thought of him from now on. Any hissy fit he threw would be passed on in anecdote sized sound bites. *Got to handle him with care. A bit touchy, that one.* He gave a brief nod.

'Excellent,' the Super continued. 'I'll let the chief constable know. A perfect example of cohesion in the community.' He was practically salivating. 'And a great example of *teamwork*. He'll want our press office involved, obviously. Won't do any harm that our newest recruit is so photogenic,' he added, his head pecking away at the thrill of it.

Ashcroft caught Daniels' flicker of a smile.

Fuckwit, he thought, smiling back.

Back in the office, Latif and Potter were waiting by his desk. 'Everything alright?' he asked, wondering if Daniels wasn't the only one he'd misjudged as a decent sort.

'It's a tradition in this nick that new team members are invited for a drink on their first day. You up for that, Sarge?'

Ashcroft's shoulders relaxed. 'I'd hate to be accused of not following protocol,' he replied, sitting at his desk so that he could log off his computer.

'Then you'll be keen to uphold the other tradition then,' Potter grinned, reminding Ashcroft of his colleague at Salford Precinct who couldn't help pushing his luck.

'And what's that then?' he asked, getting to his feet.

'Senior officer pays, of course.'

Both DCs had toiled through a double shift, if they were willing to spend a couple more hours in his company then the least he could do was pick up the tab.

'As long as I get to choose the venue, we have a deal,' he beamed, thinking of a way to kill two birds with one stone.

Rizla nightclub

'Look, Aisha's boyfriend, Tobi, is unlikely to know about her murder, given neither her name or Jamal's have been released to the press yet. Her parents didn't even know this guy existed,' Ashcroft reasoned, justifying why they found themselves standing outside Rizla's at 10pm.

Two glum faces stared back at him.

'I'm not gonna lie to you, Sarge. I'm feeling a tad out of place at the moment.'

In his Gore-Tex jacket Potter looked more like a dad taxi waiting to collect his daughter from her first disco than a clubber heading for a spot on the dance floor. 'Not exactly going to blend in, am I?'

His dress sense wasn't the only reason. The majority of the clientele waiting to be granted access were of African and Caribbean descent. As far back along the line as he could see, his was the only white face.

'Welcome to my world,' Ashcroft shrugged, patting him on the back.

'If this boyfriend found out she'd been knocking around with another fella it would give him motive,' said Latif.

'Agreed,' said Ashcroft. 'So let's see what he's got to say for himself.'

'While we're supposed to have finished for the night,' Potter reminded him.

'He's right, Sarge,' reasoned Latif. 'Before Brian here

orders tequila shots all round we need to know whether this is work or pleasure.'

'How about soft drinks tonight and we go for a proper drink tomorrow?' Ashcroft suggested.

Potter shrugged. 'Not quite the evening I had in mind, but then I've not got any better offers on the table.'

'Lovin' your dedication,' Ashcroft told him as they approached the main entrance.

The doormen eyed them up but saw no reason to bar entry. Inside, they moved along a garish corridor with a makeshift desk, then down a steep staircase.

'Let me know if you need any assistance, Brian,' Latif joked.

Potter's reply was drowned out by the increasing thump, thump, of the bass. 'I thought you said there'd be no music yet?' He jabbed an index finger into both ears before giving up when it made no difference.

'It's only the warm-up.'

'What if I'm already warm?'

'Not surprised in that get up,' Latif quipped, eyeing the zip-up jumper that he wore to work instead of a suit jacket. 'Don't you belong to the Haçienda generation?'

'The generation who went once and didn't like it, more like,' Potter responded.

'Decided the Ramblers Association was more your thing?' asked Latif, laughing.

Potter shrugged. 'Nothing wrong with a good walk at the weekend.'

According to the poster they were in for an evening of Grime and Drill.

'I don't even know what that means,' he sighed.

'Don't worry,' Ashcroft reassured him, 'by the time the rapping starts we'll be long gone.'

He'd removed his tie and unfastened the top three buttons

of his shirt. They'd taken off their lanyards earlier, placing them in pockets easily accessible if the need arose.

A young man resembling the video screenshot Sika had shown him and Latif earlier was in the DJ rig, getting his set ready for later that night. Occupying a raised platform, glass panels around the perimeter stopped uninvited punters getting too close. Amid the boxes and flashing lights he stood, shoulders hunched as he listened to his headphones, fingers busy teeing up the next track.

Potter came back from the bar with three cokes. 'Get your laughing gear round these,' he deadpanned as he placed them on the table they'd commandeered. It was all high tables and bar stools looking onto an as yet empty dancefloor.

Someone joined Tobi behind the decks. He had short dreads and metal teeth. The DJ lowered his headphones as he leaned in to listen, then nodded, before slipping his headphones on and getting back to his job. His visitor moved to an upstairs gallery where a group of men were lounging on velvet chairs in the VIP area. After fist bumping and tough guy hugs he sat down to join them, signalling to the barman for another round. Ashcroft craned his neck to get a better look. It was a champagne bar. A waitress carried a magnum of Moet in an ice bucket over to the table, was rewarded with a fifty-pound note. The economic crisis wasn't affecting everyone in quite the same way.

'That's the owner, Troy Mellor,' said Potter. 'I've watched him rise from a snot nosed kid dealing to anyone who'd stop and buy on his corner, to running the entire Abraham Road Estate. The guys with him are his lieutenants who oversee each tower block. He runs a tight ship and because of that he's been running rings around us for years. Organised Crime had him under surveillance for a while. Top brass put a stop to it. The overtime bill nearly bankrupted the division.'

'Smooth operator then.'

'Very slick. This bar will be his way of explaining his income. Oh, and did I mention the swanky pad he treated himself to, in the city centre?'

'How come you're so well informed?'

'I had the pleasure of paying him a visit about six months ago. A group of his foot soldiers turned up on a rival's patch with baseball bats and knives, gave their opposite numbers a good seeing to. He assured me he only knew the youths in passing. Knew nothing about what they got up to in their spare time. In turn, they stated they'd planned and executed the attack themselves. Who'd have thought it? They're all serving time now.'

'Can't see the appeal, personally,' Latif grunted, 'Giving up your freedom like that.'

'They don't have any choice, Naz. Their families are vulnerable once they're inside. Better to keep silent so they'll be looked after.'

The ground floor was beginning to fill up. Young men in padded jackets, gold jewellery glistening under the light from the bar. Women in figure hugging dresses and heels.

'Better get this over with,' Ashcroft said, climbing off his stool.

'Want us to come with you, Sarge?' asked Potter.

Ashcroft shook his head. 'Enjoy your drinks,' he said, placing a twenty-pound note on the table before making his way over to the DJ rig.

Potter studied his back. The grace with which he carried himself. 'The guy's all heart,' he said, tipping his coke down. 'Fancy another but with a voddy in this time?'

Latif looked at him uncertainly. 'Don't want to get on the wrong side of him so soon,' she answered, making her mind up. She shook her head. 'At least I won't need to shell out on a taxi. I'll get you one though, I won't tell.'

Potter stared dolefully at the bottom of his glass. 'No fun

drinking on your own, and believe me I've have plenty of practice.'

'Two more cokes it is then,' Latif said, wandering off in the direction of the bar.

'Can I help you, cuz?'

A fella so fat his cheeks wobbled as he spoke stepped in front of Ashcroft as he approached the stairs to the DJ's podium. The guy was no threat, but in a place like this was probably connected to someone who was.

'I need to speak to Tobi,' Ashcroft told him, deciding not to make his ID public. Places off the beaten track, where you couldn't be sure how the land lay, a police badge could double as a death warrant. He wondered fleetingly at the wisdom of showing up with two officers he'd only just met with no back up if it turned ugly. No reason it should, he reminded himself. Not if he played it straight down the middle. 'Personal business,' he stated, waiting while fat boy hauled himself up the steps after instructing him to wait.

Tobi slipped off his headphones to listen to him. Leaned in close as he spoke quietly in his ear. A tape was playing Stormzy on shuffle. *Big For Your Boots. Shut Up. Vossi Bop.*

Tobi turned, looked Ashcroft up and down before sauntering over to the edge of the rig.

'Do I know you, bro?' he called down to where Ashcroft was waiting.

'It's important,' Ashcroft called back. 'Regarding Aisha.'

He must have told fat boy to keep an eye on his equipment because he came down the steps alone.

'What is it?' he asked, a crease formed on his brow as he drew close.

'Not here,' Ashcroft told him. 'Somewhere private we can go?'

He followed him across the dancefloor to a room behind the bar. In his peripheral vision he saw Troy Mellor watching them as they made their way over. Ashcroft turned before he stepped inside, met his gaze head on.

The room behind the bar was poky. Enough space for a couple of chairs, a work surface with a sink and kettle. A cupboard above it, which Ashcroft guessed contained instant coffee and pot noodles and other staff workplace paraphernalia.

Tobi moved to the centre of the room before turning to face him. 'Dis private enough?'

He was in his early twenties. Wore a lightweight tracksuit in cream and gold. Matching high tops and baseball cap with the distinctive Prada logo.

'Can you tell me what your relationship is with Aisha Saforo?' Ashcroft asked, pulling his warrant card and lanyard from his pocket, and holding it up for him to see.

Tobi laughed. 'I don' need to see that to know you're a Fed, bro.'

'Then please answer my question,' Ashcroft persisted.

Tobi sucked air through his teeth. 'What's it to you?'

There was no good way to break bad news. No preamble that softened the blow when it came. Ashcroft decided to go for it. 'I'm sorry to have to tell you that Aisha is dead.'

'*What?*' It was an automatic reaction, not a question. He didn't need it repeating, he was trying to comprehend it. Tobi dropped into the chair behind him, placed his head in his hands as though feeling the weight of it. 'Fuuuuck…'

Ashcroft gave him a moment. 'Is there anyone I can call? Someone out there I can get to come and sit with you?' he jerked his head towards the door and the dancefloor beyond.

Tobi lifted his head, let his hands drop to his lap. 'And do what?'

Ashcroft positioned one of the other chairs to face him before lowering himself onto it.

'We didn't know Aisha had a boyfriend, otherwise we'd

have got in touch with you sooner. When my colleague broke the news to her parents, they didn't mention you. I'm afraid as far as they are concerned you don't exist.'

Tobi looked down at his hands and sighed. 'That's how Aisha wanted it. She said they were strict. Said it was easier telling them what they wanted to hear, so she could live her life the way she chose.' He lifted his head a fraction. Made eye contact with Ashcroft once more.

'How did you find out about me?'

'Her sister, Sika, told me, when her parents were out of earshot.'

Tobi started to shake his head. 'We've been seeing each other for nearly a year now. She didn't want it broadcast because her parents would have gone off on one.' His face cleared as he remembered something. 'She was building up the courage to tell them she wasn't going to Oxford. Said them finding out about me would have been the last straw.'

He pulled off his baseball cap and ran his hands over his hair, sat up straighter as it dawned on him that he wasn't in some weird nightmare that he could wake up from. 'Fuck, man.' He swiped at his face with his hands. 'How did it happen?'

'I'm sorry to say she was shot this morning. In her car.'

'No!' Tobi jumped out of his seat and planted his fist in the wall.

Ashcroft's brow furrowed. He wondered what answer would have been easier to hear. Dead was dead, after all. He was trying to deliver the information in the most relevant order. Shock made loved ones forget the bulk of the detail. Never the what, or the how, or the when, though. That would stay with them forever. Words and images that would play over and over on a loop. He tried to monitor Tobi's reaction. Was he shocked enough? Sad enough? Did he ask the right questions? He hadn't seen anything so far to raise concerns, though he wasn't done yet. He'd need to tread carefully for the next bit. Delivering the bombshell that Aisha wasn't alone when she was murdered.

'Where was she?' Tobi asked, giving him the perfect lead into what he wanted to say. He was still on his feet, his back leaning against the wall. His legs looked as though they'd buckle under him, but he refused to return to his chair.

Ashcroft told him the location of Aisha's car when the shooting happened, that a boy close to her age was in the passenger seat. That he'd been fatally shot too. As he spoke, he watched Tobi's face for giveaway tells that he already knew. That he was putting on a performance to hide the fact that in a fit of jealous rage he'd killed his girlfriend and the boy she'd been two-timing him with. Jealousy was a natural path to go down, as old as the hills. Once the red mist descended, people were capable of just about anything. Tobi started pacing around the room, the pokiness of it making him resemble a caged tiger.

'You sure it's her?' he whispered. 'I mean, could one of her mates have been driving?'

'Her father formally identified her this afternoon. There's no mistake.' Ashcroft paused. 'Was she in the habit of letting friends use her car?'

Tobi shook his head. 'No.'

'The boy in the car was Jamal Deng. Do you know him?'

Another headshake.

Ashcroft pulled his phone from his pocket. Tapped on the screen until he found what he was looking for. A recent photo of Jamal provided by his mother. He angled the screen towards him so he could see. 'Do you recognise him?'

'I already said I don't know 'im.'

'You might have seen him around,' Ashcroft reasoned.

'I've never set eyes on 'im before. That any clearer?'

'Crystal.'

Ashcroft put his phone away, giving Tobi a moment to let his anger subside. 'When was the last time you saw Aisha?'

'Last night. I was with her last night and everytin' was fine!'

'Where were you?'

'I was here, working. Aisha came here. It's what she normally does when I've got a gig.'

Ashcroft made a mental note to check where the nearest CCTV cameras were. Footage of her in the bar would help them construct a timeline leading up to her death.

'Was there anything unusual about her behaviour?'

'No.'

'What did she do while you worked?'

'She stayed with me.'

'All the time?'

Tobi cocked his head in thought. 'Sometimes she'd go to the bar and get us a drink.'

'Which bar?'

'She was allowed to use the VIP bar because she was with me. We get a coupl'a drinks a night on the house.'

'Nice perk. Did she stay with you till you finished your set?'

Tobi shook his head. 'She went home about midnight. Didn't want to aggravate her folks too much. It was hard to come up with excuses to stay out during the week, because the mates who covered for her on the weekend couldn't help in the same way on a school night.'

'Makes sense,' said Ashcroft, getting to his feet. 'I need to speak to the bar owner. Troy Mellor, is that right?'

Tobi nodded, jerked his head towards the floor above. 'He doesn't come in often but he's in tonight. In the VIP lounge with his mandem.'

'I'll go and find him,' said Ashcroft. 'Look, a couple of my colleagues are with me. Can I arrange a lift home for you?'

He shook his head. 'My car's here, but I'm staying put. I'd rather keep busy.'

Ashcroft nodded. 'I'll need you to come into the station so we can take a formal statement. Can you come in tomorrow?' He pulled out a card, patting his pockets for a pen to cross out his number at Salford Precinct station and replace it with the number of the main desk at Moss Side. He remembered something as he handed the card over. 'Sika reckons Aisha's laptop is at yours. Is that right?'

A nod.

'I need you to bring it with you when you come in tomorrow.'

Another nod.

Ashcroft paused. 'I'm sorry for your loss. I'm sorry you won't get to spend time with the people who loved her.'

Tobi's shoulders dipped in resignation. 'One o' dem tings, innit?'

'I need to ask you this,' Ashcroft added, raising his hands in mitigation. 'Can you tell me where you were this morning, around 9am?'

'Is that when it happened?'

Ashcroft nodded.

'That's easy. I don't finish here until 3am. I go home, sleep till noon most days.'

'Can anyone verify this?'

Tobi shrugged. 'Di only person who knew my routine was Aisha, and now she's dead.'

The minder at the bottom of the stairs leading to the VIP lounge was the polar opposite of Tobi's minder. Lean, angular features, he wore a black tracksuit with triple stripes down the outside of each sleeve. He grinned as Ashcroft drew near, exposing two gold teeth. 'Can I help you, Cuz?'

'I need a word with Troy.'

'"im busy wid 'is mandem right now. Yull need fi come back.'

Ashcroft moved his head from side to side. 'He might shake your lead but he doesn't shake mine. Tell him it's important.' He slipped out his warrant card to make his point.

'Sen 'im up,' a voice above them ordered.

Ashcroft looked up to see Troy leaning against the glass balcony. He was rewarded with a wide smile.

'How can I help you, *hofficer*?' Troy drawled as Ashcroft drew level.

Aware the man's cronies had quietened so they could follow the conversation, Ashcroft pointed to a small camera in the corner of the ceiling. 'I take it that thing works?'

'Why?'

'Do you know Aisha Saforo?'

A nod. 'Shi mi DJ's *empress*.'

Ashcroft locked eyes with him. 'She was shot dead this morning.'

'*What?* Fucksake, man!'

One of Troy's cronies sprang to his feet so that he was standing beside him. Mixed race with a neatly trimmed beard, he wore army fatigue pants and a khaki bomber jacket. A Yankees baseball cap on his head.

'Where did it happen?' he demanded.

Ashcroft told them. 'You were aware there'd been a shooting, though?'

When the CSI circus rolled into town it grabbed everyone's attention. There was no way these guys would have missed it, especially when it was on their doorstep. Social media would have been rife with speculation. Ashcroft made a mental note to get DC Latif to check what had been posted.

'We see de feds had put a tent over a vehicle. Knew someone had been licked 'cos o' de number of vans that were parked up. Fuck man, mi had nuh idea it was Aisha.'

Ashcroft pulled out his phone. Showed them Jamal's photo. 'You know this guy?' He clocked the glance they exchanged.

Troy shook his head.

'He was in the passenger seat, though he's in the mortuary now,' Ashcroft added, in case there was any confusion. 'Any idea who would do something like that?'

Troy gave him a look. 'You want mi fi do your job for you?'

'Reckon you could help if you wanted to.'

'Are you for real?' The crony who'd sprang to his feet spoke up. 'As tragic as it is, no one here knows nuttin' about no murder. And nobody here knows your bwoy.'

Troy nodded in agreement. 'Now tell mi what you want so you and Greater Manchester's finest waiting down there can move on.'

'I want a look at your CCTV tapes to verify what time Aisha was here.'

'We only have two cameras. Both are pointed at the cash tills. Stops any light-fingered staff in their tracks.'

Ashcroft suspected there were other, more compelling reasons why staff wouldn't want to get on the wrong side of Troy Mellor, but he played along. 'It might have caught someone hassling her when she went to the bar.'

Silence.

'I'm not interested in anything that might incriminate the dealers you let in here.'

'No idea what you're talking about...' said one of the seated cronies.

Ashcroft shook his head. 'Save it. All I'm interested in right now is catching a killer. And by the way, you've got a DJ down there who's going to carry on working tonight even though he's as good as broken. I hope you'll look out for him. Now, will you let me have those tapes and help me find who killed his girlfriend, or do I need to come back with a warrant?'

FIVE

'They believe us when we tell them that there is something better out there...'

– DR SAADIQ, HEADTEACHER, WHEATBURN COMMUNITY SCHOOL

Incident room

'As night outs go, I've had better,' Brian Potter said as he strolled into the incident room first thing the next day.

'Probably explains why you're so bright eyed and bushy tailed this morning. I'd be grateful for small mercies if I were you.' Latif was already at her desk, halfway through a pot of microwaveable porridge.

Potter grunted in reply. 'Any joy with the CCTV?' he asked as he hung up his coat.

Ashcroft noticed that yesterday's zip-up jumper had been replaced by a tank top. The fact that Nazia didn't comment on it suggested it'd had previous outings. The guy was nothing if not niche.

Troy had relented and handed over a digital copy for Ashcroft to take away. Its limited scope didn't give them much to go on. He pulled a face. 'Waste of time. You can see the top of Aisha's head as she orders drinks for her and Tobi, but that's it. I can just about make out the till and the countertop. Someone would have to have been up close and personal beside her to be captured on the tape.'

'Not the most salubrious of places for Aisha to be hanging out,' Latif observed, licking her spoon clean before putting it in her drawer. 'Put it this way, there was more dealing going on in there than the London Stock Exchange.'

'Hardly a positive environment, that's true,' Ashcroft conceded, although he'd spent many an evening in places like that at Aisha's age without being tempted to ingest pharmaceuticals. Maybe his passion for running had helped him toe the line. Or he just didn't like following the crowd. 'We'll find out from her toxicology report if she's been using anything,' he said.

'Her friends will give us an insight into that and a damn sight faster,' said Potter, 'Same for Jamal too. So far we've had their families' versions of them. Their friends will no doubt give us the true version.'

Ashcroft realised he hadn't asked Aisha's boyfriend if he was aware of her using drugs. He made a note to ask him when he came in to give his statement. He'd have to go back to the Turkish café and ask Fahri Gemici about Jamal too. Then he remembered he'd been tasked with setting up the community forum, thanks in no small part to DI Daniels pinching his idea. A case of careful what you wish for, he supposed. He added Fahri's father to his list of people to speak to.

'Fancy giving me a hand with a community forum that I'm setting up, Brian?'

Potter looked at him askance. 'Like my life isn't crap enough as it is? Then here you come with a big stinking wheelbarrow of manure which you want to offload onto me.'

'I take it that's a yes, then?'

Latif laughed. 'You know the rules Brian, manure only rolls downhill.'

'I'll put your name down as well then, Nazia,' Ashcroft volleyed, 'don't want you feeling left out.'

'As long as it's not Wednesday night. I've got Pilates on a Wednesday,' she informed him.

'And I've got model railway club on a Thursday,' said Potter.

Ashcroft laughed but the look Latif flashed at him said the DC was serious. He nodded hurriedly, 'We can accommodate that,' he said all business-like.

'It's good to see the boss was happy to support your suggestion,' said Nazia, 'at least you can go back to Refik Gemici and tell him you've fulfilled your end of the bargain.'

'You mean it was *your* idea?' Potter regarded him with wide eyes. 'Next you'll be suggesting an evening out on the pop without the pop. Oh, hang on, that was last night, how could I forget?'

'Don't worry. I keep my promises. Drinks are on me tonight at a venue of your choosing.'

'Now you're talking,' said Potter, all smiles.

'Oh, and if you're in earshot of the Super, the community forum was the boss's idea.'

'Been up to his tricks again, has he?'

Ashcroft regarded Potter quizzically.

'He has a habit of smothering good ideas then offering them up as his own, further down the line. I'm surprised he's only inspector. The amount of effort he puts into it I'd have expected him to be assistant chief constable by now.'

'I get the impression you've been here a while,' Ashcroft commented.

'I'm like part of the furniture, so I've been told.'

Ashcroft moved to a nearer desk, perched on the end of it. 'Tell me what you wish you'd known when you first came here.'

'Apart from where to get a decent coffee and where Daniels hides his single malt?'

Ashcroft nodded.

Potter's face grew serious. 'I'm the wrong person to ask.

Better officers than me have come and gone through those doors.'

'Yeah but you're the one I'm looking at.'

Potter shrugged. 'Means nothing. Just a case of last man standing, that's all.'

'More to it than that, I reckon.'

'I know how to keep my head down. At least, I do now.'

'What does that mean?'

'It means I live to fight another day.'

Ashcroft levelled his gaze at him. 'That was really insightful, thanks.'

They both new he didn't mean it.

Potter sighed. 'Look, there's plenty have come here thinking they'd make a difference. Most of them are on long term sick now. Then you get those who think a stint here will look good on their CV before putting in for promotion, and others who are transferred here as a form of punishment.'

'Where do you sit on that scale?'

A laugh. 'I'm still a DC, so I'll leave you to figure that one out.'

A punishment then, though as a result of what, he remained tight lipped.

'There are things you should be aware of though,' he said thoughtfully. 'Things that if I'd have known at the outset, my life would have been a hell of a lot easier.'

'Go on.'

'There are areas on our patch that the police no longer patrol. Streets that have effectively become "no-go" zones. If you do have the misfortune to go into these neighbourhoods you need to make sure you never go alone. You go in mob handed and loud.'

He pointed to a map on the wall behind him. 'I took the liberty a few years back of marking up — unofficially of course — said areas on here. 'We lost a WPC there,' he said, pointing to one of the alleyways that cut through the Abraham Road and Langston estates. 'And a PC here,' he said, pointing to a parking bay close to it. 'I was stabbed here,' he added matter of factly, pointing to one road, while with his other hand circled the area just below his ribs.

'When did that happen?' Ashcroft asked, pointing to the scar bisecting Potter's face. 'Five years ago. I was arresting a dealer who when I asked if he was carrying anything sharp in his pocket, turned out to be a lying bastard. Surgeons did a good job, all things considered. I did ask if they'd tighten up my jaw line while they were at it, though that seemed to fall on deaf ears. The knifing was last year. My wife left me not long after. Said she'd put up with two knocks on the door, wasn't hanging around for a third.'

'I thought you said you knew how to keep your head down,' said Ashcroft.

'Yeah, my wife said that to me as well.'

He stared at the map while Potter filled in the gaps. 'The two uniforms that were killed had responded to reports of a disturbance, totally unaware of the trap they were walking into. They'd arrested some fella the week before. Attempted robbery. Caught him in the act yet his family had taken offence. Claimed they'd needed teaching a lesson.'

He saw a look flash across Ashcroft's face. Misread its meaning. 'Every so often we send the drones in to see what's going on, but that's about it. Top Brass will never officially come out and say they've thrown in the towel, which means that every now and then some unsuspecting plod responds to a call and ends up getting their arse handed to them, worse still ends up in intensive care. I should know. A word to the wise. Memorise the names of these streets and never, ever, go there without full riot gear and the tactical firearms unit.'

Ashcroft continued to stare at the map. Tried but found it impossible to tear his eyes away. It was bad enough when residents refused to step out onto the streets, but for the police to take the same stance, where would it end?

'In criminal terms, these are among the most threatening streets in Britain,' Potter explained as though Ashcroft needed it spelling out.

In truth he was no longer listening. The map, and one particular road on that map, kept drawing him in. He racked his brain in the hope that he was mistaken, that he'd got the name of it wrong, or the location, but he knew damn well that he hadn't. He got to his feet, moving closer until he was standing right in front of it. Potter had used a red pen to mark out the roads it wasn't safe for the police to tread. He leaned in really close. He wasn't familiar with any of the street names apart from one. One that had three red circles round it.

'What does that mean?' he asked.

Potter laughed, but not in a good way. 'Sayonara,' he said, slashing his hand in front of his throat. 'Goodnight Vienna. Answer at your own bloody peril.'

There was no surprise that it was high risk. The reason being obvious once you knew what was there. Alfreton Road. The main road separating the notorious Abraham Road Estate on one side, the Langston Estate on the other. Slap bang in the middle of it, his sister's medical practice.

Potter's desk phone rang. He spoke into the receiver, said 'hang on a minute,' before turning to Ashcroft. 'Sarge, Aisha's boyfriend is downstairs. Want me to take his statement?'

Ashcroft nodded, getting to his feet. 'Ask him whether she was using. When you've finished with him I want you to go over to Jamal's school. See what you can find out from the staff and students.'

He paused on his way to the door. 'Nazia, I want you to check out what's been posted online about their murders, then make a start on Aisha's school,' he told her.

'You not coming, Sarge?'

'There's something I need to do first. I'll meet you there when I'm done.'

Hannah waited for her patient to leave before finishing the remnants of the coffee she'd brought into her consulting room twenty minutes earlier. With a full morning of appointments before her scheduled home visits, she tried to stretch the moment out. The weekly ante-natal clinic in the afternoon was something she looked forward to, gave her an opportunity to get to know the families on her list, reminded her of the reason she'd gone into medicine in the first place. The last hour of each day was spent returning patients' calls and passing on test results before catching up on paperwork. Even then there were the unexpected drop-ins, the ones who were unable to go to accident and emergency because they were undocumented, or their injuries raised questions they didn't want to answer. It was those patients, the ones with nowhere else to turn, who needed her help the most. With every minute of her day accounted for, the rare coffees she got to finish were something to savour.

The knock on her door made her look up sharply. 'Damn,' she muttered, hoping that whatever was interrupting her break merited it. She regarded the head that popped round the door, the identical brown eyes staring back at her and started to laugh.

'Two days in a row, I'm honoured!' she said, gesturing for Ashcroft to come in. She got up from her seat to envelope him in a hug, only stopping when he started to complain.

'Mind the threads, sis, spent an arm and a leg on this suit.'

'You were robbed then,' she laughed, giving his arm a playful punch before closing the door. She returned to her seat and patted the chair normally occupied by her patients. 'Have you never heard of the telephone? There's a waiting room full of people out there, so I can't be long. You'll come to dinner tonight, won't you?'

He'd forgotten how she spoke at a hundred miles an hour; how impatient she got when things couldn't be done by yesterday and how forgiving she could be with her errant brother.

'I can't stay long either, but I didn't want to do this over the phone.'

'What?' Her brow creased as he gave him an appraising look. 'You're not ill, are you?'

'Not that I know of.'

'So what is it then, you've got me worried.'

'Did you know this practice is slap bang in the middle of a police no-go area?'

She started to laugh. 'Seriously, is that it? I was panicking for a minute.'

'What do you mean, *is that it*? You do understand the implications?' He started listing his concerns, counting them off on his fingers as he said them. 'Number ONE, there's an unofficial policy with the local police NOT to attend calls unless they are of a serious nature. TWO, if attendance is deemed essential full riot procedures are followed. THREE-'

Hannah held up her hand to stop him. 'You think I don't know this? That I hadn't already worked out for myself that my patients have been left to fend for themselves?' She threw her arms wide, 'Man alive Chris, it's one of the reasons I chose to come here. To make sure their health care didn't go down the toilet along with everything else the rest of us take for granted.'

He gave her a look.

'What? You want me to set up some fancy clinic in Hale where if there's any whiff of a delay getting treatment my patients whip out their credit card and go private? Where they have nutritionists on speed dial and a trip to the spa means an aromatherapy treatment rather than the weekly shop. Is that all you think I'm good for?'

He'd forgotten how she ran rings round him when she was making a point. How it never paid to underestimate his kid sister. He held his hands up in surrender. 'Fine! Fine! I'm out of order. My bad. Pretend I never said anything.' He wasn't any happier with the situation but at least he knew she was aware of the dangers.

She rewarded him with a smile. 'All is forgiven bro, so long as you come to dinner tonight.'

He knew better than to get her riled a second time. 'I've promised my team a few drinks after work, but I'll come over after that,' he said, getting to his feet. He gave her consulting room the once over. 'Looks good.' With a pang he realised that was his first time there.

'I should hope so,' she said huffily, 'My patients deserve the same as anyone else's.'

He couldn't blame her for sounding defensive, in the same way she couldn't blame him for looking out for her. 'Actually, speaking of patients, can I pick your brains a minute? It's about a young boy by the name of Kamali Harris. Were his family patients of yours?'

'You know I can't divulge patient information.'

She'd gone from defensive to stern in two seconds.

He shook his head in reply. 'It's nothing like that, sis. I wanted to know how the community reacted to the incident. The family lived close to here, am I right?'

Hannah glared at him as though he wasn't being fair. 'A lot of the residents were terrified,' she said eventually, relenting. 'Traumatised, even. I mean, it was inhuman what his killers did to him. Tossing him away like rubbish. And all for what? To send someone a message?' She shuddered. 'Folk were scared for their lives for a long time. I'd go so far as to say for many it was a relief when his family were rehoused. Meant they didn't have to think about it quite so much.'

Her desk phone buzzed.

'That'll be reception telling me to wrap it up,' she said, smiling apologetically.

Ashcroft moved to the door and opened it. A brief scan to assess the risk in the waiting room.

'Oi. When you're here, you're here as my brother, not the police,' she reminded him. 'Don't forget the wine,' she added, whilst making a shooing motion with her hands.

Mary Seacole School was a two-storey redbrick which counted a member of the cabinet and a Nobel prize winner among its old girls. As word spread of the double murder, Aisha's face had made it onto the front page of the evening edition of several newspapers, bringing an entirely different notoriety to the school.

The head mistress was white, early fifties, her face set in a no-nonsense look. She'd already given a statement to the press, expressing the shock felt by the school community, advising that every effort would be made to help pupils come to terms with this senseless murder. 'Of all things a shooting!' she said, once she and Ashcroft were safely ensconced in her office, with no fear of eavesdroppers. 'I can't comprehend it!'

'Every murder is senseless,' stated Ashcroft.

'Some more than others,' she said stiffly.

Ashcroft levelled his gaze on her. 'What do you mean?'

'Shootings are often drug related, aren't they? According to the news.'

'Maybe you should be more selective which news channels you watch.'

After twenty years of teaching the offspring of wealthy

parents Veronica Chastaine wasn't easily thrown off her stride. 'Sorry?' she asked, when what she really meant was say it again.

Ashcroft was more than happy to break it down for her. 'Everyone who carries a gun without just cause is a criminal per se. But not everyone who gets shot is part of a criminal fraternity.'

'Yes, I know that! That's the point I'm making.'

Ashcroft was pretty sure that it wasn't, but he said nothing, happy to leave the conversation there. 'What kind of pupil was Aisha?' he asked, once he'd settled into the seat she offered him.

Veronica's smile was wide. 'She was hard working, dedicated, the top of her class,' she parroted, regurgitating her press release.

'Was she a natural scholar?'

The headmistress's face fell into a frown. 'Not really.' She breathed out a long sigh as though it was a relief to speak the truth. 'Look, you have to understand that the girls who come to this school may be privileged, but there is also a great deal of expectation on their shoulders. I take it you've met Abena?'

Ashcroft smiled in response.

'Then you can imagine what she had to live up to. Her father wasn't much better, but at least he wasn't demanding a full blow by blow explanation for any drop in marks awarded during term time.'

'Do most students go through fallow periods?' He tried to remember his time as a student. Couldn't recall anything he'd done that hadn't required hard work.

'Some. But bear in mind how exhausting that can be for the offspring of high achievers. Aisha's parents were no exception. They expected a consistent performance and outstanding success.'

'Only that wasn't the case with Aisha?'

The headmistress shook her head. 'Don't get me wrong, she was a bright enough girl but not naturally an Oxbridge candidate. She'd had countless tutors for most of her subjects, and though it was predicted that she'd do well, it wasn't with the certainty it is with other students.'

'How did Aisha cope with this weight of expectation?'

'That's not something she confided in me. Understandably she saw me as a tool to bring her parents' wishes to fruition.'

'Too establishment for her liking?'

She rewarded him with a smile. 'You could say that. I spoke to her parents briefly this morning. I didn't want to intrude. How are they?'

'As you'd imagine.' A standard phrase which was meaningless. No one really wanted to put themselves in Aisha's parents' shoes. Those that tried to empathise, their imagination wouldn't begin to scratch the surface.

Ashcroft met up with DC Latif in the school cafeteria. She had commandeered a table and several chairs from which she spoke to Aisha's friends in the presence of the guidance teacher, acting as an appropriate adult. Ashcroft waited for her to finish her current interview, thanking the young person for coming forward.

'I've spoken to the friends on the list her parents provided, including her best friend Jess, who came forward voluntarily. They all knew about the boyfriend; she was besotted apparently. She didn't take drugs; they were all adamant about that. I got the impression she was a bright girl, albeit no trailblazer, dead set against following in her parents' footsteps.'

'Pretty much what her head teacher said.'

'Did anyone have anything to say about Jamal?'

'Not a thing. No idea who he was. No one recognised his photo or saw him around. Hardly surprising. Not as though they moved in the same social circles.'

Ashcroft considered this. 'Any luck with social media?'

'I checked out the local community forums on Facebook and Twitter. Several amateur photos of the SOCO team in action yesterday were uploaded, followed by a thread of comments wondering what was going on. Put it this way, there were no cryptic posts from anyone claiming responsibility or pointing the finger elsewhere, if that's what you were hoping for.'

Ashcroft allowed himself a smile. 'OK, time to call it a day here. Go back and write up the statements you've taken. I'll head over and speak to Refik Gemici about this community shindig.'

Mikey Hassan recognised Ashcroft before he climbed out of his car. Yelling 'FEDS!' at the top of his lungs, his legs pumped the pedals as he raced along the perimeter of the market into the rat run of the flats beyond. Several youths lounging on chairs that looked like they'd been rescued from an old folks' home regarded Ashcroft as he walked towards the precinct. The youngest of the group, a wiry boy no older than thirteen muttered something which made the others snigger. Ashcroft walked on. Knew that on his own he was a sitting duck.

The men who'd been keeping watch on the first-floor balcony of the flats when he'd turned up yesterday were there again today. This time, instead of retreating into the shadows they maintained their stance, leaning against the concrete wall as they observed the activity below. Ashcroft recognised one of them as Troy's army fatigue wearing lieutenant, who'd sprung to his feet when he learned of Aisha's fatal shooting. Feeling the gangster's eyes bore into him as he headed towards the takeaway, Ashcroft turned and met his gaze. Nodded. The lieutenant nodded back.

Refik was on his own behind the counter. He wiped his

hands on his apron when Ashcroft walked in. 'If you are looking for Fahri he is upstairs. He has taken what happened to his friend badly. I thought it was best to give him some space. Let him come to terms with it in his own way.'

'Wise,' agreed Ashcroft.

'Besides, he is no use to me here.' He pointed to the lamb on the rotisserie. To the carving knife at the base of it. The deep fat fryer bubbling in anticipation of the lunchtime punters. 'The job is more hazardous than people think. No room for any lapse in concentration.'

'I can see that,' Ashcroft responded. 'As it happens it was you I'd come to see.' What he had to ask Fahri could keep.

'Yes?'

'I got the go-ahead from my boss for the community forum. The DC who was with me yesterday and another colleague are going to help with the arrangements. There's a small budget that will cover refreshments.' He wasn't sure about the last bit, but he reckoned Daniels owed him for taking the credit. He'd throw in a few quid himself if needed. Now it had been given the green light, he wanted it to succeed.

Refik's face lit up as he considered this. 'We could run it at tea-time, throw in a plate of food.'

'Budget might not be that big,' Ashcroft said quickly but the Turk was already waving away his objection.

'Leave it with me, detective sergeant, I am confident we can work something out.'

Mindful of Brian Potter's model making commitments and Nazia's Pilates, Ashcroft suggested an evening for the following week. This would give them enough time to put up posters and drop flyers through letterboxes, alongside posts announcing it on social media.

'Fahri can help with this. Take his mind off his troubles.'

'It's great that you're willing to get involved,' Ashcroft told him, 'None of this would be happening without you.'

Refik shrugged at his words. 'My part in this is easy. Yours, hmm, not so much,' he said with honesty. 'People round here do not feel listened to. They have felt this way for years and their frustration is growing. You have just one evening to make them feel heard.'

And catch the killer in a double shooting, thought Ashcroft.

No pressure then.

Sleep had evaded the man sat across from DC Brian Potter and it showed. Bloodshot eyes looked out beneath his baseball cap. Patches of stubble were visible along his chin. He'd thrown on a sweat top and jogging bottoms, both had seen better days. Must save his high-end tracksuits for when he had a gig, thought Potter. He'd declined tea and coffee but said yes to water. Tobi Harun's hands circled the plastic cup like it was a life raft.

'Where's the other cop?'

'He had to go out, he asked me to take your statement.'

'There's not much to say.'

'More than you think, in my experience.'

'He asked me to bring this in.' Tobi lifted a laptop from the messenger bag on the floor by his feet and slid it across the table. 'It's Aisha's.'

'Much appreciated,' said Potter, placing it beside his notepad. He studied the young man as he sat shoulders hunched, elbows resting on the tabletop.

'You got family?'

A nod.

'You're probably going to need them.'

Tobi's mouth slid into a smile. 'You don't know my family.'

'You sure you're alright with that water? I can freshen it up if you like?'

'Nah man, I'm good.'

'OK if we make a start?'

The smile slid away. 'I just said so, didn't I?'

When Potter returned to the CID room Latif was staring at her computer, her fingers moving lightly over the keyboard. She looked up as he made his way over to his desk.

'There's a chocolate brownie with your name on,' she called over, grinning as he turned full circle to make a beeline for the plate she held up.

'Now you're talking.' He took a bite. A look of pure pleasure flitted across his face. 'Not your birthday, is it?'

'No, my period.'

Brian shrugged. 'Happy menstruating.'

Nazia's face lit up as something occurred to her. 'Funny, isn't it. How we say MENstruating and MENopause when they don't happen to men.'

'I can honestly say it's something I haven't thought about. HIStory's also misleading, though, isn't it, if you want to start splitting hairs.'

'And MENdacious,' said Nazia, 'though I haven't a clue what it means.'

'I'd keep that to yourself,' Brian warned, 'given the career path you've chosen.'

Nazia's face screwed up in confusion, quickly followed by delight. 'Ah, Sarge, just the person,' she said as Ashcroft walked in carrying a cellophane wrapped sandwich and a smoothie. 'Would you like a chocolate brownie?'

Brian took the plate from her and offered it to Ashcroft so he could choose one.

'And before you ask, it's not her birthday,' he said quietly, his tone suggesting that the conversation be left there.

Ashcroft shrugged out of his jacket before taking a bite. Chocolate wasn't his thing, but there was no harm in joining in. 'How did you get on with Aisha's boyfriend?' he asked between mouthfuls which were, he admitted, surprisingly good.

'He's genuinely gutted,' said Brian. 'Seems she'd been planning to move in with him after she'd finished her exams.'

'What about her studies?'

'She'd had enough apparently, had already started looking for a regular job. According to him they'd thought it all through. With a couple of extra gigs a week he could cover the bills till she had an income coming in.'

'Sounds like they were the real deal,' said Nazia.

Potter nodded. 'Seems she was biding her time, plucking up the courage to tell her parents.'

Ashcroft frowned. 'Sounds like her folks had a lot of surprises coming their way.'

'Not excluding the fact Aisha's boyfriend works for a local drug lord,' stated Nazia.

Ashcroft considered this. 'Hmm…No easy way to soften *that* blow.'

'Could he be supplementing his income by dealing?' asked Nazia.

Potter shook his head. 'I can't see it, Naz. Reckons he's seen more losers than winners. Claims he's got no intention of ending up the same way.'

'And Aisha?' asked Ashcroft.

'Said she wasn't like that. Had more sense than throw her life away.'

Ashcroft considered this. 'What else can you tell me about this boss of his?'

'Troy Mellor runs everything on the Abraham Road Estate. The dealers, the trap houses that produce the merchandise, the kids on bikes who act as spotters. Even the stall holders on the market are there on his say-so. It's how every estate runs round here. Some of these guys have been in position a long time, though a couple of estates have gone through a significant turnover.' He nodded towards the murder wall in case a reminder was needed.

'Who runs the road where Jamal and Aisha were shot?'

Potter was already shaking his head. 'That's not so easy to pinpoint. If your patch covers an estate, it covers the whole territory right up to the ring road. But the stretch of road connecting one estate to another — that's a whole different story. In theory it should be no man's land — each gang needs that road to move their supplies onto their patch. Even so, every once in a while some kid comes along who thinks it's a great starting point for their career in narcotics. What they don't bargain for is that trespassers suffer the combined force of every crime syndicate, who've formed a kind of alliance to protect themselves from external threats. You know how it goes, *your enemy is my enemy*, and all that.'

'So Jamal and Aisha's presence on that road, in a car like that, would have made them an open target from several crews?'

'Agreed.'

Ashcroft frowned. 'What the hell were they doing there when they knew it wasn't safe?'

'How can you be expected to know the terms of engagement when you're not involved in the war?' asked Nazia, which was reasonable enough.

Ashcroft recalled his conversation in the nightclub. 'Going by his reaction last night, I don't think Troy had anything to do with this. And this morning, when I went to see Refik at the Turkish café, Troy's main sidekick was on the tower block balcony again, only this time he nodded at me. I think it was his way of showing we have his support.'

'That's a good thing, isn't it? These guys don't normally go out of their way to cooperate with us,' stated Nazia.

Ashcroft and Potter exchanged a look. Their experience of dealing with gangs told them nothing could be further from the truth.

'Depends. They may be hoping that if they sit on our coat-tails long enough, we'll lead them to the killer. Then slam, dunk, before we get to say *you're under arrest*, there's yet another name on that wall,' Potter explained, angling his head towards the murder board ominously.

Ashcroft recalled the look which passed between Troy and his lieutenant when he showed them Jamal's photo at the nightclub. There was something they weren't saying. Then again, in his line of work he was used to people holding things back.

Nazia shook her head. 'This Aisha's some girl. She's managed to keep two relationships secret. Makes me wonder what else she's been able to keep hidden.' Her mobile rang. 'International number,' she said before answering. She stated her name, nodding at Ashcroft to indicate it was Jamal's brother. 'Give me your flight number,' she said, reaching for her pen to take it down. When the call ended, she sat back in her chair, satisfied. 'He's booked on a flight to Manchester first thing in the morning. I'll pick him up and take him over to his mum's. See what I can glean from him on the way.'

Ashcroft nodded his approval. 'Any luck with the letting agency about that empty shop unit?'

'I've called their number several times, Sarge, it just rings out.'

'Keep trying.'

He turned to Potter. 'Mind if I tag along when you go to Jamal's school, Brian? Don't want you to think I'm stepping on your toes…'

'The more the merrier,' said Potter, 'Gimmee half an hour to type up Tobi's statement.'

Ashcroft remembered something. 'Aisha's laptop – did he bring it in?'

'He did indeed. I've sent it over to the tech guys. See what they come up with.'

They were in a pool car which Potter was driving. He drove like someone who'd just passed their driving test. Eyes frequently glancing in the rear-view mirror. Hands positioned at 'ten' and 'two' on the steering wheel, he stayed at just under the speed limit, even then, his right foot hovered over the brakes. It was as though his near-death experience in no man's land had made him risk averse. Hardly surprising.

'Did you attend the crime scene when the shout came in for Jamal and Aisha?' Ashcroft asked him.

'Briefly. The boss and Naz were next on the rota. I attended because I was closest. I'm technically working the Kamali Harris file but given that our crime scenes are close to each other it makes sense for me to be part of this investigation team too.'

'Daniels thinks there could be a connection then?' If he did, this was the first Ashcroft was hearing about it. He wondered why the DI hadn't run this possibility by him. Asked him to widen the scope of his investigation. Get him to check out Potter's list of potential suspects. The basics of murder investigation, he thought sourly.

'He's covering his backside, that's all,' Potter told him. 'It's not the first time he's had us running round like headless chickens. It's a general management technique here, closely followed by clutching at straws.'

'Same everywhere,' Ashcroft conceded.

'Not quite. The murder rate for this area has doubled, yet

the arrest rate has plummeted. Violent crime is back dominating the headlines and politicians are wetting themselves in the rush to address it. The problem is, talk is cheap. It's all very well that the Home Secretary's given chief constables the green light to ramp up the number of Section 60s carried out, but no-one's talking about how we manage the backlash that'll follow.'

Police had the power to stop and search an individual or vehicle if they had 'reasonable grounds' to suspect the person was carrying something illegal: Drugs, a weapon, stolen property, or something which could be used to commit a crime. However, a Section 60 order enabled officers to stop and search individuals or their vehicles without requiring any reasonable grounds. It usually followed a violent incident and would be limited to specific neighbourhoods for a defined period of time, but the execution of it, especially by over-zealous officers, left the force open to accusations of racial profiling and harassment.

Nice trainers.

'You'd better tell me about your investigation, then.'

Potter grimaced. 'It's been fraught with emotion — and fear — right from the beginning. Kamali was murdered in broad daylight, yet no-one saw anything, or rather, anything they'd be prepared to take to court. We carried out a fingertip search of the entire area, including the balcony he was thrown from, but it didn't give us anything.'

'Door to door enquiries?'

Potter gave him a look. 'Like I said, nothing.'

'CCTV?'

'They're broken the moment they're installed, so that was a non-starter.'

There was nothing new in that. CCTV towers in parts of Salford were regularly cut down with angle grinders by the local gangs. Keeping a watchful eye over the community was an impossible task.

'The boy's father. You said yesterday that he'd recently stopped working for a drug lord. At the risk of telling grandma how to suck eggs I'm guessing you checked out that connection.'

Potter shrugged. 'I don't mind you asking. You've been parachuted in, probably against your will, the last thing you want is to find you've been landed with a sloppy team.'

Ashcroft didn't contradict him.

'The father's refusing to say anything about the gang that he worked for or describe Kamali's killer, even though they are likely to be connected. He has another child. He doesn't believe the police are able to keep his family safe. You can hardly blame the poor bastard.'

'If he knew how dangerous the gang was that he worked for, why did he leave in the first place?'

It was a golden rule that gangs didn't allow members of their crew to walk away without reprisals. Membership was all about control.

'He found himself between a rock and a hard place. The council moved him and his family from the Langston Estate to the Abraham Road Estate because the baby has asthma, and their old place was covered in mould. A flat became vacant in Windward Tower, it was as simple as that. Problem was that meant he was moving out of one territory into another — Troy Mellor's turf. He'll have been told in no uncertain terms by the soldiers who run that block that the only product he'd be allowed to shift was theirs, and in the spirit of wanting to stay alive he'll have agreed.'

Potter glanced at Ashcroft. Decided to elaborate:

'There's a massive difference in the infrastructure of the gangs based in Salford compared to those in Moss Side. In Salford they tend to be family based, with a main lynchpin, usually the father, uncle or brother who calls the shots. Some of them live cheek by jowl but in the main they live where they like, within reason. At the end of the day, they are connected by blood.'

'Or bloodshed,' Ashcroft interjected.

'You get the gist though,' Potter said, waiting for him to nod. 'The crown is passed down along the family bloodline, same as it is with King Charlie and his motley crew. It's the children and grandchildren of those gang members that step into their rightful position when the time comes. If David Attenborough was looking for an example of the Circle of Life, crime family style, Salford would be it.

In Moss side, however – in Fallowfield, and Cheetham Hill, for that matter – the gangs are more likely to be postcode driven. When they're not naming themselves after famous rappers, they use street names or use bus routes to come up with their titles. Probably goes back to when the developers rolled in and communities were broken up, dispersed to the new sink estates that the council were creating. At the end of the day, folk need a sense of belonging.'

Ashcroft gave him the side eye. 'People can adapt, though, surely. Isn't it a form of resistance to hark back to the way things were all the time and not try to change?'

Potter considered Ashcroft's question, though he wasn't entirely sure they were talking about the same thing anymore.

'Depends where you find yourself. There's no doubt some situations are worse than others. The problem with the gang culture we're dealing with here is how transient it is. A self-appointed general selects his lieutenants who in turn recruit their own soldiers. These soldiers are typically aged fifteen to eighteen. They in turn recruit 'youngers', who range in age from thirteen to fourteen, and 'smalls', who're eight to twelve. They're the ones you see racing about the estates on bikes, watching everyone and everything, taking it all in. They're like the eyes and ears of the lieutenants. The gangs use these underage kids to move their product between areas and hold onto guns because they can't be as easily arrested and detained as the older gang members. Everyone follows orders or they're out. Only out means dead. And the general's power lasts until someone bigger and harder comes along.'

Ashcroft's nod was slower this time. It was hard keeping up with the *Drug Dealers' Code of Conduct* when it kept being rewritten.

'Who runs the supply where Kamali's family used to live?'

'An Albanian gang known as the Berati Crew, named after the leader, Ervin Muka's place of birth. They took over the block about five years ago. They have dealers on every walkway, corner and landing. It's rife.'

'What do we know about them?'

'We know that they're ruthless. That they employ ex-mercenaries to do a lot of their dirty work, but there isn't a shred of evidence linking them to Kamali's murder. It was a weaponless crime carried out with maximum efficiency. There were no defence wounds but then that's not unusual with child murders — the poor kid wouldn't have had a clue what was happening.'

A small mercy, Ashcroft supposed. 'We need a witness, then,' he concluded.

'Correction. We need a different witness.'

Ashcroft threw Potter a quizzical look.

'Kamali's dad was in the square in front of Windward Tower when Kamali was thrown off it. He saw it happen.' Potter glanced at Ashcroft to check he was keeping up. Realised he needed to fill in the blanks. It was easy, when you were all over a case, to speak in a shorthand that others not involved with it weren't familiar with. 'There are plenty of people who will tell you that they saw Kamali's father returning home in the minutes leading up to his son's murder.

That when he crossed the square heading towards the block, someone on the third-floor balcony called out his name. That what he saw when he looked up had him running with his arms outstretched. They can even describe the sound Kamali's body made when it landed on the skip, and all agree that his father didn't stop screaming until the paramedics came.'

They'd paused at the traffic lights. Ashcroft eyeballed the driver of a transit van in the next lane who was speaking into his phone, kept on eyeballing him until the driver put it away.

'What no one admits to seeing is the person who called out to Kamali's father. Or who lifted his five-year-old son over the balcony before letting go of him.' Potter moved his head from side to side, 'To think that, in this day and age, no one came forward with a single photo or video clip of the incident despite our appeals. It beggars belief.'

Straight after the murder they'd put out an appeal for digital footage, inviting the public to upload any images or videos they might have directly onto GMP's Major Incident Portal. So far no-one had availed themselves of the facility.

Ashcroft wasn't as quick to condemn. It was easy taking the moral high ground when you didn't have skin in the game. When doing the right thing meant obliterating life as you knew it. He was trying to get to grips with the fact that Kamali's father had witnessed his murder. The horror of it. 'Where was his wife?'

'She was found in the bedroom with her hands tied behind her back, the baby crying in its cot beside her.'

Ashcroft massaged his temple with his middle finger and thumb.

'Can I speak to them?'

Potter made a sound like a tyre losing air. 'Not a chance. They've been moved for their own safety and their whereabouts haven't been divulged to anyone. Security was tightened up after that fella was taken out last year. Did you hear about it? He was going up against a sex abuse network but was executed in his safe house before it got to trial. Turns out one of the senior officers on the investigation was being blackmailed. She passed on his whereabouts to the gang and that was it. Made front page of the papers the next morning. Press had a field day.'

Ashcroft remembered much more than the newspaper headlines. His equal number at Salford had been seconded to the taskforce set up to dismantle that network. He'd seen close up the damage the police leak had caused.

The repercussions that continued to be felt.

He turned to Potter and nodded. They'd find another way to get the information they needed.

Wheatburn Community School was a modern building with a large open plan reception area. Murals of inspirational people had been painted along one wall, motivational quotes on another. Ashcroft and Potter waited for the head teacher beside a large window that looked onto a central courtyard. A shrine had been erected in honour of Jamal. His photo had been taped to a wall, an array of flowers and candles had been placed beneath it, although not as many as the display at Aisha's school.

'We asked the students to organise a collection instead to go towards the cost of his funeral. Seems a more practical way of showing support.'

The detectives turned to the person standing behind them who'd spoken. Mixed race, mid-forties, hair starting to turn grey. He wore a navy-blue business suit with a striped tie. 'I'm Dr Saadiq,' he said, shaking their hands before leading them up a flight of stairs to his office. 'Can I offer you a tea or coffee?' he asked, pausing outside the staff room.

'No, we're good,' answered Ashcroft, keen to crack on.

A window ran the length of Saadiq's office, providing an elevated view of the enclosed courtyard. He moved towards it, arms folded. 'The building was designed to maximise light,' he informed them, as though addressing prospective buyers. 'And the recreational space below is a safe place for our students to socialise.'

Several benches had been placed here and there. A tree, its size denoting it was older than the school by several decades, provided shade, or shelter, depending on the season. 'There've been instances in the past where gang members have tried to intimidate certain children. Their parents owe them money, or the child owes them money, or it could be another reason entirely. Here, our vulnerable pupils can enjoy being outdoors without fear.'

'Is that much of a problem in school, gang allegiances, I mean?' Ashcroft asked.

'More a constant battle, which we're on the right side of, at the moment.'

Bypassing his desk, he moved to four chairs placed around a low table. A plant and a prospectus lay on top of it. He took a seat, invited both detectives to do the same.

'Our catchment area includes estates that have been at war with each other since my current cohort's parents attended. We can't control what goes on outside school, obviously, but we've introduced a visible presence. At the start and end of each school day staff stand at the school gates, as well as at the main bus stops used by the pupils. Our intention is to reassure our young people and their parents that school is safe.'

Ashcroft nodded. 'What can you tell us about Jamal?'

Dr Saadiq considered Ashcroft's question. 'Obviously, I knew you would be asking me this, and I've tried to think of something that doesn't sound like I'm rehearsing his eulogy. But he really was a good kid. There was never any issue with his attendance. His timekeeping was excellent, and he showed on countless occasions that he was a very considerate member of our school community.'

'We spoke to his friend, Fahri Gemici. He told us how Jamal took him under his wing back when they both started here.'

Dr Saadiq nodded. 'That was very typical of him. He was bright too. We had no doubt he'd have done well in his exams.'

'What about his brother? Do you remember much about his time here?'

The headteacher looked troubled. 'Hmm…let's just say they were very different. Fair play though, I hear he's settled into army life. Good for him.'

Ashcroft clocked his response. Filed it away.

'Did Jamal mention any issues in his home life?' Potter asked.

Dr Saadiq's brow creased. 'Not at all. He had a very good relationship with his mother. Indeed, both boys did. Safia has always been very supportive of their education.'

'Did you meet Jamal's father?'

'No, I'm not sure that he was ever on the scene. Jamal was fortunate though; his mother is such a force of nature I don't think it mattered.'

'What do you mean?'

'While AJ was in school, she enrolled at the adult education centre here. Got good enough grades to study as a legal secretary at night school. Secured a job pretty soon after, as I recall. If that isn't an example of a positive role model, I don't know what is. Mind you, I think Jamal's arrival threw a spanner in the career works,' he chuckled, 'but it's always something she can go back to, when the time's right. No education is wasted, though I'm bound to say that, aren't I?'

'Had there been any changes in his behaviour recently? Something that might not have needed dealing with formally but something that his class teachers had noticed?' asked Ashcroft.

'Something they might have gossiped about in that staff room,' added Potter.

Dr Saadiq considered this. 'I tend to stay away from there during break time so the staff have somewhere they can blow off steam. But now you mention it, a couple of his subject teachers remarked in passing that he'd been a little pre-occupied lately. Not unusual, this time of year, in the lead up to exams…' He leaned back in his seat, blew out a breath, and with it all his positivity seemed to desert him.

'We need to find a way to make this stop!' he blurted, his gaze seeking Potter's before settling on Ashcroft. 'These kids come to us, and we say to them, *listen to us, we're here for you. Put in the work and a better life is waiting.* But how can it when they return to the same broken estates night after night? Walk past the same soldiers on the street corners promising lots of cash for a lot less effort. And these kids, the ones whose spark we've managed to reach, they don't listen to them. They remember something I told them in assembly or what their class teacher said when they were finding it tough going, and they carry on. They turn up every day. They believe us when we tell them that there is something better out there, that they can have a better life if they keep on studying. And then *this.*' He threw his arms wide.

'Another assembly. Another vigil. Another memorial service where I say *let this be the last time*. When does it end? When can I step out there and tell those kids they can make their lives better and not feel like I'm the biggest phoney on this earth?' His hand shook as he ran it over his face. He dipped his head as he tried to regulate his breathing.

'Are you OK?' asked Potter, exchanging a wide-eyed glance with Ashcroft. 'I'll make a start interviewing Jamal's friends,' he mumbled when Ashcroft inclined his head towards the door.

One Good Reason

Ashcroft waited a couple of beats. Until he heard the click of the door as it closed behind Potter. 'Take as long as you need,' he said quietly. He got up from his chair. Walked over to the window. It must have been afternoon break as the courtyard began to fill with pupils. Some paused for a moment as they passed Jamal's shrine. Others walked by without giving it a second look. How many of the boys on the station's murder board came from this school, he wondered, or had fallen off its roll several years earlier?

A girl about thirteen sat on a bench close by. She pulled a book from her satchel and started to read it. He'd never thought about the toll it must take on the teachers and staff. Knowing the potential they nurtured in class stood little chance of flourishing outside the school's four walls. That the best they could hope for was the absence of a negative.

He turned at the sound of Dr Saadiq clearing his throat.

'I'm sorry about that. Can we pretend I didn't just have a meltdown in front of you? Do you think that'd work?'

Ashcroft, who'd been deep in thought, nodded before returning to his seat. He smiled as an idea wormed its way into his head. 'I think there may be a way we can help each other...'

Afternoon briefing, Moss Side station

DI Daniels perched a buttock on a spare desk in the main office, as he read out the interim postmortem reports on Jamal and Aisha. 'No real surprises here,' he said, squinting at the print outs rather than put on the glasses peeping out of the breast pocket of his jacket. Such vanity, for a man with a mullet, mused Ashcroft. Daniels provided a summary:

'Aisha's blood was present on the tip of the bullet that penetrated Jamal's skull, confirming that she was shot first.'

'So, whoever killed them saw her as a civilian then,' said Potter.

'Or the innocent party in *this* dispute, at least,' said Nazia.

There was a time when non-combatants, or civilians as they were now called, were protected from harm by the gangster code of honour. These days they were often targeted deliberately – a way of hitting rivals where it hurt most. It wasn't unusual for the civilian to be killed first – in full view of the intended target – for maximum impact.

Kamali Harris's killer calling out to the boy's father as he lifted him over the tower block balcony.

The scream.

'Any observation you want to make at this point, DS Ashcroft?' Superintendent Duncanson leaned against the back wall, like an assessment centre facilitator observing short-listed job candidates while they pretended to work as a team.

All eyes swivelled in Ashcroft's direction.

'It's too soon to say who the intended target was. I've not picked up anything so far that suggests one victim over the other. Aisha has demonstrated a pattern of deception — keeping her boyfriend secret from her parents, keeping her relationship with Jamal secret from her boyfriend and friends. Nothing at this stage suggests she had anything significant to hide, but it's a pattern, nonetheless. I've seen no evidence to indicate they belonged to any gang, nor do they move on the peripheries of one. Their assignations, if we want to use that term, were in private. No one else, apart from Jamal's best friend, knew about their relationship.'

He turned to DI Daniels, 'Do we have the results of the tox screen?'

'I was just getting round to that. Both came back negative,' replied Daniels, through gritted teeth. 'The pathologist has requested a fast track on the rest of the bloods taken. Even so it'll be a couple of days before they come back.'

'That's fine. At least we know they weren't using.'

'At their time of death, anyway,' stated Daniels.

'As corroborated by statements taken from their schoolfriends,' Ashcroft clarified. He reported on his and Potter's visit to Jamal's school — minus the head teacher's meltdown. He invited Nazia to report on their visit to Aisha's school, followed by Potter's report on the statement he took from Aisha's boyfriend, Tobi Harun, and Jamal's school friends.

'It's still unclear why they were on that stretch of road instead of being at school, so that's a line of enquiry I want to explore. Both of Aisha's laptops are now with the tech team. Is there a reason she kept one at her boyfriend's place? Actually,' he nodded towards Potter as he said this, 'Brian, if the techies are pushed for time can you get them to prioritise that laptop first. I'm guessing she didn't keep it at home for a reason.'

'Will do,' said Potter, reaching for his notepad.

'The witness statements taken at the time of the shooting tell us nothing. *One assailant wearing a ski mask and gloves* — doesn't tell us if they were black, white or somewhere in between.'

He felt the weight of Daniels' gaze on him. 'If it's alright with you, boss,' he said, returning his gaze head on. 'I'd like to familiarise myself with the investigation into Kamali Harris's murder. I understand his murder and the one I'm investigating were carried out in close proximity.'

'As long as it doesn't distract you from this investigation then that's fine with me,' Duncanson answered on Daniels' behalf.

Daniels jutted his chin out. 'Or gets in the way of the community forum,' he added petulantly.

'It's all in hand boss. A date and venue have been agreed and I'm pleased to confirm that the headteacher from Jamal's school, Dr Saadiq, will be one of the speakers.'

Daniels frowned. 'It's a residents' forum, not a conference. Where those with nothing better to do turn up and bitch about lack of police presence one minute, then over policing the next. We nod sympathetically and hand out leaflets and pens. Job done.'

Daniels was a twat, but nothing Ashcroft couldn't handle. He shifted in his chair so that Duncanson was in his line of vision.

'You've heard the phrase, *It takes a village to raise a child*?' he asked, looking around the room.

'We're in Moss Side, not Midsomer. Mind you their body count could give us a run for our money,' sniped Daniels.

Despite the DI's sarcasm, several heads nodded at Ashcroft's statement.

'Well, I'm working on the premise that it takes an estate to keep a child safe. A lot of people work damn hard in that community, but they've become disconnected. I want this forum to be an opportunity for them to step out of their silos and reconnect, and at the same time remind residents of the support already on their doorstep. Our resources are limited. We can't make promises we've got no chance of keeping, so it's in our interests to get as many organisations to engage with us — and each other — as possible, and this is the perfect occasion. I know it's not what you originally envisaged, so I can scale it back if you'd rather,' he added, tongue in cheek. 'There should be some great PR opportunities, though. All we'd need is an opening address from a senior officer.' He looked directly at Superintendent Duncanson as he said this.

The Super beamed back, already drafting his speech.

'Right, if that's us done, let's call it a day,' said Daniels, his tone neutral. His tapping foot suggesting he was anything but.

The bar was Brian Potter's choice. A shabby exterior that by no means prepared intrepid drinkers for the even shabbier interior. The décor was so dated it was almost retro, if the sticky carpet and peeling walls hadn't given it away.

'What are you having?' Ashcroft asked, as they made their way to the bar.

'They do a cheeky little red if you want to get a couple of bottles,' Potter answered before making his way to the Gents.

'He doesn't get out much,' Nazia warned, 'but it gets more palatable with every glass.'

'Good to know,' said Ashcroft, signalling to the landlord.

The bar was empty save for a couple of faces he recognised from the station. As police watering holes went, he'd been in worse. If all you were looking for was a no-frills location to get inebriated, then this place provided it in spades.

Ashcroft carried the wine to a table while Nazia wiped the rim of each glass with a clean hanky.

'Trust me,' she mouthed, once the landlord was out of range.

Potter made his way to the table, buckling his belt. 'Alright, isn't it?' as asked, indicating the wine Nazia had poured into each glass.

'It does the trick,' Ashcroft said diplomatically, avoiding her eye.

'There's only me can get away with saying this, but you're a bit of a dark horse, Sarge,' said Nazia. 'I mean, I had no idea this event you're organising had grown so big.'

Potter threw him a knowing look. The man had an uncanny knack of sniffing out bullshit.

'Well, you see Nazia, I might have exaggerated the current state of play. Just a little bit, mind,' Ashcroft admitted.

Nazia's face fell like a child who'd discovered the truth about Santa and the Easter Bunny all rolled into one. 'How much?'

Potter placed his palms together as though in prayer, then started to move them apart slowly, waiting for Ashcroft's cue.

Ashcroft took a swig of his wine. Waited until Potter's arms were fully extended either side of him. 'Okay, so maybe I exaggerated a bit more than I should have.'

'Was any of it true?'

'Er, the date and venue have been organised. And Jamal's head teacher has definitely agreed to speak at it,' he added defensively.

'If he doesn't have another meltdown,' Potter muttered, under his breath.

'What?' Nazia regarded him.

'Nothing,' Ashcroft said dismissively.

'It sounded really great, Sarge, the idea of it,' Nazia said, unable to hide her disappointment.

'Well, even if it doesn't amount to anything, it was worth it to see Daniels' face fall in on itself,' Potter observed.

Ashcroft hated not delivering on his promises, even ones made rashly. 'Look, my mouth ran away with me, but there's no reason why we can't come good on some of it.'

Potter gave him a knowing look. 'Did you hear that, Naz? All of a sudden it's *we*. I am honoured,' he added, raising his glass in a toast.

'You did say you'd help,' Ashcroft reminded him.

'Yeah, when I thought it was handing out leaflets and pens.'

Nazia looked at him bright-eyed. 'He doesn't mean it, Sarge, what do you want us to do?'

'It'd be great if you could contact sports clubs, parents' groups, health providers…' he reeled off a list of community support organisations.

'You could ask your sister to get involved,' said Nazia. 'She's a GP,' she added, turning to Potter.

'Good idea,' said Ashcroft, chiding himself for not thinking of that.

Nazia drained her glass and got to her feet. 'As fun as this has been, folks, I've got a date.'

'The sarge isn't the only one who's a dark horse then,' Potter remarked. 'You kept that quiet.'

'Hardly. I only set it up this afternoon.'

'So, who's this lucky fella then?' asked Potter.

Nazia checked her appearance on her phone before pocketing it. She lifted the bag from the seat beside her and slipped the shoulder strap over her head. 'It's a *she*, actually. I've decided to keep my options open,' she answered, giving him a sly wink as she headed towards the door.

'You two get on well,' observed Ashcroft, after she'd gone.

'She treats me like her dad, you mean.'

Ashcroft reckoned the reverse was true. Compared to the strict upbringing Nazia had described when she'd talked about her parents, Potter came across like a walk in the park, more genial uncle than Pakistani patriarch. Maybe she was projecting the kind of relationship she'd like to have with her father, onto him.

He swirled the wine in the bottom of his glass before knocking it back.

'You never said why you were transferred here,' he said.

'You're right, I didn't.'

'Sorry,' Ashcroft said, backing off. 'I didn't mean to pry.'

'Yes you did, but I understand why. You want to get the measure of everyone on your team. I get that. It's just that what brought me here isn't something I'm proud of.'

Ashcroft was intrigued. 'Go on, what did you do?'

'It's more a case of what I didn't do. I was one of those officers who looked after number one when I first joined. Reckoned the smart way to make it to my pension was to sidestep trouble wherever I could. I got a reputation for being a bit of a lazy bastard, but I didn't care. Didn't think I was doing any harm. Some officers love a bit of aggro, go looking for a ruck, especially at the weekend. I was the opposite. One night a colleague put out an urgent call for back up over the radio. I was the closest officer, but I didn't respond. I stayed in my car. When two units raced past me responding to the call it spurred me into action, but by then it was too late.'

'Your colleague didn't make it?'

'He was fine. Hospitalised for a couple of days but back to full duties within a week. No, it was my reputation that ended up dead and buried. No one wanted to work with me and they sure as hell didn't trust me. I was transferred here and I've been here ever since. There was a piss up when I left but I wasn't invited.'

Ashcroft nodded towards Potter's scar. 'Seems to me like you've more than made up for any poor choices you made back then.'

'Agreed. I've paid my debt to the universe. Paid the price in the looks department too, which was some sacrifice, I can tell you. So be warned, I'm under no obligation to do anything heroic before I retire.'

'Good to know.' Ashcroft reached for the wine bottle, topped up Potter's glass before refilling his. He'd pre-booked a taxi. Could drop Potter off on the way to his sister's. There was something he'd been meaning to ask. Something that was a lot easier with a drop of the drink inside him. 'How hard was it, working Kamali's crime scene?'

He'd worked enough child murders to know the toll that they took. How they stripped away at all that was good and decent. There'd been a case a few years back, where a little girl pumped full of drugs had fallen through a first-floor window fleeing from her abuser. The sicko had stuffed her body into a sport bag and hidden it in a closet. As vile as it was, there was something about his action that made sense. It wasn't like there was an etiquette. A right way of performing the cruellest of crimes. But the fact he'd hidden her body spoke of the shame he'd felt. The realisation that something atrocious had occurred, and the part he'd played in it.

Kamali Harris had been left spread-eagled across a pile of rubbish destined for landfill. The inhumanity of it. The skip had been left by the entrance to the block. His killer would have had to pass by him when he left. Had he avoided looking at him to assuage his guilt? Or had he sought out his broken body, the satisfaction of a job well done?

Potter stared at the bottom of his glass as though he'd find the answer there.

'It was Hell on earth for everyone working that day. Imagine your worst case.' He looked up, met Ashcroft's gaze. 'It was like *that* with bells on.'

Ashcroft looked away. He wished he hadn't asked. He hadn't meant to rake it all up, but having seen that photo on the incident room wall he couldn't rid himself of the image either.

'I'm sorry,' he said, meaning it. His phone began to vibrate. His taxi was outside.

'I've got dinner at my sister's house; I can drop you off on the way.'

'Charmin', am I the only one who made sure he wasn't double booked when we picked tonight?' grumbled Potter as he got to his feet. He lifted the bottle to his lips. 'Waste not want not,' he said, wiping his mouth with the back of his hand when he'd emptied it.

'This sister of yours,' he said once he'd climbed in the taxi behind Ashcroft. 'Where's her medical practice?'

Ashcroft told him.

'Then I'm sorry too,' said Potter.

Ashcroft's sister lived in a large semi-detached new build on the edge of Stretford. The houses here weren't as grand as the double income properties further south than her postcode, but aspirational all the same. Hannah's ex was a surgeon now working in Chicago, a move she hadn't been willing to make when he'd been offered the post of Head of Thoracic surgery. Their split had been amicable, and they co-parented their son with the minimum of fuss. Theo flew out to stay with his father every school holiday and alternate Christmas.

Ashcroft juggled the flowers and wine he'd picked up from the Tesco Metro round the corner and rang the doorbell.

'You shouldn't have gone to so much trouble,' Hannah said dryly when she flung open the front door. She took the flowers from him, peeling off the price tag before placing them in a jug she'd already filled with water. 'Decent wine though,' she said, nodding in appreciation before stepping into his hug.

He followed her into the kitchen. Accepted the glass of white she handed to him while calculating whether he'd be over the limit in the morning. He'd book a taxi to run him in, be on the safe side.

'You're allowed a night off,' she told him as though reading his mind.

'I've come straight from a team bonding session,' he told her, raising his glass to indicate that alcohol had been imbibed.

Hannah pulled a face as she moved round the kitchen island to perch on a bar stool, inviting him to do the same. 'Poor you. Was it tedious?'

He shook his head. 'Better than I was anticipating, to be fair.'

'Yeah well, I know you. That doesn't leave me feeling inspired.'

Ashcroft shrugged away her concern. 'They seem decent enough. Haven't come across too many idiots yet.'

'Amen to that,' she said, clinking his glass with her own.

'Besides, I can handle idiots on the front line. It's those higher up the food chain I need to keep an eye on. They brought me in to handle the so-called 'difficult' parents of the girl murdered alongside Jamal, but they're no more complex than any other grieving family.'

Yet it was more than that. He took a sip of his wine as he considered this. 'They're wealthy, educated and articulate, why are we so threatened by that?' He smiled ruefully. Aware he'd used 'we' when what he really meant was 'the force'. He'd spent his life shapeshifting constantly to make white people comfortable around him. Adopting a cloak of respectability that would earn their trust. As a result, his identity was confined to the parameters of an HR tick box. He was Black Caribbean, without really knowing what being Caribbean meant.

Hannah studied him but said nothing. She had the uncanny knack of knowing when to be quiet. That not everyone wore their feelings on the surface. Some folk had to dig deep. Search for words that eluded them to express how they felt. It went with the job, he supposed. She'd told him once that it wasn't the ailment her patients came in with that caused her the most concern, but the secondary issues that they mentioned in passing. The man with chest pains whose company was undergoing a restructure. The widow suffering from insomnia whose daughter had just left home. He wondered if she was analysing him. Or if she'd left her medical bag at the door and was just being his sister. He didn't want the first evening they'd spent in each other's company for ages to be maudlin.

'Ah, you'll soon lick everyone into shape,' she laughed, as though sensing his need to lighten the mood, 'Anyway, it hardly matters. Didn't you say this is a temporary gig?'

'True.'

'There you go then. You'll be hot footing it back to Salford once this double shooting has been put to bed.'

She lifted her glass to toast him once more.

Ashcroft touched her glass with his. Blinked away the image of Kamali Harris's broken body.

'Dinner smells good,' he said, eyeballing a pot of jerk chicken bubbling on the hob.

'Your favourite, when we were kids.'

He knew better than to argue. 'So, where's my favourite nephew?'

Hannah laughed as she shook her head, 'He is way too old for your corny jokes, bro.'

'Never,' he said stubbornly, throwing her a look as she took a sip of her wine.

'He's upstairs finishing off his homework. He'll be down soon.'

There was a time when Theo would have run down the stairs at the sound of Ashcroft's voice. The boy was growing up. Either that or Ashcroft was losing his magic. He preferred the former reason.

'Still working at this time?' He glanced at his watch. It was coming up to 8.30pm. No wonder his stomach was rumbling. 'The apple doesn't fall far from the tree,' he observed, remembering how much of a bookworm Hannah had been.

Theo attended an all-boys independent school two bus rides away. It meant his days were long, but he'd been attending since he was eight, so it's not as if he knew any different. After school he took the bus to his mother's medical centre, and she'd drive them home once her clinic had ended. He did his homework in the office behind reception, was usually finished by the time she was ready to go home.

'He's started playing basketball a couple of evenings a week. The trade-off is that he does his homework the moment we get home.'

'Seems reasonable,' said Ashcroft. 'Is he any good?'

'I haven't a clue,' she admitted, embarrassed. 'It's just a casual thing. He saw a few boys practicing and asked if he could join in. He gets bored waiting around for me to finish every night. I don't mind him playing so long as it doesn't get in the way of his schoolwork.'

'Speak of the devil,' said Ashcroft, looking over her shoulder.

The youth ambling towards him bore no resemblance to the knock-kneed boy just entering his teens when he'd last visited.

'Wah Gwaan,' said Theo, bumping fists before leaning in for a two-sided hug.

'Don't gi' me no *Wah Gwaan*. Last time I saw you it was 'Hi, Uncle Chris.'

'Goes to show how long it's been then.'

Ashcroft let that go. He resisted the urge to comment how much Theo had grown, didn't want to say anything that relegated him to old timer status in the boy's eyes just yet. He'd always considered himself to be a cool uncle, though the young man appraising him now didn't look that impressed.

'I hear you're a hooper now,' he said, keen to hear more about it.

A slow smile. 'Trying it out.'

'I could come and watch you some time.'

'Whatever.'

'Set the table honey, I'm ready to dish up,' Hannah instructed as she moved to the pan on the hob.

Theo huffed out a sigh then did as he was told anyway. Ashcroft kept his smile in check. He'd been on the wrong side of his sister enough times to know her tirades stung. Some things just weren't worth the hassle.

Theo looked up at him while performing his task. 'Mum said you're investigating that double shooting.'

Ashcroft exchanged a glance with his sister before nodding.

'It's been on the news,' she said hastily, in case he thought she'd been speaking out of turn.

He nodded at his nephew. 'Yeah, I'm working out of the station at Moss Side.'

'How come you got involved?'

'Resourcing issues.' It was a version of the truth.

'Did you ask to be transferred?'

'Don't forget the placemats, Theo,' Hannah instructed, spooning rice and peas onto each plate before adding the spicy chicken.

Theo went to the drawer where they were kept.

'It doesn't really work like that,' Ashcroft told him.

His nephew's eyes bore into him. 'How does it work then?'

'Theo! Salt, pepper, water glasses. Do I have to do it myself?'

Theo slammed the placemats down. 'Why do you have to talk so much? Can't you see my head's hurting?' He sucked air through his teeth.

'Don't kiss your teeth at your mum,' Ashcroft said before he could stop himself. He felt Hannah's glare pressing in the back of his neck.

'I can reprimand my own child, thank you very much.' She put his dinner plate down with a clatter.

'I didn't mean anything by it, sis. Take a breath.'

'What, I'm being hysterical now?'

She caught his eye and glared.

'Yeah, Uncle Chris, you're not my dad,' Theo informed him helpfully. 'And I'm not a child either,' he reminded his mum.

'I'd forgotten how much of a lioness you could be,' Ashcroft muttered. 'Remind me never to cross you.'

'I think that ship's sailed, don't you.' Her tone playful, keeping it light.

Ashcroft looked at the loaded plate in front of him, mentally working out how soon he could leave if he bolted it down.

'Don't you dare,' Hannah said, reading his mind once more. She threw him a challenging look. 'You don't get to go until that pot is empty and you've demolished dessert,' she told him in a tone that reminded him of their mother, 'Moody teenager or not.'

SIX

'Life can be a bastard like that.'
— DI DANIELS

The CID room was quiet. Nazia was at the airport picking up Jamal's brother. Brian Potter had gone to Windward Tower, the scene of Kamali Harris's murder, knocking on the same doors he'd knocked on six weeks earlier. There was always that slim chance, he reasoned, that someone would remember something they'd forgotten to mention, when they'd originally given their statements. He'd taken a couple of uniforms with him, hoped going in mob handed sent out a message that they weren't giving up.

DI Daniels was in his glass cubby hole, engrossed in a report he hadn't given a toss about until Ashcroft walked in. This suited Ashcroft fine. He walked over to the murder wall, sipping half-heartedly at a blueberry smoothie he'd made after his morning run. The headache he'd woken with first thing reminded him that he wasn't a drinker, but he'd stubbornly ignored it, climbing into his running gear as a form of penance. Two paracetamol and a long shower later, he wasn't exactly raring to go but close enough. Having the office to himself gave him the chance to mull over the investigation, albeit at a slower pace. To reflect on the progress they were making, or weren't, depending on whether you were a glass half full or half empty sort of person. Ashcroft was an optimist. He preferred to work with the hand he'd been dealt, rather than dwell on what might have been.

Jamal and Aisha stared back at him from their incident board. Their photographs, provided by their families, showed all that was different between the unlikely pair.

Aisha's photo had been taken at a family gathering to celebrate her unconditional offer from Oxford. She wore a figure-hugging dress with expensive looking shoes and the designer bag found with her at the crime scene. Her parents must have just presented her with the car, as she stood beside it, grinning, one hand resting on the bonnet while the other held a glass of champagne. What would have become of it when she told them her plans, he wondered. Would they have taken it back, or let her keep it with their blessing? Was their gift to her as unconditional as her university offer? Not that it mattered now.

In contrast, Jamal's photo had been taken in his mother's front room. Slouching on the sofa where the women from Safia's church had sat when they'd come to pay their respects. The colour had faded on the hoody he was wearing, his tracksuit bottoms a tad too short. Safia had explained to Ashcroft that she'd taken the photo as leverage. In the world of Instagram moments Jamal was by no means looking his best, and she'd threatened to post it online if he didn't get off his backside and tidy his room. He'd done as she'd asked and though she'd kept her side of the bargain and hadn't posted it online, she couldn't bring herself to delete it from her phone. Now she never would.

Ashcroft drained his smoothie, the rumbling in his stomach telling him it wasn't enough to get him through to lunchtime. He toyed with the idea of a fried egg sandwich. Pushed it out of his mind.

He slipped his phone from his pocket, tapped on the photograph icon, scrolling through the images until he found the one he'd taken of Jamal's bedroom two days before. His eyes scanned the photo even though he didn't know what it was he was looking for. The boy's room had certainly been tidied. Even the contents of his wardrobe had been neatly folded into piles. He used his fingers now to zoom in and get a closer look: jogging bottoms made from cheap material, knock-off designer sweatshirts, old trainers. He moved over to his desk. Opened the case file, skimmed through until he found the mobile number for Anita, the FLO assigned to the boy's family. He typed the number into his phone and hit 'call'. She picked up immediately.

'Good timing, Sarge. Safia's in the shower. She wants to go shopping, get something nice in for when AJ arrives.'

'I'll give them a bit of space this morning, but I'll need to come over and speak to him later, although that's not why I'm calling,' he informed her. 'I want you to take a look at the clothes in Jamal's wardrobe and text me a list of the brands. Same with his trainers. Oh, and there's another pair that looked pretty new by the front door, I want you to include those as well.'

'Will do, Sarge, I'll get onto it now.'

Ashcroft ended the call, his attention turning to the wall of incident boards. One had been wiped clean, meaning a suspect had been charged and the investigating officer's efforts would turn to preparing a file for the CPS. In a world that kept evolving, it astounded him that there'd been no progress in reducing the murder rate. Despite the lull during the pandemic when the public had been told to stay indoors, murders were back to pre-covid levels — and rising. The largest increase was males under the age of twenty.

He stared at the blank whiteboard. Wondered how long it

would be before another name was written on it, another crime scene photo placed at its centre.

'Penny for them.' Daniels stood in the doorway of his office; arms folded.

Ashcroft inclined his head towards the whiteboard. 'Wondering when the next name will appear there.'

Daniels blew out his cheeks. 'It's like waiting for a bus. Nothing on the horizon one minute, then blink and three bodies turn up.'

'Like Kamali, Jamal and Aisha.'

'Exactly.'

'Brian Potter's straddling both cases because you think they're connected.'

A shrug. 'Hardly rocket science.'

'What do you mean?'

'Kamali's dad was a dealer who got on the wrong side of his boss. We're pretty sure one of the Berati Crew killed him but we haven't a hope in hell of proving it. Now this couple wind up dead down the road from where the boy was killed. Just because their toxicology screens came back clear, doesn't mean they weren't dealing too.'

Not this again, thought Ashcroft. 'Their friends say otherwise,' he reminded him.

Daniels raised his hand for silence, like Kanute trying to stop the tide from coming in.

'Well, they would, wouldn't they?' he said as though explaining something really simple. 'They're hardly going to rat on their mates, alive or dead.' He caught the look that flashed across Ashcroft's face. 'Sorry, but sometimes the simplest answer really is the right one.'

'There was no evidence of dealing in the car. Nothing found in their personal belongings recovered at the scene to suggest any form of criminal behaviour.'

Daniels spread his hands wide. 'Look, for all we know it could have been their first time. That'd explain why they weren't geared up for it. Life can be a bastard like that. They tried dabbling in a viciously protected area and paid the ultimate price.'

Ashcroft regarded him. 'You're serious, aren't you?'

'One way or another they stepped on somebody's toes.'

Ashcroft laughed but it came out flat. He ran a hand over his mouth, his gaze darting around the room as though seeking out an imaginary audience. He moved his hand to the back of his neck, his fingers massaging a knot that had formed at the top of his spine.

'You've heard of confirmation bias, haven't you, boss?'

'I've no idea what you're talking about.'

'It's where we have a theory, right? An idea that's stuck in our head. And to support that theory we go looking for examples that prove it. You know, like left-handed people are creative so everything we find that supports that theory — regardless of the examples that show the exact opposite — prove our point.'

'Thanks for enlightening me, though I'm not entirely sure why you bothered.'

'The problem is when we do that, we stop looking for other possibilities. Close our mind to the idea they even exist. You're so stuck on this narrative that Jamal and Aisha are wannabee dealers you're not receptive to an alternative explanation.'

Daniels' face stiffened. His body drew back a little. 'Focus on the crime, not the victim, detective sergeant.' His tone changed. Had hardened several degrees.

Ashcroft took a step forward. 'And that, right there,' he said, his tone matching the inspector's as he jabbed a finger towards him, 'Is why murders that don't fit the textbook go unsolved. Because no one bothers to look *beyond* the crime.'

'The number of homicides we deal with every year-'

'-Matches the number of broken families who deserve

justice no matter what. You know, it really is about the victim, boss. If we forget about that then what's the point of us?'

Ashcroft took a breath, but he wasn't done yet. 'Now you don't have to like me being here, and to be honest I wasn't exactly wild about it either. But I was brought in to do a job and I'll do that job the best way I know how — and that means considering *every* possibility. If you have a problem with that then I suggest you take it up with Superintendent Duncanson.'

His phone buzzed signifying an incoming text. A glance at the screen told him it was Anita. 'I need to check this,' he said, but Daniels had already returned to his desk.

Ashcroft tapped on the text to open it. The list of clothing brands in Jamal's wardrobe was as he suspected. Mid-priced sports shop labels with a few market 'specials' thrown in. Yet the trainers left by the front door were a high-end designer label, as were the clothes he'd been wearing when he was shot. Ashcroft turned back to the murder board. Peered closely at the crime scene photo once more. If you ignored the blood and fragments of skull that clung to them, the clothes Jamal died in were the best he had.

'You said we could go shopping!' Safia said accusingly to Anita.

They were in Safia's living room, sat around the dining table just as they had been during Ashcroft's first visit.

'I want to make something nice for AJ,' she said for the umpteenth time.

'This isn't going to take long, Safia. DS Ashcroft wants to clear up a couple of things before we head out. We'll be back in plenty of time, I promise.'

Safia let out a long sigh. Nodded.

Anita angled her head towards Ashcroft, a pleading look on her face. Safia was agitated, but the sooner she cooperated the sooner they could continue with their plans. She only hoped that the detective sergeant stuck to his side of the bargain and kept it brief.

Ashcroft leaned forward in his seat. 'Did Jamal have a part time job, Safia?'

Safia's face brightened. This wouldn't take long at all. 'He worked Saturdays at the sports shop on the main road. They offered him evenings as well, but I said he shouldn't let anything get in the way of his studies.'

'What did he spend his money on?'

She gave him a look. 'What do all boys spend their money on? Computer games and clothes to strut around in. That was why he was pleased when he got a job there. Meant he got a staff discount. A good one too, going by his new trainers.'

The trainers in the hall weren't from any sports shop. Ashcroft had checked them on his way in. They were seriously designer. Little change out of £500 if he was hazarding a guess. Nothing a trip out to the Trafford Centre wouldn't be able to confirm. He'd need to check with the Evidence Management Unit, but he suspected the ones Jamal had been wearing when he was murdered would be in the same ballpark.

Nice trainers.

'OK, that'll do for now,' he said, getting to his feet. 'Thanks for your time.'

Aisha's family home

'We gave Aisha an allowance,' her father told Ashcroft when asked the same question as Safia an hour earlier. 'She had very little spare time, what with all her study groups. It seemed unfair to burden her with a meaningless part time job on top of everything else.'

Ashcroft kept his features neutral. He'd stacked shelves in a supermarket while studying for his 'A' levels. He wasn't clear how any job was meaningless when it put money in your pocket. Besides, as well as the obvious employment skills like timekeeping and communication, he'd learned a valuable lesson which had prepared him for his career in the force. Normalising criminals — not their crimes, which was a different matter entirely — made them a lot easier to track down. Few killers lived up to the grotesque caricature created by the press. Even murderers went grocery shopping.

They were standing in the kitchen. Remnants of breakfast remained on the work surface. A plate of half-eaten toast and a yoghurt drink. Empty cereal bowls and glass tumblers stacked around a juicer, waiting to be loaded into the dishwasher.

Ozwald was dressed for work. He had a client meeting in his chambers, which he'd been reluctant to postpone. 'Besides, it's easier keeping busy,' he said, as though trying to convince himself.

Abena was dressed, but make-up free. 'I can't face anyone yet,' she'd said simply when she'd answered the door. 'If I don't see other people, I can pretend none of this has happened.' Her movements were flat-footed, heavy-limbed, like someone who'd had the fight knocked out of them.

Sika had joined them for breakfast but, returned to her room soon afterwards.

'Don't think she can bear being around us,' Abena had added as she showed him through to the kitchen. 'Can hardly blame her.'

Ashcroft had accepted the offer of a coffee. Wasn't something he drank a lot of, but today's foggy head merited it. His hands circled the mug as he brought it to his lips. 'That's good,' he said, meaning it.

Ozwald glanced quickly at his watch before picking up a stack of files from a side table.

'What kind of things did Aisha spend her allowance on?'

Ashcroft prompted when it became clear no further information was forthcoming.

The lawyer's mouth turned down at the edges. 'Clothes, going out, I didn't keep track of it. I suppose by most standards what we gave her was generous, but it was also teaching her to budget. She had to make it last.'

'Apart from those occasions when she came to you for a top-up when she got carried away,' said Abena, not unkindly. The smile she'd been attempting fell away. 'I'm glad she did now. I'm glad she went on mad shopping sprees and had wild nights out with her friends.'

Ashcroft regarded her.

'I was young once, DS Ashcroft. I know the nights she stayed at her friends' homes they'll have gone out drinking. Let their hair down after working so hard at school. What does it matter now? None of us knew how short her life was going to be. If we'd have known…' Her words fell away.

'I'll be applying to Aisha's bank to get a record of her financial transactions,' he told them.

'Is that relevant?' Ozwald asked.

'I don't know,' Ashcroft replied honestly. 'But it may throw up something useful — a place she visited regularly, for example — which no one thought important enough to mention…' Or, going by her track record, no-one had a clue about. 'It could be something completely obscure that leads us to whoever killed her.' With any luck it would show that she had bought the new clothes AJ had started to wear, though how significant that was in the grand scheme of things he was unsure. He was reluctant to share his discovery with DI Daniels just yet. The man would claim the designer clothing was evidence of criminality. Not unreasonable, he admitted. He just wanted the opportunity to find a simpler explanation.

'Are you following the same line of enquiry with the boy?'

Ozwald demanded. It was the first time either of Aisha's parents had referred to him voluntarily.

'In a manner of speaking, yes, even though he earned considerably less than your daughter and spent most of it on essentials.' He tried not to make it sound like a criticism.

'Look, I'd better get going,' said Ozwald. He turned to his wife. 'I'll come straight back once I've finished; I promise.'

'Take your time.' She turned her cheek towards him to receive his kiss as he passed her on the way out.

Ashcroft tipped his head back slightly to finish the remnants of his coffee.

'Have another,' said Abena, already on her feet and fussing round the Nespresso machine before he had a chance to say yes or no. 'He'll not hurry back, regardless of his promises,' she stated, almost to herself. 'The place hardly feels like home anymore,' she admitted, her gaze sweeping the bouquets of flowers that kept arriving. The house smelled of pollen and sorrow.

'I've always been the pushy parent as far as my daughters are concerned. I've tried to raise strong women who are proud of their heritage. Aisha, being the eldest, kicked against it the most. Preferring to read *Grazia* magazine rather than *Maya Angelou*. We never seemed to reach a compromise that worked for us both and I admit I was disappointed.' She regarded Ashcroft. 'It's possible I'm not the easiest of parents,' she acknowledged with a smile.

He perched on a bar stool, resting his forearms on the island's granite surface. He handed over his mug when prompted. 'I can still arrange for a liaison officer to come here to support you through the next few weeks.'

Abena moved her head from side to side. 'They can't give me what I want,' she said sadly, sliding the freshly made coffee with a splash of milk towards him, 'So I'm not sure there's much point.'

He nodded, blowing across the top of his coffee to cool it.

'It's funny really. Considering how stand-offish he can be, the girls have always worshiped their father. He's strict, but in ways that they seem willing to accept, rather than rail against all the time. His relationship with Aisha has always been an easy one. She'd ask him about every step of his career and being the showman that he is, he loved telling her, knowing she hung on every word.' Her face clouded over, 'However, when you came round the other day you asked us something that we didn't answer entirely truthfully, although I've no idea why. Pride, I suppose.'

Ashcroft waited.

'You asked if we'd noticed any change in her attitude or behaviour. We both said no.'

He recalled asking the question. Remembered that her husband had answered first. That when she'd given the same answer moments later, it hadn't been with the same conviction.

'The truth is that things had been a bit strained between Aisha and her father the last couple of months. Nothing specific, that I could put my finger on, just little digs here and there, a few caustic comments that I know got to him as they were normally very close. I think that's why he feels he can't be here. Because his most recent memories of their time together aren't good.'

'Any idea what caused this friction?'

'It wasn't really friction. In my mind that suggests both of them were rubbing each other up the wrong way, when in truth it was Aisha whose behaviour became antagonistic towards Ozwald.'

'What did she do?'

'At first it was more what she didn't do. She stopped spending time with him. Didn't ask about his work which had fascinated her from being small. Snarky comments here and there. It wasn't like her. She was normally so proud of him, you know, fighting for people's rights.'

'Not that dissimilar to you.'

'Thank you. I happen to agree, though Aisha failed to see how what I did empowered minority groups. She preferred her father's courtroom confrontations, the dismantling of his opposition to win his case. She was young, privileged compared to many. How could she understand that the law itself, favours few? The course I run reaches far more people, shows them how to embrace their culture rather than be shamed by it.'

The room fell silent, save for the sound of the coffee machine pumping a decaffeinated blend into her cup. 'Was this boy in a relationship with my daughter then?'

Ashcroft moved his head slightly. 'I don't know. She hadn't mentioned him to any of her friends.'

Abena considered this. 'Maybe it was early days.' She lifted her cup from the machine. Blew across the top of it. 'Do you have children?'

Ashcroft shook his head. He wasn't against the idea. He just hadn't met someone he wanted to share that level of vulnerability with.

'You try to protect them the best way you know how, and when it goes wrong you can't help but lash out. My first thought, when we were told she was with this boy, was that she was dead because of *him*. But we have to face facts, don't we? See our offspring without the rose-tinted glasses we wear whenever we think of them. My daughter was a strong-willed young woman, detective sergeant. There's part of me wondering if this boy's dead because of *her*.'

'Let's wait until we know more before apportioning blame.'

'I wish we hadn't been so strict with her! She was a young woman and we kept her in a gilded cage. I wonder if she hated us? Blamed us for all she was missing out on? What I wouldn't give to have her back. I'd do it all differently, I promise you. Let her live the way she wanted to. Listen to her talk about boys, rather than tell her to concentrate on her books. Help her pick an outfit for a date, then stay up until she came home to find out how it went.' She swallowed back a sob. 'I'm so sorry she didn't have any of that. That she didn't know what it was like to be loved by someone other than a relative.'

Ashcroft sipped at his drink as he listened to her. This time, once his coffee was finished, he stood up to leave.

'Have you said any of this to Sika?'

'How can I when we're barely in the same room for five minutes?'

Despite her claims that she wished the opposite were true, learning about Tobi from her younger daughter could drive a wedge between them. No wonder Sika was steering clear.

Truth had a way of coming out though. Only not in the way those affected were ready for.

Moss Side station

'How was dinner with your sister?' Potter looked up from behind his computer screen. Today's ensemble was a brown shirt and tie that wouldn't have looked out of place in Burtons' shop window circa 1975.

After confirming details with the Evidence Management Unit, Ashcroft had driven out to the Trafford Centre to check out shops selling men's designer footwear. Aisha's bank details were now with the forensic accounting team. An application to her bank for access to her current account and credit card would be submitted by close of play. He put a mental tick against each item on his actions list, satisfied.

He acknowledged Potter's question with wide eyes, before flopping into his chair. 'You've got family, right?' he answered, blowing out his cheeks.

Potter gave him a look that stated *enough said*.

Following the initial awkwardness after reprimanding Theo for giving cheek to his mother, Ashcroft had feared the evening was doomed. Not so. Whether it was a case of blood being thicker than water or they all decided to put in the effort, the atmosphere improved as quickly as it had darkened. Theo's attitude disappeared, and for the remainder of the evening he listened enraptured as Ashcroft shared parts of his job he was able to. When it was time for him to go to bed — when Hannah tapped her watch several times and raised her eyebrows — he paused in the doorway.

'It was great seeing you, Uncle Chris,' he said, rewarding him with a shy smile.

'Listen, about earlier,' Ashcroft had said when he heard Theo's bedroom door close behind him. 'I didn't mean to step on your toes.'

Hannah flapped her hand at him. 'Forget it. I was caught off-guard, that was all. You sounded so like Dad when we were little. *No disrespecting your mother now*, do you remember that?'

Ashcroft rubbed at eyelids that were starting to feel heavy. 'Oh, God, did I? They were so stuck in their roles, weren't they? Mum the soft touch, who's worst threat was *Wait until your father gets home* and Dad, the disciplinarian.'

'We were good kids. The threat of what he'd do kept us in check.'

Ashcroft smiled at the memory. 'I don't think that made any difference, to be fair. Most people toe the line.'

Hannah lifted the bottle, felt the weight of it in her hands. Satisfied there was enough wine to share she made to pour some into his glass.

'I'm done, thanks,' he said, placing his hand over the top of it. 'Too much of a good thing, and all that.'

Nodding, she tipped the contents of the bottle into her glass. 'Waste not, want not,' she muttered, her grin ever so slightly lop-sided. She glanced at Ashcroft then looked away, the way she always did when she was building herself up to say something.

'Go on, spit it out, I need to be going soon,' he said good naturedly.

'I've been thinking. It's Dad's seventieth this year. Why don't we fly over and surprise him. He and Mum would love that.'

Ashcroft sobered immediately. This wasn't what he'd been expecting at all. 'I don't know.' He tried to think of a way to put the idea to bed without sounding lame. 'It's not that easy taking time off.'

'About as easy as it is for me,' she reasoned, her answer proof that he'd failed miserably.

'I thought they were coming to stay with you later in the year?'

'They are. But if we go over, we could make it into a holiday. Imagine. The feel of serious heat on your skin.'

He'd been undecided between a sailing holiday in Corfu and a cooking holiday in Bologna. Both came with their fair share of sunshine. He tried to look like he was giving the matter some thought.

'No need to decide now, just promise me you'll think about it?'

'Okay,' he'd said, reluctantly, getting to his feet. He'd slipped his phone from his pocket and ordered a taxi via his Uber app. 'I'll definitely think about it,' he'd said, injecting more enthusiasm than he'd felt. Especially since he'd had a favour to ask…

Potter peeled back the lid of his Tupperware box and lifted out an egg and cress sandwich.

'My sister's agreed to speak at the community event,' Ashcroft told him, trying not to wrinkle his nose at the smell. 'Reckons she can rope in a community nurse to run a *well-*

being stand offering blood pressure checks and free diet sheets.'

'She should send 'em here, this lot'd keep 'em busy,' Potter said between mouthfuls.

'Any luck with the house to house?'

Potter frowned. 'Depends on what you mean by luck.' He swilled his sandwich down with a plastic cup of apple cordial which he kept in a bottle in the kitchen labelled 'Urine Sample'. Unsurprisingly no one ever touched it. 'One couple we'd spoken to previously who remembered seeing a fella leave the tower block in a hurry was able to give a description of him this time: White, thirties, wearing a Hi-Viz jacket.'

'Hi-viz jacket doesn't sound promising.'

'It isn't. I checked with the council housing team to see if it was someone who worked for them. Sure enough, the wife of one of their maintenance workers upgrading the door entry system went into labour the day Kamali was killed — it was their skip he ended up in — and before you ask, they sent through a photo of the bundle of joy who arrived after a twenty-three-hour labour.' He smiled despite his obvious disappointment. 'It explains why the killer gained entry to the block without having to be buzzed in. Then again, all he had to say was 'Deliveroo' and it would have been *Open Sesame* anyway.'

Ashcroft nodded in sympathy. 'Whatever was going on between them, Aisha had started buying Jamal clothes,' he told him. 'High end designer gear. His mum thought he'd been buying his new stuff from the sports shop he worked in on Saturdays. I've checked with the EMU, the clothes he had on when he was shot were top end designer brands sold in the Trafford Centre, same as hers. Obviously, it needs to be cross checked against her bank account and credit card, but her parents confirmed they gave her a generous allowance to spend how she wanted.'

'So what were these purchases in aid of then? Gifts from a besotted girlfriend?'

'I'm struggling to think of another reason,' Ashcroft admitted. 'Though I've no experience of anyone ever wanting to lavish gifts on *me*.'

'Why would they? Can't improve on perfection,' quipped Potter. 'You'd think though,' he said, his face growing serious, 'that his mate would have picked up on it. I'm guessing he never mentioned his pal's new clobber when you spoke to him?'

'No, he didn't,' Ashcroft replied, wondering why that would be.

DC Latif's mobile phone was clamped to her ear as she entered the CID room. 'It's the letting agency, Sarge,' she said, holding the phone away from her ear. 'Although it's empty at the moment, someone's about to take over the lease of the retail unit close to the locus. The person I'm speaking to is checking with their manager that they can pass the name of the organisation on to me.' The sound of pan pipes filled the room.

'Do you want me to speak to them?' offered Ashcroft.

Nazia's chin lifted. 'I've got it, thanks,' she said stiffly.

Ashcroft nodded before returning to his desk.

'Thanks, you're a star,' Nazia said into the phone, 'Now is there any chance you can give me their mobile number?' She wrote something onto her note pad before sending a triumphant smile in Ashcroft's direction.

'It's a refugee advice agency,' she said aloud once the call had ended. 'Goes by the name of The Dignity Centre. I've got the number of the person the agent has been dealing with, do you want me to give them a ring?'

Ashcroft wasn't sure there was any point. As lines of enquiries went, they'd reached a dead end. 'I can't see how the new tenants can help us with anything, but call the agency back and tell them we'd like to have a look round.' He checked his watch, 'See if they can meet us there in half an hour.'

Nazia made the call, giving Ashcroft the thumbs up when her request was met with a yes.

'There's a couple of things I want to check out with Fahri Gemici so we might as well head over to the café when we're done.'

'Yes, Sarge.'

They were in the pool car heading to the vacant shop unit on Abraham Road. They'd driven the last ten minutes in silence, which suited Ashcroft, given he was still worse for wear. Even so, though he couldn't claim to know her well, Nazia seemed quieter than normal. He remembered she'd left the pub early to go on a date the previous evening. Either it had been a spectacular success or a monumental failure, in his experience there was never anything in between. 'Late night, was it?' he ventured.

'Think I'm a convert,' she said, flashing him a grin.

They left it there. No one wanted to jinx the prospect of a new relationship by speaking out of turn.

'Any issues when you picked AJ up at the airport?' he asked, returning to familiar territory.

'Not really,' she shrugged, 'He had a lot of questions, obviously, none of which I had any answers to, though I reminded him its early days. That didn't go down too well, as you can imagine.' She sounded pensive.

Ashcroft had been gazing through the passenger window. He turned towards her. 'What kind of questions did he ask?'

'Who we'd spoken to so far. Names of potential suspects — I didn't tell him anything,' she added quickly. 'Not that there's much to tell.'

'Questions family members often ask,' he reminded her.

'Mmm…' She didn't sound convinced. 'It was more than that though, Sarge…' Her eyes were on the road ahead but in reality she was running through their initial meeting that morning.

AJ was the opposite of his brother. Taller, heavier. Solid muscle, biceps that looked as though they'd been sculpted in a gym. His hair was closely shorn, military style. He'd stood out from the passengers around him as he waited for her outside Arrivals. Holidaymakers returning from two weeks in the sun. Family members waiting to be reunited with loved ones for a special occasion. He'd been eyeballing every vehicle as it approached the pick-up zone, his gaze moving on to the next one when they didn't stop. He was already striding towards her car as she pulled into the parking bay, his brooding eyes locked onto hers as she lowered the window and called out his name. He'd tossed his rucksack into the back of the car before climbing into the passenger seat, acknowledging her condolences with a curt nod. Then began what had felt like an interrogation:

'Who've you got down for this?'

'What do you mean you haven't brought anyone in yet?'

'You've been speakin' to someone though, or is it a case of just another black boy?'

'This might sound mad, but I got the impression he knew who killed Jamal. That the questions he asked were to ascertain how much *we* knew.'

Nazia checked her rear-view mirror before indicating left and pulling into a space outside the row of shops on Abraham Road, which were open as normal. Apart from shards of broken glass wedged into the tarmac there were no visible signs of the massacre that had taken place two days earlier. Jamal and Aisha had already been erased from the present.

A woman in the laundrette folded clothes into a laundry

bag while a student holding a bulging bin bag waited for a machine to become available. In the salon next door, a young mother had nail extensions while her toddler slept in his buggy. The African clothing store had a half-price sale poster in the window. Life went on.

Jay Crozier, the agent Nazia had spoken to, was waiting for them outside the vacant shop unit. 'Happy to help,' he said once the introductions were out of the way, though his face looked anything but.

'You won't mind if we take a look around on our own?' Ashcroft asked, his tone making it clear he wasn't seeking permission.

The agent perked up at the prospect of half an hour scrolling through social media. 'Knock yourselves out,' he said good naturedly.

Ashcroft wasn't entirely sure what he was hoping to see. He'd carefully studied the shop's exterior before they'd walked in. There were no CCTV cameras that they'd missed when they'd checked the street two days earlier. No hidden entrance that the killer could have waited in. He shrugged his shoulders. No action was wasted, he reminded himself.

The interior was open-plan style with built-in shelves against one wall. He checked out the vantage point from the large shop front window in case the killer had scoped the road out from here in the weeks leading up to the murder. 'Have you shown anyone round the property recently?' he called out.

The agent frowned as though he'd been interrupted from doing something important. 'No, there's no point now we've got new tenants lined up.' He went back to scrolling or texting or whatever he'd been doing before he'd been rudely interrupted. He paused from his screen, angling his head towards Nazia. 'The new tenants sent their office manager over one afternoon to measure up. Does that count?'

Ashcroft and Nazia shared a look.

'Remind me who they are,' he asked her.

'The Dignity Centre. An advice agency for refugees,' she told him.

'The number I gave you is the office manager's direct line. They're good clients, they rent multiple offices from us throughout Manchester,' Jay told them.

'Give them a ring, Nazia,' Ashcroft instructed, deciding it would do no harm. 'Ask if they saw anything unusual the day they came round.'

Nazia stepped outside to make the call. If the shooting was pre-planned — though for the life of him he couldn't see why, Jamal and Aisha were looking more and more like they'd been in the wrong place at the wrong time — there was an outside chance the killer may have looked for the best angle from which to exterminate his target.

'You manage those units?' He nodded towards the other shops on the row.

Jay shook his head. 'Not anymore. The owner sold them during the pandemic.'

Made sense, what with everyone being told to stay at home. 'What kind of rent can you expect for something like these?'

''Bout a grand a month.'

Ashcroft moved back to the window. Stretched his mouth into a frown as he considered this. 'That's a lot of manicures. Business must be better than I thought. Any idea who the new owner is?'

'Can't say as I remember.'

Ashcroft looked at him sharply. 'What would it take to help your memory along?'

Jay threw his arms wide. 'I don't deal with sales.'

'But you speak to your colleagues who do?'

'I suppose.'

'Someone walks in off the street and buys a row of shop units. That must be worth a mention during your tea break?'

'I don't drink tea.'

Ashcroft smiled. Folk liked to play the police for fools then moan when they got arsey. He wasn't the sort who threw his weight around to get what he wanted, but he wasn't averse to sharing a few simple truths.

He leaned in close. 'I can see that,' he said, taking in the dilated pupils and attitude. 'How would your employer feel knowing *that's* what you get up to whenever you nip out to meet your clients.' He indicated the fine dusting of white powder beneath the agent's nose.

'It was a one-off,' Jay said, startled. His face was flushed but it was more likely a by-product of a dopamine rush than embarrassment.

'If you knew how many times I get told *that* little pork pie…' Ashcroft gave him time to weigh up the pros and cons of engaging with the police. The fella was law abiding mostly. Wouldn't want to make the situation bigger than it needed to be.

Jay looked at the ceiling as though inspecting it for cracks. 'Like I said, I wasn't involved in the sale, but my mate was. I remember him saying the guy who bought it had a few dodgy connections. That's all he said, honest. Look, if I give you the buyer's name can you make sure nothing comes back to me?'

'No reason why it should. I'm just curious.'

Jay gave him the name.

Ashcroft nodded his thanks. Though he wasn't done yet.

'What about this unit?' he asked. 'Who owns this? And don't try telling me you don't know the name of the client you're acting for.'

Jay sighed. 'It was a lot simpler when it was the Baby Boomer generation. They'd leave us to manage their properties while they sat back and watched the rental income roll in. The pandemic put the frighteners on them. They sold up and brought premium bonds instead.'

His face was a lot paler than it had been when he'd greeted them on the pavement. That was the problem with regular drug use. The highs never lasted and the lows felt like a sucker punch.

'We let this guy's property out. That's all. We don't have any other dealings with him.'

'I'm not suggesting you do,' stated Ashcroft. 'But you know how it works. A reluctance to co-operate can look a hell of a lot like obstruction from where I'm standing.'

The agent sighed. 'We're supposed to keep client details confidential.'

Ashcroft couldn't be bothered going toe to toe with him about Data Protection.

'How about I give you a name, and if I'm right you nod?'

Jay nodded. Realised he was jumping the gun. Said 'Yes,' then waited.

Ashcroft gave him two names. Supressed a smile at the vigorous nod he received in respect of the second one.

Nazia met Ashcroft on the threshold of the shop unit. A quick shake of his head told her not to bother coming in. 'We're done,' he said, turning to thank Jay for his time. The agent raised a hand in farewell, the other was busy dabbing at his nose with a tissue.

'Hay fever's a bugger,' she called over sympathetically. She caught Ashcroft's glance as she climbed into the car. 'I'm not a complete knob end. I can see he's partial to a bit of Mancunian Marching Powder.'

Ashcroft's eyebrows merged into his hairline. She'd certainly perked up from earlier. 'Is this how you carry on with DI Daniels?' he asked, only half joking.

'Sorry, Sarge, am I overstepping boundaries again? He has spoken to me about it if that's what you mean.'

'Don't change anything on my account,' he said, meaning it, 'But learn to read the room. DI Daniels and the Super are old school and sufficiently narrow-minded to want their world to stay the same. Unfortunately, there's more of them in the force than the likes of you.' And me, he wanted to add, but didn't. 'So, if you want to progress your career, you'll need to navigate your way round them.'

Nazia nodded solemnly.

He hoped she didn't think he was crushing her spirit. 'I've worked with a DS for the past five years who, if there was any justice in this world would be DCI by now,' he told her. Maybe DCI was pushing it, admittedly, when he took into account the complaints that had been raised against him — mostly unfounded — but sometimes it helped to embellish a story.

'What did he do?'

Ashcroft considered this. 'He did his job. Brilliantly. Went above and beyond on every shift. Only problem was that he spoke his mind. Didn't care who was on the receiving end and by that, I mean top brass. Made a lot of enemies.'

'But I bet he slept at night, Sarge.'

Ashcroft wasn't sure that he did. The cases they'd worked together. The damage one investigation in particular, had wreaked on his family. 'All I'm saying, is if you want to move through the ranks then you need to choose which of the bosses' nerves to get on. You can't stomp over them all.'

'Be Nazia Lite, you mean.'

An unfortunate turn of phrase, given the allegation of institutional racism metered at GMP following a report commissioned by the mayor, though it summed up the approach he'd taken during several flashpoints in his career. 'Perhaps not as drastic as that,' he said, cautiously, 'Just a little less Nazia Max, if you want the higher ups to take you seriously.'

Nazia nodded, satisfied, as though this was something she could do. She stopped at the traffic lights, going across the junction when they turned to green. They turned into

Walcott Avenue; Appleton House loomed in front of them. To their right, the shopping precinct, the Turkish café mid row.

'Anyway, Sarge, I've got some belting news.'

Ashcroft raised an eyebrow. 'Better not keep it to yourself then.'

'I managed to get hold of the new manager of the retail unit, like you asked. She confirms going over there a couple of weeks back to take another look around and work out where the office furniture should go. Only she didn't go on her own.' She paused, milking the moment.

Ashcroft waited her out.

'Aw, you're no fun, Sarge, you're supposed to ask me who it was.'

'It doesn't work that way Naz, remember what I said about reading the room.' He showed her his serious face.

'Sorry! Sorry! But this is a game changer. It has to be. She told me she'd brought her new assistant along. She wasn't due to start officially for a couple more weeks, but she thought it would be good for her to familiarise herself with the layout — and the locality — as soon as possible.' She nodded at Ashcroft, like a puppy who'd mastered fetch for the very first time. 'It was Aisha, Sarge! She'd only gone and got herself a job there!'

Ashcroft allowed his eyebrows to fly into his hairline for Nazia's benefit. 'It was right what her boyfriend said then. She had no intention of going to Oxford,' he mused.

'Bit of a coincidence, Sarge, that she's murdered so close to her new place of work.'

Nazia wasn't wrong. What had they missed? What had *he* missed? This discovery opened up a whole new line of enquiry which would need to be explored before he was happy to relegate it to the strange but true book of coincidences. He put a call through to Brian Potter. Told him what Nazia had discovered. 'Did Aisha's boyfriend mention anything specific about employment that she'd applied for?'

'No, Sarge, I'd have included it in his statement if he had.'

He deserved the rebuke he detected in Potter's voice. Sometimes you had to double check details, regardless. 'I'm sure you would have done, Brian,' he said, placating him, 'Still finding my feet and all that.'

'No problemo...want me to ring him and find out if he knew about the job offer?'

Ashcroft smiled into his phone. 'I'd appreciate that,' he said, ending the call.

He turned to Nazia. 'While you were speaking to the office manager, I was pumping the letting agent to find out who owned the shop units along that row.' He told her that Troy Mellor had started buying up the units during lockdown, though Vasif Muka was the new owner of the unit the refugee centre was about to be moved into.

'Funny how some industries thrived during COVID,' he surmised.

'Folk still needed to get off their faces, I suppose.' She regarded Ashcroft. 'Are you starting to think this is a turf war after all?'

He began to shake his head then stopped. He wondered how objective he was being. It was easy to become entrenched when there was a principle at stake. He'd not been parachuted into the investigation because Top Brass wanted unbiased transparency. He was there because Aisha's family were wealthy, influential and Black, and his presence disrupted allegations of social stereotyping.

He was GMP's silver bullet.

Truth was, he'd become so hell bent on finding a motive that wasn't down to drugs or gangs, he wondered if he'd lost his focus. He'd widened the scope of the investigation but had that been the right decision? If he was running around like a paid-up member of DI Daniels' *Headless Chickens* club, he had no one but himself to blame.

'Too soon to rule anything out,' he replied.

A row of concrete bollards along the perimeter of Walcott Precinct's parking bay prevented vehicles from mounting the pavement and ram raiding the shops or joy riding around the square. A poster with Kamali Harris's face on it had been tied to one bollard. Jamal and Aisha's faces now appeared on another.

Mikey Hassan watched them climb out of their vehicle before pedalling like mad towards the clustered stalls announcing their presence. 'Fuck, man, it's the Feds!'

Ashcroft looked up at the overhead walkway connecting Appleton House to Windward Tower. The two men who normally observed proceedings from the tower block's first floor landing were nowhere to be seen.

Inside the café, Fahri was back in charge of sharp implements once more, cutting slices of doner to make up kebabs for a group of boys who should have been in school.

'My dad's at the cash and carry getting supplies for the community evening,' he called out to Ashcroft, over their heads.

'No matter. I've come to see you.'

Several of the boys turned in Ashcroft's direction, then started elbowing each other.

'*Babylon!*' '*Coconut!*' they hissed.

Nothing he hadn't heard before.

One of the boys clocked Nazia. 'Jih-'

'Don't even think about it, Twinkle Toes.' Nazia jerked her thumb towards the exit, watching as they picked up their kebabs and left, pushing and jostling each other through the door.

Fahri wiped his hands down the front of his apron before joining the detectives at the counter. 'What is it?' His face paled. The bearers of bad news turning up at his door once more.

'Nothing to worry about,' Ashcroft reassured him. 'There's a couple of things I wanted to check with you about Jamal, that's all.'

'Like what?'

'He was dressed head to foot in designer gear when he was murdered. We came across a pair of expensive trainers in his home, as well. Any idea where he'd got them from?'

Fahri's head bobbed up and down as he spoke: 'She bought them for him, innit? Started dressing him like a roadman. I told him to his face that people would get the wrong idea, but he told me to shut up. Said he had no interest in what other people thought. Said she liked treating him, that's all. Not like she was breaking no laws.' He paused, though it was clear he had more to say on the matter. 'She'd turn up out of the blue and take him out for coffee. A couple of hours later he'd come back with a shopping bag in his hand and a daft grin.'

'And you're sure he never got involved dealing drugs?'

'I already told you no last time!' he said, shaking his head.

'Did he mention to you that Aisha was looking for work?'

'What, instead of going to that fancy university?'

Ashcroft kept his gaze on him.

'No, I swear down that's news to me.'

'Would he have told you, though?' asked Nazia, needling him.

'He was my best mate, of course he'd have told me!' he bridled. 'He'd have been made up knowing that she was staying around. Not being funny but there's every chance she'd have forgotten about him once she moved away. Bin him off for some law graduate who reminded her of her old man or some rich white guy who wanted to look street.'

The café door opened and Fahri's father walked in carrying an armload of boxes.

'There's more in the boot,' he barked, flushing when he saw they had company. 'Detective Sergeant Ashcroft, I wasn't expecting you! Or *you*!' he said, smiling at Nazia. He placed the boxes on one of the bolted down tables. Swept his arm in the direction of the door while addressing his son in Turkish. Going by Fahri's reaction he'd been told to get a move on.

'OK Baba! I'm going!' he said, hurrying to follow his father's instructions.

Refik turned his attention back to Ashcroft and Nazia. Opened his arms wide to show his frustration. 'He's my son, it's my blood that runs through his veins, but that, I think, is where the similarity ends! Please, sit! I bet he didn't even offer you refreshments.'

'It was busy with customers when we came in, to be fair,' Nazia told him.

Refik's eyes narrowed. He stepped behind the counter and moved to the till. Keyed in a code then studied the contents when it opened. 'These customers. They were schoolkids, no?' he asked them.

Nazia nodded.

'Bastard thieves. They come in when I'm not here. They never pay. He thinks they are his friends if he gives them things. That friendship is a transaction. He is a foolish boy!'

He slammed the till shut, rounding on Fahri as he staggered into the café carrying the remainder of the boxes.

'Aptal çocuk!' he shouted, adding 'Stupid boy!' in case a translation was needed.

Fahri's cheeks reddened as he carried the boxes through to the back room.

'Want some help taking those through?' asked Ashcroft.

'He can do it. Since he acts like a donkey I will work him like one,' Refik muttered, tirade over. 'Please, let me make you that tea.'

'Another time,' Ashcroft told him, eyeing the food

containers that Fahri was carrying through. 'There's enough supplies there to feed an army. You have remembered the community event is only two hours long?'

'We said we'd put on a meal for people, no? So they will come? I have roped in several volunteers. Between us we are going to cook up a feast.' His face broke into a grin before it clouded over once more. 'That is unless idiot features bankrupts me!' he shouted towards the back room.

Jamal's home

The flat resembled a funeral home. Sombre flower arrangements on every surface. AJ eyed the *With Sympathy* cards placed between old school photos on top of the fireplace. A tealight burned in front of them.

'There's more chicken stew if you've got room.'

He shifted his gaze away from the photos. To the peeling wallpaper and faded cushions. To the ornaments on the windowsill they'd bought her every Mothers' Day.

They.

'AJ?' The female cop wittered in his ear. She'd never let up from the moment he'd arrived until he'd escaped to his old room, slamming the door behind him. Correction. *Their* old room. The one they'd shared since the rug rat had come along. He'd dug his old weights out from under his bed. Lifted them until his arms hurt.

'I'm good,' he said. It was all he could do to keep it civil. He pushed himself to his feet. Restless, he prowled around the living room. 'I'm going out,' he said eventually to no one in particular.

The female cop asked him to hang tight, said the detective running the investigation wanted to speak to him.

AJ shrugged. Not like he had much to say.

The air in the flat was heavy. Made it hard to breathe. How long could he hold it together with this rage burning inside him? He'd put his neck on the line for this country, yet no one had been there for his brother. He'd never have left if he'd known this was coming…

He knew what it was like to not have a father. To endure the gap that could never be filled. At least he'd a memory of his own old man. A series of moving images etched into his brain. His height. His strength. His face breaking into a grin whenever he saw him.

His body lying prone in the dirt.

Jamal had no memories to cling onto. Unlike AJ, his father had never been present. For as long as they remembered his absence loomed large in Jamal's life, making AJ all the more determined to fill the gap.

Except he hadn't been there when he'd needed him.

'Sit down, son.'

His mum looked small. Her voice was even smaller. He did as he was told. She had enough to deal with without him acting up.

'All this food,' she said. 'I made too much.'

He lifted the ladle resting in the pot of stew. Spooned a second portion onto his plate. He wasn't hungry but he ate it anyway. If all he could do right now to make her feel better was eat what she made him, then that was what he would do.

He swallowed it down, trying not to look at Jamal's empty chair. 'This is good,' he said, reaching across the table to hold her hand.

The female cop got to her feet when her phone started to ring. She stepped into the kitchen to take the call.

He put down his fork. Glared at it like it was the cause of his pain. His brother's killer was out on the streets while he sat filling his face. He clenched his fist. Kept it good and tight.

Some fucker out there knew who had done this. All he needed to do was track down who that fucker was.

'DS Ashcroft's on his way,' the FLO said breezily as she returned to the table.

AJ unclenched his fist. Nodded. Estates were secretive places. The people in them lived by a certain code. He would wait for this cop. Do and say what he had to, before slipping out to make his own enquiries.

He had people to see.

The FLO greeted Ashcroft and Nazia with wide eyes when she opened Safia's front door, her smile suggesting the cavalry had arrived. 'Safia's having a lie-down. I'll be through in the kitchen if you need me,' she told them, indicating they made their own way to the living room.

AJ was positioned at the window, staring at the pedestrian square below. He turned at the sound of Nazia's voice, accepted Ashcroft's outstretched hand as she made the introductions. He'd changed into tracksuit bottoms and a gilet over a slim fitting top. White sports socks that had turned grey over time.

'Shall we sit down?' Ashcroft asked.

AJ looked about to argue, then thought better of it, dropping into the nearest dining chair, resting his hands on the tabletop. His fingers found the same bit of loose thread his mother had picked at the first time Ashcroft had gone round.

'I want you to know that we are doing everything we can to find the person who did this,' Ashcroft began. Nazia had been the one who'd informed him of his brother's murder, and the bare bones of the circumstances surrounding it. He was bound to have questions. If they wanted him to cooperate with them they'd need to provide him with answers first.

'Did you recover any bullets at the scene?' AJ asked.

Ashcroft nodded. He hadn't been expecting that to be his first question, though he kept his surprise in check. 'A bullet casing, yes. I hope you understand that I can't share any further information relating to it with you, at this present stage.'

'Does it help you identify his killer?'

'No. But it may be evidence we rely on later to prove their involvement.'

It was AJ's turn to nod. He got up to close the living room door. When he returned to his seat, he sat hunched forward, his elbows on the table supporting him.

'Where was he...' He paused to take a breath. 'Where was he sitting in the car?'

Ashcroft told him.

'Who was shot first?'

'Aisha.' Ashcroft opened the file he'd brought with him. Pulled out a copy photo of her taken from the incident board. The one of her standing in front of her new car. He placed it on the table in front of him. 'Do you know her?'

AJ shook his head. 'Who was she to him?'

Ashcroft clocked his choice of words. *Who was she to him?* Rather than *Is she his girlfriend?*

A quick glance at Nazia confirmed she'd picked up on it too.

'We were hoping you'd be able to tell us,' she said.

He looked at the photo once more. 'I haven't seen her before.'

'He never mentioned her in his texts?'

'If he had I'd have known who she was, wouldn't I?'

'Your mum said you were close,' said Nazia.

'We are.' His face clouded over. 'Were. But that doesn't mean we were in each other's pockets. Hard to be that when you're on patrol two thousand miles away.'

Nazia's comment had sounded like an accusation. No wonder he was getting defensive.

Ashcroft told him the car had been stationary on Abraham Road when their killer struck.

'Can you think why they would have been parked there at that time in the morning?'

'No. He should have been in school.'

'They both should.'

'So he knew her from school, then?'

'No, Aisha attended a private school.'

AJ nodded. 'Car like that, it figures.'

'Know anything about a refugee centre that's opening on Abraham Road?'

He gave him a look as though he'd misheard him. 'How would I know anything about that? And what does it matter anyway?'

Ashcroft hesitated before answering. He was torn between preserving new information until they understood the relevance of it and progressing the investigation any way they could. He decided on the latter. 'Aisha was due to start work there in a couple of weeks.'

'So this is down to her then.' AJ sat back in his chair, as though he'd made his mind up about something.

'Why do you say that?' asked Nazia.

'Why else would they have been there?' he shot back.

'This isn't about blame,' said Ashcroft, attempting to take the tension down a notch. 'Whatever reason took them there should never have resulted in their deaths.' He waited. Shook his head quickly at Nazia who'd been about to ask another question. He didn't want him rattled. Not yet. Not when the question he was about to ask would be like lighting the touchpaper.

'Abraham Road links two estates with a history of gang

violence against each other. Do you know if Jamal was aware of that?'

'Every kid round here knows that. It's one of those things you learn without needing to be told. The places to avoid. The people to stay on the right side of…'

'Is it possible that's what your brother was doing? Trying to stay on the right side of someone?'

'You mean was he in a gang?' AJ demanded, incensed. He jumped to his feet cursing, brought his fists down hard on the table. His voice shook with rage as he leaned towards Ashcroft. 'It took you ten whole minutes to get to what you really wanted to say. Are you for real?' He sucked air through his teeth. 'Take a look at yourself, man. You think you're any better than me?' He turned to glare at Nazia. 'Do you?' He covered his face with his hands. breathed out long and slow. He dropped them to his side, regarding the detectives as he spoke. 'You think that badge you carry makes you immune? That if you were found dead in an alley with a shot to the head, the Feds wouldn't assume you were bent?' He raked a hand over his scalp, dropped back into his chair. 'You reckon you're accepted right? That by being one of them no one thinks you're one of us?' He jerked his thumb towards his chest. 'I'm a squaddie. I've completed two tours tracking down Al Qaeda. Trust me, I know what I'm talking about.'

Ashcroft raised his hands. 'Hear me out. You have my word that this isn't the only angle we're looking at. But I can't ignore the nature of their murder. I wouldn't be doing my job properly if I didn't consider every possibility.'

AJ closed his eyes. Massaged his eyelids with his forefinger and thumb. 'He wasn't in a gang.' He sounded tired.

Ashcroft understood how isolating it felt to be judged, not on attitudes or behaviours, but on assumptions based on something outside your control. He knew this, yet he'd still needed to ask.

AJ's eyes opened. 'Now I don't know this girl, or anything about her, but if Jamal was willing to spend time with her, I'd say she wasn't either.' The look he threw at Ashcroft told him he was done.

There were parts of his job that Ashcroft detested. The murders, obviously. And the lies people told to sidestep suspicion. But what he hated more than anything was the pain the investigation caused to the victims' loved ones; having to answer invasive questions, become an advocate for the victim at a time when all they wanted to do was howl at the moon. Like they hadn't suffered enough.

'I'm sorry for your loss,' Ashcroft told him. He got to his feet even though he was reluctant to leave. He knew what he'd be doing if he was in AJ's shoes. 'Leave us to get on with the investigation,' he cautioned. 'You've every right to be hurt and angry, but the best thing you can do right now is support your mum.'

Hurt. Angry. That didn't even touch the sides. AJ wanted to laugh out loud but more than that he wanted them out of there. The Fed standing opposite him probably meant well but no one had the right to tell him how to behave. He slumped back in his chair to show he had no strength for a fight. Stretched his mouth into something resembling a smile. 'I appreciate you coming by,' he said eventually, pushing himself out of the chair.

The detective handed him a business card with his mobile number handwritten across the top. 'Any time of day or night, you call me,' he said, looking as though he meant it. AJ made a point of putting it in his pocket.

Satisfied, the detective turned to leave. 'We'll see ourselves out,' he said, pausing in the kitchen doorway to say something to the annoying liaison officer.

AJ resumed his position at the window. Waited until he saw

them climb into their car. Watched the Asian detective reverse out of the parking bay before driving away.

'Fancy a cuppa?'

He screwed his eyes shut at the sound of the FLO's voice behind him. Now her colleagues had gone he was free to do what he wanted. He opened his eyes, blinked back the tears that threatened. He turned and without acknowledging her, left the room.

'I take it that's a no, then?' Anita called after him.

The front door slamming behind him was his answer.

Ashcroft hadn't been in the car long when his phone began to ring. He slipped it from his pocket, hit the 'answer' button. It was Brian Potter:

'Aisha's boyfriend had no idea about her job. As far as he knew she was still applying for work. He hadn't heard of the refugee centre — and doesn't remember her speaking about it or showing any particular interest in that line of work.'

'How did he react when you told him about it?'

'He's taking it as a positive. Said it showed how much she was into their relationship. Reckons she must have been planning to surprise him with the news, but didn't get a chance.'

It was certainly one way to explain a partner's secretive behaviour. Time would tell if it was the right one.

'Oh, and the boss has told me to tell you Superintendent Duncanson will be at this afternoon's briefing. The press are braying for an update.'

There was certainly a lot of new information, Ashcroft reasoned when the call ended. Though it was the kind of information that led to more questions, rather than answers.

SEVEN

> 'You know how the saying goes, blud: Everyone's a gangster till another gangster walks in the room.'
>
> – TROY MELLOR

Amid the boarded-up shops on Ludgate Grove, one business continued to thrive despite the recession. Forget-Me-Not Florists: *Funeral flowers a speciality*, the sign in the window boasted. Inside, several wreaths had been placed by the window, waiting for collection. A football shirt in City's colours. White carnations that spelled out the word Mum. A teddy bear.

The shop owner looked up from the bouquet she was making when the bell above the door jingled. She studied the distracted looking man who walked in, offered him a solemn smile.

'Would you like to see our brochure?' she asked, sensing his discomfort.

AJ hadn't meant to walk in. Wasn't ready to make *arrangements*.

'Do you have a date yet?' She was used to customers enquiring about flowers for murdered relatives not yet released for burial. It could be several weeks before they came back with a date, but when they did, she'd pull out all the stops to give them what they wanted. She understood the limbo they were in. The need to step up, take charge. Perform this last act of love.

AJ blinked twice. Started backing away. 'I made a mistake,' he said, turning to leave.

'Come back when you're ready,' she told him, thinking the mistake he referred to was walking into her shop.

With the neon lights off, the exterior of Rizla nightclub looked unimpressive during the day. Shabby even. A lone bouncer standing by the entrance moved so that his bulk blocked the door as AJ approached. As he drew closer the henchman looked less sure of his stance.

'Wah Gwaan,' he said, stepping sideways. 'Mi not know it's you.'

AJ nodded as he stepped past him into the narrow passageway. The place felt soulless. The club wouldn't open for another few hours. This was the in-between time when the bar was re-stocked and any maintenance needed was carried out. A cleaner, wearing earbuds, pushed a hoover over the red carpet leading to the stairwell. Instead of following the sign down to the dancefloor, AJ headed upstairs to the VIP area. When the club was in full swing, patrons using the invitation only section preferred to flaunt their favour by using the stairs beside the DJ's rig on the dancefloor. The backstairs AJ used now were for those who didn't want to advertise their allegiance.

The bartender looked up from polishing glasses, acknowledging him with a nod. His line of work, it paid to see everything but say nothing. Three men sat around a low table, in front of each of them a mug of herbal tea. Their soldiers lounged on the velvet sofas close by, sipping high energy drinks.

One of them looked over as AJ came into sight, tipped his chin at his boss to warn him.

AJ looked on as Troy Mellor's foot soldier alerted him to his presence. Watched his mini dreadlocks dance as he turned his head to check out the interloper.

'Wah Gwaan.' Troy sprang to his feet, his metal teeth gleaming in the glare of the overhead light.

AJ felt himself pulled into an embrace. Over Troy's shoulder his companions raised their fists in readiness to bump his, AJ leaned across the low table to bump them back.

'Sorry fi yuh loss,' said Troy.

AJ spun round. 'That's all yuh can say? We grow up like we blud an' that's all you can say?'

The foot soldiers lounging nearby moved into a sitting position, ready for action if needed. A nod from their leaders and they'd be on their feet.

AJ eyeballed each of the trio in turn. Troy Mellor. Kwame Kuma and Leyton Appiah. It had been a couple of years since he'd last seen them, longer still since they'd spoken. He thought they'd said all they'd needed to. That their business was concluded.

'If I find out one of you was behind this-' he spat.

Troy pointed a warning finger at him, 'You and Jamal were like fam, blud. You better shut up before yuh say sometin' yuh regret.'

'Regret?' AJ kicked the table onto its side, the mugs shattering as they collided with each other before hitting the floor.

'Pussy!' Kwame hissed, inspecting his clothes.

Leyton sucked air through his teeth.

'There's only one thing I regret,' AJ grunted, moving in on Troy.

Troy's foot soldiers got to their feet. Kwame and Leyton's men did the same. Troy raised his hand to stop any further movement. He was the five star General. The Overlord. Everyone around him did his bidding. 'Leave we,' he said, looking at his own crew to take the initiative.

He waited while the foot soldiers filed past. Jerked his head at Kwame and Leyton to do the same.

'In a bit, bruv,' said Leyton, bumping Troy's fist.

Kwame was less pleased about being told to do one. Gave AJ a sideways look while he bumped fists with Troy. 'In a bit,' yeah,' he muttered while staring him down.

'You got a nerve, you know. I'll give you that,' Troy said once they were alone.

'How?' AJ threw his arms wide. 'A minute ago we were fam, according to you. W'appen?' He shook his head in confusion.

What Troy claimed had been true. They were family in every meaning of the word apart from blood. They'd grown up in the same tower block. Their mothers were friends, had minded each other's kids while they juggled shifts. AJ had had as many home cooked dinners at Auntie Rochelle's house as Troy had eaten at Auntie Safia's. They'd copied each other's homework after school and chased after the same girls. Jamal had been a younger brother to them both, which made AJ's suspicions all the more unpalatable. But he had to start somewhere.

'Keep shaking your head bruv. That's some bad memory you got.'

Troy pulled up his top to reveal the result of multiple skin grafts that had been carried out on his chest and abdomen. 'Eddie Richards carved his initials onto me with a drill while you were off playing Action Man, remember?' He tugged his top back into position.

AJ shrugged. 'We had a deal.'

'Yeah, an' I'm just reminding you I stuck to it.'

'Oh yeah? Then how come Jamal is in the mortuary?'

'I don't know, bruv.'

Troy motioned for AJ to sit down. 'Can I get you a drink? A brandy or something?'

AJ shook his head, worried that if he started drinking, he wouldn't stop.

'Something to take the edge off, then? Got some sniff downstairs that'll blow your mind.'

AJ shook his head once more, the last thing he needed was coke. 'I don't do that stuff no more, or did you forget?'

'Ironic, really, since I only got into the food business because of you,' Troy reminded him, using the slang term dealers used for drugs, to avoid incrimination.

Drugs had been the catalyst that had taken them down an unwanted path. An addiction that AJ couldn't afford. The dealer he was in debt to, who threatened to break his legs. In hindsight, that would have been the easiest option, though whether he'd have stopped at AJ's legs was debatable. The threat, at fifteen, had kept them awake for several nights until Troy came up with the bright idea that they join the roadmen trading on the estate.

'We pay off your debt and make money on the side. Easy innit?' he'd grinned.

Neither of them realised they were playing into the hands of local gangster, Eddie Richards. That this was how he recruited his foot soldiers. Hand out enough free stuff to kids to get them hooked, then start charging them, only by then they couldn't afford what they were using.

They'd started working for Eddie straight away, yet no matter how much cash they handed over, AJ's debt never went down. In fact, with all the compound interest, the amount he owed kept increasing. It was a time in his life he preferred to forget. Jamal's murder forced him to remember every last detail.

'When you left here, I promised you that Jamal wouldn't

get caught up in it all the way we had, and I stood by that. Everyone on my firm knew to keep their distance. *Don't deal to him, don't recruit him*, and I never turned a blind eye. I made sure trouble didn't come his way — for him or his little Turkish mate.'

'So what went wrong?'

'I swear down I don't know, blud. But if we put our heads together we'll work something out. Like we used to back in the day.'

'Are you for real? We're not fifteen anymore. And you're a proper gangster now. You can make this right.'

Troy shook his head. 'You know how the saying goes, blud: Everyone's a gangster till another gangster walks in the room. I can't do anything that'll fix this.'

AJ stared into the distance. Pictured his mother poring over Jamal's photographs. The stoop in her back that hadn't been there before. What Troy said was true. They could never make it right.

'Then we mek it even,' he said, his tone deadly. 'We find out who did this, and we lay 'im out.'

Incident Room

DI Daniels was all too keen to run the afternoon briefing. Nothing to do with the fact they'd made huge inroads in the investigation and Superintendent Duncanson had booked a ringside seat. Only a cynic would think that. Daniels ran through the new information that had come to light concerning Aisha's new job, and wrote the names of the owners of the retail units on Abraham Road along the top of the whiteboard.

Troy Mellor and Vasif Muka.

'They're building quite the empire for themselves,' he said

as he underlined both names. He looked around the assembled group of detectives, pleased with himself.

'Jamal and Aisha were shot dead less than fifty metres from Aisha's new place of work. Thoughts, anyone?'

'A far-right group protesting against the opening of a refugee facility?' asked a DC sitting at the back of the room. Daniels looked as though he wanted to chew him up and spit him out.

'Seriously? I give you a bloody great clue by stating two rival gangs are jutting up against each other, and that's what you come up with? The far right prefer knives or explosives to make their point. Besides, there are plenty of similar advice centres already up and running. The victim count would have been a lot higher if they'd put their mind to it.'

'Yeah, but they'd need brains to start with,' chimed Nazia, dipping her head when Ashcroft threw her a look.

'We could run it through HOLMES, widen the parameters, see if there've been incidents with similar MOs,' he suggested helpfully.

'Fine,' said Daniels, his tone clipped. 'DC Latif can do the honours with that, seeing as she's got a lot to say on the matter.'

He moved over to a map of the locus pinned beside the incident board. Traced his finger along Claremont Road as it segued into Walcott Avenue. He kept his finger in place as he turned to the team once more. 'We need to focus on the significance of *this* stretch of road. Yes, Aisha was due to start work at The Dignity Centre in a couple of weeks. But we've also established the unit is owned by Vasif Muka, a prominent member of the Berati crew who run the Langston Estate. Is the refugee centre a cover for other activities? And more importantly, was she targeted because of that?'

Ashcroft spoke next. 'I'm going to meet with the office manager tomorrow morning. I'm interested to know what

Aisha told them about herself, whether she mentioned something that hasn't yet come to light.'

'Wouldn't surprise me. There seems no end to her deception,' DI Daniels observed, enjoying himself. 'Still adamant she isn't mixed up in anything gang-related?'

Ashcroft chewed the inside of his cheek. Wondered how many people returned home from work each day thinking their job would be so much easier if it wasn't for the tosser they reported into. How much simpler the decision-making progress would be if they didn't have to take other people's opinions into account. If those same other people didn't get off on spouting hot air for the sake of it.

'The fact that the rest of the units on that row are owned by Troy Mellor doesn't change my opinion,' he stated. 'Yes, it's possible there's friction between both gangs regarding taking ownership of the whole row—'

'—I'd say it's more than possible!' Daniels chimed.

Ashcroft ploughed on, 'Even so, it's a big leap to conclude the Abraham Road gang would take out civilians just because they work in a building owned by Vasif Muka. Not only that, how would they have known who was going to work there when Aisha hadn't told anyone? Don't forget that Aisha's boyfriend works for Troy. She was known to him. He seemed genuinely shocked by her murder.'

'Maybe his shock was real,' Daniels conceded. 'Maybe he'd ordered the hit without knowing her involvement.'

This was the most plausible thing Daniels had said. Ashcroft took it into consideration. If there was a power struggle in Troy's team then it was also possible someone else had ordered the killing. Even so.

'It's not impossible,' he said eventually. 'I just can't see what brought them both to that stretch of road on that particular morning? The office isn't due to open for another couple of weeks.'

'Perhaps she was showing lover boy her new place of work,' stated Daniels.

'And their killer just happened to be passing? Too many *ifs* and *ands*, for my liking.'

'If this refugee centre is dodgy, then anything is possible. Get a full financial work up of the centre's accounts,' instructed Daniels, 'See where that takes us.'

'I've already written up a request, I can submit it to the Business Investigation Unit this evening if you're happy to sign off on it.'

Daniels gave him a slow smile. 'Be happy to,' he said eventually.

Troy parked his Range Rover at the rear of Windward Tower, head bobbing to the rap music thumping through the window. A crowd of youths gathered nearby stood to attention as he stepped out and made his way towards the main entrance.

A boy doing wheelies on his bike cycled after him. 'Wah Gwaan, Troy!' he called out, causing the youths to laugh at his bravery.

The kid reminded Troy of what he'd been like at that age. Cocksure. Too big for his boots but a joker with it. He smiled, pulled a twenty from his pocket and handed it to the boy.

'Luk what mi get!' Mikey shouted as he circled back towards the youths, his North Face parka flapping in the wind.

Kwame and Leyton stood in their usual position on the first-floor walkway, observing the activity below. The youths milling around the square returned to their established positions, their actions resembling a well-oiled production line. One youth took the punter's order. Another handled the cash. A 'runner' collected the order and delivered it, or left it where it could be collected, if the punter wasn't known. The process was slick, though the threat from rivals or the Feds, was ever present, hence the need to always be on the lookout.

Both men turned in unison as Troy made his way towards them. He eyed them steadily, wondering what they saw. A gangster whose money talked so loudly the Feds had been a fixture outside his home for several months. He'd send coffee to their car every morning, let them know they were fooling no one. Knew damn well by camping there they were saying the same to him.

He meant what he'd said to AJ. He'd never wanted to get into this game. Back when they were kids, he'd wanted to complete his education and get a job he could be proud of. Find a girl that didn't want him for his money. Raise a family. Only shit happened and now he was stuck. AJ had escaped, and he was glad for him. When his own chance had come he hadn't taken it. He'd seen the money the big players were making, looked at the bling they were wearing and knew deep down that he wanted that more.

'What did AJ want?' Kwame asked.

'What would you want, in his position?'

Kwame didn't hesitate. 'I'd want to kill the fuckers.'

Troy nodded, satisfied. 'So what you should really be asking, is how do we help him?'

EIGHT

'You can look at some people and see the future mapped out for them.'

– FEMI UKEJE

The Dignity Centre was situated between a unisex barbers and an internet café. The woman who greeted Ashcroft at the door introduced herself as Femi Ukeje. Of Nigerian descent, her long braided hair fell across a kaftan style top which she wore over a patterned skirt. She ushered him inside, locking the door behind him. 'The centre doesn't open for another hour so we will not be interrupted,' she told him as she showed him through to her office.

The interior was basic. A reception area with chairs set out like a doctor's waiting room. Posters in several languages explained this was a drop-in centre and the wait to be seen by an advisor could be several hours. *If all the seats are taken, please come back another day,* stated a sign Sellotaped to a low table in the centre of the room.

'Please, sit down,' she said, indicating the chair positioned at the side of her desk. She seemed to slump the moment she lowered herself into her own.

'I'm struggling to take it in, to be honest.'

Ashcroft gave her a sympathetic nod. 'You're bound to. It's been a shock for everyone involved.'

'I'm so grateful that your colleague telephoned me.'

'You didn't hear about the shooting on the news, then?' he asked her.

Femi shook her head. 'I've been away on a residential course. I only got back yesterday evening.'

'Something useful, I hope.'

She pulled a face. 'A Home Office run programme in Folkstone. Updating humanitarian agencies on the government's latest policy for dealing with migrants. These things can get very intense.'

'I can imagine.'

Her desk was piled high with legal textbooks marked with post-it notes. On the shelf beside her several box files contained information booklets: Credible Fear Interview, Emergency Support, Family Reunion Visas.

A framed print on the wall behind her stated: *Don't tell me how to tie my laces until you've walked in my shoes.*

'How long have you been doing this?' Ashcroft asked her.

Femi puffed out her cheeks. 'Well, I'm 40 next year, and this is the only job I've had since leaving school. Even then I used to stick up for the underdog. I guess that fight never left me.'

'It must be very rewarding.'

She eyed him steadily. 'Hmmm. What would you think if someone said that about your job?'

Ashcroft didn't hesitate. 'That they didn't have a clue what it entailed. My bad,' he said, raising his hands in mock surrender.

'We're all guilty of it,' she said, shrugging away his apology. 'The need to sugar coat everything. To make even the most soul-destroying work seem better than it is.'

She was silent for a moment, as though remembering why he was there.

'I never thought something like this could happen to

someone like Aisha,' she stated. 'You know how it is. You can look at some people and see the future mapped out for them — not always in a good way,' she admitted, 'not in my line of work. But for Aisha I predicted great things. I was relieved to be finally getting her on the payroll to be honest. I was worried we'd lose her.'

Ashcroft's brow creased. 'Sorry, you told my colleague she was due to start work at your new office as a trainee advisor.'

'That's correct. But she'd been volunteering here for several weeks. A few hours a week, after school and during the holidays, but she'd made such a difference.'

Ashcroft patted his pocket for his notebook and pen. 'How did that arrangement come about?'

Femi's face broke into a wide grin as she remembered a happier time. 'She literally walked in off the street one day and without knowing it came to my rescue! Due to the nature of our client base, we don't run an appointment system here. People seeking advice turn up and wait. And yes, before you ask, I'm the only one based here permanently. My title may be office manager but I'm also chief cook and bottle washer. We have a larger office in the city centre. That's where our legal team is based. The rest of us work in outreach offices referring cases to them on an *as and when* basis.'

Ashcroft looked up from his note taking and nodded.

'The day Aisha walked in, the waiting room was full. A lot of my job is form filling and explaining rights of appeal for deportation orders. Time consuming and laborious. Aisha waltzed up to my desk and offered to help. I thanked her but explained she'd need a criminal record check to work here. "Then we can apply for that this evening!" she'd said, adding that in the meantime she could do the filing and keep me topped up with coffee. I am not ashamed to admit, she had me at filing. Within a couple of weeks, she was triaging walk-ins and helping fill out basic forms, taking phone messages.

Becoming indispensable, really. I also knew someone like her would want more. When head office said they'd secured funding for a satellite office in Moss Side, I knew this would be a great opportunity for her. It was a part-time post with training provided. She was thrilled when I mentioned it to her.'

'She had an unconditional offer from Oxford.'

'She told me. She said she didn't want to go. I'll admit I was worried she was using her job here as a way of rebelling against her parents, but she assured me that wasn't the case. She said she wanted to make a difference at grass roots level, now, and she didn't need a degree from Oxford to do that.'

'We don't think her parents knew about her work here,' Ashcroft said, making a mental note to speak to them to make sure this assumption was correct.

'They must be devastated.'

It occurred to Ashcroft that Femi had spent more time with Aisha than he'd originally thought.

'Did you notice any change in Aisha over the last couple of weeks? Anything that might indicate that she was worried about something?'

Femi shook her head. 'No, nothing at all.'

'Anything unusual in her behaviour generally?'

Femi paused, as though giving it some thought. 'She was very inquisitive. Keen to learn the ins and outs of everything. I worried sometimes that she was getting ahead of herself.'

'What do you mean?'

She hesitated, as though weighing up the consequences of what she said next. 'She was a bright girl and such a big help...'

Ashcroft waited.

'I ended up giving her full clearance on our database. It meant she could enter client details directly onto our system...'

'Which gave her unlimited access to client records,' Ashcroft finished for her.

Femi nodded, embarrassed. 'There were a couple of

occasions when I found her loitering on the computer, as though reading records she had no business accessing. She told me she was interested in the outcomes we'd achieved for previous clients. I wasn't very comfortable about that, so I asked her to stop.'

'And did she?'

'To my knowledge, yes.'

'You didn't check though? Or put any restrictions in place?'

'No, I told you.' She shifted in her seat. 'I valued her help. Volunteers like that don't grow on trees.'

Ashcroft nodded.

'What kind of information does your database hold?'

Femi shrugged, 'Usual housekeeping stuff. Contact details, date of birth, origin of birth. Who we referred them to and the result.' She tapped several keys on her keyboard. 'Here, I'll show you.' She turned the screen to face him. 'I've hidden the client names to protect their identity, but you can see from this report the details of the clients recently referred to our head office, for example, and further on...' she tapped an arrow key to move the screen along the page, 'whether their application to stay has been granted. We also provide training to help clients secure employment. In fact, some of our workforce consists of former clients, who bring a wealth of personal experience. That was why I was a little uncomfortable seeing Aisha opening records she had no place accessing, but I didn't want to make a big thing out of it.'

Ashcroft considered this. 'We're trying to get a timeline of her movements in the lead-up to her murder and her work here puts a whole new slant on things. Are you aware of her falling out with a client, or upsetting someone unintentionally?'

Femi looked shocked. 'People are fearful when they come to us,' she told him, her tone defensive. 'They are facing deportation, separation from their families with no end date in sight. They are usually very grateful for our services, very compliant.'

'But what if their application isn't successful? Or that of a family member?'

'Well, the solution would hardly be to shoot someone.'

'It isn't a solution to anything, last time I looked,' he commented.

Femi's face took on a pained expression. 'They already deal with a lot of prejudice and suspicion. It's disappointing that you think one of them could be her killer.'

'Her killer has come from somewhere. I can't rule anyone out yet, regardless of how it will make them feel.'

Her smile was slow. 'I guess we're both representing our clients the best way we can.'

Ashcroft showed her Jamal's photo. 'This boy was killed alongside Aisha. Have you seen him before?'

Femi studied his photo. 'No, I'm sorry.' She shook her head. 'I thought her boyfriend was older than that, from how she spoke about him.'

'This isn't her boyfriend,' Ashcroft told her. 'We're not sure what their relationship is. I take it Aisha spoke about her boyfriend to you, then?'

'She was a teenage girl; I couldn't have stopped her if I'd tried.' She smiled, 'She sounded very happy about the future they were planning together. Although…there were times when she was unusually quiet.' Her face clouded over, 'I put it down to the inevitable conversation she'd need to have with her parents about not going to university. I'd hate to think it was something more. Something to do with what's happened.'

A thought formed in Ashcroft's head. 'Where are the majority of refugees from, who seek your help?'

'Iran, Iraq, Afghanistan, Syria, though the largest group is from Albania. Albanians are now the biggest single nationality making this journey, with 12,000 arriving on our shores over the last six months, of which 10,000 are single, adult men. This is compared with fifty in 2020.'

Ashcroft wrote down her answer, underlining Albania. He felt Femi's eyes on him. There was no nice way to ask difficult questions. 'Are you aware of any in-fighting between them? Particularly the men. Anything that could have taken a sinister turn?'

'Nothing that would involve the shooting of a popular volunteer, DS Ashcroft!' she said irritably. 'A young woman is murdered and you're quick to blame the very people she was trying to help.'

'No blame, just a line of enquiry,' he stated.

Femi got to her feet.

Ashcroft did the same. No point outstaying his welcome. He left a business card on her desk, then waited while she unlocked the door and held it open for him. 'I would have expected better from you of all people,' she muttered.

'What do you mean?' It was hard keeping the irritation from his voice.

'You know what it's like to have people make snap judgements about you. The unfairness of it. Yet here you are doing the exact same thing.'

The skin around his eyes creased. 'Sometimes that's all we've got,' he said, stepping out onto the pavement. He swore to himself as he remembered something. 'I'm sorry to drop this in at the end of our meeting, but do you know the owner of the new premises you've taken on?'

Femi looked confused. 'No, we deal with the letting agent. Why?'

'There's not a lot I can disclose at the moment. However, I must inform you our financial investigation team will be in touch regarding accessing your organisation's accounts.'

Femi shook her head at him. 'Why doesn't that surprise me?' she said as she closed the door.

Nazia had spent the morning searching HOLMES for incidents of far-right attacks against staff working in centres supporting refugees. DI Daniels had been right. Their standard weapons of choice were knives and petrol bombs. The odd bit of arson if they really wanted to make a point. There was nothing to indicate their involvement in Jamal and Aisha's shooting. She logged out of the HOLMES database and sighed.

'No joy?' asked Potter, glancing over from his own online research.

'Useless. Up there with chocolate teapot and a suede raincoat I bought in the sale last year. I mean, what was I thinking?'

'At least you haven't had to spend the morning trawling through social media accounts.' He shook his head slowly. 'The drivel people want to preserve for posterity these days. There was a time when photographs commemorated significant events. The moon landing. Muhammad Ali felling Lister in '65. Tiananmen Square. All anyone posts these days is what they've had for lunch.'

'It is the most important meal of the day.'

'No Naz, that's breakfast.'

'You sure about that?'

Potter shook his head. 'The youth of today…'

'Were *you* ever young, Brian?'

'As a matter of fact I was. The summer of '83. A group of us hitch hiked down to Brummie to watch Bowie in Concert. I had bleached blond hair and eyeliner. My dad didn't speak to me for a month, but it was worth it.'

'Respect,' said Nazia, bumping her chest with her fist. 'Not bad for an old geezer.'

'Who. Me?'

'Totally. You've still got it, Brian, despite your age.'

'Erm, thanks. I think.' Potter returned to his screen, slightly embarrassed by the compliment.

'Were Jamal and Aisha friends on Facebook?' Nazia called over after two minutes of silence.

Brian nodded. 'Yeah, they started liking each other's posts about three months ago, which ties in with when we understand they met.'

'Any other friends in common?'

'Nada. I've been comparing pages they've liked though and apart from a shared interest in music and fashion this was the only page they were actively following,' he told her, indicating his screen.

Nazia went over to his desk to take a look. 'I wasn't expecting that,' she said, brow creasing. 'You gonna flag it up to DS Ashcroft?'

'Someone taking my name in vain?' Ashcroft pulled at the knot of his tie as he entered the room. Dropped his car keys onto his desk.

'Brian's got something to show you, Sarge,' said Nazia.

'It can wait,' said DI Daniels, standing at the threshold to his office. 'A word in your shell-like,' he said to Ashcroft. 'NOW.'

Ashcroft glanced at the others. A quick shrug from Potter told him they were none the wiser. Ashcroft followed Daniels into his room and closed the door.

'You certainly know how to make an impression,' Daniels said as he lowered himself into his chair.

Ashcroft waited. Reckoned if he let Daniels wring as much pleasure out of whatever it was as he could, there'd be less need for a sanction.

'Tell me, on a score of one to ten, how well your meeting with the manager from that refugee centre went this morning? Ten being you made each other friendship bracelets and one being she phoned the station the moment you left, demanding your head on a plate.'

Ashcroft dropped into the chair opposite. 'She may have interpreted some of my questions as finger pointing,' he conceded.

'More than finger pointing, according to her. I think she used the phrase witch hunt, in her phone call.'

'That's disappointing,' said Ashcroft. 'I'd just learned that Aisha had been working there on a voluntary basis long before her job offer. Made sense to ask about the clients she came into contact with.'

'Hmm, that's all very well, but you're here to build bridges, not burn them down.' If Daniels looked like he was enjoying himself earlier, he was having a field day now. 'Bit of a turn up for the books. I doubt Top Brass expected you to encounter problems like this.'

'Like what?' Ashcroft repeated, long and slow.

'Problems the rest of us face when we're dealing with the Black community.' Daniels looked flustered, 'You know what I mean. You were brought here to help with cohesion.'

'And solve a murder,' Ashcroft reminded him.

'Anyway, I've done my bit. Off you fuck.' Daniels made a shooing motion with his hands.

'That's it? Don't you want my written account for your records?'

'Last thing I want is a paper trail.'

'She's entitled to have someone follow her complaint up.'

'And that someone was me. I'll report to the Super that no harm was intended so we can all move on.'

Ashcroft felt grubby. He'd been more blunt with Femi than he should have been because she was black and he hadn't wanted it to look like he was making allowances. Now her complaint about his attitude would be swept away because *he* was black and therefore they cancelled each other out. There was no win-win here.

'My attitude towards her was less than professional,' he admitted.

'Save it,' said Daniels, 'No one's listening. Now go and find this bloody shooter. Oh, and the Super wants a press appeal. Tomorrow. Is that going to be a problem?'

'Leave it with me,' said Ashcroft, getting to his feet.

Incident room

Ashcroft kept his face neutral as he stepped out of the DI's office. Nazia was staring at something on her computer and Potter was busy with a call, both failing miserably at pretending they weren't watching him. 'I wouldn't bother applying to do surveillance work any time soon,' he said, tutting, 'You'd have been more subtle cutting two holes in a newspaper and holding it in front of your face.'

'Everything OK, Sarge?' Nazia asked, pushing her chair away from her desk so she could view him properly.

He turned so that he was facing away from Daniels' office window when he spoke next.

'Nothing I can't handle. I screwed up when I interviewed the refugee centre manager. She decided to share her frustration with Superintendent Duncanson, who in turn let it roll downhill to the boss. You know how it goes.' He raised his eyebrows. Didn't want to elaborate further, not within earshot of Daniels anyway.

'It's not all bad though. While I was out today I learned that Aisha had been volunteering at the centre for several weeks before they offered her the job.'

'You're kidding me,' said Potter. 'What about school?'

Ashcroft talked them through the arrangement Aisha had set up with Femi, and her *access all areas* on the client database.

'She could have been searching for someone specific when her manager caught her snooping,' said Nazia.

'Maybe she found them, given that she's dead,' Potter added.

'Thanks for that, Brian,' said Ashcroft, though he'd been thinking something along those same lines.

'Most databases have an in-built audit trail,' Nazia informed them. 'It shouldn't be too difficult to trace which files Aisha was accessing.'

'Yeah, though I'm in no rush to float that by the boss just now, given I'm not in Femi's good books,' he admitted.

'While you were in getting your chestnuts roasted I took a call from NABIS — the DC I'd spoken to previously about the bullet casing found in Aisha's car.'

'Go on.'

'He was calling to give me a heads up. If you remember, the bullets used came from a shipment of guns seized in Cheetham Hill a while back. One consignment is obviously still in circulation, and so far they've been unable to track it down. Seems there's been a development. A reliable informant has confirmed it was bought by the Berati Crew.'

Ashcroft swiped a hand over his chin. 'Let me get this straight. The gun was in *their* control when it was used to kill Jamal and Aisha.'

'Yes.'

'Apart from Vasif Muka buying the refugee centre building, what do we know about them?'

'They're headed up by Vasif's father, Ervin. Been in the drug trade for over forty years, though he's more of a figurehead these days. He doesn't get involved in the day to day running of the business, leaves that to his son. He's old school.

With him at the helm, the organisation is treated with respect by suppliers and other players in the industry.'

'So the son is the one more likely to have ordered the hit on our victims?'

'Yes, though it's unlikely he'll have done so without clearing it with his father.'

'If the decision to execute them came from the top of the organisation and was ratified by the figurehead, it was hardly a hot-headed retaliation. How on earth can this couple have come to their attention?'

'Maybe the question should be framed in a different way?' said Potter.

Nazia eyeballed him. 'Meaning?'

'What level of threat could a young couple pose to the Berati Crew, that obliterating them was the answer?'

'Something that would have exposed the gang to even greater threat,' Ashcroft answered for him.

'Yeah, but who from?' asked Nazia.

Potter shrugged. 'Business rivals. The police.'

'What did they know that Vasif Muka didn't want broadcasting?'

Potter's face closed in. 'Everyone knows it was one of them who threw Kamali Harris off the balcony.'

'Knowing isn't proof,' Ashcroft reminded him.

'Yeah, but what if it was something to do with that?' said Nazia. 'Maybe Jamal and Aisha had proof. Maybe they witnessed it and were planning to come forward.'

Ashcroft's pulse quickened. How easy would it be to check their whereabouts when Kamali was murdered? See if it was possible that they'd witnessed his killing?

'Aisha's interest in the refugee database *could* be connected,' he said, thinking aloud.

'What if she saw the killer and recognised him?' asked Nazia. 'It's possible she was searching the database for his ID.

The office manager was pretty sure that she stopped when she asked her to. Perhaps by then she'd already found what she was looking for.'

Ashcroft regarded Potter. 'Where does the Berati Crew operate from?'

'There's a warehouse in Hulme. Father and son live in a swanky house in Cheshire although Vasif hangs out with his cronies in a flat on the Langston Estate a lot of the time.'

'The refugee centre manager, Femi Ukeje, told me they get a lot of Albanian refugees passing through their doors in need of support. This may well be where Vasif recruits his members. If they're undocumented, it would explain the difficulty you've been facing finding Kamali's killer.'

Potter nodded eagerly. 'That's a good enough reason to get the tech team to trawl through the refugee centre database, see if they can find out which files Aisha accessed.'

'I'll go and pay Aisha's parents a visit. See if they had any inkling what their daughter was doing in the lead up to her murder. I need to see them and Safia anyway to tee up a press appeal The Super's scheduled for tomorrow. I'd like you to come with me,' he said to Nazia.

'Thought you'd never ask, Sarge, there's only so much desk top research a girl can do.'

'Actually, there's something else,' said Potter. 'Before you go, I think you'd better see this.' He typed something onto his keyboard before sitting back, so Ashcroft could see his screen. 'I've been looking into their Facebook accounts. Neither of them had any friends or family in common but they did both follow this business page.'

Ashcroft stepped closer so he could get a better look. 'A genealogy site?' he asked, disappointed. He wasn't sure what he'd been expecting but he was certain it wasn't that.

'It's where people go when they want to find out about their family tree, Sarge,' Nazia explained.

'I know what it is, Naz. I'm just not sure of the relevance.'

'It'd do no harm to ask the families about it since we're going there anyway,' she suggested.

Ashcroft nodded. They had bigger fish to fry but as Nazia said, it would do no harm.

He didn't want to jinx it by saying anything aloud. But today felt different.

Like they were actually making progress.

Aisha's family home

Abena stared at Ashcroft blankly as though he'd spoken in another language. She'd taken them through to the kitchen, explaining that her husband was out, but would be back soon. Unless he was in court, or had a client appointment, he'd continued to work from home. 'I think he feels the same as me. That returning to our routine before Aisha's murder is disrespectful to her memory.'

'You're both reeling from what's happened. It's understandable to take things slow,' Ashcroft had sympathised.

She'd poured Nazia coffee from a pot, then handed Ashcroft a tumbler of water from a bottle in the fridge. She regarded her half-drunk cup of fruit tea and sighed. 'I prefer my drinks steeped in caffeine, but it's hard enough to sleep at the moment as it is.' She'd refused their suggestion to take a seat, telling them, 'I've spent too long in that damned chair.' She'd studied their faces, 'You don't have to wait for my husband to get back, you know,' she insisted, 'You can tell me.'

Which is what they'd done. The whole kit and caboodle. Only now she was staring at them like they'd insulted everything she stood for.

'I don't understand,' she said eventually. Her gaze scanned the kitchen as though searching for something familiar.

Something she could cling onto since the rug beneath her had been pulled away once more.

'Perhaps I will sit down after all,' she said, moving towards the sofa by the window.

The front door slammed shut and Ozwald entered the kitchen carrying groceries. 'Thought I could cook us that Thai meal you like…' he slowed when he saw the detectives in his kitchen. 'What's happened?' he asked, dropping the groceries onto a work surface when he saw his wife slumped on the sofa. He angled his head towards Ashcroft and Nazia.

'Where's Sika? he demanded; his voice laced with fear.

'She's at school. She's fine,' Abena told him quickly. 'It's about Aisha.'

He moved over to his wife, placed an arm around her shoulder. 'Can someone tell me what's going on?'

'Several facts have come to light over the last couple of days that we need to talk to you about.'

'Regarding Aisha?'

Ashcroft nodded.

'Get on with it then.'

Ozwald sat on the arm of the sofa coiled, ready to spring. He'd the benefit of forewarning, would be readying himself to defend his daughter to the hilt if needed.

'Do you know anyone by the name of Tobi Harun?' asked Ashcroft.

'No,' said Ozwald without missing a beat.

'He's her boyfriend!' Abena told him.

'That's not possible!'

'Let me show you a photo,' said Nazia, tapping onto her smartphone before turning the screen to show him.

Ozwald turned his head away. 'I don't need to see it; you must be mistaken.'

'Her friends knew about him,' said Ashcroft, careful not to drop Sika in it.

Nazia's arm was still outstretched.

Sighing, Ozwald took the phone from her, studied the picture on the screen. 'I've never seen him,' he said after several seconds. He handed the phone back then turned to his wife. 'Did you know about this?' His arm fell from her shoulders, the earlier concern in his voice replaced with accusation.

'Of course not!' she snapped. 'What about you? Did you know she wasn't going to Oxford?'

Ozwald's face screwed up in confusion. 'What are you talking about?'

'Aisha had a job lined up with an organisation she'd been volunteering with for the last two months. She was due to start there in a couple of weeks,' Ashcroft informed him.

Ozwald looked from Ashcroft to his wife. 'How is this possible? She had school…' He was working through the logistics, rather than rejecting it out of hand. It was progress, of sorts.

'A couple of hours here and there when she had a free period. During the holidays…' Ashcroft informed him.

'She told me she was working on a project.'

'She was, in a way,' said Nazia, not altogether helpfully.

'Where?' he asked, eventually.

'She's been volunteering at The Dignity Centre in Rusholme, which helps refugees. She was going to take up a permanent position in their new office on Abraham Road.'

Ozwald flinched. 'Where she was shot?'

'Yes.'

'Could one of the refugees have done this?'

'We've no evidence to support that at the moment,' Ashcroft said carefully.

'But that's what you're thinking! Come on, it makes sense! One of them may have taken a shine to her only she sends him packing and he follows her…'

'We'll be looking into every possibility,' Ashcroft assured him. 'I take it you had no idea about your daughter's change of plans?'

Ozwald regarded him. 'I think our reaction is answer enough, don't you?'

'Did Aisha have a particular interest in this line of work?'

'Nothing that she spoke to me about,' said Abena.

Ozwald merely shrugged.

'Was the boy who was shot alongside her a refugee?' Abena asked.

'Perhaps he encouraged her to work there,' stated Ozwald. Still keen to pin the reason they were in that spot that morning on Jamal, rather than consider it had anything to do with their daughter. Only natural, Ashcroft supposed.

'No, we're not aware of anything that connects Jamal to the refugee centre.'

'Keep looking. There's bound to be something.' Oswald reached down to grip his wife's hand.

'Please be assured we're looking into every possibility. With that in mind my Superintendent wants to run a press appeal tomorrow. There may well be a witness out there who doesn't realise the importance of something they might have seen that morning. I can call you with the details later. Send a car to pick you up, if you feel up to it?'

'We'll do it,' said Abena. 'If you think it will help.'

'Thank you.' Ashcroft paused. They'd been inundated with a lot of information. Their energy reserves would be running low, but there were still a couple of things he wanted to clear up. He started with what he hoped was the least contentious.

'My colleagues have been looking at Aisha's social media accounts. She and Jamal both shared an interest in a genealogy site. Was this something she was specifically interested in?'

Abena's face brightened. 'I can't believe she was actually taking something I said on board!'

'What do you mean?'

'I've been encouraging her to learn more about the origins of her heritage for a while. She kept shrugging my suggestion off.' She smiled at the curiosity on Ashcroft's face. 'My work brings me into contact with many culturally-disconnected Brits of Afro-Caribbean descent. There are so many assumptions about us. We're allegedly blessed with two homes — one in our parents' country and another the UK — yet the reality is very different. With each passing generation, many of us feel removed from our ancestry, yet Brexit has compounded the alienation we feel here. We find tenuous links to where we're *from*, through food, music and often-mispronounced birth names, yet many have never even visited the country of their heritage. For many, a dual identity feels more like one fractured in half.'

Ashcroft dropped his gaze.

'I encourage my students to research their history and discover the prevalence of their African roots. Embrace their past. Aisha used to tease me that my views were outdated but then at her 18th birthday party she surprised me by wearing a dress she'd had made out of Kente cloth, which she'd sourced from a village in Ghana where my parents were born.' Her smile broadened at the memory. 'It proved that not everything I told her over the years had fallen on deaf ears. Her interest in genealogy would have been a natural progression.'

'How do the sites work?'

'They may differ slightly in the way they operate and the fees they charge, but the principle will be the same. Someone interested in learning more about their heritage sends off a DNA sample and it's checked against a global database. When I did it, I discovered I was eight percent European, which makes sense, because of the slave trade, as well as thirteen per cent middle eastern, which opened up a whole new aspect of my history to explore. It can be a life changing experience, though not always in the way anticipated. The neo-Nazi that discovered he was quarter Jewish might be the headline grabbing example but many people who enter the process with a specific belief about their history, learn something entirely new about themselves.'

Researching ancestry had certainly become popular over the years, given the number of TV shows following celebrities as they delved into their past. It was possible that Jamal's interest in the topic came from Aisha. He wouldn't be the first person whose actions were influenced by a friend or romantic partner.

Ashcroft steeled himself as he broached the more contentious topic. 'Just one more thing. There was an incident, a couple of months ago now. A five-year-old boy was thrown from a balcony on the Abraham Road Estate. Did you hear about it?'

'Briefly, on the news,' said Ozwald.

'Terrible,' observed Abena. 'Why do you ask?'

'Did Aisha say anything about it to you?'

'No. Nothing.' Ozwald eyed him suspiciously. 'You didn't answer my wife's question. Why exactly are you asking?'

'I'm wondering whether Aisha or Jamal witnessed something that day. Kamali Harris — the little boy — was murdered Thursday 10th March at approximately 4pm. Do you know where Aisha would have been at that time?'

Abena pulled out her phone to check her calendar. 'It was term time. She'd have been at school. Getting ready for hockey practice-'

'-I think, given today's revelations,' stated Ozwald, cutting her off, 'that we're the last people who can give you any reliable help with her whereabouts, don't you? You'd have more chance finding out where she was from her friends, or this so-called boyfriend of hers.'

'We will be asking them as well,' said Ashcroft. 'We just wanted to speak with you first.'

'And make us aware how little we knew our daughter.'

'Would you like to meet Tobi. Her boyfriend?' Nazia ventured. 'You may get some comfort from meeting someone who was important to her.'

'You really think we'd want to meet someone who encouraged her to lie to us? He's probably the reason she gave up on her promising future.' Ozwald shook his head. 'Now if that's everything,' he concluded, making a sweeping motion with his arm, 'My wife and I would like to be on our own.'

Ashcroft caught Nazia's eye. Better leave it there, he signalled, getting to his feet.

Jamal's family home

'Have you come with news?' Safia asked as the detectives walked into her front room.

'More questions, I'm afraid,' Ashcroft told her, 'But hopefully they'll result in answers that will help move the investigation along.'

She was setting the table for lunch. The smell of garlic, ginger and dark sugar filled the air.

'I've made plenty, if you'd like to join us?'

'Thank you, but I don't intend to take up too much of your time,' he said, ignoring the disappointment on Nazia's face. 'When I spoke to AJ yesterday I mentioned that Aisha had been offered a job at a refugee centre that's opening soon on Abraham Road.'

'Yes, he told me.'

'Did Jamal mention anything about it to you?'

Safia looked troubled. She shook her head and sighed as she looked over the table. She'd set three places. 'I keep doing it. I'm sure Anita will join us. I haven't the heart to clear Jamal's place away once I've set it.'

She turned to face Ashcroft. 'Sorry, I was miles away. What did you want to know?'

'Whether Jamal knew about the refugee centre that's opening on Abraham Road. Aisha had been about to start work there.

'He never mentioned anything about it to me. Then again, he didn't mention this girl either, did he?'

'That's true.' He nodded at Nazia as though saying, *over to you.*

'Safia, we've been looking through Jamal and Aisha's laptops and we can see they both follow a page on Facebook related to genealogy. Did Jamal ever discuss his interest with you?'

'I don't even know what it means,' Safia said, frowning. Her brow creased even more as she listened to Nazia's explanation. 'I can honestly say he's never mentioned it,' she said, after giving it some thought. She shrugged. 'Maybe he was only interested because she was.'

'It's possible,' agreed Nazia.

'A colleague of mine is investigating a murder that was committed not far from here, several weeks ago,' said Ashcroft. 'Kamali Harris. A little boy who was thrown from a balcony.'

Safia's head dipped onto her chest. 'It's turned into a cruel world.'

'Despite numerous appeals, no witnesses have come forward. Then a short time later Jamal and Aisha are murdered in cold blood. I have to consider whether the murders are connected.'

Safia looked at him sharply. 'What?'

'I'm wondering whether he and Aisha might have seen something that day and they were too scared to tell the police.'

Ashcroft told her the date and time of the murder.

'He'd have been on his way back from school with Fahri at that time. They often called into the café on the way home even when Fahri didn't have a shift, so his father would give them pizza — despite a perfectly good meal waiting for him here! What is it with that generation and fast food?'

'So it's not impossible then? That Jamal saw something that day?'

Safia blinked. 'I suppose not,' she said slowly. 'But if he'd seen something as wicked as that, he'd have told me.'

'Maybe not if he wanted to protect you.'

Safia held onto the back of a dining chair for support. 'This estate has changed while we've been here,' she said, taking a breath. 'The gangs have us all in a chokehold.' She moved to the window. Took up the position AJ had taken the day before. 'It's time we stood up to them.' She looked out onto the horizon. The walkways and rat runs that joined one tower block to another.

'Is AJ here?'

'He went out earlier. He promised he'd be back for lunch, though.

'Did he mention where he was going?'

Safia shook her head. 'He's a grown man. He goes where he wants.'

'Does he keep in touch with any of his old friends?'

She eyed Ashcroft. 'Some, I suppose. You'd have to ask him.' She forced her mouth into a smile. 'Fahri's father came to see me. He told me about the residents' forum he's helping you arrange.'

'He's doing most of the heavy lifting,' Ashcroft admitted.

Safia nodded. 'He is a good man. If I can help in any way…with the food…'

'There's no need, honestly. I asked Refik to keep it simple. A couple of sandwiches, a bit of coleslaw…'

'Our community is fractured, Sergeant. We need to tend to

it. The same way we would with someone who is sick. With love and food. Let those who want to help do so, it helps them heal too.'

The sound of a key in the lock made them turn. AJ stepped into the hall, removed his trainers before heading into the living room. He made a point of patting his pockets as though looking for something. Placed the leaflet he'd picked up from the florist the day before onto the table. 'For when the time comes,' he said. He looked from his mother to the detectives standing close by. 'Did I miss anything?' he asked, his expression suggesting he already knew the answer.

'My superintendent wants to put out a televised appeal for witnesses tomorrow. He asked me to check you are both available to take part.' Ashcroft waited for his reaction.

'I'd be glad to,' said AJ, inclining his head.

Nazia pulled into the parking bay nearest Refik's cafe.

'Feds!' yelled Mikey Hassan, scrambling onto his bike. He'd been sat on the edge of the kerb when they'd arrived, blowing smoke rings with what looked like his first cigarette.

Ashcroft grabbed the boy's jacket one handed as he stepped out of the car. 'Not so fast,' he said, gripping onto the bike's handlebars with the other. Mikey's cigarette fell from his mouth, he didn't bother picking it up. Didn't bother putting up any resistance either. He was in his own neighbourhood, after all. Help was close by if he needed it. He sat back on his seat, folded his arms.

'Shouldn't you be in school?' Ashcroft asked, letting go of him.

'School is for pussies!' Mikey shot back. He glanced at Nazia and grinned. Nazia stared through him, picked at something in her teeth.

'Is that so?' Ashcroft looked him up and down. 'I used to love seeing my mates every day and playing sport at breaktime. The school dinners weren't too shabby either.'

'So, what you tellin' me bro?'

'I'm saying I can't see what you're getting out of this. Sitting on a pavement smoking a cigarette you don't even like.'

'I'm just watching and waiting, bro,' Mikey told him with confidence. 'One day I'll be like the mandem up there.' He jerked his head towards the men keeping watch from the tower block balcony. Ashcroft didn't need to look to know who was there: Troy Mellor, Kwame Kuma and Leyton Appiah. That their eyes were on him.

'You arresting me or what, bro?'

'Do I need to? Have you committed a crime?'

Mikey dropped his gaze. Shook his head.

Took Ashcroft's silence as his cue to leave.

Ashcroft stared after him. They weren't social workers; Top Brass expected them to operate in a vacuum, but if they carried on doing that then nothing would change. Might as well move the maternity ward into the Magistrate's court and be done with it.

'Anything wrong, Sarge?' Nazia held the café door open, a quizzical look on her face.

'All good,' he answered, stepping inside.

Fahri was behind the counter. Dipping fillets of fish into batter before dropping them in the fryer. 'Dad!' he called through to the back as Ashcroft and Nazia approached the counter.

Customers waiting for their order turned to study them.

'You de one running dis community ting?' one of them asked, pointing to a poster on the café wall advertising the residents' forum the following evening.

Ashcroft nodded. 'You coming?'

He was rewarded with a slow nod. 'Me come fe hear your big ideas…and de food.' The man grinned at the prospect.

'It's more about hearing from you how we can help…' Ashcroft began, his words falling on deaf ears. The man took his wrapped-up fish and chips from Fahri, threw Ashcroft a look as he passed him. 'Nuff me come, widdout you expecting me to do your job fe yuh,' was his parting shot.

Refik joined his son behind the counter. He'd been in regular contact over the phone while preparations were made for the forum. 'There's nothing left to do,' he told them, looking pleased with himself. 'Other than show up and win everyone over.'

As though it were that simple. Ashcroft felt like a political candidate in the run up to an election. Even though there was no formal seat to win or lose, he'd be judged on the event. Not just by the local community, but by those who had influence over his career. Would too many residents turn up, or not enough? Would their questions be too provocative, their emotions too high? Worst still, had he set Superintendent Duncanson up to fail? Everywhere he turned there was a trap door.

'Relax, everything is in hand,' Refik reassured him as though reading his mind. 'The speakers and agencies have all confirmed they will be in attendance. I must thank your colleagues for their help with that,' he said, turning his attention to Nazia, rewarding her with a full beam smile. 'Looks like we can expect a large turnout.'

That was something, Ashcroft supposed. 'I wanted a quick word with Fahri, if you can spare him?' he ventured, looking from Refik to his son.

'Yes, of course.' Refik shooed his son towards the other side of the counter. 'I've got everything covered here.'

'We've been following the activity on Jamal's socials,' Nazia stated once they'd settled into the seats they'd occupied when they'd first broken the news of his murder. 'He was following a genealogy page on Facebook. It's a site for people interested in their family tree-'

'I know what it is!' said Fahri, offended, 'We covered it in school.'

'Any idea why he was interested?' asked Ashcroft.

A shrug. 'As long as I've known him, he's wanted to find out about his dad. Maybe he thought the site would help.'

Ashcroft thanked him. Made a mental note to speak to Safia's FLO, see if she could delve into the family background a little. 'Did you walk home from school together every day?'

'Yeah, like I said, we were pretty much in each other's pockets.'

'Apart from when Aisha was around,' stated Nazia.

'Suppose,' Fahri conceded.

'Only I've been wondering whether what happened to them is connected to the murder of the little boy who was thrown from the balcony not far from here.'

'Kamali Harris,' added Nazia, in case he'd had forgotten the name of the boy whose face was plastered across posters throughout the estate.

'Is it possible Jamal witnessed something, given his route home from school would have taken him passed the balcony. Or rather the skip below the balcony, where Kamali landed.'

Fahri winced.

'But then if you and Jamal always walked that route together, you'd have witnessed something too.'

'Only you'd have mentioned something as massive as that, wouldn't you?' Nazia added helpfully.

Fahri looked as though he was going to be sick. 'You can't tell anyone!' he said quickly. He glanced round at his father, who was engaged in banter with a customer, while piling chips into a lidded cardboard tray.

'We didn't see it happen; I swear! But we heard it, and we

did see a group of men run away from the block as we turned into the square.'

'Can you describe them?'

'Are you kidding me? You see a group of guys run away from anything round here, you look away, not consign them to memory.'

'Seems they remembered Jamal.'

Fahri blinked. 'You think they killed him?'

'I don't know, but I need to speak to them. Can you give me any descriptions at all?'

Nazia pulled out her notebook and pen, lay them flat on the table when Fahri shrugged.

'Let's start with the basics. Were they black or white?' she prompted.

'White.'

'How were they dressed?'

Fahri thought about this. 'They were all dressed in black.'

Nazia opened her notebook and began to write. It was a start, she supposed.

'All? How many of them were there?' asked Ashcroft.

Another shrug. 'Five or six?'

That was a lot of men to be running out of a building. There was no way that number would have gone unnoticed. 'Can you describe their clothing?' he asked.

Fahri looked confused.

'Tracksuits, hoodies, ski masks,' Nazia prompted. 'All or none of the above.'

'Not tracksuits…jeans maybe, and bomber jackets?'

'You askin' us or tellin' us?' said Ashcroft.

'Yeah, it was jeans, bomber jackers, a couple of hoodies.'

'Did you and Jamal tell anyone about what you saw?'

Fahri shook his head.

'Even when news of Kamali's murder was made public?'

'If they can do that to a little kid, what would they do to a rat?'

'I think we know the answer to that,' said Ashcroft.

'Everything alright?' Refik called over to them. The queue of customers waiting to be served had grown. It was hard to be sure whether he was checking his son was OK, or telling them he needed him back behind the counter.

'Did they see you?' Ashcroft asked quickly.

'N-no, I don't think so. They were in too much of a hurry to get away.'

'And you've spoken to no one about this?'

'No.'

'Did Jamal tell anyone else?'

'Why would he? He'd be a dead man walking if they blabbed to someone else.'

'Not if it was someone he trusted. A teacher maybe. Someone from church. Or…'

'Or Aisha.' Fahri finished for him.

Aisha hadn't grown up there. Didn't understand the rules of the estate. Was that why she'd been searching through the refugee database? Was she trying to help Jamal identify Kamali's killers?

'Did you hear any of them speak?' asked Ashcroft. An accent would be too much to hope for but it was worth checking.

'No. It all happened so fast. We didn't think too much about the men until later. All we heard was Kamali's dad screaming, followed by a thud.'

'What did you do then?'

'We saw people gathering around the skip but we didn't want to get too close. The sound he made when he landed…I didn't want to see what something that sounded as awful as that looked like.'

Ashcroft gave him a moment. When he spoke next he kept

his voice low. 'Would you be willing to give a formal statement at the station?'

'Why?' Fahri glanced over at his father. Refik was ringing up the last customer's order on the till. 'What I told you doesn't count for much and I'd be putting myself at risk for what?'

He was right. A partial description from a reluctant witness wouldn't count for much in court, assuming they found suspects to fit it. Rather than place him in danger, they could use what he'd told them to refine their search for Kamali's killers. If there was the slightest chance that by doing this they would unearth Jamal and Aisha's killers too, then that was a win in his book — providing they found evidence capable of securing a conviction.

'We'll leave it there for the moment,' Ashcroft said, getting to his feet. 'I wish you'd told us this at the beginning. By keeping this to yourself there's every chance the killers have gone to ground.' He regarded Fahri's stricken face. 'From what you've told me there's no reason to think you're in any danger. If you were, you'd be dead by now.'

The boy shrank into his chair.

'What I mean is it's a lot easier to predict your whereabouts than it was Jamal and Aisha's. You're a sitting target in this shop at certain times of the day if someone wanted to harm you, yet for some reason *they* were the target instead.'

This did nothing to reassure Fahri. He shoved his hands between his thighs as though seeking warmth.

'I was going to make you some mint tea since my son's hospitality skills haven't improved,' said Refik as he approached them. He smiled, oblivious to the tension around the table.

'Thanks, but we'd better get back to the station,' Ashcroft told him, 'I'll see you tomorrow evening.'

'Splendid,' said Refik. 'Don't worry about a thing, I have it all under control,' he called out as they reached the door.

Ashcroft wished he could say the same.

One Good Reason

Troy Mellor watched the detectives leave the Turkish café from his vantage point on the first-floor landing. The male cop seemed troubled as he closed the door behind him. A lot less sure of himself than he'd appeared on the way in.

'Wonder what that's all about?'

Kwame looked pleased with himself as he filled his boss in. 'The Feds have asked the Turk to organise a residents' meeting. He was in the laundrette handing out leaflets the other day, gave one to my nan.'

Troy sucked air through his teeth. 'Did the blud look like 'im been talking 'bout seating plans?' He reached in his jacket pocket for his mobile. Tapped on the number saved in his contacts list. Let it ring.

NINE

> 'We're well placed to cause a little disruption here and there, then make them an offer they can't refuse.'
>
> – VASIF MUKA

Ervin Muka looked up from the paperwork he'd been reading in the back of his chauffeured Bentley, angled his head towards the passenger beside him. 'The shipments are operating like clockwork. We've expanded our distribution channels and revenue has increased thirty percent on last year, whilst our expenditure has remained the same.'

He nodded his approval, dropping the papers into the case by his feet. 'What is that phrase the English use?' He studied the air around him as he searched for the right words. 'Ah yes, chip off the old block. You are indeed your father's son.' He smiled benevolently into a pair of eyes identical to his own, bar the creases. Vasif was his youngest child but his only son. He'd all but given up hope when his third wife held him up like a trophy after his birth, her future with Ervin assured.

'I've had the best teacher,' Vasif answered, smiling.

Ervin leaned back in his seat, tired. He'd been feeling every one of his sixty years, lately. A lifetime defending his territory was bound to take its toll. He'd kept his promise to his wife and stepped back from the business, but he couldn't be complacent.

Plenty of rivals would have his head on a stick given half the chance. He'd installed panic rooms into the family home, and his driver was an ex-mercenary. It didn't pay to take chances.

Vasif studied his father. Decided to take advantage of his pensive mood. 'Business is booming. We have money to burn, Baba. We need to find new channels to hide it.'

Ervin nodded. 'Go on.'

'You already know my view, Baba!' Vasif swallowed down his frustration at having to repeat himself. Maybe this time the old man would look on his proposal more favourably.

'We start buying up the land around the Langston Estate. I've spoken to some of our partners. They are keen to establish a consortium, move into large scale property development. My contact at the council has told me the housing department has been haemorrhaging money for years. It can't afford to maintain its existing stock; it won't take much for them to throw in the towel.' He flashed his father a winning smile, 'We're well placed to cause a little disruption here and there, then make them an offer they can't refuse. Five years from now we could be leasing out luxury offices and apartment blocks with rooftop pools and underground gyms. Just think of it.'

'It's a lot of money to explain away.'

'That's the whole point, Baba. The consortium will consist of legitimate investors as well. Banks, insurance companies, any unpleasant whiff regarding where the money originated will be rinsed clean away. Our accountants and legal team are on extortionate retainers. That's their problem, not ours.'

Ervin looked sceptical.

'I've bought a retail unit on Abraham Road. A bit of friendly persuasion, and I'm confident we'll acquire the others this year. Why don't we take a detour, and I can show you?'

'It may have escaped your attention, but I'm not exactly dressed to go on an expedition round some sink estate.' Ervin indicated his velvet jacket and bow tie. He glanced at his Patek Philippe watch. 'Your mother is expecting me at the reception she's hosting in fifteen minutes. She doesn't like to be kept waiting.'

'What charity is it this time?'

'As long as it makes her happy, I don't care. You could join us, if you like? I'm sure we can magic up a shirt and tie from somewhere.'

With Ervin as a major donor, no one would bar Vasif's entry, but there were standards to maintain. Ervin knew he was considered old school. That said, his son's preferred uniform of black denim jeans and army boots could hardly be described as elegant. He dressed like someone who lived on a military base, rather than a gated mansion in Cheshire. Ironic really. But then when you were running an operation like theirs, it did no harm to look as though you could handle yourself. The tattoo on his neck was very convincing, in that regard.

Vasif shook his head. 'I'll leave you to your fundraising, Baba. There's some business I need to attend to.'

Ervin looked at him quizzically.

'The Abraham Road gang are planning something. I can feel it. I need to make sure our men are ready when they show their hand.'

'I thought you'd sent them a message.'

'Seems they didn't understand it.'

'I'm not surprised.' Ervin looked pained. 'About that boy.'

Vasif waited.

'What you did, throwing him off that balcony…'

'Jesus Christ, Baba, what else could I do! Someone joined their firm who used to work on our patch. I had to teach him — and them — a lesson.'

Ervin held up a hand to silence him.

'But what have they learned? That you can only do half a job?'

The look he gave his son was cold and hard. 'You should have thrown the mother and baby off too.'

Fahri was about to turn the sign on the café door to 'closed' when it opened unexpectedly, causing him to stumble backwards. They normally shut for an hour before the teatime rush. It gave him and his dad a chance to eat a proper meal before spending the rest of the evening serving doner kebabs and pizzas for folk too idle to cook for themselves.

'Hey, watch it!' he cried out as the door swung towards him. 'Can't you read the sign?'

'Surely that doesn't apply to me?' AJ asked as he stepped inside. 'You and Jamal were so tight, it was like I had two kid brothers, not one.'

'Of course,' said Fahri, stepping to one side so that he could pass. 'Sorry, I didn't realise it was you. How are you?'

'I'm not gonna lie, I've been better.' AJ leaned against the counter as though he was about to place an order.

'Can I get you anything?' Fahri asked, 'On the house, of course.'

'That's very good of you.'

He had a way of stretching out his words that made him sound menacing even when he was being nice. Fahri had always been a little afraid of him. An only child, he had no experience of sibling rough and tumble. The insults and wind-ups, Chinese burns and wedgies that seemed part and parcel of adolescent males growing up in close proximity. Jamal had worshipped him though, and the next best thing to having a mean looking older brother was having a best mate who had one.

'What's going on, blud?' AJ demanded.

'I don't get you.'

'We both know that isn't true.' AJ moved suddenly, making Fahri blink.

'Can't believe you're still falling for it after all these years!' he joked, 'Even Jamal got wise to me and he was soft as shit.'

He gave Fahri a pretend punch on the arm. 'Remember what I used to tell you both. You gotta learn to stand your ground. Not show any fear.'

'Guess I'm a lover, not a fighter,' Fahri said, sheepish.

AJ's grin fell away. 'Mum said you went round to see her the day it happened. To pay your respects. That means a lot.' The confidence he normally exuded had all but deserted him. He leaned back against the counter. Kept his eyes on Fahri the whole time.

'I hear the Feds came to see you again.'

Fahri swallowed. Nothing went down on the estate without Troy Mellor knowing about it. He'd heard rumours that Troy and AJ were tight back in the day but Jamal had never spoken about it, so he'd left it alone. Old friendships, like wounds, run deep.

He knew better than to spin AJ a line. 'They think his murder is connected to that little boy,' he told him, 'The one who-'

'-Yeah, I know which one.' AJ tilted his head as though giving the matter some thought.

'Tell me something I don't know,' he said eventually.

'I'm not sure what you mean.'

'When they came round to the flat, they made it sound like it was only a theory. The way you say it sounds like they've made up their mind. I'm wondering what you told them that would make that happen.'

Fahri blinked, even though AJ hadn't made any sudden moves. He remained still, like a statue, his eyes empty. AJ looked more menacing than the roadmen in the square and Troy Mellor's henchmen combined. Right now he looked more menacing than Troy Mellor himself, for fucksake, and he was the meanest motherfucker there was.

'The thing is…' He squirmed under AJ's gaze. Weighed up the consequences of spilling his guts versus keeping shtum. The outcome would be the same, going by the deadly look on the squaddie's face. Better the Devil you know, he reasoned. He hauled in a breath. Walked over to the door. Flipped the sign to closed.

'There's something I need to tell you,' he said, turning to face AJ once more.

It was nearly closing time. The last appointments of the day were done with, so she'd let the other girls leave once they'd cleaned down their work area. No point keeping them back for the sake of it, she believed in playing fair. She checked through the appointment book for tomorrow — all the time slots were full, a blessing given how close the salon was to that shooting. She glanced out of the window to where the couple had been parked. Broad daylight too. To think she'd been bustling about in the back, opening up. She shuddered. The killer would have laid her out if he'd seen her. The place was going to the dogs and no mistake.

She checked the money in the till against the receipts, placed the cash in her bag ready to pay into the bank deposit box on her way home. She'd already slipped her jacket on when the salon door opened, causing her to glance at the clock. Five minutes to five.

'I'm sorry, we're closing!' she called out, hoping it wasn't one of her regulars. She was relieved when a man stepped forward. Probably after a last-minute gift voucher for his girlfriend, she reasoned. The smile she gave him fell away when she got nothing back. She took in his black denim jeans and bomber jacket. The army boots that none of the men in this neighbourhood wore, and felt a moment of unease.

'Can I help you?'

'I'm your new business partner,' he said, offering her his hand.

By the time Vasif entered the maisonette on the Langston Estate which he used as operational headquarters, he'd pocketed the best part of a grand. The nail salon owner hadn't been too thrilled about parting with the day's takings, but as he'd pointed out, it was a small price to pay for peace of mind. He'd said the same to the neighbouring laundrette and clothes shop owners when he demanded their takings too, would have hated anyone to feel left out. They could expect him the same time next week, he'd told them, and every week thereafter. If they had any sense they'd terminate their leases as soon as they were able, leaving empty properties which he'd snap up should the owner decide to sell. He grinned at that thought. Troy Mellor would have no choice in the matter. He might give the impression business was going good for him right now, but he'd need a lot of cash behind him to keep three vacant properties with no sign of a return.

The interior of the flat resembled an underground bunker. Big men lounged on chairs that looked as though they'd been rescued from a fire sale. Vasif had summoned them an hour ago, made no apologies for keeping them waiting. He handed the cash to Aljan Vata, his bag man, who counted it, entering the total onto his phone before dropping it into the sports bag beside him, like a portable bank.

Vasif told his henchmen where the money was from.

'You know those units are owned by Troy Mellor, don't you boss?' asked one of them.

'Of course he knows, that's the whole fucking point!' Aljan countered, nodding in admiration.

Vasif was allowed to feel pleased with himself. He was on track to achieve his dream of part owning the luxury development he'd described to his old man.

Things were looking up.

TEN

'Without the right resources we're just catching damaged fruit when it falls, nothing more.'

– DI ALEX MORETON

Incident room

Since the start of his shift, Ashcroft had paced the length of the murder wall while sipping water from the sports bottle he'd brought from home.

Potter watched him, a bemused look on his face. 'I'm as frustrated as you are, but I'm not sure wearing holes in our already threadbare carpet tiles will help.'

'To be fair Brian, you have just shown him a photograph of the crew you think are responsible for Kamali Harris's murder. And three of them are wearing clothes that match Fahri Gemici's description of the men he and Jamal saw running from Windward Tower immediately after.'

Ashcroft continued pacing, apparently oblivious to the conversation going on around him.

'Whoa, you need to back up a bit there Naz,' countered Potter. 'Firstly. I'm not saying these men killed Kamali, but his father, Petro, definitely worked for them. They're part of the Berati crew who run the Langston Estate. The drugs they supply are embossed with an image of a sports car — their way of keeping tabs on their supply chain, if you like. A snap bag of amphetamines stamped with this design was found in Petro Harris's flat after Kamali's murder, so it's safe to say there's a direct connection.'

'What, their version of a calling card?'

'Seems so.'

Nazia took the photograph of the men from Potter's desk and held it aloft. 'I refer you to Exhibit A, your honour, a photograph of six thugs identified by my learned friend here as running the Langston Estate. Three of the men in this picture are wearing clothing described by our witness who saw them hurrying from the tower block after Kamali's murder. Note the black bomber jackets worn by two of them. A black hoody worn by another. And to finish off the look they're all wearing regulation black jeans, suggesting a distinct lack of imagination, or they like to buy in bulk.'

'It's not enough,' said Ashcroft, who'd been following their conversation after all. 'Even if we bring them in we've got nothing to keep them, and certainly no grounds to charge them. A half decent lawyer and they'd be out of here and on the first plane back to the Eastern Bloc in no time. Fake passports, new IDs, never to be seen again.'

'Until the dust settles,' Potter added. 'When they come back and pick up where they left off.'

'Then we put Fahri into witness protection and we get him to testify,' said Nazia.

'To what? That he saw a group of men who dressed like them coming out of a tower block? Sarge is right. What we have is weak to say the least.'

'So what do we do now?'

Ashcroft stopped pacing. He'd needed to focus. To work out the order of the actions he wanted to assign, according to the results he thought they'd bring in. Fahri's statement on its own was flimsy, but combined with Brian Potter's hunch regarding the Berati Crew it was a direction of travel he wanted to pursue.

'Naz, check Alisha was where her mother said she was at the time of Kamali's killing — school hockey practice. She might not have witnessed the murder, but she's the one with closest links to any migrants who might be working illegally for the gang. I want to be clear of the facts, before I present them to the boss.'

'I'm on it,' said Nazia, returning to her desk.

'If Jamal had described the men he'd seen leaving the tower block after Kamali's murder to Aisha it's possible that something rang a bell. Thanks to the database at The Dignity Centre, she'd know where to find them.' A thought occurred to him. 'I've got a contact in Organised Crime. I'll give them a call. They may be able to help me join up some of these dots.'

He returned to his own desk and dialled their number. Smiled at the sound of the familiar voice. He explained the information he was looking for, listened to their response for a couple of minutes, wrote down the address they gave him before ending the call.

The next person he rang was Anita, Safia's FLO. There was something he needed her to check. 'Are you able to talk right now?' he asked when she answered her phone.

'Yes, I offered to get some shopping in for them. Safia prefers to talk to AJ now he's back, which is understandable, but his mood's so damned unpredictable. They've had words a few times, which ends up with him storming out then coming back hours later full of apologies. Don't get me wrong, I get it. Just doesn't make it any easier being around him.'

'Has there been any talk of Jamal's father?'

'Not that I'm aware of. I know he's not on the scene.'

'The kind of not on the scene that'll see him show up for the funeral and spout rubbish to the press?'

'I dunno, Sarge, but I can try and sound Safia out. Use that scenario as a conversation starter.'

Ashcroft thanked her. He picked up his car keys, told the others to call him with any updates.

Ashcroft parked outside the address he'd been given, texted the occupant to tell them he was outside, then waited. Within a matter of seconds the front door flew open and two overexcited boys ran to his car. 'Mum says we can show you round,' said the older of the two. Gangly, with a mop of hair that fell into his eyes, he manoeuvred his brother out of the way so that Ashcroft could open the car door.

Empty cardboard boxes lined the hallway. The younger boy pointed them out. 'We're going to make a den out of these,' he said, stepping into one to give Ashcroft a mini demonstration.

'No we're not, dummy, the removal men want them back,' the older one chimed.

'Whose got the messiest bedroom?' Ashcroft enquired in an attempt to head off the fallout that threatened to follow.

'Me!' the boys cried in unison, the younger one taking his hand as he led him upstairs.

A quarter of an hour later he stepped into the kitchen where Alex Moreton had made them both coffee.

'Ben told me you said they could watch cartoons on their iPads for half an hour,' he said, taking the mug she held out to him.

'God, yes,' Alex answered, rolling her eyes, 'anything to give us a bit of peace.' She offered him an oat flapjack which he declined. 'Who in their right mind moves house with small kids?' She made one hand into the shape of a gun and pointed it at her head before pulling the trigger. 'School's closed today because of the teachers' strike, and the childminder can only take them for a couple of hours so it's been challenging, as you can imagine.'

Ashcroft wasn't sure that he could. He saw how his sister juggled her career with being a parent, a single one at that. Yet to anyone looking on from the outside, both women made it look easy. At work, Inspector Alex Moreton was a stickler for protocol, a dedicated rule book cop who expected nothing less from those around her. Since her move to Nexus House in Tameside, where GMP's Serious and Organised Crime Division was based, Ashcroft had become accustomed to seeing her impeccably turned out in her dress uniform on the rare occasion their paths crossed. A far cry from the sweatshirt and jeans she wore now, her mid length hair held back in a scrunchie. She was luckier than most, he supposed. The boys' father worked from home, was able to structure his work as a computing consultant around their school and nursery hours.

'Where's Carl?' he asked, expecting to see him walk in any minute with a hammer and an armful of pictures that needed putting up.

'He's gone to the supermarket. My earlier attempt at stocking up failed miserably. So,' she said, leading him through open French doors onto a raised patio that looked onto Haughton Dale Nature Reserve. 'We can talk uninterrupted.'

'Nice part of the world,' he observed, as he sat down.

Alex nodded in agreement. 'Easy decision. My workdays are getting longer. At least now I'm only fifteen minutes away from home when I do eventually clock off.'

'Makes sense.'

'So, come on then,' she said, cocking her ear towards one of the bedroom windows above them. 'It won't be long before the Chuckle Brothers up there turn into Jekyll and Hyde. Let's get down to what it is you want to know.'

Alex had participated in several division-wide operations aimed at dismantling organised crime. She was the best chance he had of finding out the extent of the Albanian network without having to submit a request in writing or blow smoke up some desk jockey's backside because they had information that he wanted.

'I'm interested in the Albanians who run the Langston Estate in Moss Side. What can you tell me about them?'

'The Berati Crew?'

Ashcroft nodded.

Alex widened her eyes. 'I can tell you that they're highly regarded in the drug community, particularly in relation to the supply of cocaine. They've single-handedly driven the price down in Manchester, as have their equal numbers across the UK. Put it this way, they've done for cocaine what Aldi has done for grocery shopping. More than that though, they have a reputation for being reliable and ruthless. In the same way that the Italian Mafia members swore to uphold the oath of silence, known as Omerta, the Berati Crew keep to an ancestral code of Besa, *'To keep the promise,'* and Kanun, *'The right to take revenge.'*

'Nice.'

'Times are changing though. Whilst the old guard believed discretion was key to their success, the younger generation are a lot more obvious about their activities, going so far as posting videos on YouTube in an attempt to lure new recruits.'

She pulled out her smartphone. Tapped on the YouTube icon and typed the name of the gang into the search bar. 'See for yourself,' she said, handing the phone to him.

Ashcroft hit the 'Play' button, watched in disbelief as a group of Rolex wearing gangsters postured for the camera, miming to the lyrics of a rap song while parading around with a gun in each hand.

'They think they're untouchable,' Alex said when the video had finished.

Ashcroft handed the phone back to her. 'What about surveillance?'

'They're too widely spread, and we just don't have the resources,' she said, looking glum. 'Never mind that, you're on a murder team, what's your interest in them?'

Ashcroft told her about his temporary move to Moss Side following the murders of Aisha Saforo and Jamal Deng. 'We've reason to believe their murder is connected to the killing of Kamali Harris, a five-year-old-'

'-Don't,' said Alex, holding up her palm to stop him from saying any more. 'It turned my stomach when I heard about it. Even now I can't have the image in my head. Not that.'

She glanced up at the bedroom window then looked away. Some things you couldn't allow to get under your skin.

Ashcroft nodded. 'We've reason to believe Jamal saw the men leave the tower block after Kamali's murder.'

'Sounds feasible. I mean, I've got colleagues who'd stake their pension they were behind it.' Alex shuddered as she spoke. 'Problem is, with your witness dead, how can anyone prove it?'

'I was hoping you might have something we could use. Seems to me no-one's gone after them for anything significant. Mid-tier drug related stuff, but nothing more. Makes the headlines on the court pages but nothing that makes any meaningful difference.'

'That's what happens when you're up against high level criminality. This gang has long roots and a considerable reach. They've established themselves in record time compared to their counterparts. Take your Langston Estate as an example. They started to move in during the early noughties following the unrest in Kosovo. Within ten years, Albanian was the second language spoken on the estate.

It's no wonder the gangs are able to recruit so many members. Albanians arriving in the UK illegally are taken to the Langston Estate deliberately. Many will have a debt they need to repay from paying traffickers to bring them over. They soon discover that they can earn £10,000 working on a cannabis farm for two months, as opposed to potentially £50 a day cash-in-hand working in construction or car washes.

It might look like easy money but there are consequences. Albanians are the third largest foreign nationality in UK prisons. UK Home Office figures reported that in 2019 Eastern European gangsters committed more than one in four of all crimes in the UK. That includes nine out of ten drug offences.'

He could rely on Alex to back up what she said with evidence. There were too many rumour mongers out there all too happy to peddle their opinion and claim it as fact.

'It's happening everywhere, Chris, even Counterfeit Alley.'

This was the local name used for an area of Cheetham Hill because of its prevalence of outlets flogging fake gear. 'We carried out a spate of arrests last month. Forty 'stall-holders' turned out to be vulnerable child asylum seekers who'd been abducted from outside hotels run by the Home Office. They're coerced into organised crime groups in an attempt to extort money from their families. They're seen by the crime gangs as low-level cannon fodder. Expendable. That's why so many end up in jail. If you want to make any real difference you need to go further up the tree. But without the right resources we're just catching damaged fruit when it falls, nothing more.'

She gave him a stern look. 'Though I'll deny it if you tell anyone I said that.'

She took a sip of her drink. 'One of the reasons this particular gang is impenetrable is because of the support they receive from professional enablers, operating within the 'legitimate community'. The likes of accountants and security guards helping people who have arrived make a life in the UK. This cloak of legitimacy makes it so much harder for us.'

So many people paid to turn a blind eye. That or they've been blackmailed into it, Ashcroft reminded himself.

'The Berati Crew have been unstoppable because they control so much of the drug supply. These are dangerous men, Chris. Any street gangs who stand up to them tend to disappear.'

'So they're going to get away with Kamali's murder?'

'You know how the saying goes. *No face, no case.*'

Ashcroft sighed. If he'd been hopeful that Alex could offer him a magic bullet he was mistaken.

'Have you come across Troy Mellor yet?' she asked.

'The guy who heads up the Abraham Road gang, yeah.' Ashcroft nodded.

'We received intel a while ago that he was trying to gain territory.'

Ashcroft considered this. 'Sounds about right, he's bought up some of the retail units close to where my victims were found.' All of the units bar one, if his memory served him correctly.

'Have you considered the possibility that he arranged to have your couple killed to deliberately incite a turf war. *Your enemy is my enemy and all that.* If the neighbouring gangs think the Albanians are getting out of control then they're more likely to join him against them.'

Ashcroft pulled a face. 'Aisha was known to him though.'

Alex shrugged. 'Since when does that make a difference?'

'*Mu-um!*'

'And that,' Alex dead-panned, 'is my two-minute warning. Any longer and I'll have World War Three on my hands.' She got to her feet. 'It's been good seeing you,' she added in between calling up the stairs as they passed them that she was on her way.

'Have you seen much of Kevin?' she asked as Ashcroft stepped onto the driveway.

'Still on light duties.'

'Lynn was walking much better, last time I went round,' she

informed him, though they both knew their friend's return to normal duty had nothing to do with his wife's recovery and everything to do with his feelings of guilt. 'Tell him I was asking after him, next time you see him,' she called out before closing the door.

Ashcroft nodded, though given the last two calls he'd made had not been returned, he wasn't sure when that would be.

He checked his phone for messages as he climbed into the driver's seat. There was one from Nazia: Aisha's school confirmed that she was at hockey practice when Kamali Harris was murdered. She hadn't been killed for something *she'd* seen, then. Though that didn't rule out that her murder was as a result of something she'd found on the refugee centre's database.

Despite knowing Brian Potter would call him if he had anything to update him with, Ashcroft phoned him anyway.

'*The boss has signed the Production Order off, Sarge,*' he said before Ashcroft had a chance to ask him anything. '*Me and Naz are going over to the refugee centre now with a couple of uniforms. Don't want the grass growing on this, do we?*'

Ashcroft smiled. 'No, we don't Brian.'

'*Any luck your end Sarge, with your contact?*' Potter asked.

Ashcroft considered his answer. 'This gang recruits a lot of refugees as foot soldiers, albeit through kidnapping and coercion. This supports our theory that Aisha was searching for something on that database that would prove that link.'

'*Maybe someone went to the centre for support, then later disappeared?*' Potter suggested.

'It's as good a theory as anything else on the table right now, Brian. Let's keep it in mind.'

Potter was on a roll. '*If that theory proves to be correct, it begs the* question whether the centre manager was involved in informing the gang about potential recruits.'

'If she was, she'd have good reason to not want Aisha snooping.'

'One more thing that ties the Berati Crew into her and Jamal's murder.'

'It'll be great to get some hard evidence to support all this conjecture.'

'Hopefully my trip to the refugee centre will do just that.'

'Agreed.'

'Oh, and DI Daniels has been informed by the press office that tomorrow's briefing is scheduled to go out during the lunchtime news. I've organised the relatives to be brought here half an hour before so we can talk them through it.'

'Thanks, Brian.'

'The Super'll be beside himself, what with his shiny buttons getting two outings in one day.'

'Don't remind me.' Ashcroft groaned, thinking of the forum he'd naively thought would be a good idea.

'Just picture the rapture on his face tomorrow evening if he can stand at the lectern and announce that several arrests have been made.'

That's what worried him. The pressure they'd be under to pull a result out of the hat. He looked on, grim-jawed. Tomorrow's forum would be a resounding success or an abject failure. As far as Top Brass were concerned, there was nothing in between.

CID room

Ashcroft sat at his desk, sipping water from his sports bottle as he checked through his emails:

DCI Mallender asking how he was settling in, followed by a casual enquiry as to the progress the investigation was making.

His old boss's tactful way of asking how long he thought he'd be there, without asking him straight out. His transfer here had helped Moss Side station, but it had left his old team short-staffed. It didn't help that Chief Superintendent Curtis was notoriously slow at signing off requests for overtime or acting-up duties. Ashcroft allowed himself a smile. He wasn't going to lie; he felt some comfort knowing he was missed.

The business unit had sent through a copy of Aisha's latest bank statement. Several transactions from designers stores at The Trafford Centre matched Jamal's expensive trainers, as well as the clothes he was wearing when they were killed.

An email from Nazia, attaching a running order for tomorrow evening, for his approval. In the body of her message she informed him that the Super's assistant had requested it, along with an approximate number of those likely to attend. Sounded like he was determining how much effort to put into his speech. Ashcroft typed a quick reply to Nazia thanking her, suggesting she liaise directly with Refik for numbers, before forwarding it to DI Daniels and the Super.

An out of office message from Daniels bounced into his inbox.

Ashcroft looked over at the DI's office and frowned. He could have sworn he'd seen him at his desk earlier. A DC on his way to the photocopier filled him in:

'Got a call from his wife reminding him it was their anniversary. Never seen him move so fast.'

Ashcroft tried to remember what it was like having someone in his life who gave a toss. He'd done most of the heavy lifting in his previous relationship. Moved to London when his partner got a job with the Met. Truth was she'd have gone anyway, same as she stayed put when he decided he'd had enough. She was a DCI now.

'Actually, Sarge,' the DC added, stepping into Daniels' office to retrieve a post-it note stuck to the top of his monitor. 'I took a message for the boss while you were out but it's regarding the case you're working. Professor Clemont was keen that one of you called her back.'

Ashcroft recognised the name as the pathologist who'd carried out the postmortems on Jamal and Aisha. The scrawled note included her office number, followed by *blood results*, which had been underlined. DI Daniels had attended the postmortem for both victims, had circulated Professor Clemont's interim report when she'd emailed it over. Cause of death had never been in doubt, their tox screens had been negative and routine blood samples collected had been sent to the lab for tests. No doubt the professor wanted to run through the blood results with the SIO or his deputy before submitting her final report.

Ashcroft dialled her number.

'*Ah, many thanks for returning my call,*' she said after he introduced himself. '*Just bear with me while I get the files.*'

He heard a series of tapping noises and the shuffling of paper. The sound of a drink being slurped if he wasn't mistaken.

'*OK, so I noticed during Aisha Soforo's postmortem that she had atopic dermatitis — that's eczema, to the uninitiated — on the back of her elbows. It can present itself differently in people of colour, due to increased levels of collagen. So, unlike Caucasians, who can get scaly, people with darker skin experience lichenification.*'

'I'm hoping that sounds worse than it is.'

Professor Clemont laughed. '*Yes, sorry. Let me explain. It means the thickening of affected patches of skin. You'd feel the ridges if you ran your hand over an affected area. Also, rather than the redness you see in white skinned eczema sufferers, patients of colour can present with a dark grey 'ashiness.' I'm telling you this as it is often overlooked.*' She sounded pleased with herself.

Ashcroft tried to make suitably impressed noises.

'*I noticed Jamal had the same condition, appearing on the same parts of his body too. Conditions like this are often familial, and when their blood results came back showing they were the same blood group, I realised I needed to compare their DNA, just to be certain.'*

Familial.

Same blood group.

Ashcroft sat up straight in his seat. 'What? You're saying they're related?'

'That's correct. Their DNA results indicate that they are half siblings. Not full ones, but family all the same. Their mitochondrial DNA, which they inherit from their mother, is different, which means they share the same father.'

Ashcroft remained silent.

'I take it you weren't expecting that?'

'No way. I suspect the families won't be either.'

'Are both 'so called' fathers on the scene?'

'No, just Aisha's.'

'OK, well a DNA swab from him will help clarify who the daddy is, or isn't, no pun intended.'

Ashcroft was already working his way through the ramifications of breaking this particular nugget of news.

'I don't need to tell you to tread carefully,' Clemont added. *'These things aren't always proof of infidelity.'*

'What do you mean?'

'There's a whole raft of offspring coming forward these days who are the product of their biological father selling his sperm to fertility clinics to fund his way through university. Maybe it's something he did before settling down.'

'Jamal and Aisha were the same age, remember.'

'Crap.' The sound of more papers shuffling. *'So they are. Scratch that, then. Looks like someone's not been able to keep it in their pants, after all. Good luck with that,'* she added, ending the call.

When Brian Potter and Nazia Latif returned to the CID room in full spirits an hour later, they found Ashcroft pacing the same patch of floor as he had first thing that morning. Potter had been about to crack a joke, but the concentration on Ashcroft's face told him it wouldn't be appreciated. Exchanging a glance with Nazia he returned to his seat, logged into his emails to see if the clue to Ashcroft's perplexed look lay there. He wasn't quite sure what he was expecting. A letter of resignation from The Super would surely have elicited a happy dance, even from one so new to the team. There was an email from Ashcroft which he'd marked as urgent. Attached was the blood test and DNA results that Professor Clemont had sent through to him after their conversation. The professor had highlighted the relevant text, which Potter read before signalling to Nazia that she should do the same. He watched Nazia read the email before throwing her arms wide in a *what the fuck* gesture.

Jamal and Aisha were brother and sister.

Each officer contemplated what difference that made to the investigation.

Two youths shared a spliff as they walked along Windward Tower's second floor landing, oblivious to the man following them. The first they knew about it was when something cold and metal pressed into the back of their necks.

'What the fuck, blud?' said one of them, mainly because his mate was there. He was white but spoke with a blaccent. A shiny tracksuit hung from his skinny frame.

'Mek a noise an' you're dead,' came the reply. 'Do as you're told, and I might let you live.'

The gobby one tried turning to get a look, saw angry eyes, a scarf covering the nose and mouth.

'You got a death wish or sometin'?' The youth was rewarded with a blow across the back of his head. Not enough to concuss, just to scare. 'All you pussies need to do, is open that door. You get me?'

'An' you'll let us go?' the quiet one asked. He was mixed race. Light brown afro hair with pale eyes.

'That's not how it works, cuz,' the gobby one cautioned, reaching into his pocket for a key. It was why they weren't supposed to leave their post. Why they were told to stay inside and bolt the door.

'That's it. Nice and slow. Any sudden moves and I'll blow your fuckin' head off,' AJ threatened as he slipped into the flat behind them.

ELEVEN

'Let the dog see the rabbit.'
– DI DANIELS

Inside the once abandoned flat, unemployed teenagers chopped and sieved cocaine for twelve hours a day for minimum wage. It was their job to cut the cocaine with anything from baking powder to flour to make it go further. They did it without ventilation, protective clothing, or gloves. Not like there was a union they could complain to.

It was the generals, like Troy Mellor, who made the big bucks. The mark up on the coke earned him five times more out of each shipment than he paid. In the meantime, kids like these worked in squalid conditions.

Too cool for school, this was their fast track to a better life.

Two toddlers slept in their buggies in the middle of the room. Their mothers worked at a table beside them. They were paid to bag up the final product in £10 and £20 plastic snap bags before handing them to the soldier boys, who sold them through a small makeshift hole, called a trap, cut out of the flat's front door. To keep ahead of their rivals – and the police, the trap house would close down after a few months, move somewhere else.

No one bothered looking up when the soldier boys walked in. Life was a whole lot easier if you kept your head down, did what you were paid to do.

Chop and sieve.

'I need information,' AJ said, nice and slow. 'And if I get that information, it'll be like I was never here. You get me?'

One of the women glanced up. Saw the fear on the soldier boys' faces and nudged her friend.

'Hush up!' the woman yelled at the teenagers on the other table, causing them to look at AJ too.

'Six weeks ago a kid was thrown from the upstairs landing. I've been told that the person who did that, shot my brother and his friend because he saw them do it. What I want from you is that bastard's description.'

'What, so we can get shot up too?' muttered one of the teenagers.

'Better sometime in the future than right this fucking minute,' AJ warned him.

'How can we see anything when we're in here all day?' said one of the women, and in that moment AJ knew she was the one who'd tell him.

'That your kid?' he demanded, nodding to the infant beside her. The woman jerked her head up and down, placed a hand protectively on the pram handle. The pram was shabbier than the one beside it. The wheels were worn down and the chassis was scuffed. Used by at least one other baby at some point, he reckoned, thinking. A job like hers could easily be done round school hours, especially with a mate to share the load.

'You'd gone to pick up your older kids from school, hadn't you?' he asked.

The woman looked down. Started fiddling with the bag of coke in front of her.

'What's your name?' he asked her.

'Shakira.'

'How would you feel if your kid was thrown off the landing, Shakira?' he persisted.

The woman started to shake. 'Please don't hurt my baby,' she whispered.

AJ swallowed. That wasn't what he'd meant at all. 'I just want to stop him doing it to anyone else,' he told her.

'Fucksake tell him!' Gobshite pleaded; his head bent forward due to the metal pressing into his neck.

Shakira heaved out a breath. Turned to look at her baby as though seeking reassurance. 'I was late going to pick my daughter up. I left the baby here,' she admitted. 'It meant I could use the stairs. While I ran down them, I passed a man going up. He was talking to someone on his phone. He spoke with an accent.'

'Just the one?' Faz had told him there'd been more than one. Maybe this fella was phoning for reinforcements.

A nod.

'Describe him.'

A beat. 'He was white.'

AJ glared at her.

'I wasn't really paying attention!' she said quickly. 'I just wanted to get to school.'

'Come on, make an effort!' AJ prompted.

'He had a beard. Trimmed. Round his jaw like this,' she said, moving her hands around her own jaw to demonstrate. 'And a tattoo!' she added, relieved. 'On his neck, though I didn't see what it was,' she said, pre-empting AJ's next question.

'What was he wearing?'

She looked up at the ceiling as she considered this. 'Black jeans. Bomber jacket. Army style boots.'

'You seen him before?'

She shook her head. 'That lot don't normally come round here, do they, unless they're looking for trouble?'

The teen on the cutting table spoke up once more. 'He needs to be lit up, for what he done to that kid. Yours too, blud.'

AJ had seen him hanging round Appleton House. He had a kid brother, not yet out of primary school and working as a spotter for Troy's gang.

He looked around the shabby room. His addiction had changed the path that Troy's life had taken. His friend had only got into dealing to help him pay off his debt and now… now he was the master of a vast production line that extended way beyond this flat. There'd be another dozen like this throughout the estate, the same again on other estates round the city. *If I didn't do it, then someone else would,* Troy had told him on more than one occasion. *There'd still be soldiers working those corners.*

Kids sat at tables learning to chop and sieve.

AJ couldn't hack the life he'd got them into. He'd wanted out. The only problem was his debt to Eddie Richards needed to be paid off. In many ways they'd become victims of their own success. They ran the most profitable corner, there was no way he'd ever let them go. By then Troy was enjoying the money and the girls; the lifestyle that came with being a player. After a while, when he admitted he didn't want to leave, they'd come to an agreement. AJ would walk away empty handed, handing his stake in the business to Troy. In return Troy would take any punishment that came his way for allowing AJ to split.

The week after AJ packed his bags and left for the army, Richards sent his henchmen to Troy's home. They set about him with a drill and an iron. The paramedics who attended had to pick chunks of his skin off the linoleum, took it along to the hospital in a freezer bag from his kitchen. Six weeks later

Richards had been killed in a drive-by shooting outside his home. A drill bit and a cord from an iron had been left on his chest, sending out a message: there was a new general on the block. Troy Mellor had taken over, had held the top position ever since.

Despite his protestations he *was* a ruthless gangster.

But he was also AJ's friend.

The kids in this room had given him what he wanted. There was no need to take his anger out on them. He lowered the metal dumbbell bars he'd been holding against the rude boys' necks. Began walking out of the room.

'He wasn't even tooled up! Bumba Clart!' the gobshite yelled after him, keeping his distance all the same.

CID room

'So what if they were brother and sister, does it change anything relevant to the investigation?' Nazia said out loud what they were all wondering.

Ashcroft moved over to her desk, perched on the end of it. 'It explains Aisha's actions, perhaps. Why she wanted to help Jamal, even if that meant putting herself in danger,' he reasoned. 'But, on the face of it, no, it doesn't alter anything.'

He folded his arms. 'Unidentified members of the Berati Crew are key suspects in two murder enquiries.'

'It sounds to me that the key to their identity is on that database. I'll call the techies, let them know this is critical to our investigation, tell them to green light it through their system,' Potter offered.

'Pretty much what you'll have said to them earlier?' Ashcroft enquired.

Potter nodded.

'Then let them do their stuff. We don't want them missing something in haste.'

Potter held his hands in the air, a gesture suggesting he'd leave well alone.

'Probably explains why she was so free and easy with her cash when it came to treating him,' he said as an afterthought.

'Think my sister would have something to say about that,' said Ashcroft.

'Mine too,' said Nazia. 'Though to be fair Aisha was loaded. Having money puts a different slant on things.'

'I wouldn't know — on either count, being an only child,' added Potter.

Ashcroft was only half listening. 'Assuming they knew, of course. I mean, we're making assumptions based on how they behaved towards each other, we've nothing concrete that proves they knew they were related.'

'True, but where does that leave their families? I'm guessing they're as much in the dark as we are. Remember, Aisha's family were insistent they didn't know Jamal, just as Safia and AJ have stated they didn't have a clue who Aisha was.'

'Or they've been covering up a fairly supersized skeleton in the closet.'

'Well, if the families didn't know, we can't assume that Jamal and Aisha knew either.'

'But then our theory about that being the reason Aisha looked out for him no longer stacks up,' reasoned Nazia. She had a point. They were going round in circles.

Ashcroft's phone rang. Anita Lam, the FLO. He told her he was putting her on loudspeaker so that Potter and Nazia could hear.

'Fraid there's not much to report, Sarge. I tried getting Safia to open up about Jamal's father, but she wasn't having any of it. For a quiet, church-going woman she can be stubborn when it suits.'

'Did you try AJ?'

'Yes, Sarge, and he gave me the brush off too, though I got the

impression he was being awkward for the sake of it. Not sure he knows anything, to be honest, and just didn't want to admit that to me.'

'OK leave it there for now. There's been a development which I'll talk to you about as soon as I can. I just need to run it by DI Daniels.'

He eyeballed the others as he ended the call.

'Which leaves me with no option but to ask Aisha's father for a DNA sample,' he stated, sighing at the prospect.

'That won't be a walk in the park. He's likely to do a number on us, what with him being a human rights lawyer and everything,' added Potter.

'Yeah, Brian, I'd worked that much out.'

Talk about timing. Neither family had visited the murder site, preferring to carry out their mourning in private. Tomorrow both families would meet for the first time, in front of TV cameras. This needed careful managing or the Super's press conference would blow up in his face.

'We need to let DI Daniels know now,' said Potter.

Nazia glanced at him and nodded.

'What, this evening? And ruin his romantic dinner.' Ashcroft looked at his watch. He wasn't convinced pulling the DI away was in anyone's best interest. Besides, he'd be on his main course by now. Definitely over the limit to drive. He wasn't sure sending a car for him was warranted either. Brian and Naz looked at him expectantly. They knew Daniels better than he did and their demeanour was telling him the boss wouldn't thank him for holding back, even if it was for the sake of his marriage. The corners of Ashcroft's mouth turned downwards as he made his decision. He would send him a text to alert him to the medical report he'd circulated. Offer to pick him up if he insisted in coming in. He pulled out his phone and cobbled a message together. Just the facts as they stood, along with a suggestion they push tomorrow's press appeal to later in the day, so they could speak to both families first. This would buy them some time. Take the pressure off Daniels from doing anything hasty.

He pressed send.

Ashcroft looked at Potter. 'I think it's worth you calling the tech team, after all. Get them to search through Jamal and Aisha's laptops for any interactions with that ancestry site they were following.'

'Now you're talking, Sarge.'

Ashcroft stood by the answer he'd given Nazia earlier. The fact that Jamal and Aisha were siblings was likely to have little bearing on the investigation. But they couldn't ignore it.

His phone rang almost immediately.

'What the fucking hell's going on?' No prizes for working out it was Daniels.

'Your guess is as good as mine, sir,' Ashcroft answered, raising his eyebrows at Potter.

'Have you spoken to the families yet?'

'No sir. Thought it better to update you first.'

'I bet you did.' Daniels wasn't pissed, but he'd been working towards it. The drink had loosened his tongue, though it was hard to imagine how 'merry' he'd been before Ashcroft's text. He wondered what the DI planned to do. Where his wife was. He soon got his answer.

'I'm in a cab, on my way in.'

'There was no need to do that, sir, I would have picked you up.'

'Makes no odds now. My missus is staying put. Has refused to leave until she's worked her way through the tasting menu we'd ordered. Said she'll get mine bagged up.'

'Suppose that's something.'

'For the dog.' A pause. The sound of several slurred swear words. *'This is a real ball-ache, you know that?'*

'I'm with you on that,' said Ashcroft, 'which is why I'm

suggesting we push back the press appeal. Gives us time to break the news to the families.'

'*Bollocks to that. Someone's been stringing us along and it doesn't take a genius to work out it's that snooty fucking lawyer. I'll have great pleasure rocking up to his front door with a swab kit.*'

'That might not be your finest hour, career-wise, sir. Better leaving it to me.'

'*Oh, because he'll take the news so much better from you?*'

'No,' Ashcroft conceded, 'but I've got no reason to enjoy it.'

'*Hmmm.*'

'Why don't you head back to the restaurant, sir. I'll work out a strategy for approaching the families, then once we've pushed the briefing back we'll have time to work out how we-'

'*-Not happening, Ashcroft,*' Daniels said, speaking across him. '*The Super won't agree to it either. We need to stick to the schedule we've got in place.*'

'This is a lot for the families to take in. We've no idea how this might affect Safia, or Abena for that matter. The situation needs handling with kid gloves.'

'*Yeah, I was worried you'd say that. Do nothing. I'll be there in half an hour.*'

They plied him with coffee and an egg roll someone had left in the fridge.

'Best not to worry too much about the use-by date,' said Potter, pressing it into the DI's hands before retreating.

Aware that he couldn't speak to either of the families reeking of overpriced plonk, Daniels ate what he was given, burping into his hand to check on his breath.

'Nothing a couple of strong mints won't sort out,' he hiccupped.

Potter rummaged in his desk drawer, found an open packet

of Trebor Mints, gave it a wipe with his tank top before throwing them across the room to Ashcroft.

'I never go out,' Daniels lamented. 'And the one time I do, what happens? I end up sitting here with you lot, trying to make out that I'm not partial to a swift half like anyone else when they clock off.'

'You didn't need to come in,' Ashcroft reminded him. It smelled like more than a swift half had been imbibed, although that would be splitting hairs.

'I'm the SIO in case you've forgotten. It's me who'll get neutered if the press decide to take a swing.'

'No reason for that to happen. We've made a discovery, not cocked something up,' Ashcroft countered.

'I'll agree with you on that, Ashcroft, but we need the press to be one hundred per cent sympathetic to the families when this appeal goes out. The last thing we need is them being judged because of bad choices someone made nineteen years ago.'

That seemed remarkably compassionate, thought Ashcroft, giving him the side eye.

'I'm not a complete moron, you know,' the DI added, as though reading his mind.

Which was why they had called Ozwald Saforo on his mobile and asked him to come into the station. There'd been some development that they'd like to discuss with him, was how Nazia had put it when he picked up. She thanked him for his cooperation, ending the call before he had the opportunity to push for more information.

DI Daniels answered his land line phone when it rang. Acknowledged the civilian on the desk with a grunt before saying he'd send someone down.

Nazia, already on her feet, took that as her cue.

Daniels locked eyes with Ashcroft. 'Let the dog see the rabbit,' he said, rubbing his hands together.

Satisfied Aisha's father had been left long enough to stew over what reason they had to call him in, Daniels breezed into the interview room.

'Sorry to keep you waiting,' he said, not meaning a word of it.

Ashcroft followed him in and shut the door, though not before clocking the scowl on Ozwald's face. Daniels needed to tone down his delight, they didn't know the facts yet. The two things he was certain of right now was that Ozwald was a hot shot lawyer and drink had made the inspector over-confident.

'It sounded important,' said Ozwald, his gaze travelling reluctantly to Daniels when Ashcroft remained silent. They'd agreed, or rather Daniels had insisted, that he should take the lead on this. This way Ashcroft would remain 'onside' in case he needed to play good cop to Daniels' bad cop as the interview progressed.

'It is,' Daniels acknowledged.

He took his seat opposite the esteemed lawyer, placed the briefcase containing the swab kit on the floor beside him. Ashcroft took the remaining seat, placing the file he'd been carrying on the table between them so they both had access to it. Daniels moved the file so that it was squarely in front of him. He positioned his hands either side of it like a preacher about to deliver a sermon, before thinking better of it and clasping them together.

'There's no easy way to say this…'

'So get on with it.'

Daniels cleared his throat. 'DNA results that came back on Aisha and Jamal show that they are half brother and sister.'

Ozwald looked as though he'd been punched in the chest. 'I'm sorry?' Even though the question was reflex, Daniels repeated what he'd said. Like Ashcroft, he was studying the lawyer's reaction.

'DNA results that came back on Aisha and Jamal show that

they are half brother and sister. Their mitochondrial DNA, which a person inherits from their mother, is different, which means that-'

'Yes, I know what it means,' Ozwald snapped. 'I'm just trying to understand how it happened.'

Ashcroft, sensing that Daniels was about to say something tactless, spoke up. 'I'm sure this has come as a terrible shock. The pathologist who conducted their postmortems, noticed that they shared a skin condition which can run in families. It prompted her to make further comparisons, resulting in the DNA test.'

'Her eczema,' Ozwald concluded, his hand moving to scratch an area above his wrist.

Ashcroft slid the file that Daniels had commandeered over to his half of the desk. Removed a photograph which they'd printed out from Jamal's Facebook page. He slid it across the table. 'This is Jamal's mother, Safia Deng.'

Ozwald stared at the photo and swallowed. 'This can't be happening,' he said, pushing it away. He leaned forward onto the table, placed his head in his hands.

This wasn't the reaction Ashcroft was expecting. Denial, certainly. Anger most definitely. When backed in a corner, many cheaters came out fighting. Then again, he was a lawyer, and evidence was evidence.

The look on Daniels' face suggested he was just as surprised. 'So you remember her then?' he prompted.

'What kind of person do you take me for? Of course I remember her. We had a relationship. Albeit a brief one.' He looked down at his hands. 'My wife and I had been going through a difficult patch.'

'Your pregnant wife, going by their ages,' Ashcroft corrected him.

'Yes, indeed.' Ozwald lowered his gaze. 'It was a blip, that's all. Once I came to my senses, I ended it immediately.'

Ashcroft wondered if Safia had known that he was married. Whether finding that out was the reason she excised him from her life. From the life of their child.

'And there's been no contact with Ms Deng since?' Daniels continued.

'None.'

'You had no idea you'd fathered a child?'

Ozwald shook his head.

'We'd like to take a DNA swab from you, to confirm the match with Jamal. Do you have any objection?'

There was a slight pause. 'No, of course not…I understand these procedures need to be followed.'

Ashcroft wondered whether it had occurred to him yet. Originally, Jamal's name had meant nothing to Ozwald. When he'd been shown his photo, all he'd seen was a boy from a sink estate. Now he'd learned the shooting had robbed him of two of his children.

Ozwald spread his fingers wide on the table. Addressed his next comment to Ashcroft. 'I'd like to be the one to tell my wife, but is it possible to wait until after the press appeal? The thought of her having to deal with this on top of everything else we're going through right now…'

Ashcroft shared a look with Daniels. This bombshell had the potential to derail the press appeal, which the DI was adamant must go ahead. Safia needed to be told. They couldn't let her walk into the station tomorrow and walk slap bang into Jamal's father without some sort of warning. Unless they delayed telling her too. Ashcroft racked his brain for another solution. 'The only way that'll work is if you stay away from the appeal,' he stated.

Daniels nodded in agreement.

Ozwald regarded him, flabbergasted. 'How am I supposed to explain that to my wife?'

'I think that's the least of your concerns, right now,'

Ashcroft reminded him. His wife wasn't the only one impacted by this news. His daughter would learn she had a brother she'd never get to know. She'd question her relationship with her sister, wonder why she'd kept Jamal to herself. Assuming she knew.

Ozwald's face looked pained, as though he was already picturing the shit show he'd caused. 'Let's get this over with, then,' he said, nodding at the case by Daniels' feet.

TWELVE

'You just learn to stop asking questions, especially if they cause someone else pain.'

– AJ

Press briefing room, Moss Side station

Amid flashing cameras, Superintendent Duncanson led Abena and her daughter Sika towards the row of tables in the station's briefing room. Ashcroft and AJ, flanking Safia, followed close behind. They'd run through this part before the press arrived. Told them how to walk in, where to sit.

Abena had been upset when Ashcroft collected both families from reception. Her husband wouldn't be able to attend after all. A judicial issue that couldn't be pushed back. Ashcroft reassured her that Ozwald's absence wouldn't be a problem. The main thing was that both families demonstrate a united front. The women had embraced while AJ and Sika looked on.

They blinked as they took their seats. AJ poured water from a jug and placed it in front of his mother. He poured another for Abena and passed it across. Both families had been told not to speak unless they were addressing the press. Several microphones had been positioned in front of them, every word they uttered would be picked up.

A widescreen TV behind them displayed photographs of

Jamal and Aisha, while banners either side of it displayed the GMP and Crimestoppers logos. After an introduction from the Superintendent, both mothers read from the notes that they'd written.

A lifetime of love reduced to a sheet of A4.

Click. Flash. Click. Flash.

The Super cleared his throat to signal it was his turn to speak again.

'I would like to reassure the local community that we have a large number of officers patrolling the area to ensure the public remain safe, in addition to a team of experienced detectives working on the case.'

He nodded at Ashcroft to wrap it up.

Ashcroft looked directly at the camera he'd been told to address: 'We would like to hear from anyone who drove or cycled along Abraham Road using a Dashcam that morning. Please do not think that the footage you have is unimportant. Let us decide that. The number to contact us on will appear on screen at the end of this appeal. Thank you for watching.'

He shuffled the papers in front of him to signify he'd finished. After a nod from the Superintendent, he got to his feet. Waited while the others did the same, before leading them out of the room. The Super was staying on to field questions from the journalists. He'd had media training, unlike the bereaved family members who looked wrung out.

Ashcroft walked with them to reception, just as Nazia and Potter pulled up outside the main door in pool cars. 'My officers are ready to take you home. You did well today. I have to hang on here in case the press want to know anything specific about the investigation, but I'll call round later to see how you're getting on.'

'That's very good of you,' said Safia.

'I don't need you holding our hands,' said AJ, 'I want you to find whoever did this. You get me?'

'Then we want the same thing,' Ashcroft assured him. Nazia and Potter climbed out of their cars and held the rear doors open. Potter said something encouraging to Safia before she stepped inside. Ashcroft blocked AJ's path, felt him tense at the proximity.

'I can only imagine what you're going through, but any resource I use watching you will slow this investigation down. You get *me*?'

AJ shrugged past him. Climbed into the car. Once seated he turned to eyeball Ashcroft, kept staring until the car had pulled away.

Ashcroft made a call to Refik Gemici as he headed back into the building.

'Fahri and I saw you on the news, DS Ashcroft. Praise be to Allah that those poor families get justice soon. How is Safia holding up? I'm sure AJ will be a great support to her.'

'It's taking its toll,' Ashcroft informed him. 'And something's come up which means I need to spend time with both families this afternoon. It means I won't be there in time to do much setting up for this evening.'

'And nor should you. We have plenty of volunteers who can do the shifting and carrying. We're all very keen to hear about the safety measures your Superintendent has put in place following the shooting.' He said it without any sarcasm. *'I'll not be short of people willing to give me a hand.'*

Ashcroft thanked him and ended the call. A quick glance at his email inbox told him that Jamal's mobile call log was in from his network service provider. Deciding to check it later he returned to the press room in case reinforcements were needed.

Afternoon briefing

'Response to the incident room number has been sluggish.' DI Daniels looked on, unsurprised. 'Though immediately after the broadcast, the Crimestoppers line was inundated with calls blaming the Berati Crew or Abraham Road Gang depending on where the callers' allegiance lay.'

'A dead loss then,' a DC muttered at the back of the room, out of earshot of Superintendent Duncanson, who was sitting in.

'It's been a useful exercise in terms of keeping it in the public's mind,' said Daniels diplomatically. 'It's going to be repeated on the tea-time news and again at ten o'clock. Remember, the success of these appeals is cumulative. Viewers need to see them several times to be spurred into action. A bit like when they buy a new sofa or change their car.'

'How very public spirited of them,' said Potter.

'Any luck with the tech team, Brian?' Ashcroft asked.

'They're interrogating the data on the refugee database. They said they'll need a couple of days to work through it and see which files have been accessed recently, specifically files opened by Aisha.'

'What about the genealogy site they'd both shown an interest in on Facebook?' asked Daniels.

'Aisha set up an online account with a site called *Small World Ancestry* six months ago, selecting the option to find where her ancestors were from.'

'That fits in with what her mother told us,' Ashcroft confirmed.

'The company sent out a DNA collection kit, which, according to the online account, she returned to them a week later, along with their fee. The following month a notification arrived in her inbox with a list of the geographical locations her ancestors were from. Her DNA markers showed she was

85% Ghanaian with trace percentages of other African countries which they list.'

'No shock surprises there, then,' stated Daniels.

'I suppose not. I did notice a disclaimer on the website which advises it keeps results of DNA tests indefinitely, with reviews every 10 years.'

'One way of boosting its data bank,' observed Ashcroft.

'Indeed. Where it gets interesting is that about three months later, Jamal sets up an account with the same site, only he selects the option to find biological relatives. We know he was keen to learn more about his father, and given his mother remained tight lipped about his identity, this makes sense. So, he goes through the same process as Aisha, except he gets a notification a week later that tells him they've found a relative whose DNA blueprint overlaps his, confirming they are half siblings: Aisha. He contacted her through the site, and for the first couple of weeks their communications were via each other's inbox. It's clear from her initial reply how shocked she was — this revelation meant that her father had been unfaithful. Equally, Jamal was impatient to learn about his father. They exchanged mobile phone numbers and didn't communicate through the website again.'

'Speaking of which, Jamal's call log came in this morning,' Ashcroft informed them. 'It's comprised mainly of texts between him and Fahri Gemici — including the texts Fahri told us he'd sent at midnight the night before Jamal's murder and the following morning, asking why he hadn't heard from him. There were texts from his brother, nothing of note, along with a couple of texts he sent to Aisha thanking her for the clothes and trainers she bought him. A reply from her saying she wanted to make up for 'Daddy Dearest,' — a term she'd begun using when referring to their father, for not being around for him when he was growing up. These all tally with the call log we received from Aisha's network provider. In one text she says she's thinking of selling her car and giving him the money, but he makes her promise not to. Said all he really wanted was to get to know his dad.'

'We still need to address this sibling angle,' stated Daniels, glumly. 'We've managed to keep it away from the press, but is there a chance we've narrowed our line of enquiry too soon?'

Ashcroft shook his head. 'If they were shot because Kamali's killer thought they knew his identity then I don't see the fact they are related matters. What we do need to be mindful of, is the impact this information will have on both families and how *that* impacts the investigation. Safia has kept the identity of Jamal's father a closely guarded secret all his life. How she'll react to hearing Aisha was his half-sister is anyone's guess. As for Abena, she's going to discover her husband was unfaithful and that Aisha, having become aware of it, had chosen not to tell her.'

'Oh, what a tangled web we weave...' muttered Nazia. 'What?' she said defensively when Potter looked over at her. 'I didn't spend all my time at school pranking the teachers, you know. I loved my English Lit class.'

'You never cease to amaze me,' he said, shaking his head.

Ashcroft could only imagine the turmoil the teenagers must have felt. Both thrilled to discover a sibling that felt like a soulmate, knowing they couldn't announce it to the world. Blurting it out would have caused shockwaves through Aisha's family. She was about to drop the bombshell that she didn't want to go to Oxford and was planning to move in with her boyfriend.

The impact would be no less for Jamal's mother. There was obviously a reason why she'd remained tight lipped over the details surrounding his father. Had he broken off their affair without warning? What if her unplanned pregnancy been the cause of her split with AJ's father?

Ashcroft's phone began to ring. A number he didn't

recognise. They needed to wrap the briefing up anyway, given the house calls he needed to make to both families.

'OK if I take this, sir?' he asked DI Daniels. He waited for a nod before hitting the answer button.

'I want us all on point for this evening,' Superintendent Duncanson instructed everyone as the briefing was brought to a close. He regarded Brian Potter. 'And that includes dress.'

'Wasn't planning on wearing one,' muttered Potter, rewarded with a glare from Daniels.

Ashcroft pocketed his car keys as he stepped into the corridor to take the call.

'*DS Ashcroft, It's Femi Ukeje, from The Dignity Centre.*' There was an awkward pause. '*Look, about the other day. I wanted to apologise for firing off that angry email to your boss. I promise you that isn't normally my style.*'

He took the stairs down to the ground floor, mulling over which family to visit first. Aisha's or Jamal's. 'Don't worry about it. I shouldn't have responded the way I did.'

'*Yes you should!*' Femi insisted. '*I was making it personal when I had no right to. I'm sorry for making your day more difficult than it needed to be.*'

'Water under the bridge.'

Out through the rear doors, he pressed his key fob and climbed into the pool car.

Another pause.

'So, if there's nothing else…' he prompted.

'*Actually, there is. The reason I'm calling is that I saw the press appeal on TV. Those poor mothers, sitting at that table with all those cameras flashing. My heart went out to them. But then, well. The strangest thing happened. At first, I thought my eyes were playing tricks on me but the moment the appeal ended I rewound it and played it over and over until I was certain.*' Another pause. '*It might be nothing, but I thought you'd want to know.*'

'About what?'

Femi continued as though he hadn't spoken. '*The moment I saw her she looked so familiar it got me thinking. I mean, what are the chances, after all these years?*'

Ashcroft's brow creased as he wondered which woman she was talking about.

'Who? Abena?' he ventured, after all Femi had been working closely with Aisha for several months, she was bound to see the resemblance.

'*No. Jamal's mother. Safia.*' She gave an embarrassed laugh. '*It probably isn't important, but I thought you should know. We used to work together.*'

'When was this?' Ashcroft pulled his notebook and pen from his pocket to write down what she said.

'*Oh, let me see. Nearly twenty years back? Perhaps not as far as that. She was quite serious for someone so young, but then she'd been through such a lot already. She was very pretty, too. We're not allowed to say it these days but back then girls like that could be too pretty for their own good. Sometimes it hampered their progress. She was certainly a hard worker; the team had come to rely on her, then one day she upped and left without warning. I can't help but wonder now if her departure and Jamal's arrival were linked in some way.*'

Ashcroft was way ahead of her. He recalled his conversation with Jamal's headteacher. About how Safia had taken adult education classes to train as a legal secretary. 'Did she work with you at your office in Rusholme?'

'*No, back then we were both based at the head office in Manchester.*'

'Where the legal team were based?'

'*That's right.*'

'Was there a lawyer by the name of Ozwald Saforo working there around the same time?'

'*Yes, that's correct.*'

'Do you remember Safia working for him at any point?'

'*Not really. She was inexperienced so would have been working in the typing pool rather than be assigned to any specific lawyer.*'

'And when did Ozwald leave?'

'*That was a good few years back too.*' A pause as she joined the dots. '*He was married, to Aisha's mother, it seems…*' she added, her words trailing off.

Ashcroft thanked her before ending the call. He sat back in the driver's seat as he considered her words.

'Jamal's it is then,' he said, starting the engine.

There was a commotion outside Appleton House. An altercation between two men who looked worryingly familiar. Ashcroft climbed out of his car, muttering 'Bollocks,' as he hurried towards them.

AJ had pinned Aisha's father against the bonnet of his car.

'Get this maniac away from me!' cried Ozwald, as AJ's arm swung back ready to take a punch.

Ashcroft grabbed the squaddie's wrist, yanked it behind his back. 'Let him go!' he ordered, putting pressure on his bent limb. 'I said, let him go!'

AJ sucked air through his teeth as he released his grip.

'I could have you done for assault!' shouted Ozwald, straightening his tie before opening his car door.

'Then I'd better mek it worthwhile,' retaliated AJ, struggling against Ashcroft who had grabbed his other arm.

'Don't make a bad situation worse,' Ashcroft warned them. 'You,' he said, addressing Ozwald, 'Go home and stay there. I'll be with you when I've finished here.' He glared at the lawyer until he did as he was told, holding AJ still until he was a safe distance away.

'You pussy!' He rounded on Ashcroft once he'd let go of his arms.

Ashcroft shrugged. He'd been called worse, often by colleagues who thought he was out of earshot.

'Why are you making this so difficult? I'm trying to help your family, yet you're hell bent on getting yourself arrested.'

'I'm trying to get justice for my brother.'

'That's my job.'

'Do it, then!'

'I can't if I have to keep second guessing who you're going to ambush.'

'No ambush here. He came to my yard, remember?'

He had a point. Ashcroft exhaled a breath. 'What did he want?'

'I don't know. I was in the kitchen when Mum answered the door. Next thing I hear is her crying and him offering her cash. I just wanted him gone. Upsetting her like that, he needed teaching a lesson.'

'By you I suppose.'

'What choice do I have?' AJ railed at him. 'No one cares when things go wrong for people like us.'

He was right. There were times when Ashcroft felt that too. He just didn't go round hurting people as a result.

'I need to speak to your mum.'

'What about?'

It sounded like Ozwald had already stolen his thunder. Giving AJ the heads up might get him on side. He jerked his thumb in the direction of the main road. 'That fella there, who's head you were about to remove from his shoulders…'

'Yeah, what about him?'

'He's Jamal's father.'

Safia was in the living room, sipping at tea that Anita had made after her ordeal. Her eyes were red rimmed. She reached for a tissue from a box on the table and blew her nose.

'I turn my back for five minutes,' Anita muttered, embarrassed, when Ashcroft returned with AJ.

'No harm done,' said Safia, keen to draw a line under it.

Ashcroft drew up a chair. 'There's something we need to discuss.'

He'd asked AJ to let him do the talking. That if there was any sign of Safia refusing to speak in front of him, he'd need to leave. Overwhelmed by the amount of information he'd been presented with; he'd been too distracted to object.

Ashcroft kept his voice low. 'I understand Jamal's father has been here.'

Startled, Safia looked from him to AJ.

'He knows,' Ashcroft added.

'Knows what?' She took in the confusion on her older son's face as he tried to process what he'd been told. 'Don't listen to him!' she spat.

Ashcroft leaned forward in his chair. 'Safia, we're waiting on a DNA test to confirm the man who left here just now is Jamal's biological father. However, he is Aisha's father, and we have DNA that already proves that Jamal and Aisha are half brother and sister.'

He let that sink in.

'That girl was Jamal's sister?' she whispered.

'Yes. He sent a sample of his DNA to an ancestry site in an attempt to trace his father. It came back as a match with Aisha. At least we now understand the nature of their relationship.'

Safia covered her mouth with her hand.

When she'd first been told the name of the young woman murdered alongside Jamal, it had meant nothing to her. Even her photograph meant nothing. Beneath the Love Island makeup favoured by a lot of young women it was hard to make out any features she shared with esteemed lawyer, Ozwald Saforo. Even then, you'd need to know where to look.

'He did ask about his dad a lot when he was younger,' said AJ.

'I hoped he'd grow out of it,' admitted Safia, swiping at a tear.

'It's not something you grow out of. You just learn to stop asking questions, especially if they cause someone else pain.'

'What did Ozwald say to you when he turned up?' Ashcroft asked.

'Nothing.' She sent an accusing look at AJ. 'Seeing him was a shock, that's all.'

'It was more than that Mum! I told him what I heard,' he said, jerking his head towards Ashcroft. 'That he offered you money.'

'Why was he offering you cash, Safia?' Ashcroft asked.

'I don't know!'

'When did you last see him?'

'When do you think!' She lowered her head.

Anita moved so that she was beside her. Placed a reassuring hand on her shoulder. 'Seeing him turn up like that, must have been upsetting,' she said. The look she sent Ashcroft told him a heads up would have been nice. He took it. Femi's call had thrown him off his stride, but that was no excuse.

'How would he know where you live?' he asked.

'Are you for real?' AJ's voice was full of scorn. 'We get journos knocking on the door every day. Ask anyone where the boy who was shot lived and they'll take you right to the door for a tenner.'

Ashcroft blinked.

'No harm done,' said Anita, throwing him a bone.

He hoped not, because he wasn't done yet. There was something he needed to straighten out. 'Why would a man you've not seen for the best part of nineteen years offer you money, Safia?'

Jamal's mother covered her face with her hands. 'He made

me promise not to tell a soul. He said if I broke that promise, I'd lose the right to stay here. He's a lawyer. If he wanted to make that happen, he could.'

'What do you mean?'

Safia dipped her head, wiped at her nose with a tissue.

'We came here from the Sudan when I was a child,' AJ explained. 'Even though she has the right papers, Mum worries that one day she'll be deported.' He turned towards his mother. 'But why would he threaten you?'

Ashcroft signalled to AJ to be quiet. 'Safia, are you able to tell me about what brought you here?'

Safia nodded before taking a breath. 'Our village was ransacked by the Sudanese Military. I had taken AJ with me to get water. It was the only reason we survived. From our hiding place, we saw soldiers on horseback bludgeon the men and boys to death — including my husband.' She looked at AJ. 'No child should ever have to see that.'

'*Nobody* should see that,' said Anita.

Safia regarded her son. 'I grabbed your hand and we ran for our lives, eventually finding shelter in a humanitarian camp. We stayed there for six months, before seeking asylum in the UK.' She turned her attention to Ashcroft. 'It was 2004. During that year alone over a hundred thousand people were killed by the Janja Weed, as they were called, in what would become known as the Darfur Genocide. They called it ethnic cleansing, though what drew them to rape women and children before they killed them, I'll never understand. With support from a refugee centre, I applied to remain in the UK and was granted the right to stay in 2005.'

'And what has life been like for you here?'

'It has been good. While my asylum claim was being considered I wasn't allowed to work, so I used that time to go to adult education classes. I learned English and secretarial skills while AJ was in school, then volunteered at the refugee centre's main office to gain experience while I waited for my visa. We were safe, and we had a future to look forward to.'

'And that's when you met Jamal's father.'

Her face grew serious. 'It wasn't like that.'

'What do you mean?'

'You make it sound like one of those romantic films on TV. There was nothing romantic about it.' Her voice caught as she spoke.

Anita reached for her hand. 'Safia, did he force himself on you?'

Safia's nod was barely visible. 'It happened just once. His secretary was off sick and I was asked to cover her work. He approached me at the end of the day and said I'd made several errors in the letters I'd typed and that they needed to be corrected immediately. I telephoned a friend from church, asked her to pick AJ up from school. When I went into his office, he'd laid the letters out on his desk, but when I read through them there were no errors. By then the office was deserted. He pushed me against the desk and...' she looked from AJ to Ashcroft, her gaze settling on Anita. 'Do I really have to say it?'

'Not here,' Anita said, giving her hand another squeeze.

'What happened, afterwards...' Ashcroft prompted.

'When he finished, he told me that if I ever said a word to anyone he would get my visa revoked, send me and AJ back to Darfur so the Janja Weed could finish what they'd started. I left to pick up my son from my friend's house and never went back.'

'And now he's trying to buy your silence,' said Anita.

'I should have killed the bastard!' yelled AJ springing to his feet. He'd reached the front door when Ashcroft grabbed him, pinning him to the wall, the way AJ had pinned Ozwald earlier.

'I'm running out of patience,' he growled in his ear.

'You heard what he did!'

'Yes, and I will deal with it.'

'My way's better, trust me.'

'You think she wants a son in jail, on top of everything else?' Ashcroft felt AJ slump beneath his grip. He let his hands drop by his sides, stepped back a little, though close enough to lunge at him should the need arise. 'You've got to start trusting me.'

'Why? You're either one of them or you're not.'

It wasn't the first time that had been volleyed at him. That he couldn't be Black *and* Blue. He was at peace with that now. All he wanted was to be a better cop than the young men in these communities were used to.

Ashcroft levelled his gaze at him. 'I can't be everywhere all at once AJ. Can I get to the end of my shift without hearing you've been thrown in the slammer? Do you think you can manage that?'

AJ held his hands up to show he'd not give him any trouble.

'Good. Now I'm going back in there to let your mum know I'll send a car for her tomorrow to bring her to the station. Specially trained female officers will take her statement — but only if she wants to. What she needs from you is support without a running commentary on what you'd like to do to everyone. So how about you do your job, and I do mine. Do we have a deal?'

AJ inclined his head. 'I won't go rushing in anywhere until you've shown me what you can do,' he offered with a smile. It wasn't the deal Ashcroft was hoping for and they both knew it, but he'd take it for now.

'Yo, Fed, hang on a minute.' Ashcroft had been about to join the others in the living room. The catch in AJ's voice made him turn.

'There's something you should know.'

One Good Reason

The front door of Aisha's home was open. Ashcroft walked past several bin bags which lay haphazardly on the driveway. Clothing spewed out of one that had split along its seam. Abena appeared at an open bedroom window, lifting a bin bag onto the window ledge before letting it go. He sidestepped another that landed by his feet.

'Now's not really a good time,' Sika told him when he entered the hall after ringing the doorbell.

'Never is,' Ashcroft told her shrugging. 'Where's your dad?'

'Gone to stay at his brother's. Said he'd pick his stuff up later, though if he's got any sense he'll get my uncle to do it.'

'I need to speak to your mum.'

'Good luck with that.'

'Do you know what the row was about?'

Sika gave him a look. 'I've been eavesdropping on their conversations since I was three, though I'd be surprised if the whole street didn't hear this one.'

'Did you know?'

'Thanks for the vote of confidence! I've only just got those two off my back. Mum even threatened to throw *me* out if I didn't come clean.'

'That's anger talking.'

Sika's lip curled. 'Whatever. Look, I'm just as cut up about this as Mum is. Me and Aisha were hardly close, but I'd have thought she'd tell me something as epic as this, if for no other reason than to share the burden of knowing our dad was a cheat.'

He was a lot more than that, going by what Safia had alluded to, though that could keep for the time being.

'She even kept quiet that we had a brother. Would've been nice to get to know him.'

'What are you doing here?'

Ashcroft turned at the sound of the voice behind him. Abena glared at him, her face twisted in anger.

'He told me you were in on it.' Her tone full of accusation.

'Then he told you wrong. We only got the report from the pathologist yesterday. Ozwald persuaded me to let him tell you himself. Either way he knew I was coming round this afternoon to make sure you were aware of the situation.'

'The situation?' Abena sneered. 'More like a shit show. Was it your idea to wait until after the press appeal? Didn't want to risk losing the public's sympathy?'

'Our main priority is finding the person who killed Aisha and Jamal. We're not marriage guidance. Anything else is secondary to the investigation.'

'Of course,' Abena said, stung. 'It's been a lot to take in, that's all.'

'Can I speak with you alone?'

'Fucksake,' hissed Sika, 'when will everyone stop treating me like I'm a child?'

'It won't take long.' Ashcroft waited her out. For the stomping upstairs to be replaced by the slam of a bedroom door.

Abena regarded the serious expression on his face. 'I'm not sure I can take any more.'

'Then you'd better sit down for this,' he warned.

Moss Side station

Brian and Nazia joined Ashcroft in DI Daniel's office, while he brought them up to speed regarding Safia's allegation. Daniels sat behind his desk. Both DCs occupied the chairs on the other side of it, while Ashcroft paced the floor as he highlighted the facts.

'Safia has agreed to give a statement. The threat Ozwald

made all those years ago has hung over her, and she's desperate to be finally rid of it. It's why she became a cleaner, rather than look for work as a legal secretary with another firm when she left her job — in case their paths crossed again.'

'Why didn't she say any of this when you told her Aisha had been due to start work at the refugee centre? Didn't it ring any bells?' asked Daniels.

'Only unhappy ones, and without knowing how they were connected, none of it seemed relevant. Certainly nothing she wanted to dredge up voluntarily.'

'Did Jamal know about his mother's life in Darfur?' asked Daniels.

'A potted version of it, if there's such a thing,' Ashcroft told him. 'AJ, once he'd calmed down, said that he spoke of it often with Jamal, especially the last sighting he had of his own father, who'd been killed by the militia. He said he wanted him to know that he missed having his dad around too, albeit for different reasons.'

'This is what you call a game changer,' said Nazia, when Ashcroft had finished.

Daniels eyed her. 'How so?'

'Before Jamal entered Aisha's life, she'd hero-worshipped her father, lapping up every nugget he'd told her about his career. Jamal's existence outed him as a cheat, but his mother's history must have really set her antenna twitching. If Jamal told Aisha his mother had come over here as a refugee, then it would explain her sudden interest in The Dignity Centre. She made it look like she'd walked in off the street to volunteer her services, but there's every chance she'd targeted them, because she knew her father had worked for their legal department before she was born. When the centre manager caught her snooping around on the database, we thought she'd been looking up Albanian gangsters. What if she'd been trying to find out more about Safia?'

'It's plausible,' said Ashcroft.

'What would be the point, though?' asked Potter.

'Maybe she was trying to find out how she and her father's paths crossed.'

Daniels' face was glum. 'We won't get the tech team's report until tomorrow to confirm any of this, one way or another.' He regarded Ashcroft. 'Where's Ozwald staying?'

'He's at his brother's. Uniforms have been round to check,' he confirmed, anticipating Daniels' unasked question. 'He's aware Safia's statement will lead to his arrest, although he's more concerned about the state of his marriage than his liberty.'

'Easy to say when you can come and go as you please,' remarked Potter.

'How did his missus take it?'

'Learning that he's been accused of rape?' Ashcroft considered this. 'Dealing with his infidelity was one thing. When I told her the bare facts of Safia's allegation her demeanour changed. Whatever professional respect she had for Ozwald vanished in that moment. For him to do what he did, to someone who'd fled from a country where rape was used as a weapon against women. It was the last straw.'

'Too right,' said Nazia.

Daniels considered this. 'There's no doubt he'll have been aware of his wife's views. Question is, how desperate was he to keep her from finding out? What if Aisha hadn't kept shtum? What if she told him about Jamal, and the work she'd been doing at the refugee centre? Bound to unnerve him, pillar of the community and all that. If he's capable of rape, then is he capable of murdering his flesh and blood to keep his dirty secret quiet?'

'Seems extreme,' said Ashcroft.

'Murder is extreme.'

Ashcroft frowned. 'I don't buy it. This was a cold-blooded execution.'

He thought some more. 'Then again, the fact he said nothing when I'd gone round to tell them Aisha had been volunteering at the Dignity Centre doesn't go in his favour. I can understand his wife not attaching any significance to it, the number of charities he's worked with over the years, representing hundreds of clients, but for him not to say anything...He even had the cheek to suggest Jamal was the reason Aisha was working there. It proves he can't be trusted. Having said that, he has an alibi for that morning.'

'Yeah, yeah, on his way to meet a client in Liverpool, I recall. Even so. Naz, I want you to double check his route there with ANPR, see if he made any stops on the way.'

Nodding, Nazia recorded the action in her notebook. Oswald's journey on the morning of the shooting had already been checked against the automatic number plate recognition cameras along the route, but it paid to be thorough. Killers were caught because of the simple errors they made. It was up to the investigating team to find them, and the art of that was to check, then check again.

'We're not taking our eyes off the Berati Crew, though?' Ashcroft asked.

'No, they're the more likely fit for this,' Daniels agreed. 'Let's just see where this takes us.'

Ashcroft looked thoughtful. 'If they were so close, why did she keep all this from her boyfriend? They were planning on moving in together, weren't they?'

Potter nodded.

Nazia tilted her head as she considered this. 'It's a lot for anybody to take in, let alone a teenager. I think she decided not to tell her sister in case she blabbed to her mum, whether in solidarity or simply as revenge on their father. Either way it wouldn't have been pretty — as we're finding out, and who'd want to be the cause of that? As for her boyfriend, well, it's all very well bitching about your dysfunctional family as a unit, but it's much harder to admit that someone you've always looked up to has done something shameful. Maybe she worried that he'd judge her. Sometimes secrets are better never to be told.'

Daniels stifled a yawn. 'This is all well and good but it isn't getting the baby bathed. Speaking of which I need to get home and remind the kids what I look like before reconvening with you ugly lot in two hours at the West Indian Social Club.' He pushed himself to his feet. 'I'd like to say how much I'm looking forward to it but well, I'd be lying. Oh, and Potter, try and take on board what the Super said earlier. He doesn't want to see you in anything woollen, got it?'

Neighbourhood Forum, West Indian Sports and Social Club

The room was set out theatre style, with rows of chairs facing a low-rise stage. Two tables had been placed side by side at its centre, along with seats for the guest speakers. Several more tables had been set up around the periphery of the room, manned by representatives from local services: Mental health support, adult education, citizen's advice. A nurse from the medical centre had set up a blood pressure monitoring corner. A stand displayed healthy eating recipe cards and a form to sign up for the wellbeing clinic held on the third Tuesday of every month.

At the back of the room, catering sized trays of food had been placed along the bar's counter, where tea, coffee and non-alcoholic punch was being served by a local residents' group.

Ashcroft's stomach rumbled as he eyed the food.

'Welcome,' said Refik proudly, stepping out from behind the bar to greet him. 'Please help yourself. There is plenty to go around.' He leaned in closer. Lowered his voice so that the women hovering by the food station wouldn't hear. 'You must of course accept everything that's offered, so as not to cause offence.'

'Thanks for the heads up,' Ashcroft responded, picking up a plate while calculating how long tomorrow's run would need to be to work this lot off. He read along the labels in front of each tray: Nigerian Egusi soup. Jamaican Curried Goat. Antiguan Pepperpot Stew. Trinidadian dumplings stuffed with mackerel and chickpeas. Indian Chana Bhatura. Moroccan Lamb, Turkish Kofta meatballs. It smelled so good he decided whatever he needed to put himself through in the morning would be worth it.

'Now you're talking!' said Potter, eyeing the buffet as he walked in. He moved along the food line, nodding with gusto at everything on offer, no fear of him causing offence to anyone.

'Awesome,' said Naz, joining him in the queue, 'Almost makes the prospect of listening to the Super rambling on worthwhile,' she added with a grin.

'Such cynicism in one so young,' Potter observed, shaking his head at her.

Several early birds, having finished at the food station, gingerly made their way to the information stands. A queue had started to form at citizen's advice.

A woman wearing a burka had her blood pressure taken while her companion looked on. An elderly couple were adding their names to the wellbeing clinic, and Hannah was in discussion with a pregnant woman who looked as though she was nearing her third trimester. Ashcroft waited until she'd finished her conversation before going to join her.

'Thanks for coming.'

'Happy to.' She smiled up at him. 'You thought any more about Jamaica?'

'I haven't had a chance!'

'Which means you don't want to go but you're too chicken to say so.'

Ashcroft sniffed. 'Chicken? How old are you, ten?'

He wondered why she was so het up about it. Whether she saw it as some sort of homecoming? That the plane would touch down and he'd look at the lush green landscape and feel that he belonged. He remembered the visits during their childhood. How daunted he felt. The patois he never understood, let alone got the hang of. The endless relatives who greeted him warmly, who as an adult he'd never gone back to see. He felt himself squirm under her scrutiny.

'It's not really my thing,' he admitted. 'Is it going to cause a problem with us if I say no?'

'Of course not,' she said, though it sounded forced.

'Look, my boss has just arrived.' He nodded towards DI Daniels who was casting a critical eye around the hall. 'Can we do this another time?'

'Nothing more to say on the matter, is there?' Hannah turned away from him, her tone dismissive.

Ashcroft made his way over to Daniels.

'This isn't how we normally run these shindigs,' the DI said as he drew close.

'That was the general idea, sir.'

Daniels' gaze moved to the residents as they entered the hall. The initial trickle had turned into a steady throng. 'They'll only be here for the grub, mind.'

'Provided for the residents, by the residents,' Ashcroft reminded him. 'You should try some, it's good.'

'No, you're alright. Promised the wife I'd pick up a takeaway on the way home.'

Ashcroft kept his smile in check. 'I'm sure someone would make up a doggy bag for you.'

Daniels shuddered. 'I like to know what I'm eating. No offence, like.'

Ashcroft gestured with his hand. *It's alright* or *fuck off*, it was hard to decipher.

The room began to fill, albeit a wider age range than he'd expected. He'd anticipated the mothers and the elderly. The number of young men sauntering in surprised him. He'd chosen not to put uniforms on the door, thought it sent the very message he was trying to dispel. He questioned this decision when AJ arrived looking shifty, his mouth forming a grim line. Ashcroft stared in his direction until he caught his eye. Held his gaze. AJ shrugged.

You never said anything about me not coming here, his response seemed to say.

Dr Saadiq, the head teacher from Jamal's school, arrived accompanied by two colleagues. Ashcroft greeted him warmly. 'This your doing?' he said, indicating a group of teenagers in uniform, walking in behind him.

Dr Saadiq nodded. 'I want our pupils to stop feeling threatened when they cross paths with the police. I hope meeting you will go some way towards that.'

Ashcroft swallowed down his guilt as each of the group shook his hand and introduced themselves. No one other than the team he'd been assigned to knew that he was on temporary loan, that for all intents and purposes he was merely passing through. He eyeballed Potter and Nazia, signalled for them to come over and meet the pupils too. Daniels had already found his seat on the stage, was busy reading through the agenda.

Superintendent Duncanson turned up with the press officer, flanked by several minders, like a bride arriving at church with her retinue. The press officer, spotting the school pupils, organised a group photo, before whisking him over to the food station where he was photographed biting into a bhaji. The room quietened to a low murmur as he strode towards the stage, Ashcroft, and Dr Saadiq in his wake. The uniformed officers who'd accompanied him lingered at the back of the room eyeing the buffet.

A hush descended as Ashcroft approached the lectern. He felt a sensation similar to how he felt before a big race. His heart rate rose, he began to sweat.

He stared at the audience.

The audience stared back.

Every seat in the hall was taken.

His mouth ran dry, making his voice sound strange as he introduced himself.

'Pussy clart!'

The words shot out from somewhere in the hall. He tried to ignore them.

'Bumba clart!'

This time the heckling came from the other side of the room.

'Coconut!'

The speakers to Ashcroft's right shifted in their seats. The uniforms at the back of the room took a step forward, waiting for their cue. Removing the hecklers would be a PR disaster. A PR disaster that would go viral on social media before the hour was out. He scanned the crowd for AJ. Was he behind this? Was this his way of showing he wouldn't be silenced? He located him sitting in the second row. He regarded Ashcroft with a shrug.

Superintendent Duncanson looked on, stoney-faced. He and DI Daniels were waiting for him to handle the situation, as though he was a magician and all he had to do was pull a rabbit from his hat to keep the crowd happy.

He swallowed down his frustration.

Placing a hand either side of the lectern he leaned into the microphone. 'I'd like the people who've got something to say, to stand up.' He regarded the officers at the back of the room, shook his head before returning his attention to the audience. 'Don't be shy now, there'll be no repercussions, I promise you.'

Smirking, several of the youths who'd sauntered in earlier got to their feet.

'I see you,' said Ashcroft, 'And I think everyone here heard you. But let me ask you something — do you see me? Or do you see the lanyard around my neck and think you know what that means?'

He pointed one of the youths out. He'd been one of the group who'd minded his sister's car when she'd called in on Safia. Hannah had told him his name was Nezim Hassan. 'You belong to a gang but I see more than that. I see a boy whose mother is sick, and has a kid brother who trails after him on his bike because he wants to fit in. He should be in school, by the way, so when this man stands up to talk,' he pointed to Dr Saadiq, 'I want you to listen to him good.'

He regarded the other youths, who looked smaller, now the spotlight was on them. '*We* get accused of assuming criminality on the part of the victim when they happen to be young and black. Yet here you are. You don't *know* me, but you've made your mind up that everything I stand for is a waste of time. You've no idea how much that offends me. My job is to dispel assumptions, and investigate the murders that are happening on our patch, thoroughly. My question to you is, how are you going to give me these minutes back — the minutes I've spent focussing on you, so I can do just that?'

One of the youths glanced at a shadowy figure leaning by the door. Troy Mellor's dreadlocks bounced as he shook his head in reply. Head down, the youth dropped into his seat, followed by his cronies. Relieved, Ashcroft looked on as The Super took his place at the lectern.

'I would like to reassure the community that we are making headway in regard to the murders of Jamal Deng and Aisha Saforo, as well as

Kamali Harris, whose life was cruelly taken in a separate incident. We are leaving no stone unturned.'

Ashcroft tried not to wince. Duncanson had had a week to come up with a reassuring message and this was the best he could come up with.

'We fully understand that the local community is shocked by recent events, and as a result will continue to provide visible reassurance in the form of on-foot patrol officers, vehicle patrols and covert patrols.'

Ashcroft caught Brian Potter's raised eyebrow. Had it been too much to expect the bosses to come up with something more innovative? The look on Potter's face suggested he'd heard it all before. Bang on the allotted time The Super returned to his seat before inviting the audience to ask questions.

'What developments have there been regarding the double shooting?'

'What can we do to keep our children safe?'

After fifteen minutes of fielding questions, Ashcroft was relieved when it was the headteacher's turn to speak. His message was more positive than it had been when they'd met, then again everyone had bad days. He spoke of hope, and education, and how they were linked. Ashcroft looked purposefully at Nezim, hoped that some of the head teacher's message hit home.

Once the forum had drawn to a close, Ashcroft moved around the room, thanking each resident for coming.

'Pleasure's all mine,' drawled a familiar voice behind him.

He spun round, his face splitting into a grin when he locked eyes with his old partner.

'What the hell are you doing here?' he demanded, slapping his arm.

'Charmin', and there was me thinking you'd be glad of the support.'

Ashcroft made a wafting motion with his hand, 'I didn't mean it like that. I meant how did you hear about it?'

'You're not the only one on Alex Moreton's speed dial, you know. She likes keeping tabs on us all. Especially me, obviously, since I'm her favourite. She sends her apologies, by the way. She wanted to come as well but it's parents' night. Anyway, you got me, the better looking, more charismatic one, though probably better not to tell her I said that, you know how tetchy she can get.'

As well as being a straight down the middle cop, Kevin Coupland was one of the few people Ashcroft felt he could be himself with. There was no side to him. You were either in his tent peeing out of it, or outside it peeing in, and if you were in, he had your back for life.

'How long have you been here?' Ashcroft hoped he hadn't witnessed the heckling and his impression of a rabbit caught in the headlights.

'Long enough to wonder whether you needed your hand holding up there,' Coupland answered, indicating the lectern. 'Trust me,' he added when Ashcroft's face fell, 'You did good. They were flexing their muscles, that's all, you know how it goes. Likely someone else was pulling their strings. You dealt with them without getting bent out of shape. I told the fella beside me I taught you everything you know.'

'Why doesn't that surprise me?' Ashcroft gave him the side eye. 'Mind you, it's easy to talk a good game from the bench. When are you planning on returning to the real world?'

Coupland's face grew serious, 'Just as soon as it stops spinning, mate. Early days yet. Besides, nothing wrong with working burglary, makes a pleasant change reuniting folk with stuff that's been taken from them. Gives me a warm feeling inside.'

Ashcroft wasn't convinced. 'Lynn's doing fine though, isn't she?'

A pause. 'She's doing better...' was all Coupland would

commit to. Then, changing the subject, 'This case sounds like a handful.'

Ashcroft pulled a face. 'They brought me in as window dressing.'

'Got more than they bargained for, then.'

'Suppose.'

Coupland punched him playfully on the arm. 'Forget about the politics. Do what you're good at and get justice for those families.'

Ashcroft looked thoughtful. 'The team's divided. Some think the motive's gang related, others like the girl's father for it — trying to cover his tracks regarding an historical crime.'

Coupland huffed out a breath. 'Opinions are like arseholes, everybody's got one. Hear the others out, but only change course when you're happy to do so — or willing to take the fall if it goes tits up.'

'DS Ashcroft, the Super wants a photo with you on stage.' The press officer flashed him a no-nonsense smile.

'I'll leave you to it. I can see you're busy,' said Coupland. He headed towards the exit, turning briefly when he reached the door. 'One of these days it'll be you in that pristine tunic,' he said, giving him the thumbs up.

It was 9.30pm when Ashcroft let himself into his flat, though it felt a lot later. He'd spent the last half hour at the forum smiling and nodding and shaking hands for the benefit of the press officer.

'Teacher's pet did well,' Daniels observed, once the Super had left the building. 'Though for a minute there I did worry we were going to have a riot on our hands.'

Ashcroft recalled his friend Coupland's words. 'They were just flexing their muscles, nothing I couldn't handle.'

'Yeah, well, it doesn't pay to be complacent. It could have escalated just as quickly.'

Ashcroft took it. Daniels was right, even though it sounded condescending, coming from him. The boss hadn't been the only one who wasn't sure how the heckling was going to pan out. He couldn't help feeling that that was the intention. The headshake from Troy, to show how quickly he could bring the youths to heel.

Which reminded him. By the time he'd had a chance to seek out Nezim Hassan, he was long gone. He'd catch up with him another time, see if he could get that brother of his back into school.

He picked up his mail, kicked his shoes off on the stripped wooden floor. Padded into the kitchen in his socks.

The mail — all junk — went straight into the recycling bin. He draped his jacket over the back of a stool, opened the fridge, allowing himself a cold beer. At least he didn't have to think about cooking.

His kitchen was modern. Granite worktops cluttered with high end gadgets. Bread maker, food processor, blender. He applied himself to cooking in the same way he applied himself to running. His job too, for that matter. *If you put the work in, then you reap the rewards. And you never, ever cut corners.* He knew it wasn't as simple as that. That there were other factors which determined the outcome. Like timing. Each second mattered, for that was the difference between success and abject failure. In terms of his job, the blink of an eye was the difference between life and death. Then there was luck. The biggest game changer of them all, the one component no one had control over.

He walked through to the living area, which consisted of two grey leather sofas facing a glass and chrome coffee table. There was a book the size of a doorstop at its centre. A head shot of Muhammad Ali on the front of it. His father was a boxing fan, a passion they didn't share. The book was an attempt by Ashcroft to meet him halfway.

He dropped onto the sofa facing a wall mounted TV, picked the remote control up from the armrest. He cursed when his mobile rang, its muffled tone reminding him it was in his jacket pocket. He returned to the kitchen to retrieve it.

His sister's name flashed up on the screen. Ashcroft closed his eyes. When he'd told her they could discuss the holiday later, he hadn't meant now.

'*Theo isn't home yet and isn't answering his phone!*'

She sounded calm but the fact she'd called him told him how worried she was.

'Has this happened before?'

'*No!*'

'Have you checked to see if he's with any of his friends?'

'*Of course I have! He's not with them.*'

'Did he go into school today?'

'*Why wouldn't he? They'd have called me if he hadn't. The secretary phones the parents of any pupil who has an unexplained absence.*'

'Maybe the secretary phoned in sick today. Or had to leave early. Or the school had engineers in working on a new phone line.' He didn't want to add that if Theo hadn't arrived at school that morning, whatever he was up to he'd had all day to do it.

'Call his friends back, sis, ask if he showed up for school, then we know what we're dealing with.'

The phone went silent. He tried Theo's number. Listened as it rang out, unanswered. While he waited for Hannah to call back he went into his bedroom, changed into his running gear and trainers. Picked up his car keys from the hall table.

He'd almost reached the parking bay when his phone rang. When all he could hear was Hannah whisper '*Chris...*'

He listened, grim-faced, as she told him Theo's friends

admitted he hadn't gone into school. '*They didn't want to get him into trouble, but what kind of trouble is he in if he isn't answering his phone?*'

'I'll find him, sis, but I need you to sit tight, you hear me?'

He drove to Theo's school, circling the darkened building before following the route to his sister's medical practice. Theo did his homework there while he waited for her to finish. He phoned the local hospitals next, checking admissions, calling Theo's mobile over and over.

The last time they'd spoken had been over dinner at Hannah's place. The conversation had become stilted, especially when Theo started acting up. Although the tension eased after a while, there'd been no mistaking the undercurrent of resentment.

He wasn't a child anymore, though he wasn't a man either.

I hear you're a hooper now.

Tryin' it out.

Ashcroft nodded to himself.

He knew where Theo would be.

He parked outside the medical centre, the security lighting offering some form of protection should anyone fancy their chances with his car. He jogged around the rear of the building along a path which cut through the Abraham Road Estate. Windward Tower stood on one side of the path; Appleton House loomed on the other.

Behind a row of maisonettes he heard the thud of a ball hitting the ground interspersed with shouts of encouragement. He ran towards the sound, slowing his pace when the light from the basketball court illuminated several players.

Theo was there.

Ashcroft texted Hannah to let her know that he'd found him, then switched his phone to silent for the call that he knew would come. He walked up to the fence. Called out Theo's name, then waited. Without his blazer and tie he looked like any other kid playing with his mates after school. The boys he was playing with were similar in age, and looked as engrossed in the game as Theo. It was the young men watching them that made Ashcroft frown. More suited to street corners and trap houses, they gave each player an appraising look, potential recruits in the making.

'Theo!' Ashcroft called again, trying not to let his concern show.

His nephew looked over and raised a hand. Ashcroft pointed to his watch, signalled for him to wrap it up. Theo moved sulkily to his sports bag. Threw it over his shoulder before fist bumping the other players.

'It's sweet blud, he's fam…' he explained when one of them pointed Ashcroft out.

He'd changed his pattern of speech to match theirs. 'In a bit,' he said to one boy, 'Safe,' he said to another. He hunched forward as he walked. Hands shoved inside his trouser pockets.

Ashcroft gave him space as they walked back to the medical centre, when what he really wanted to do was clip him round the ear for worrying his sister, not that she'd thank him.

He waited until they were in his car.

'Why were you speaking like that when that's not who you are?'

Theo angled his head towards him. 'Who am I?'

'You're just a kid.'

Theo bristled.

'A young man, then,' Ashcroft conceded.

Theo's slender, willowy frame made him seem older than he was. He wondered if it had started yet. The double takes by strangers who thought he was going to mug them.

'Either way, it doesn't stop you being vulnerable,' Ashcroft warned.

'To what?'

'To the surroundings you find yourself in. To the choices you might make.'

'So, you think I'm stupid?'

'Bunking off school wasn't one of your brightest moves.'

Theo sank into the passenger seat. 'Does she know?'

'Of course she knows! Check your phone.'

Theo did as he was told. Thirty missed calls between them both. 'Fuck,' he muttered into his chest.

'Your mum's been worried sick. Why didn't you answer her calls?'

'Because she'd have told me to come home.'

Ashcroft swiped his hand over his eyes. 'Where've you been all day?'

Theo sighed. Inclined his head in the direction they'd come from. 'Nowhere special. We went to a café in town, walked round the shops, it was boring really.'

'So why did you do it?'

'Didn't want them thinking I was different. I can hardly tell them I go to a fee-paying school or that my dad's a surgeon.'

'I can see that might be difficult.'

'Or that you're a Fed,' he added, glaring at Ashcroft.

'Guilty as charged.'

'Sometimes you gotta blend in. Show any weakness and you're history. Dog eat dog an' all that.'

'Since when did you want to become someone's dog food?'

'Funny,' said Theo, shooting him a look.

'What about those guys who were watching you? They give you any trouble?'

'I know they're roadmen, if that's what you're getting at,' Theo told him. 'Relax. They offer to buy us stuff now and again but none of us are stupid. We know they'd want something in return.'

'You were daft enough to bunk off school. God knows what else you'd do. Some kids have no luck, and you have it all.' He'd said it in frustration, instantly wishing he could take it back. He looked around them in an attempt to find common ground.

'Nice trainers,' he said, eyeballing Theo's footwear.

'Now you *sound* like the Feds.'

Alone together for five minutes and already he was the object of hatred. They turned away from each other, lost in their own thoughts.

'The other night,' Ashcroft ventured. 'Was there something you wanted to say, about the investigation, or my transfer? I got the impression something was bugging you.'

Theo regarded him. 'Don't you feel a bit like Uncle Tom?'

Ashcroft flinched.

'I mean, two kids get shot in a postcode no one gives a shit about. The big guns bring you out, but let's face it…' Theo gave him a withering look, '…all you're good for is toeing the party line.'

Ashcroft's hands shook as he started the engine. 'Let's get you home. Way past your bedtime,' he grunted.

When did it happen, he wondered, this subtle shift in their fault line? They shared the same blood but breathed different air.

VIP lounge, Rizla nightclub

AJ moved towards the men sitting by the champagne bar. Troy and his lieutenants, Kwame and Leyton turned to watch him approach. They'd all attended the meeting at the West Indian Sports and Social club, along with the soldiers gathered behind them. These were the youths who'd heckled that Fed. He recognised one of them from the trap house he'd gained entry to, working on the cutting table, lacing coke before it was bagged.

He'd wondered how long it would take before word of his visit made it back to Troy. Now he had his answer. He threw his arms wide, decided to brazen it out.

'What you call me for?'

'Sit down,' ordered Troy.

AJ gave him a long stare. Did as he was told.

'Me hear you been throwing your weight around.'

'I didn't hurt no one Troy. I just wanted to get to the truth.'

'By stepping on my toes?'

'I needed answers. Not like anyone else is riding out for me.'

'You want to bring the Feds to my door?'

He remembered what that cop said to him. 'They're focussed on looking for Jamal's killer, not watching me. If you're looking for discretion you might want to tell those pussies not to smoke skunk on the landing.'

Two of the youths standing behind Troy dropped their gaze.

'Even so. Wasn't your risk to take.'

'Faz told me he and Jamal saw that kid get thrown off the balcony. If they saw the killer then there's every chance he saw them. It's got to be him who pulled the trigger. All I wanted from your posse was a description and now I've got it. It's definitely the Berati Crew. Your girl described the guy she saw. The tattoo on his neck should narrow it down…'

'Shut up, blud.' Troy threw him a look he couldn't decipher. Anger. Pity. Whatever it was, after a moment his face cleared as though he'd made up his mind about something that was troubling him. Beside him, Kwame got to his feet.

AJ swallowed. 'I didn't mean no harm, Troy.'

Kwame moved to AJ's side.

'If I caused you any disrespect, I'm sorry.'

Troy held up his hand to silence him. 'I know who he is,' he said simply. 'His name's Vasif Muka. Yesterday he walked into the retail units I own. Took the day's takings off each tenant. Told them to expect him same time every week. Pussy didn't even hide his face.'

'Him cyan't disrespect yuh like dat, bro,' said one of the soldier boys.

AJ's brow creased.

'He's after my turf.' Troy explained. 'He's been yapping at my heels for the last few months. He's more of a threat now he's taken over from his old man. He's got the ways and means to do whatever he likes.'

'So you knew something was brewing…' AJ said slowly.

'Nothing like that!' Troy said quickly. 'He's never come at any of us directly. Me knew it was him who threw that kid off the balcony. Me felt for the family and all but it was a beef he had with a roadman who used to deal for him, nothing more. There was no need to get in the middle of that.'

'It happened on your territory. You know how these things escalate. You come at them for stepping on your turf, they come at you, bigger this time. You do nothing, they come back at you anyway. Either way you're screwed. If you'd gone after him when he killed that kid, Jamal would still be alive.'

Troy's head dropped onto his chest. 'There was no way me could have known something like that was going to happen. Jamal has never played a part in any of this. Me gave you my word, blud, and me stuck to it. We made sure no one touched him so he could get on with his life. Build something better than dis. When Jamal was killed it was like I'd been cut down too, blud. Let me mek it up to yuh.'

'I'm listening.'

'What yuh sayin' is true. We got no choice but to deal with those motherfuckers or we get fucked. Me need to strike before they shut me down. It's all arranged. We go after them tomorrow, and we go in heavy. We'll take care of his men but will leave Vasif for you.'

The look he gave AJ went deep into his soul. 'I want your face to be the last one he sees.'

Troy nodded at Kwame.

Looked on with satisfaction as he handed AJ a gun.

THIRTEEN

'Everybody wants more, don't they?'

— NOZZA HASSAN

Moss Side station

There was something different about Ashcroft when he walked into the CID room the next morning. Nothing specific that his colleagues could put their finger on, after all they hadn't known him long, in the grand scheme of things. When Brian Potter congratulated him on the previous evening he appeared distracted, managing a brusque 'Thank you,' before moving on to his desk.

At 9am Potter took a call from the tech team. A couple of 'Uh-huhs' and a 'that's great, mate,' and he replaced the handset with a cheer. 'Sarge, the tech guys confirm that Aisha was searching the refugee centre database for information on Safia Deng, specifically the information she gave in support of her application to remain in the UK. Ozwald Saforo is listed as legal counsel, but here's where it gets interesting.'

'Go on,' said Ashcroft.

'Aisha carried out several searches using her father's name as a parameter, cross referencing it with widowed or single female refugees referred to the legal team over a five-year window. These names appear in a file she created on the laptop she kept at her boyfriend's house.'

'How many are we talking about?'

'Including Safia, there were four women on her list who'd received legal representation from her father. Two have since had their visas revoked.'

Ashcroft stared at him.

'Christ, is this going where I think it's going?' asked Nazia.

Potter regarded her. 'The last known address of the other woman granted the right to remain, is in the file Aisha created. There's only one way to find out…'

They both looked at Ashcroft expectantly. He'd kept pace with the conversation despite his silence.

'We can't ignore this,' he said eventually. 'Speak to this woman, Naz, see what she's got to say.'

His desk phone rang.

'*A gentleman downstairs wants to speak to you,*' said the civilian in reception.

'Who is it?'

'*Doesn't want to give his name. Says you spoke to him last night at some forum.*'

'Did he now?' he said before replacing the receiver.

'I take it this isn't a social call?'

Ashcroft led Nezim Hassan through to one of the interview rooms and closed the door. He perched on the edge of the table, folded his arms. 'To what do I owe this pleasure?' he prompted when Nezim remained silent.

The youth leaned against the wall, his arms mirroring Ashcroft's. Ashcroft dropped his arms to his side, placed his hands either side of the tabletop.

'I'm not a mind reader, Nezim. You asked to see me, remember?'

'Mates call me Nozza.'

'So we're mates, now? Only after last night's performance it's hard to keep up.'

Nozza gave him a look. 'This comes back on me, I'm dead. You get me?'

Ashcroft nodded. Watched as the teenager put a hand in the pocket of his tracksuit bottoms. Pulled out a scrap of paper. Held it out to him.

'What's this?' he asked, taking it.

An address had been scrawled in black ink.

'The Berati Crew run the Langston Estate from there. The big boss, 'im moving in on Troy's territory an' Troy ain't standing for that. We're going there tonight, tooled up, an' we gonna tek em out.'

Ashcroft regarded him. 'Why are you telling me this?'

'I didn't join a gang so I can drive a BMW and wear bling around my neck. We're broke, you get me? My family rely on me to pay the bills. I can't afford to get sent down. Mum's health isn't so good, I need to be around for my brother.'

'You could start by getting him back into school,' Ashcroft told him. 'Let him discover what his options are.'

Nozza sucked air through his teeth. 'Fat lot of good if he ends up in care because I'm in the slammer.'

Mikey was heading there anyway if his truanting didn't stop, but now wasn't the time to go down that particular road. Not now there were more pressing matters to deal with. Ashcroft ran a hand over his head.

'This is definitely going down?'

'It's happening, blud. Troy says you've got to hit your enemies first. Show them who's boss. You can't lose face in this game. Once you've put a hit on someone, you've gotta see it through.'

This was dangerous work for anyone, let alone a kid barely in their teens.

'What's got Troy bent out of shape?'

'Vasif has got his tenants by the nuts. He's started demanding protection money.'

'The shop units on Abraham Road?' The units Troy had bought after lockdown.

Nozza inclined his head.

'Why now? Troy's had them for a while.'

'He doesn't tell me his business.' Nozza sucked air through his teeth. "im say something about Vasif wanting that territory to build on but there's nothing unusual about that. Everybody wants more, don't they?'

'Who was he talking to when he said this?'

'His mandem. And the pussy whose brother was shot up with that girl.'

Ashcroft narrowed his eyes. 'Is AJ part of Troy's gang?'

'No, but they go way back. He said the Turk Jamal used to hang round with told him the Albanian killed him and that girl.'

'Does AJ know about this evening?'

A nod.

Ashcroft swore under his breath. 'OK,' he said, sounding more confident than he felt. 'I need to run this by my boss, but we can help you. Sit tight.'

DI Daniels' office

DI Daniels listened as Ashcroft gave him the lowdown.

'Why's he come to us? He wasn't exactly on side last night when he was lobbing insults at you.'

'He hadn't been ordered to play executioner at that point,' Ashcroft reasoned. 'He's a bright lad. He's done the maths.

They'll have to obliterate the Berati Crew for there not to be any reprisals. If he isn't looking over his shoulder for them, he'll be looking for us. He knows damn well that it's the bottom feeders who do the time. He's got an invalid mother and a kid brother who'll end up in care if he's not around to look after him.'

'Should have thought of that before he signed up for Easy Street.'

'Is that all you've got?' Ashcroft looked at him wide-eyed. 'Maybe this is his teachable moment. The moment he realises the criminal life he's chosen isn't for him, and he wants to change.'

'You been watching that Disney Channel?'

Ashcroft tensed. He swiped a hand over his mouth, one hand resting on his hip while he gesticulated with the other. 'He's virtually signed his own death warrant coming here. Thanks to him we've got a chance to seriously dismantle two rival gangs, not to mention avoid civilians getting caught in the crossfire. He's looking for immunity.'

He looked on as the DI considered this. 'Lifelong protection is what him and his family will need. Come on, you know how it works.' Daniels got to his feet. 'I'll take this to the Super but in my view we've got enough to exercise a warrant for this address. Armed response. Trojan Unit, full shebang.'

'And protection for Nozza and his family?'

'That too.'

Ashcroft accompanied Daniels to the lift, waited while he jabbed his finger on the call button as though he couldn't be trusted to keep his word. He watched the senior officer step inside before returning to the interview room. 'A word to the wise,' Daniels called out before the doors closed. 'Make it clear that he mustn't go in tooled up. When it all kicks off I can't guarantee his safety if he's holding a weapon.'

'Understood.'

The breaktime bell had sounded and Fatima Liban stood back to let thirty excitable children push their way into the corridor. 'No running!' she called out, looking on as they changed into their outdoor shoes before heading into the playground.

The class teacher regarded the slender woman who'd started working at the school at the start of the year. Quietly spoken, she had a habit of touching her hijab when she spoke as though checking it was in place.

'You coming, Fatima?' Mrs Coben asked, slipping her bag over her shoulder before heading to the staff room.

Fatima shook her head. 'There's only so much tea I can drink,' she answered, smiling. 'Besides, I like to put up their drawings while the children are outside. I love seeing their faces when they come back in and see the result of all their hard work on display.'

Mrs Coben beamed at her. 'I certainly won the lottery when you were allocated to this class. Speaking of which, you shouldn't be spending your own money on all this stuff,' she said, indicating the pots of glitter and crepe paper the classroom assistant had bought at the weekend.

Fatima waved away her concern. 'It's my pleasure. I've always loved art; I just want them to enjoy it as much as I did.' Besides, with no children of her own and elderly parents to care for, there was little opportunity to spend it on other things.

She'd wanted to be an art teacher when she was at school. The outbreak of war in her country put paid to her completing her education. Working with children in a school setting was the next best thing.

Neither of them noticed the head teacher step into the

classroom, a young woman similar to Fatima in age beside her. The woman held up her police ID, asked Fatima if she'd mind helping her with an ongoing enquiry.

The day was spiralling in a way Ashcroft could never have predicted before Nozza Hassan had walked in. If his intel was correct, they had the opportunity to put two gangs and a double murderer behind bars.

If.

Once the duty solicitor arrived, Ashcroft had asked Brian Potter to join him in the interview room while Nazim gave his statement. In it, he confirmed that one of Troy Mellor's trap house workers saw Vasif Muka going up to the flat where Kamali Harris lived with his family, on the afternoon of his murder. This, along with the Albanian taking money with menaces from Troy's tenants, was enough for Troy to want him dead.

For reasons known only to him, Fahri Gemici had admitted to AJ that he and Jamal had witnessed members of the Berati Crew run from the tower block shortly afterwards. Little wonder this had inflamed AJ, but if word got out it would put Fahri at risk from the Berati Crew as well. For a boy used to being under threat before his friendship with Jamal, he was slow on the uptake not working that much out.

Nozza was starting to regret coming forward.

'I gotta go into the Albanian's yard heavy,' he'd spluttered when Ashcroft had given him DI Daniels' orders.

'Trust me, even I wouldn't risk it,' Ashcroft had admitted, realising that was the truth. He didn't blame him for looking petrified when he'd left, two hours later.

Back in the CID room Ashcroft helped himself to water from the cooler. He wasn't sure Nozza could be relied upon to do as he was told. Then again, the courage it must have taken to walk into the station. To betray the gang he considered his family. It had to count for something.

AJ was a different kettle of fish altogether. There was no way he could warn him to stay away tonight, without revealing there'd been a leak. It wouldn't take Troy long to work out who the weakest link in the chain was. Ashcroft shrugged. He'd warned him enough times, now it was out of his hands. The squaddie was heading for a death sentence or jail.

Ashcroft's phone rang. Nazia's name flashed up on his screen.

'It was easy enough to trace Fatima, Sarge. Her family's last known address was in a housing association block of flats which has since been demolished. I spoke to the housing officer, who was able to give me their new address and her mother told me where she worked when I called round.'

'Was she willing to speak to you?'

'Not at first. She doesn't like dredging up her past. Can't see any value in raking over old coals. Told me she'd said as much to the other woman who'd tried poking her nose in.'

'Aisha?'

'The very same. I told her what had happened and she was genuinely sorry. Said she was willing to tell me everything she'd told Aisha.'

Ashcroft waited.

'She'd become separated from her family as a teenager about fifteen years ago. They'd been trying to board a boat in the middle of the night on the Libyan coast. Traffickers took her to Tunisia, where she was abandoned for six months before a Red Cross volunteer helped her trace her family to the UK. Her family sought advice from The Dignity Centre. Aisha's father was the lawyer appointed to help reunite them. All well and good, you'd think, wouldn't you? Only he arranges a meeting with Fatima once she gets over here — in private — where he pretty much tells her that she owes him, and it was time to pay him back.'

'Nice guy.'

'*Not quite the words she used. She never reported the rape, but made sure she was never alone with him again. She informed Aisha that she didn't want to take it any further. Her parents had no idea that Ozwald had abused her, she didn't want to cause them distress by speaking about it after all this time.*'

Ashcroft thanked her and ended the call. He relayed the information to Potter. 'Aisha's interest in the refugee centre was all about her father and the extent to which he abused his position. It was nothing to do with identifying who killed Kamali,' he concluded.

Potter considered this. 'The business team has sent over their report on the centre's financials. No irregularities were detected, certainly nothing to link them to any criminality. I think you're right about Aisha. This was all about her old man, yet Naz found nothing to cause concern when she checked his alibi a second time.'

'He's a piece of work, but he's no killer. Vasif's still in the frame for that. Nozza Hassan's statement makes it pretty watertight.'

DI Daniels appeared in the doorway, a grin splitting his face in two. 'The Super's been on to his opposite number in the Firearms Unit. All systems are *go*.'

Vasif was buzzing. He'd taken delivery of a shipment of coke that morning that once distributed would net him two million. An afternoon in the casino followed by a lap dancing bar, had put him in good spirits. He telephoned his girlfriend, informed her he'd made a reservation at that restaurant she'd been going on about. He grinned as she squealed down the phone, pleased with himself. It was notoriously hard to get a table there, even booking months in advance. Vasif's father knew the owner and the owner knew better than to get on the wrong side of the Muka family. He'd assured Vasif the best table in the house would be ready upon his arrival.

'You can show me how pleased you are later, babe,' he drawled down the line, instructing her to use his credit card to buy something new to wear. Something hot. He didn't add that they were meeting two business associates and their wives, financiers he hoped to persuade to invest in his property dream. No harm in mixing business with pleasure, especially when there was plenty of cash to throw about. He was on a roll.

There was only one thing that could top this feeling. He opened an ornately carved box on the makeshift table in front of him. Lifted out a slim scoop which he used to tap out two lines of fine white powder. Taking a bundle of fifty-pound notes from his pocket which he tossed onto the centre of the table, he invited the men gathered around to join him. He rolled one of the notes into a tube, made short work of the lines he'd tapped out.

'Living our best lives, gentlemen…' he said, wiping under his nose with his forefinger and thumb.

He lounged back on his chair, closed his eyes as he visualised his dream. His eyes snapped open as Troy Mellor's face loomed into view. Troy was the one blot on his horizon. Even if intimidating his tenants worked and the tin pot gangster put his shop units up for sale, there was no way he'd sell them to Vasif. His face clouded over. He should have thought that bit through, warned Troy's tenants not to say anything. Once they told Troy he was extorting money from them there was no way he'd play ball. Worse than that, he'd come after Vasif himself. Everyone knew the best form of defence was attack.

'We need to take Troy Mellor and his crew out,' Vasif

announced to the cronies lounging beside him. The men nodded as though orders like this were inevitable.

'When do you wanna go after them, boss?' asked Aljan, his trusted bagman.

Vasif glanced at his Rolex. Three hours yet before he was due at the restaurant. A quick call to the person storing their weapons to have them ready, and they'd be all set. He felt his heartrate quicken, whether from the sniff he'd inhaled or the anticipation of a ruck, he wasn't sure.

'No time like the present,' he answered, grinning.

Outside, a drone circled the tower block like an angry bird.

'Where's AJ?' Kwame asked, scanning the back seat of Troy's Range Rover as he climbed into the driver's seat.

'Relax,' Troy ordered. "im already in place. 'E keepin' watch over the exit points in case Vasif mek a run for it.'

AJ knew the rat runs on the Langston Estate better than anyone. He and Troy used to dare each other to go over there when they were kids, back when the worst thing they'd get if the old gangsters caught them was a hiding. 'Besides, he can handle himself,' he added confidently. 'He's army trained. Was a sniper in Mali.' He caught the look of apprehension on Nozza's face in his rear-view mirror.

'What is it with everyone today? Remember, we've got the element of surprise over dem pussies. We'll be in and out, two minutes.' He made the shape of a gun with his hand. Imitated the sound of a shot being fired. 'Just so long as you keep your aim straight,' he added, turning to grin at the boy. He liked to bring one of the promising soldiers along. Did no harm to give 'em a bit of match experience, so long as they did as they were told. A bead of sweat ran from Nozza's hairline over his forehead. Troy narrowed his eyes.

One Good Reason

'I'm giving you a chance to step up,' he said, 'You better be up to it.'

'Course I am, Troy,' said Nozza, 'I won't let you down.'

'Show me your kit,' Troy ordered.

Nozza's hand shook slightly as he lowered the zip on his tracksuit to show his bullet proof vest. With his other hand he held up his ski mask and gloves.

Troy waited him out.

Nozza tried to slow his breathing down as he reached inside his tracksuit for the gun he knew wasn't there.

'Keep it hidden!' Troy ordered him. 'Too many nosey fuckers round here.'

Nozza heaved out a breath as he did as he was told.

'What you waiting for?' Troy turned his attention to Kwame. 'Time to roll out.'

Incident room, Moss Side station

The surveillance officer operating the drone spoke into his radio.

'Apart from getting a takeaway delivered there's been no other activity. At least we know there's someone inside. Several of them, going by the size of the order that was dropped off.'

'Copy that,' responded DI Daniels.

Ashcroft let out a sigh. When Daniels confirmed that all systems were 'go,' he imagined that he'd be in the thick of it. Instead, once Superintendent Duncanson, acting as Tactical Strategic Commander, briefed the assembled firearms unit an hour before deployment, he'd been relegated to the sidelines. He been about to follow the armed officers into the car park when DI Daniels grabbed the Kevlar vest he'd been carrying and shrugged into it.

'Not like you'll be needing it,' he said when Ashcroft looked at him, confused.

'What are you talking about? The Super's appointed me Intel officer, I'm needed at the scene.'

Daniels was already shaking his head. 'Intel Officer stays at the command base. That's here, for the uninitiated,' he said, trying but failing to hide his glee. 'I'm the SIO on this case, or have you forgotten?'

'Not much chance of that,' Ashcroft muttered, as he turned and walked away.

'If it's any consolation,' Daniels called after him, 'the big man thinks you're better placed to analyse any intelligence as it comes in. Seems all I'm good for is preserving the scene and collecting evidence.'

He was playing his role down. They'd been granted a warrant to search for the missing weapons brought in illegally the year before, one of which was used to kill Jamal and Aisha. If successful, there'd be enough evidence to decimate a rainforest with the number of charges the Berati Crew would be facing.

Ashcroft didn't begrudge him, though it rankled that he wouldn't be part of the action. He stood in the station car park, watching as Daniels joined officers wearing boilersuits with bandanas covering their faces, climb into three unmarked BMWs. He watched them drive off, staying until the last vehicle's taillights disappeared, then trudged back inside.

Superintendent Donaldson was in the CID room staring at a bank of computer screens. From here they would monitor every stage of the raid, via the surveillance camera mounted onto a drone, hovering above the Berati Crew's den. Ashcroft went to join him. Together, they studied the screens in silence.

The cars parked in front of the tower block wouldn't have looked out of place outside a high-end hotel. A Maserati, alongside several top of the range beamers. It demonstrated

One Good Reason

Vasif's level of confidence that he didn't feel the need to conceal their HQ from the outside world.

'*Confirmation required that Target A is in the property.*' The operational commander's voice came over the radio.

'The car registered to Target A is parked outside the property,' Ashcroft confirmed, eyeballing Vasif Muka's Maserati.

Something bothered him. 'Bit early for a spicy meat feast, though,' he muttered, consulting his watch. It was 5.30pm. Frowning, he pressed the rewind button on the computer keyboard, watching the surveillance footage flash by in reverse until he found what he was looking for.

'I know these guys keep different hours to regular folk,' he said, more to himself than any of the officers within earshot. 'And that getting off your face regularly increases your appetite, but THAT does seem excessive.'

He'd paused the footage on the screen at the point where the takeaway delivery driver handed over an insulated food bag to the henchman that answered the door. The bag was large enough to contain a dozen supersize pizzas.

'We've no idea how many people are in there,' said Potter, wandering over.

'No. But if every car that's parked there arrived with two occupants, that's still a shed load of food.'

The delivery guy wore a baseball cap pulled low over the front of his face. Ashcroft used the zoom button to see if he could get a close-up. The image was blurred. He zoomed out, moved the footage along until he got a view of the delivery vehicle's registration number.

'Brian, check who the car's registered to. Give them a call to verify the order.'

'Will do,' said Potter, taking a photo of the car with his phone.

'Looks like we're on,' said the Super as a black Range

Rover turned into the car park. They watched as the driver executed a three point turn so that it faced the opposite direction, before coming to a stop. All the better to make a quick get-away.

There was a crackle of static before the operational commander spoke into his radio.

'*Confirmation required that this is target B.*'

'The car belongs to Target B,' Ashcroft confirmed, after checking the car's registration against historical surveillance photos taken with Troy Mellor at the wheel.

'Please remember that one of the occupants is unarmed,' he added, hoping that Nozza hadn't lost his nerve and turned up carrying a weapon.

'*We act on what we see,*' the OC responded.

Ashcroft turned to Superintendent Duncanson. 'We wouldn't be here if it wasn't for his intel,' he reminded him.

'The kid needs to make it clear he's unarmed the moment he steps out of that vehicle...' the Super left the consequences if he didn't do that unsaid.

Ashcroft asked the drone operator if they could get a close-up view of the car's occupants.

The drone couldn't fly any lower without its cover being blown. He watched the image on screen magnify as the camera's lens was zoomed in to its maximum setting. Five occupants could be made out in the vehicle, their faces obscured by ski masks. Even so, Ashcroft was certain they were looking at Troy and his two lieutenants, which left Nozza and AJ as the other two passengers.

Ashcroft turned to The Super. 'Jamal's brother, AJ is likely to be one of them…'

'We know that,' Duncanson stated. 'He's a soldier. He of all people knows the consequences of not dropping his weapon when he's told.'

It was easy in the control room to theorise about how it

would play out. What none of them watching on-screen could take into account, was the adrenaline pumping through everyone's veins at the scene.

'Sarge,' Potter called across the room as he came off the phone. 'Drawn a blank on the delivery driver's car. False plates.'

'Worth a try,' Ashcroft said, his eyes fixed on the screen.

The drone continued to hover above Troy's vehicle, giving an aerial view of the car park.

Police firearms units were positioned behind a row of lock-ups opposite the block of maisonettes. Armed officers were already in position either side of them. Around the side of the block an officer holding a battering ram pulled his helmet's visor over his face.

Upon the operational commander's signal, the vehicles would drive out and block the car park's exits while the tactical team swooped to disable the shooters.

Satisfied everything was in place, Superintendent Duncanson instructed the operational commander to proceed. The airwaves fell silent, waiting for his signal.

In the control room, they watched as the doors of the Range Rover started to open.

It was now or never.

Ashcroft looked on as the OC gave his signal over the radio.

'ARMED POLICE! STAY WHERE YOU ARE!'

The sound of tyres screeching came over the airwave. Officers' boots on the ground as they surrounded the vehicle.

'DROP YOUR WEAPONS! PUT YOUR FUCKING HANDS UP!'

Behind them the maisonette door caved on impact. Armed officers pushed inside.

Ashcroft watched as the occupants of the Range Rover were dragged onto the tarmac and handcuffed.

DI Daniels stepped into view, holding a video camera, the footage live-streamed onto a third screen in the control room. He filmed each gang member as he removed their ski mask.

Ashcroft watched and waited.

Troy Mellor was identified, along with his lieutenants, Kwame Kuma and Leyton Appiah. Nozza Hassan. He held his breath as the last ski mask was removed.

It wasn't AJ.

'Do you know who he is?' demanded Duncanson.

Ashcroft regarded the skinny rude boy in his adidas striped tracksuit. 'He was at the nightclub the evening we gave Aisha's boyfriend the death message. He's definitely one of Troy's inner circle.'

Duncanson nodded, satisfied.

A shot rang out, followed by another, causing Daniels to duck for cover. Two armed officers ran towards an unmarked BMW and sped off, blue lights flashing.

Moments later the OC's voice boomed over the airwave. 'Vasif Muka has absconded! He jumped out of the kitchen window after opening fire. Officers in pursuit.'

'They'll not get near him if he stays on the Langston. All those concrete bollards,' said Potter.

Duncanson gave the order for the helicopter waiting on standby to be scrambled.

'If he stays beneath the maze of walkways he'll not be seen from above either.'

They looked on as Daniels entered the maisonette once Vasif's men had been brought out in handcuffs. His video camera captured the upended furniture, the over-sized pizza box containing an array of Glock pistols. 'Looks like they were expecting company,' he said into his radio.

'Good work,' responded Duncanson.

'We've still got a killer at large,' Ashcroft reminded both of them, his comment earning him a glare from The Super.

'Bastard won't get far, he's got a gunshot wound to the shoulder,' chipped in the operational commander.

Not to mention a trained soldier on his tail, Ashcroft didn't wonder. Revenge eats away all the good a person has in them. Leaves sorrow in its wake. Not that he'd lose any sleep if the Albanian got what was coming to him. If anything, he'd sleep better knowing he wouldn't be pulling the gang's strings from his jail cell. What mattered to him was that AJ didn't become another victim. Locked up for life was no way to honour his brother.

He tried calling AJ's phone. Was unsurprised to find it was switched off.

Vasif knew the estate like the back of his hand. He'd grown up here, before his father's business had transported them to a better life. Each housing block was linked by interlocking walkways that made it easy to hide from rivals and the police. He moved stealth-like, sticking to the shadows so the drone couldn't find him.

'Fuck.'

His shoulder throbbed where the bullet had lodged into it. Blood leaked down his top, leaving a trail of drips on the ground. The path ahead forked into two. Turn right and the tarmac flyover above Alfreton Road provided an unofficial border between the estate and the world beyond. Turn left and a twisting maze of walkways would return him to the sanctity of the Langston Estate.

He continued along the pedestrian flyover. The concrete jungle of the Abraham Road Estate lay ahead.

Before it, the medical centre.

'ARMED POLICE! STAY WHERE YOU ARE!'

AJ had been hiding on a walkway behind the maisonettes, when the police raided Vasif's yard. He saw them surround Troy's car, saw another group push their way into the Albanians' den. He'd started to back away when the sound of gunshots set him on alert. He had to get closer, check Troy was OK. He edged forward as far as he dared, saw Troy and his men lying on the tarmac in handcuffs. Two armed officers ran to an unmarked BMW and set off at speed. Blues and twos suggested they were in pursuit of something, but what? He slunk into the shadows, made sure he stayed out of sight as he watched Vasif's henchmen as they were led out of the building in handcuffs. It wasn't the outcome he'd wanted. Putting a bullet in Vasif's head would have given him a great deal of satisfaction, but seeing the bastard behind bars was a close second. Looked like that cop had been as good as his word after all.

'Vasif Muka has absconded!' he heard an armed officer say into his radio.

AJ felt a surge of rage, like a simmering pot boil over. The bastard he had come to kill hadn't been apprehended after all. He was on the run, sticking two fingers up at everyone because he thought he was above the law. What a joke.

'Bastard won't get far, he's got a gunshot wound to the shoulder,' he heard the same officer say into his radio.

AJ allowed himself a smile. The injury would slow him down. Make it less easy for him to blend unnoticed into a crowd. He'd need to get it seen to if he held out any hope of escaping this concrete maze.

He headed back along the flyover that joined the Langston Estate with Abraham Road. The droplets of blood he stepped over confirmed he was going in the right direction.

He would find Vasif, and when he found him, he would make him pay.

They were in a pool car. Potter driving. Ashcroft going out of his mind.

'Do we have any confirmed sighting of Target A?' he barked into his radio. Held his breath while the air filled with radio static.

'Negative.' This was from the firearms officers who'd left in pursuit of Vasif after he'd absconded.

'Negative.' From the helicopter pilot.

'Negative.' From the rapid response firearms unit now circulating the Langston Estate.

The officers involved in the raid could not be re-deployed, as they were needed to provide an armed escort for the vans transporting the Bereti Crew and Abraham Road gang members into custody at two different police stations.

Ashcroft tried his sister's mobile one more time. All he'd got from the reception phone line was an engaged tone. He dialled it again, letting out a breath when it started to ring. A voicemail kicked in advising patients the medical centre was now closed. 'Fuck,' he said, ending the call.

'Try your sister's number again,' said Potter. 'Remember, hers isn't the only GP practice in the area. There's another one, a couple of miles further up the road.'

'Yeah, but hers is the closest, and it's the only one in No Man's Land. The perfect choice for someone trying to evade capture when they need medical help. I reckon a gunshot wound to the shoulder counts as that, don't you?'

'Suppose.'

'Come on, man, don't play it down! You were the one who told me about the injuries you sustained along that road, about the officers killed while trying to do their job. How it's a no-go area for anyone who values their life.'

'Which is why armed response units have been dispatched

to both premises. We'll hear soon enough if there's anything to report. Now do us both a favour and try her number again.'

Ashcroft hit the redial button on his phone. Listened as Hannah's number rang out.

'Shit!' He remembered that Theo took the bus to the medical centre after school. That he'd started playing basketball while he waited.

'My nephew will be on his way there now. I'll call him and tell him to stay away until we know Hannah's OK.'

'Sounds like a good idea.'

He hit Theo's number. Felt his heart thud as his phone rang out.

Ashcroft tensed. 'C'mon Theo, don't do this now. Pick up the phone.'

Theo's voicemail kicked in after four rings.

'It'll be fine,' said Potter, pushing his foot down on the accelerator.

The sound of sirens could be heard from the neighbouring estate as Theo shrugged on his jacket and hoisted his rucksack over his shoulder. He raised his hand to the other boys leaving the basketball court, called out that he'd see them later in the week.

Blue lights flashed in the distance.

He slipped his phone from his coat pocket. Saw a missed call from Uncle Chris. He was about to hit reply when a text flashed up on his screen from the sister of one of his mates. A group of them were going ice-skating at the weekend. Would he like to join them? He grinned as he tapped his reply. Uncle Chris could wait.

He used his key to unlock the medical centre's back door.

Knew instantly something was wrong. Felt something cold against the back of his skull.

'Don't make a sound,' said a deadly voice behind him.

The call from Control was just what Ashcroft didn't want to hear.

'A member of the public has reported seeing someone with a gun heading towards the medical centre on Alfreton Road. An armed unit has confirmed its location is close by and a second has been dispatched. The emergency department is on standby.'

'ETA two minutes,' stated Ashcroft, wondering what scene they'd be greeted with when they arrived.

The tactical unit had surrounded the building. The operational commander stared expectantly at Ashcroft and Potter as they drew close. The inspector that normally handled hostage situations was off sick and DI Daniels was tied up overseeing a dozen warring gang members as they were taken into custody.

Ashcroft had passed the National Negotiator's Course during his time in the Met. Had never in his worst nightmares expected the first time he'd put it to use would be in a bid to rescue his sister. Not that he'd mentioned that little detail to Superintendent Duncanson when he'd asked to attend the scene minutes earlier, and he wasn't going to mention it now. Potter had intuitively kept his mouth firmly shut on the matter.

Theo hadn't called him back. He suspected that both were being held inside the medical centre against their will. There was no way they could risk waiting for someone with more negotiating experience to come along. Men like Vasif were trigger happy. If he could throw a child from a balcony he'd have no qualms killing Hannah and Theo if his demands weren't met.

The operational commander passed bullet proof vests to Ashcroft and Potter, which they put on.

'Keep your radios on,' he instructed. 'Good luck.'

Side-stepping a discarded BMX bike beside the medical centre's main entrance, Ashcroft paused at the threshold. He turned to look at Potter. 'Sure you want to do this, what with you opting for the easy life now?'

'I'm here, aren't I?' Potter responded. 'Let's get on with it.'

They stepped through the automatic doors, taking in the scene that greeted them:

Hannah was standing in the middle of the waiting area. Vasif stood beside her, a gun aimed at her head.

'We're police,' said Ashcroft, keeping his distance.

'I know who you are.'

Blood was leaking from a wound in his shoulder. He stood lop-sided, though it wasn't affecting his aim.

'Put the gun down,' ordered Ashcroft.

Emergency vehicles would take up positions around the perimeter. There was no way out.

Ashcroft drew in a breath as he readied himself. Moments like this, when a gunman felt cornered, could only end one way.

'You're injured. How can she help you when you're pointing a gun at her?'

The Albanian straightened himself as he considered this.

Ashcroft studied the gun in his hand. Exchanged a look with Potter to see if he'd clocked it too. A Glock pistol, same as the other guns found during the raid on Vasif's den.

Identical to the one that had killed Jamal and Aisha.

Potter's nod confirmed that he'd seen it too.

Ashcroft studied the Albanian's face, looking for something, anything, to suggest his words were getting through. 'Let her help you,' he said through gritted teeth. 'Drop your gun.'

Vasif did as he was told.

Hannah swallowed. Stole a glance at her brother who kicked it out of reach.

Ashcroft nodded.

'I'll need to take a proper look,' she said, turning so that she could tend to his injury.

'You've got to be kidding me, right?'

The raised voice came from the office behind reception. AJ stepped towards them, holding a gun. He stared at Hannah wide-eyed.

'You're going to help the bastard that killed my brother and that girl? He threw a kid over a balcony! What kind of monster does that?'

A gasp coming from the office made them all turn.

'THEO!' cried Hannah.

'Mum, I'm so sorry, he pushed his way in!'

'THEO GET BACK!' yelled Ashcroft, assessing him visually. The boy looked unharmed, which was how he intended to keep it.

'I was never going to hurt him!' cried AJ.

'I know you wouldn't, what with everything you've been through,' said Hannah. She tried to slow down her breathing. In through the nose. Out through the mouth. Her eyes dropped down to the gun in his hand. 'This isn't the answer though.'

'There are no answers.' He turned to Vasif. 'You've destroyed my family. You have to pay for that.'

Ashcroft moved towards him. Arms wide. 'He will pay, AJ. I promise you that.'

AJ laughed but it came out fractured. 'You mean jail? If he doesn't kill the witnesses first? My family deserve more than that.'

'You point your gun at him and the armed officers out there will blow your head off before you've even pulled the trigger. How does visiting two graves help your mum?'

'I have to do something!'

'Then let us do our job!'

A flurry of static on Potter's radio told them the firearms officers were in position. He threw Ashcroft a look. All they needed was a clear line of sight.

It didn't matter that AJ wasn't the cold-hearted killer in this tableau. That he was Jamal's brother and was grieving. That he was a serving British soldier.

All they would see was the gun in his hand.

Ashcroft glanced at the waiting room window. AJ was partially obscured by a pillar. Right now that pillar was the only thing keeping him alive.

'I need you to stay where you are and drop your gun,' Ashcroft instructed him.

'Why are you trying to save that killer?'

'I'm trying to save you!'

'Don't worry about me bruv, sometimes you gotta step up, you know what I'm saying?'

'You shoot him and you'll leave here in a body bag. That what you want?'

'At least he won't be here.' He took a step closer to the Albanian. He was now in clear view of the window.

'Drop your weapon!' yelled Potter.

'Do it quick!' yelled Ashcroft.

AJ extended his arm. 'I can't let this bastard li-'

THUD.

The bullet sent him flying backwards.

Hannah screamed as the Albanian grabbed AJ's gun as it fell and pulled her in front of him. Now the tactical unit had taken AJ down, their weapons would be trained on Vasif, only he had a human shield.

'It'll be OK, sis,' Ashcroft said without thinking. As the word came out he collapsed in on himself.

A cruel smile played on the Albanian's lips as he placed his gun against her temple.

Potter's words of warning rang in his ears:

They like to take out your loved ones in front of you.

This was the man who'd called out to Kamali Harris' father as he lifted his son over the tower block balcony. Who listened to his screams as he let him fall.

'NO!' Ashcroft yelled, stepping forward.

A shot rang out.

Ashcroft's eyes closed as a spray of blood hit his face. When he opened them his sister was slumped against the pillar. The Albanian, lying dead at her feet.

'Sis?'

'I'm OK,' she whispered.

Potter yelled into his radio: 'TARGET IS DOWN, HOLD YOUR FIRE!'

Ashcroft squinted his eyes as he took in the scene. Everything about it was wrong. Vasif had been facing the window, yet it was the back of his head that had been blasted away.

The bullet that killed him hadn't come from outside the medical centre.

It had come from within.

'Mum!' yelled Theo. He started running towards her.

'Theo stay back! Drop onto the floor. Don't move until I tell you!' Ashcroft ordered. Shaking, Theo did as he was told.

Ashcroft remembered the discarded BMX by the entrance. He moved round the perimeter of the waiting area, scanning the treatment rooms.

The door to one of them was ajar.

He stepped towards it. Mikey Hassan stood in the centre of the room, trembling. In his hand was a converted handgun.

Weapons like these could be bought from most street corners if you knew where to go. Cheap. Untraceable. Deadly. The dealers gave them to their boy soldiers to defend their territory. They carried them in their rucksacks the same way most people carried phone chargers. This was the gun his brother Nozza had left at home when Troy and his henchmen raided Vasif's yard.

Ashcroft swiped his hand over his face. Nozza had given evidence so that they could start a new life. What would that life look like now?

'You need to put the gun down,' Ashcroft instructed. He waited until Mikey had done as he was told before stepping nearer. Using the tip of his shoe to push the gun out of reach, he placed him under arrest. The boy hugged his North Face coat around him as Ashcroft read him his rights.

The first time he'd clapped eyes on him he and his brother had been minding Hannah's car. 'They look out for me,' she'd told him at the time.

Mikey had certainly looked out for her today.

Ashcroft placed his arm around the boy's shoulders as he guided him from the room.

Potter spoke into his radio once more: 'Stand down. The building is secure. I repeat, the building is secure. Urgent medical assistance required.'

They watched as Hannah worked on AJ, checking his vital signs while stemming the flow of blood from a wound below his ribs. She looked up at them and nodded. He'd live.

The tactical team carried out their own search of the building before the paramedics were permitted to enter. Once they took over from Hannah, she moved to where Theo and Mikey waited with Ashcroft. Blood had spattered into her hair, seeped into her clothing, dried into the creases in her fingers. In her peripheral vision, the body of Vasif Muka lay prone.

'Mikey, did you do this?' She was torn between comforting

her son and helping the little boy who'd save her life. The little boy who'd called into the clinic for his mother's prescription. Who'd run into the treatment room to hide when Vasif burst in holding a gun.

Ashcroft placed a hand on her shoulder.

'He's under caution, you can't speak to him.'

'What's going to happen to him?' she demanded.

'Not here. Not now,' Ashcroft said before accompanying Mikey to a waiting police car.

The mood in the CID room was electric. Two opposing gang leaders had been taken off the streets, along with their henchmen. Raids on their businesses and private properties were planned while they were in custody. Further charges would follow, along with further arrests; those low down the pecking order not sharp enough or fast enough to cover their bosses' tracks.

Cold blooded killer, Vasif Muka, was dead. Ashcroft couldn't think of a single person outside the thug's family who'd weep for him, but his death brought no satisfaction. The way it came about. For his killer, the future looked grim. Instead of the new life Nozza had hoped for his family, his brother would spend time in a residential facility.

There were no winners here.

DI Daniels had been waiting for Ashcroft when he returned to the station. A quiet word was needed, in his office. Superintendent Duncanson was prepared to overlook the fact Ashcroft hadn't disclosed the GP held hostage was his sister. 'No point making an issue of it,' he'd said, 'Don't think any of us can be arsed with the paperwork. Besides,' he admitted, 'I need you stay on a while longer to get the evidence over the line for the CPS.'

It was the closest they'd get to a truce, Ashcroft reckoned, so he took it.

A brief knock on Daniels' door followed by Potter's head appearing around it. 'I think you're going to want to hear this,' he said, advancing. He was holding an iPad, which he tapped to replay the taped call he'd just taken from a member of the public.

Ashcroft and Daniels listened.

'*Hello? It's about that shooting. I saw the appeal you put out for witnesses. I don't know if this is important or not, and I've been wrestling with whether or not I should call so I thought it was better to let you decide.*'

'*You did the right thing, sir.*' Potter's voice, coaxing him to get on with it.

Potter switched from the audio recording and opened the incident room email account. Tapped on an uploaded video. 'After waffling for ten minutes he sent this over.'

He pressed 'Play', turning the screen to face them.

'The caller sent over footage recorded on his dashcam. He's a courier, and on that particular morning he had a delivery to drop off in the vicinity, which was why he was crossing that junction.'

The junction on Westward Street and Abraham Road.

Which coincided, going by the date and time shown in the corner of the screen, with when Jamal and Aisha had been shot dead.

Ashcroft peered closer.

He stared at the footage of a person dressed in black as they ran along Westward Street pocketing a gun, before stopping and being sick.

Beside him, Daniels started to swear.

'Pound to a penny you're both thinking what I'm thinking,' Potter stated.

Ashcroft began to pace the room. What he wouldn't give to be on a running track right now.

'Cold-bloodied killers don't vomit after committing murder,' he muttered.

The footage didn't lie. This wasn't a professional, or a gang member used to handling hardware. This was a novice, sickened by what they'd done.

The euphoria in the CID room was quickly replaced by disappointment.

'So Vasif didn't kill Jamal and Aisha?' Nazia wasn't the only one who was perplexed. Officers who'd worked on the investigation crowded round to make sense of what they were hearing.

'The Dashcam footage shows a much slighter person than Vasif running away from the scene. There's none of his intimidating muscle, put it that way. And the fact that this person throws up indicates they're not a natural born psychopath, which he clearly is.'

'But we're sure he killed Kamali?'

'No doubt on that score,' said Potter. 'Now he's dead his so-called right-hand man, Aljan Vata, is squealing like a stuck pig. There'd been no plan to kill Kamali, he's claiming. When he'd driven Vasif to Windward Tower on the day of his murder, Vasif had ordered him to stay in the car. Said he wanted him to watch and learn. He saw him lift Kamali over the balcony and drop him. When he returned to the car he was cool as a cucumber. "That's how I deal with people who let me down," he told him, easy as you like.'

Several DCs shook their heads.

'That's something, I suppose,' Nazia observed, 'Even if we are back to square one with the other investigation.'

'I don't think we are.' Ashcroft spoke slowly, as though trying to work something out in his head.

Daniels eyed him sharply. 'What do you mean?'

He hadn't broken the news to Superintendent Duncanson yet that Vasif was out of the frame for the double shooting. He'd been building himself up to it while secretly holding out for a miracle. Perhaps Ashcroft was going to offer him one. 'Reckon it's a crime of passion after all? Aisha's boyfriend sees her with Jamal and decides to take them both out.'

'He's certainly the right build,' said Ashcroft, mulling it over.

'His devastation over her murder seemed pretty real to me,' said Potter.

Ashcroft nodded as he considered this. 'Brian, remember me asking for the original statements taken at time of Kamali's murder, so I could familiarise myself with the investigation?'

'Uh-huh,' said Potter.

'After reading through them, I agreed with you that they weren't particularly helpful in terms of evidence.'

Potter shrugged. 'That's what happens when folk are scared to speak out. You get all the emotion but none of the facts.'

'Yeah, then Naz and I returned to the café to speak to Jamal's best friend, Fahri Gemici, and this time, after a bit of two-ing and fro-ing he admitted he and Jamal had witnessed Kamali's murder. I remember he said something along the lines of-' he paused as he tried to bring the exact phrase to mind.

'-I've got it, Sarge,' said Nazia, flicking through her notebook until she located the notes she'd taken during that visit. 'This is what he said about Kamali:

"The sound he made when he landed…I didn't want to see what something that sounded as awful as that looked like."'

'-Wait a minute, I'm sure one of the statements I took said something like that,' said Potter. 'Hang on, I can soon find it on the system.'

'Thanks Brian. What he said jarred with me. I mean, for a

young person to say something like that. It makes me wonder, what if Fahri was paraphrasing this other witness? The other details he gave us are at complete odds with what we now know happened. For a start, he mentioned multiple accomplices, when in fact Vasif killed Kamali on his own. We weren't to know that at the time, so we took what he said to be true. So why would he want to claim he and Jamal witnessed a murder when they didn't? The only reason I can come up with, is to provide a motive for his friend's murder.'

'It seemed odd at the time that he wasn't concerned for his own safety,' said Nazia.

'He deflected that by claiming he'd kept shtum about witnessing the incident, suggesting Jamal must have confided in Aisha.'

'Neither of whom could confirm or deny it.'

'Here you go,' said Potter, after pulling up the statements taken after Kamali's murder. 'This was taken from an elderly neighbour the next morning: "He made an awful noise when he landed, poor little mite. I didn't go out. I didn't want to see what something that sounded as awful as that would look like". If this old dear went round saying that to all her cronies, and they in turn quoted her, then there's every chance Fahri could have heard — you know how this stuff spreads like wildfire. Before you know it he's got a pretty emotive description of what happened without witnessing anything.'

Several heads nodded in agreement.

Ashcroft shoved his hands in his pockets. 'The problem with when you catch someone out in a lie is that it casts doubt on everything else they've told you. I think we should focus on Fahri Gemici. Look at his alibi a lot more closely.'

Nazia frowned. 'What was his motive, Sarge? Jamal was his best friend.'

'A best friend who's been usurped by Aisha, though not in the way he imagined.'

Nazia considered this. 'He claimed he was at the cash and carry at the time of the shooting. We checked his till receipt and everything,' she said, shrugging.

'Then we start with that.'

He searched through the case file until he found a copy of the till receipt, the time stamp stated 09.12. 'I was satisfied at the time that this was evidence enough that Fahri was where he said he was when they were killed. The date and time fitted, and he seemed plausible, but now we know his evidence is unreliable. Naz, I want you to go and check the CCTV at the cash and carry. Cross check that he was there during the time it states on the receipt, just in case he got someone else to do his shopping for him.'

He handed her the receipt.

'By the sounds of it I don't think he has any friends, Sarge. Not the sort who'd cover for him.'

'Let's dot all the 'I's and cross all the 'T's anyway.'

'Will do.' Nazia reached for her jacket and car keys.

'I'd better go and update The Super,' Daniels said, wrapping up the briefing.

'Want me to come with you?' offered Ashcroft.

'Nah. You've been in the line of fire enough for one day. Speaking of which, you and Potter, your shift ended hours ago.'

'So did yours, boss.'

'Yeah, but all I'm saying, if you want to call it a night, I wouldn't blame you.'

'I'm not about to leave a job half done. If there's a chance of locking up a double killer before I clock off tonight then I'd prefer to keep going, if that's alright.'

'Appreciate that,' said Daniels. He threw a glance in Potter's direction.

'What he said,' Potter replied, earning a nod from the DI.

Potter's features gave nothing away until Daniels left the

room. He let out a long sigh.

'Not like I could say anything else without sounding like a jobsworth. Especially while you two were having your little bromance.'

'No bromance, Brian. We've just come to a mutual understanding.' Ashcroft grinned. 'For the record, I'd work with a jobsworth like you any day of the week.'

'Don't start getting sentimental,' Potter quipped, 'next minute you'll be telling us you've decided to stay.' He caught the look that flashed across Ashcroft's face. 'Don't worry, I'm joking. I don't blame you for wanting to get back to your old station. You'll get quite the hero's welcome, I don't doubt.'

There wasn't a malicious bone in Potter's body, but his words rankled. He was right, Ashcroft conceded as he returned to his desk. He would be glad to go back to Salford. He just wished he didn't feel so damned guilty admitting it.

He rang his sister. Informed her that SOCOs would complete their evidence collection by the close of play tomorrow.

'I'll move my appointments to the community centre. We'll manage.'

'How's Theo?'

'Shaken, but he'll be fine. He says he wants to speak to you, hang on…'

He heard a muffled conversation in the background, the next voice on the line was his nephew.

'Uncle Chris…'

'It's OK, Theo,' Ashcroft told him, trying to make it easy.

'No, it's not. I said some crappy things to you the other night. I wanted you to know I didn't mean them.'

'It's all good,' said Ashcroft, meaning it. 'How about I come down to that basketball court tomorrow so you can show me how to shoot some hoops?'

'Sure you've got time?'

'I'll make time. How does that sound?'

'*I'd like that.*'

More muffled voices then his sister came back on the line.

'*Thank you.*'

'What for?'

'*He came off the phone smiling. That doesn't happen often with moody teenagers, trust me.*'

'Glad I could help.'

'*Since you're in such an amenable mood, I don't suppose you've had a chance to think about Jamaica?*'

'Seriously? You're asking me that now? I said I'd get back to you and I will.'

'*OK, OK, you can't blame me for asking.*'

'Look, I've got to go. I'll check in on you tomorrow.'

His mobile rang the moment he ended the call. It was Naz, phoning him from the cash and carry. '*You were right, Sarge. Though not in the way any of us expected.*'

'Tell me.'

'*There's no sign of Fahri on the CCTV footage from the cameras situated by the checkout at the time the till receipt was printed. However, he is caught on camera entering the car park fifteen minutes later, on a camera located above the store's entrance. He parks in a disabled bay before hurrying into the store, emerging with a trolley load of supplies ten minutes later. Internal cameras capture him racing up and down the aisles like a contestant on Supermarket Sweep.*' Nazia sounded pleased with herself, thought Ashcroft. Rightly so when he heard what she had to say next.

'*I thought about the ticket he gave us. The goods itemised on it were fairly innocuous, weren't they? Cooking oils, margarine spreads, soft drinks, frozen chips. They were plausible, but the stuff he carried out in his trolley on the CCTV footage included a number of meat packs, so I replayed the external tapes, watched everything he did after he packed the goods into the boot of his car and returned the trolley. Only instead of returning to his dad's car he walks over to a bin by the entrance and starts pulling out bits of paper which he reads and discards until he finds what he is looking for.*'

'A receipt that shows he was at the checkout at 09.12.'

'*Exactly.*'

'Great work, Naz.'

Ashcroft got to his feet. 'Get yourself over to the café and wait for me.'

'*Are we bringing him in then?*'

'Damn right we are.'

The first thing Ashcroft noticed when he pulled into the parking bay on Walcott Avenue was the young girl on a BMX who pedalled towards the market shouting 'Feds!' at the top of her lungs. The sun hadn't gone down on Mikey's arrest and already he'd been replaced. Ashcroft glanced up at the balcony that overlooked the square. With Troy and his henchmen in custody, three different faces stared back at him as he climbed out of his car.

Life went on.

Nazia hurried towards him from a parking spot on the other side of the road. 'Didn't want to give the game away by getting here too early,' she told him, though by the look of things something was already amiss.

The cafe was closed.

'They live in the flat upstairs. Let's give their front door a rattle,' said Ashcroft, walking round to the rear of the shop units and up a flight of steps where he started banging on the front door.

'Finally!' said Nazia when Refik threw the door open.

'I thought it was kids mucking about,' he told them, though he didn't invite them in.

Ashcroft peered around him, eyed the suitcases standing in the tiny hall. 'Going away somewhere?'

'We are moving to my brother's in Smethwick. The rents

are too expensive here. A shop unit has become available to lease close to where he lives which would be ideal for me and Fahri.'

'Mind if we come in?' Ashcroft asked as he stepped inside, Nazia behind him.

Refik grunted reluctantly as though he'd been given some say in the matter. It was a studio flat. A combined lounge, diner and kitchen with doors leading off to a bathroom and a couple of bedrooms. The place was clean albeit untidy. Drawers and cupboards left open, contents lying in a jumble. 'Trying to decide what to take and what to leave behind isn't easy.'

He gave them a weak smile.

Ashcroft stared him down. 'How long have you known?'

Refik made a poor job of pretending to look confused. 'I don't know what you are talking about.' His gaze darted to what Ashcroft assumed was Fahri's bedroom door.

'That's how we're playing it, is it?' He walked over to the kitchen, pocketing Refik's car keys which were lying on the work surface.

'What the hell do you think you are doing?' Refik demanded.

Ashcroft eyeballed him. 'I'll ask you again. How long have you known that your son murdered his best friend? Was it right from the beginning? When you lectured me about the police not doing enough to control the gangs? Or when you helped set up the residents' forum, so your neighbours could share their fears about violent crime?'

Refik's chin dropped onto his chest. 'I didn't know then, I swear it!'

'He's telling the truth!' Fahri stood in the doorway leading to his bedroom, a shopping bag stuffed with clothes in each hand. 'He only found out a couple of days ago. He walked in on me when I was wrapping the gun up.'

Ashcroft angled his head towards Refik. 'And you had no

suspicions anything was wrong prior to that?'

Refik looked away. 'When you came here that first time, to tell my son the news about Jamal, I heard him tell you that the last time he'd seen him had been the evening before, when he'd called round after school. He told you I'd given him a pizza to take home. It wasn't true — that had been the day before. I asked him about it later, when we'd finished up for the evening. He told me the shock of it had made him confused. I had no reason not to believe him…yet whenever I tried getting him to talk about Jamal he shut the conversation down, started acting…' He looked around as though searching for the right word.

'Shifty?' Nazia suggested, 'Like you were acting with us, just now.'

Refik looked shamefaced. 'I suppose so, yes. I kept badgering him, asking what was wrong. That's when he told me he and Jamal had fallen out. I told him he had to call and tell you this, not that I thought it would make any difference to the investigation.'

'I never got that call, did I, Fahri?' Ashcroft stated, turning to look at him.

Fahri lowered his head.

Ashcroft turned back to Refik. 'No reason why you couldn't have told me instead.'

'And said what? *This might be nothing, but my boy argued with his friend the day before he was gunned down.* I couldn't do that. Despite everything he's my flesh and blood. There's nothing I wouldn't do for him. If keeping quiet was all it took, then that's what I was prepared to do.'

Ashcroft eyed a baseball cap discarded on the arm of the sofa. What else had Refik been keeping quiet about? he wondered.

Fahri sank down onto the sofa once he'd been cautioned, as though whatever energy he had left, deserted him.

'How did you know it was me?' he asked.

'We've got footage of the killer throwing up after Jamal and Aisha were shot dead. Like he'd just committed the worst mistake imaginable.'

Fahri's head dipped. 'I never wanted to hurt Jamal.'

'But you'd gone there fully prepared to kill Aisha?'

A nod.

'Why Fahri, you never told me why…' His father whined from the corner of the room.

'Jamal meant everything to me. He was my best mate, my world really. I felt safe when he was around. Like I belonged, and that matters, especially in a place like this. Then she came along and spoiled everything.'

'Aisha was his sister.'

'What?'

'Jamal found her on the ancestry site he joined while looking for his father.'

Fahri shrugged the information away, 'Either way she was stealing him from me, and I couldn't let her do that.'

Jealousy had a way of eating away all the good a person had in them. Left nothing but bitterness in its wake. He'd decided Aisha had to go and that was the end of it.

'So what did you do?'

'I saw her drop him off outside his block of flats the night before. I waited while he let himself in. Neither of them knew I'd been watching them. I went over to her car and tapped on the window. She was surprised to see me. I mean, I wasn't exactly nice to her whenever she was around. That's why things got a bit tense between me and Jamal, I suppose. Anyway, we'd started giving each other a wide berth. I asked her if we could meet up and sort our differences out once and for all. It wasn't fair that Jamal felt torn between us. She said she'd be happy to. Then she said something stupid like she'd love it if we could be friends. Like that was ever going to happen. We arranged for her to pick me up on Abraham Road the following day. We'd go for a coffee or something, clear the air.'

Fahri slumped in his seat. 'How was I supposed to know it would go so badly wrong?'

'What do you mean?'

'I turn up the next morning and wait. After a couple of minutes her car comes into view, only she's not on her own. Jamal is in the passenger seat. I should have known she'd tell him. They were probably laughing all the way there at how pathetic I was.'

Nazia had heard enough. 'Maybe they'd decided to let you into their secret. They chose not to tell their families about each other for a reason. Perhaps they felt they could trust you.'

Ashcroft's look said, *easy now*.

Nazia sat down, folded her arms to indicate she had nothing more to say.

Fahri picked up his story: 'The moment I saw Jamal I wanted to turn and run but how could I without making him wonder what the hell I was up to? I had no choice but to see it through.'

'You arrived there with the intention of shooting Aisha at point blank range?'

'Yes, only now I had to kill Jamal too.'

The logic of the unhinged.

'I didn't mean to do it. Not to Jamal anyway,' he corrected himself. 'He meant the world to me.'

Ashcroft had been debating whether he should say anything. Decided what he was about to tell Fahri had no baring on the investigation, though its impact would be huge on his soul.

'Jamal confessed to his brother that he had feelings for you,' he said.

Three pairs of eyes locked onto him.

It was the day he'd prevented AJ from assaulting Aisha's father, that the squaddie decided to confide in him. They were standing in Safia's hallway. AJ was troubled:

'There's something you should know…I don't think it's relevant, but Jamal told me his feelings toward Fahri had changed. Intensified, if you know what I mean. I think it scared him. He was trying to work it out I suppose. It's why when you asked me about Aisha, I knew that whatever she was to him, she wasn't his girlfriend.'

Fahri stared ahead, comprehending the enormity of what he'd done. Of what he'd lost.

Ashcroft cleared his throat. He wasn't done yet.

Guns were easy to come by if you knew where to look and who to ask, but even so. Fahri must have been confident he'd get his hands on one so quickly after arranging his meeting with Aisha. Or had it already been in his possession?

'Where did you get the gun, Fahri?'

Fahri leaned forward and covered his head with his hands.

'We'll find out one way or another, you might as well tell us,' Nazia warned him.

After a couple of moments, he lifted his head. Levelled his gaze at his father as though apologising for what he was about to do.

'I found a container of guns the week before, in Baba's bedroom.'

Ashcroft's head swivelled in Refik's direction.

'I can explain!' Refik said quickly, as though there were circumstances that would mitigate harbouring lethal weapons.

'Vasif Muka came into my shop a few months ago, demanding cash. I told him I didn't have any and instead of breaking my legs he offered me a deal. The Berati Crew had guns that needed hiding. If I agreed to keep them here, then I wouldn't need to give him any money. I didn't know what else to do.'

'Bad decision,' said Ashcroft, 'because now I'm going to

have to arrest you too.'

While Nazia arranged for transportation to take father and son into custody, Ashcroft's attention returned to the baseball cap on the sofa. 'One last thing,' he said, remembering where he'd last seen it. 'You delivered those weapons to Vasif earlier this evening, hidden inside a stack of pizza boxes.'

It wasn't a question, but Refik nodded anyway.

FOURTEEN

'I want to put things right for people when they go wrong.'

— DS CHRIS ASHCROFT

Aisha's family home

'Thank you for coming.'

Ashcroft followed Abena through to her office. Waited for her to take a seat before dropping into the chair opposite. She'd poured coffee for them both. 'I knew you'd be punctual,' she said, 'but please, drink it while it's hot.' A plate of sandwiches which neither of them would eat had been placed between both coffee mugs.

Ashcroft studied her as he sipped his coffee. She'd aged since he'd seen her last. Deep lines had formed around her eyes and mouth. Her cheeks had hollowed, and her clothes hung from her as though she'd lost weight.

'I wanted to come and speak to you anyway,' he said, returning the empty coffee mug to the table. 'Will your husband be joining us?'

'Soon to be ex-husband,' she corrected him. 'I'm afraid there's no way back from what he did.'

Ozwald's DNA test had come back as a match for Jamal. No surprise there, but it was the circumstances surrounding the young man's conception that had proved too much to bear.

One Good Reason

Ashcroft nodded sympathetically. She'd lost her marriage as well as her daughter, no wonder she looked done in.

Abena summoned a smile. 'I wanted to thank you for looking beyond the constituent parts of my daughter's murder. Two young people shot dead in a top of the range car in an area rife with drugs. Black too. Anyone reading that news headline was bound to jump to conclusions. *No prizes for guessing what was going on there.*' She looked away. 'But I was just as guilty. Heaping blame onto a boy who'd done nothing wrong, just because I didn't know him.'

'You had a lot to deal with.' He was being generous, and they both knew it.

'Even so, when you called to say that his friend had been charged with their murder, I was shocked. I don't think any of us saw that coming.'

Ashcroft's sigh was heavy. 'Good old-fashioned jealousy. He thought Aisha was usurping his position in Jamal's life.'

Abena wiped away a tear. 'And Jamal's mother? Safia? How's she coping?'

'Much the same as you, from what I can see. No charges were brought against her older son, which is something, at least. He's returned to his unit. Flew out to Germany, last thing I heard.'

They sat in silence for several moments. 'You said you wanted to come and speak to me anyway. What about?'

Ashcroft cleared his throat. 'I just wanted to reassure you that, although I'll be returning to my old station, you can reach me there any time. We don't walk away easily just because a case is solved, and we never forget the victims. So if ever you want to talk…'

He handed her one of his old cards from Salford Precinct station.

Abena took the card from him. Turned it over in her hand as though she couldn't believe what she was seeing. 'You're not serious? You're going to return to your old job just like that?' she said, clicking her fingers.

'As I said, you'll still be able to reach me…'

She shook her head in frustration. 'That's not the point and you know it. Besides, I'm not thinking about me.' She looked about her as though searching for the right words. 'Look, I get it. You want to go back to your old job, work hard at not rocking the boat…'

'That's hardly fair!' he responded, stung.

'I know, I know, why should it be down to you?' She wasn't being sarcastic, which made her comments worse, somehow.

'-It isn't like that…' Even as he said it his words sounded hollow.

'It doesn't matter. I'm sorry if I came on too strong. Can I ask you, though, why did you join the police?'

Ashcroft didn't miss a beat. 'I want to put things right for people when they go wrong.'

'And you can't do that here?'

He was saved from answering by the doorbell.

'That'll be Tobi,' she told him, smiling as she registered the surprise on his face that Aisha's boyfriend was about to step over the threshold. 'I decided to reach out to him, get to know the person who'd made memories with her. Who if I'm lucky, will share some of them with me.'

'Mind you.' She glanced at her watch. 'He's early. Too young to realise that's as bad as being late.'

Ashcroft got to his feet. 'I'll leave you both to get acquainted.'

'You don't have to rush off.'

'Yes, I do. My nephew's teaching me how to play basketball. I suspect it's going to be a long day.'

Epilogue

Salford Precinct station

It was turning into a habit. A 10K run. The rhythm of his body propelling him forward, the sound of his feet hitting the pavement. The joy of the solitude.

Now here he was, suited and booted outside Chief Superintendent Curtis's office, his feet wearing holes in the carpet as he paced up and down.

It hadn't been easy leaving Moss Side. There'd not been a whip round, just a piss up followed by a curry. Promises made to keep in touch. The last couple of days had been awkward. Filing reports while new faces appeared on the murder board. New investigations in which he had no part to play.

He was there, but not there.

It felt like a jolt when it came to him. The realisation that he'd already moved on. That returning to his old job was no longer an option.

That he was here, but not here.

The Chief Super wouldn't need persuading. Probably played right into his hands if he thought about it. He pictured the delight on the senior officer's face, his mind already formulating the announcement. He'd ask him to hold off sharing the news until the following week. Give him time to see his old team. Break it to them. They'd mostly take it in their stride. He could only think of one person who'd get arsey about it.

Since he was chancing his arm, he might as well ask to take some annual leave, go on that bloody trip to Jamaica before he changed his mind.

He knocked on the Chief Super's door. Waited for permission to enter.

'Wondered if I could have a word, sir…' he said, approaching Curtis's desk.

THE END

Acknowledgements

I thought it was about time that Ashcroft got his own series. He's been a loyal 'sidekick' to DS Kevin Coupland, his equal number at Salford Precinct station for several years now and deserves a medal, never mind his own storyline. I hope readers who've followed Coupland enjoy getting to know Ashcroft as he begins his journey.

The books I read whilst researching this novel include *Kill The Black One First*, by Michael Fuller, *Forced Out*, by Kevin Maxwell, *Black and Blue*, by Parm Sandhu, and *The Real Top Boys*, by Wensley Clarkson.

Writing is a lonely job carried out by social misfits trying to make sense of what's going on around them. It is also the best job in the world. That said, getting a book out into the world is a whole different ball game and wouldn't be possible without a team.

Grateful thanks to Betsy Reavley, Tara Lyons (especially for her patience!), Hannah Deuce, Lexi Curtis and everyone at Bloodhound Books for getting this second edition of One Good Reason across the line, and for the awesome cover design.

Thanks to my beta readers Sue Barnett and Sally Howorth, and to Lin White, for her editorial services over the years. I'm very grateful to ex police sergeant Stuart McGuire for his police procedural advice and answering my many questions. Lynn Osborne, friend and reader, as ever, your keen observations help me stay on the right path. Any remaining errors in the book are mine.

Thanks to my family for their continued support: Stephen, Matt and Tom, and to Cat for being the world's best cheerleader. My brother Anthony, for peppering our conversations with buzz words that find their way into my stories one way or another.

About the Author

Emma writes gritty crime fiction that focuses on the 'why' dunnit as well as the 'who'. Her previous job working with socially excluded men and ex-offenders provided her with a lot of inspiration. When she's not writing she has been known to frequent bars of ill repute, where many a loose lip has provided the nugget of a storyline. Find out more about the author and her other books at:

https://www.emmasalisbury.com

A note from the publisher

Thank you for reading this book. If you enjoyed it please do consider leaving a review on Amazon to help others find it too.

We hate typos. All of our books have been rigorously edited and proofread, but sometimes mistakes do slip through. If you have spotted a typo, please do let us know and we can get it amended within hours.

info@bloodhoundbooks.com

www.ingramcontent.com/pod-product-compliance
Ingram Content Group UK Ltd.
Pitfield, Milton Keynes, MK11 3LW, UK
UKHW010507270525
458898UK00004B/8